BAD SEED

BETH SAULNIER

—

BAD SEED

AN ALEX BERNIER MYSTERY

WARNER BOOKS

An AOL Time Warner Company

WARNER BOOKS EDITION

Copyright © 2002 by Beth Saulnier

Cover design by Diane Luger

Warner Books, Inc.
1271 Avenue of the Americas
New York, NY 10020

Visit our Web site at www.twbookmark.com

 An AOL Time Warner Company

Printed in the United States of America

Originally published by the Mysterious Press

First Paperback Printing: February 2003

10 9 8 7 6 5 4 3 2 1

To Paul Cody
who's always been in my foxhole
and
Miss C.A. Carlson
who'd make an excellent murderess,
if she put her mind to it.

ACKNOWLEDGMENTS

With many thanks to:
Bill Malloy
for taking me on
Sara Ann Freed,
my beloved new editor
Jimmy Vines,
agent, gentleman, dad
Mark Anbinder
for always saving me from my iMac
Aimee Mann
for the best tunes to write by
Professor Susan McCouch,
Cornell University Department of Plant Breeding,
for some hows and whys of rice science
&
special thanks to
David Bloom
for being David Bloom

CHAPTER 1

The nastiest marriage in Walden County history ended a couple of yards from where it started, on the supernaturally green lawn of the university chapel. The fact that it ended surprised exactly no one—especially those who'd attended the ceremony, which had culminated in such aggressive rice throwing on the part of the bride that the groom spent most of his wedding night in the emergency room, having little white grains plucked from his eyes.

No, it was *how* it ended that got people; nobody would've thought the match would actually turn out to be till-death-do-us-part. But exactly fourteen years and two days after the wedding, the groom expired on his way across campus. And as for the bride—she did the last thing anyone expected. After fourteen years and forty-eight hours of swearing up and down that she hated his guts, she cried so hard she had to be sedated.

Then she was arrested for his murder.

It didn't happen right away, of course. In the first few days after Lane Freeman keeled over in front of a particularly hideous cherub, the grieving widow act held up; his death was assumed to be from natural causes. Yes, his wife had always told anyone who'd listen (including their five kids, aged six to thirteen) that she wished to hell he'd drop dead *right this minute*. But when it finally happened, nobody could believe she'd actually done it. They figured he'd had a heart attack, or an aneurysm, or whatever it is you die from when you're a middle-aged white guy who eats crap all day and never exercises. Then the toxicology report came back, and Mrs. Freeman was in a whole lot of trouble.

In the weeks following the arrest, rumor had it that she was dying to cop a plea. But the Walden County D.A. isn't what you'd call a forgiving sort—it's endlessly frustrating to him that Singapore has caning and we don't—and he saw no reason to deal. He even made noises about going for the death penalty, which was completely ridiculous under the circumstances. But in the end he figured no jury was going to send a desperately unhappy mother of five to the chair (or even the needle), so he set his sights on twenty-five to life. And the hyper-educated denizens of Gabriel, New York, settled back for the ultimate in civic entertainment: a really juicy murder trial.

I had a ringside seat for this spectacle, seeing as I was covering it for the local paper. It wasn't my usual job—I'm on the city government beat, not cops and courts. But since the *Monitor*'s search for a new police reporter was taking several lifetimes, the trial coverage was being assigned to whoever was vaguely qualified to write about whatever was happening that day. The paper's science writer (my beer-swilling buddy Jake Madison) therefore had the joy of sitting through hours of testimony on the chemistry of plant-based poisons, while I got sent to record all the ugly details of the Freemans' miserable relationship.

I'm not quite sure what to make of that.

The fact is, though, I had another connection to the unhappy couple: They both worked at Benson, which falls into my beat. Shelley Freeman was an associate dean at the agricultural college; her husband wrote pithy press releases for the university news service.

He was also, as it happened, an alumnus of the *Gabriel Monitor.* You'd think that would make us go all soft and squishy at his demise, but that wasn't quite the case. Freeman had jumped ship from journalism to flackery—and as far as we were concerned that was a capital crime. Plus, considering what a royal pain in the ass he'd been pre-mortem, it was a miracle that the members of the Gabriel Press Club hadn't offed him en masse years ago.

But that honor had gone to his wife, a former Benson student council president who'd come to campus at seventeen and never left. She'd graduated with a bachelor's in plant pathology, earned a master's in agricultural economics, then taken a job vetting prospective Ivy Leaguers in the ag-school admissions office. She'd worked her way up to associate ag dean—and if she hadn't made the mistake of killing her husband on university property, she probably would've wound up as vice president for Obsequious Grant-Mongering, or some such thing.

Lane himself had had a less satisfying career trajectory. He'd been editor in chief of the Benson student paper, which is more impressive than it sounds; the *Bugle* is a daily that has been known to scoop the pros every once in a while. After graduation, he got a perfectly respectable job covering towns for the *Monitor.* But three years and two kids later, his wife decided (a) there was no way she was leaving Gabriel to follow him to some midsize fish wrapper and (b) he'd better start making some real money or else. So he turned in his press pass and went over to the dark side, where he spent the next decade trumpeting the glory of all things Benson to anybody with a tape recorder.

If the job made him unhappy, nobody ever knew it—not

because he seemed content but because he was always so depressed it was impossible to dissect the causes of his misery. There was his dead-end career, the notoriously awful Gabriel weather, the stress of five kids, and, last but not least, the fact that he and his wife loathed each other.

You're probably wondering why they ever got together in the first place; having seen them go ten rounds in the pickle aisle at the Shop 'n Save, I've wondered that myself. All I can say is that, from what I hear, their romance was based on aggression from day one: He was covering student government, she was running it, and apparently they'd have raging fights over campus politics and wind up screwing like rabbits. They didn't just rub each other the wrong way, in other words; they rubbed each other *exactly* the wrong way. They fit together like Lego blocks, neurosis snapped to neurosis.

The question of why they got hitched is considerably more straightforward: She was Catholic, and she got pregnant. So, on a typically gloomy Saturday two weeks before spring break, her parents hosted an elegantly catered shotgun wedding at the Benson chapel. And fourteen years later, exactly two days after he forgot their anniversary for the third year running, she put him out of her misery.

The Freeman story was a cautionary tale, one that offered more than a few lessons about love, marriage, and life in general. And not the least of them was this: If you decide you want to poison your husband, don't leave traces of the stuff you killed him with all over the backseat of your Subaru Forester.

∾⳯⳯ॐ

The Shelley Freeman trial was front-page news for a solid month. That may sound a wee bit provincial, and it probably is. But the truth is that although we get our fair share of murders around here—way more than our fair share, come to think of it—we don't tend to have very many *trials;* for whatever reason, our homicidal maniacs tend to be the confess-or-die-by-gunfire variety.

The Widow Freeman was the exception. Although the scuttlebutt had her angling to plead to a lesser charge, when it came to facing down a quarter-century in the slammer she started swearing up and down that she was absolutely, totally, and completely *innocent.* Her lawyer, a Yellow Dog Democrat named Jim Collier who's intimately familiar with lost causes, figured he might as well put his client on the stand and let her do her swearing under oath, on the off chance one juror out of twelve might buy it. And since I'm the paper's resident sob sister (by default, anyway), I got to spend a day and a half in the courthouse watching her weep into a hankie and pledge eternal love to her dear departed Lane.

The funny thing was . . . I believed her. Not that she hadn't offed him; it was pretty obvious that she had. But that, when all was said and done, she actually loved the guy. Go figure.

"You want to hear my theory?" I asked across a wobbly table in the Citizen Kane, the newshound's bar of choice. My drinking companion didn't answer, just kept staring down at the beer sloshing around in his mug. "Earth to Madison," I said after a minute. "You want to hear my theory or what?"

"Not particularly."

As always, we were sitting in the window seat—a tiny clutch of three tables on a platform two grimy steps up from the rest of the bar. This gave Mad plenty of options for avoiding looking me in the eye. Besides his beloved beer mug, he could gaze at the gaggle of underage Bessler College sorority girls bellying up to the bar with their tummy shirts and fake IDs, the various wares (blown-glass bongs, used bell-bottoms, aromatherapy massage oil) on sale in the shops across the way, and any number of local freaks lounging on the Gabriel Green, our paved pedestrian mall.

"Christ," I said finally, "you *are* in a mood."

"Piss off."

"What's your problem tonight, anyway?" He finally looked up from his liquid supper. "Ah. I get it. You're having an Emma relapse."

"Am not."

"Come on, Mad. Don't sweat it. It's only natural that you feel—"

"I do *not*."

"She only left a week ago. Nobody says you've gotta be over it by—"

"What theory?"

"Huh?"

"Why don't you tell me about your stupid theory?"

"Oh. It's about what happened with the Freemans."

"She poisoned him."

"No shit she poisoned him. I mean my theory about their marriage."

"You mean why they hated each other so much?"

I downed the rest of my gin and tonic and shook my head. "Nah, why they stayed together."

"Five kids'll do it."

"I know, but I kind of think that in a weird way, they made each other happy."

"Come on, you know damn well they had the worst—"

"Yeah, but you know what I think? I think as long as they were together they could point at each other and say, 'If it weren't for *you,* I'd be happy, you jerk.' That way they could avoid the fact that they were just miserable people, right?"

"Since when are you the queen of psychobabble?"

"And since when are you the king of pain?"

That shut him up. "So when is it going to the jury?"

"End of the week, looks like. I don't know why they even bother."

"Woman's entitled to be shit-canned by a jury of her peers."

"I meant why Shelley and her lawyer don't just plead out and throw her on the mercy of the court. I mean, have you checked out how the jury's looking at her? It's like she's the bastard stepchild of Lizzie Borden and Lady Macbeth."

"Aronofsky's still in no mood to take a plea. Why should he? He's got her dead to rights."

"Mrs. Freeman is a very sloppy murderer."

"No kidding. You wanna be a good girl and get me another beer?"

"If it'll improve your mood, you got it."

I made my way to the bar and tried to figure out if there was any way I was going to get Mad to open up. Doubtful; the man has always been something of a clam when it comes to personal matters. But truth be told, I was starting to worry about him. Jake Madison has always been a study in contradictions—an obsessive exerciser and consumer of low-fat foods who drinks like a giant mackerel—but usually his personal chakras are more or less in alignment. Recently, though, he's been tilting toward the depressive way more than usual. And yes, I know: According to the chemists, alcohol is a depressant. Mad, however, sees this as some sort of conspiracy of disinformation by losers who wish we still had Prohibition.

The happy-hour crowd had besieged the bar three deep, so it took me a while to get the goods. When I finally got back with the drinks and a bowl of crunchy rice snacks, I found Mad slumped over the table with his head in his oversize hands.

"You sure you're okay?"

"I don't wanna talk about it."

"I miss her too, you know."

"I don't wanna—"

"Sorry. Let's change the subject. What horrifying science thing are you working on?"

"Forget it." He started to get up. "I'm gonna go home and watch *Shark Week*."

"And waste this perfectly good Labatt's?" I wagged the mug at him, and some of the stinky stuff fell on my shoe. "Come on, don't leave me here all by myself. Cody's not getting here for, like, an hour."

He sank back down with a sigh. "One more drink."

"There's the spirit."

We sat there not talking for a while, me overdosing on salty snacks and Mad tapping his enormous fingers on the table until I wanted to spank him. Finally, he looked up at me and said, *"Abrus precatorius."*

"Huh?"

"You asked me what science story I was working on. That's it."

"Oh."

"It's the poison Shelley used to kill Lane. Bill's got me doing a big take-out on it."

"And?"

He cracked the first smile of the evening. "It's very nasty stuff. Makes you feel like your gut's full of steak knives and broken glass."

"Lovely image."

"Actually, *Abrus precatorius* is the plant the poison comes from. Commonly known as the rosary pea. Grows in the tropics. Not here."

"Unless you count the Benson University greenhouses."

"Aronofsky's point exactly. In case you care, the poison's a protein called abrin. Also a glycoside called abric acid."

I slouched in my seat and put my feet up on one of the two empty chairs. "Please don't tell me what a glycoside is."

"The plant's kinda pretty. Has bright red seeds with little black dots on the end. You eat 'em, you die."

"And Lane ate them."

"Not on purpose."

"Man," I said, "love drives you *nuts*."

"Your point being?"

"Well, Shelley Freeman seemed like a perfectly normal lady most of the time. But she and Lane just totally brought out the worst in each other, right? I mean, can you imagine being so pissed off at somebody you actually *kill* them?"

"Sure."

"I mean somebody you used to *love*."

He shot me a look straight over his beer mug. "Sure."

"I take it you haven't heard from her."

He slammed the aforementioned mug onto the table. "Christ, Bernier, which part of 'I don't wanna talk about it' don't you get?"

"Don't you think you'd feel better if you—"

"So how long do you think it's gonna be before your boyfriend moves back to Boston?"

I stuck my tongue out at him, which was the highest level of discourse I could come up with on short notice.

"Come on, Alex," he said with an icky tone in his voice, "don't you think you'd feel better if you—"

"You're not a very nice man."

He picked the mug back up gently, like he wanted it to know the slamming had been nothing personal. "Given."

"How about we change the subject?"

"Deal."

"Okay," I said. "How well did you know Freeman, anyway?"

"Professionally, too damn well. He was always on my ass

about covering some big donor who endowed a new john in the biotech building, or some damn thing. Bought the Benson party line in a big way. Damn waste, if you ask me."

"You think he might've made a decent reporter?"

"I think he *was* a decent reporter. I've run through some of his old clips doing research. Guy could've gone places."

"But he stayed here."

"Staying here wasn't the problem. Flacking his ass off was."

"It's a dirty job, but somebody's gotta do it, right?"

"Gimme a break."

"So, like, apart from the flackery and all that, what'd you think of Freeman as a guy?"

He shrugged his big bony shoulders. "I didn't really know him personally. Hardly ever came into the Citizen except to schmooze us up every once in a while. I guess the wife kept him on a short leash."

"You ever get a load of the two of them together?"

"Who in this town didn't?"

"You know, I heard one time she threw a plate of chicken curry at him in Thai Palace. Cracked a window and everything."

"Poor guy."

"Yeah, well, maybe he drove her to it."

"What does your boy Cody have to say? He think there's any chance she's getting off?"

"Nope."

"She ever admit to anything when he grilled her?"

"What grilling? Woman like that isn't dumb enough to talk to the cops. Cody barely got her into the interview room and she lawyered up."

"Not," said a very hunky voice off to my left, "that I wouldn't have gotten her to cop to it if I'd had the chance."

I turned around and there was Cody, all green eyes and red hair and muscles. *Yum.* "You're early, Detective."

He leaned down and pecked me on the lips. Then he deposited himself in the empty chair between me and Mad, took off his jacket, and smacked his hands together. "You people call this *spring?*"

I pecked him back. "And you call yourself a Yankee?"

"We had spring in Boston. This is not spring."

"Little hail never hurt anybody."

"I got the next round," Mad said, and took off toward the bar.

Cody watched him go, then gave my knee a little squeeze. "What's eating him?"

I wrapped my hands around his and rubbed for warmth, like they taught me in the Brownies. "Emma thing."

"Ah. Probably best if we lay off the . . ."

"Couple stuff. Yeah."

"She coming back anytime soon?"

"Doesn't look like it."

"Poor guy."

"You men sure as hell stick together." He cocked an eyebrow my way. "Mad was just expressing a similar sentiment about Lane Freeman."

"Well, he *is* dead, you know."

"He meant vis-à-vis his miserable marriage."

"Oh. Poor guy."

"From what I saw, he gave as good as he got."

"Except that she's still breathing."

"Except for that, yeah."

I checked to make sure Mad wasn't within viewing distance, then gave Cody a respectable kiss. The man was definitely worth kissing, what with his perfect bod and great laugh and manly-but-not-macho demeanor—all of which make me overlook the fact that in a previous incarnation he was a goddamn navy SEAL.

And, okay . . . Though I know a ban-the-bomb peacenik like me should be above such things, I gotta admit the *Officer and a Gentleman* thing is pretty damn sexy. We've been going out a year—for me, this qualifies as several consecutive lifetimes—and I've yet to develop the ability to keep my hands to myself. He doesn't seem to consider this a character flaw.

"You know," I said when I was done assaulting him, "you looked awful cute in court today. What were you doing there, anyway?" Again with the eyebrow. "And no, this is not going to wind up in the *Monitor* tomorrow."

"In that case . . . Aronofsky needed some last-minute stuff for his cross. Nothing too exciting. Hey, by the way, were you in court when he demolished Shelley's tox guy?"

"Mad covered it. Said it was quite the scene. Collier tried to salvage it on redirect, but I hear it was pretty pathetic."

"How's he doing, anyhow?"

"Collier? Not too damn—"

"Madison."

"Oh. Honestly, he's kind of freakish at the moment. I've never seen him this upset over a girl before. Half the time he's crying in his beer, or else, *poof*, he's just off someplace. But then a couple days ago he was totally manic, talking a mile a minute and pacing like crazy. If I didn't know better, I would've thought he was on something."

"You think he might be?"

"Mad? No way. He does alcohol and he does caffeine. The problem is he does them in excessive quantities every once in a while."

"So you really think he and Emma are over for good?"

"Probably. I mean, London's pretty damn far away. Plus

which, I'm kind of worried she maybe got back with her ex. He was calling a lot the past couple of months."

"And I take it that's not good news?"

"Alcoholic M.D. Real piece of work, from what she told me."

"Well . . ."

"Yeah, I know what you're gonna say. Change doctor to reporter, and you've pretty much got Mad."

"Not that I don't like the guy . . ."

"But he can be a real piece of work."

"And you really think she's gone back to her ex?"

"She told me a while ago she never really got him out of her system. And like I was just saying to Mad, love makes you do some crazy shit."

"Sometimes in a good way."

"Tell that," I said, "to Lane Freeman."

CHAPTER 2

Closing arguments came two days later. Aronofsky went first, unfolding his spidery frame from behind the prosecution table and stalking over to the jury box with more righteous indignation than you'd think would fit into a guy that thin.

"Michelle Freeman," he began, "is a sad woman."

I glanced over at her, and found that even if his tone was less than conciliatory, his description was right on the nose. Shelley sat at the defense table with her hands not so much folded as clenched together, tension bringing her shoulders up to her earlobes. Her frizzy black hair was pulled back so tightly it looked like she'd had an overnight face-lift—which was kind of fortunate, because the trial had aged her ten years inside of three weeks.

"She's a *very* sad woman," Aronofsky went on. "As you've heard over the past three weeks, she's a woman who never knew happiness in her marriage, who struggled to raise five children with a husband she despised." The sad woman in question opened her mouth like she was actually about to interrupt him, but—thank God—her lawyer reached over and shushed her.

"Michelle Freeman made some unfortunate choices in her life. She decided to marry too young. She decided to stay in a bad relationship. She decided to subject her children to a household in which their parents fought constantly."

He took a deep breath, and even the flaky-looking hippie covering the trial for the weekly *Gabriel Advocate* could tell he was about to go for the gusto.

"But four months ago," Aronofsky said, "Michelle Freeman made the worst choice of her life. She decided to kill her husband. And she did it not in a fit of rage, but with cold, calculated precision. How did she do it? She poisoned him with a substance *she* had access to in her role as an associate dean of the Benson agricultural college. She used a method *she* was familiar with as a graduate of the college's plant-pathology program. You've heard testimony that *she* studied this class of plants as an undergraduate. . . ."

I wondered what was up with all this emphasizing of the pronoun, and figured it was probably something they teach you in prosecutor school. I made a mental note to ask my lawyer mom the next time she called to remind me how much she'd enjoy some grandchildren with Cody's Republican DNA.

"You've also heard police testimony that the very same poison was found in the backseat of Michelle Freeman's car," Aronofsky continued. "You've heard that on numerous occasions, Mrs. Freeman not only wished her husband dead, but threatened to kill him herself. You've heard that just a day before Lane Freeman died, he and his wife had a bitter argument over his failure to remember their anniversary. Now"—his voice shifted from authoritative to smarmy— "anyone can understand that a wife would be disappointed if her husband forgot their anniversary. But, ladies and gentlemen of the jury, *it is not a capital crime.* Even if Lane Freeman were still alive, you couldn't convict him of being a bad

husband. That's not against the law. And you can't convict
Shelley Freeman of being a bad wife. But what you can convict her of—what you *must* convict her of—is depriving
their five children of the father they loved. . . ."

He went on like that for another twenty minutes, with
Shelley getting more and more agitated until I definitely
thought she was going to stand up and whack him over the
head with a yellow legal pad. I also thought that—though his
ham-fisted speech was probably going to land her in the
slammer—Aronofsky was a piss-poor public speaker who
had no business being head judge of the annual Gabriel High
Forensics Jam.

Then it was Collier's turn to pontificate. Clad in a shiny
suit that screamed *I do way too much pro bono,* he gave a
stirring little talk aimed squarely at the *Oprah* crowd—about
how Shelley was a victim of circumstance, and how she really and truly loved her husband even though she had a damn
funny way of showing it, and how nobody outside a relationship can ever really know what's going on inside it, now
can they?

His closing lasted even longer than Aronofsky's; the fun
part came at the beginning when he looked each juror in the
eye and practically dared them to answer him. "Do you understand the Freeman marriage?" he asked. "*I* don't. Do you?
How about you? Or you, sir?"

He was making them damned uncomfortable, which
didn't seem like a good idea considering they had the power
to lock his client up for the next several decades. But then his
voice took on a lighter tone, like he was letting them all in on
the joke.

"Would you want to be married to either one of these people?" he asked, and this time nobody thought he expected an
answer. "No? Well, you know what? Neither would I.

"But as my esteemed colleague Mr. Aronofsky so aptly

said, you can't convict Shelley Freeman of being a bad wife, any more than you could have convicted Lane Freeman of being a bad husband. Why did they stay together? I couldn't tell you. But the point is that they did just that. *They stayed together.* They made noises about getting a divorce, but neither one of them ever took one single step toward a separation. And yes, they also made noises—ugly, unfortunate noises—about how thrilled they'd be if the other one dropped dead."

He walked from the jury box to the defense table and picked up a legal pad with a flourish. "Let's take another look at what they said, shall we? As Mr. Aronofsky's own witnesses have testified, on various occasions Mrs. Freeman said the following, and I quote"—he cleared his throat for dramatic effect—"'I hope he trips and falls into the gorge and breaks his neck and drowns in the waterfall *and then gets eaten by a shark.*'"

He shook his head with a rueful little grin, waved the pad toward the jury, and cleared his throat again. This time, I could swear it was to keep from cracking up. "And here's another thing Mrs. Freeman said. She said, 'I swear I'd like to run over that idiot with a John Deere tractor.' Not just any tractor, ladies and gentlemen. A *John Deere tractor.*" This time, a couple of jurors actually giggled. The judge didn't look amused. "'I wish,'" Collier quoted again, deadpan and slow, "*'that he'd come down with the flesh-eating bacteria.*'"

He paused to let the sheer stupidity of it all sink in. "Now," he said after a minute, "Mr. Aronofsky and I may not agree on much about this case. But I think we can fairly say that Lane Freeman did not die from flesh-eating bacteria. He did not fall into a gorge. Neither was he run down by farm equipment, driven by Mrs. Freeman or anyone else."

More titters from the jury box. Aronofsky looked inclined

to object—and the judge, for that matter, looked inclined to sustain it—but Collier knew when enough was enough.

"I don't mean to make light of this," he said. "A man is dead. But my point, ladies and gentlemen, is that all the threats Mrs. Freeman supposedly made were nothing more than hyperbole from a woman who was unhappy in her marriage.

"But, you may point out, harm *did* come to Lane Freeman. He *did* die. But, ladies and gentlemen of the jury, there is nothing tying my client to her husband's murder. Our expert has testified that the substance found in the backseat of her car was not the poison that killed Mr. Freeman, but may have been a common organic herbicide. A *weed killer*. You also heard him testify"—he cranked his voice up a notch— "that it was the incompetence of the Gabriel Police Department's toxicologists, not any wrongdoing on the part of Mrs. Freeman, that led to the arrest and prosecution of an innocent woman.

"Don't let her be victimized any more," he said, giving the jury a heavy dose of his pleading puppy eyes. "Please, do the only decent, honest thing, and send this mother of five back to her family."

It was a damn moving speech, and I thought Juror Number Three was actually in tears as the judge gave his final instructions. Then the jury went off to deliberate, and the rest of us hunkered down in the diner across the street to await the verdict and eat large quantities of Greek food.

There's always a festive atmosphere over at Yanni's on such occasions. The place, which is claustrophobic to begin with, gets jam-packed with reporters, lawyers, friends and relatives of the opposing parties, and various and sundry court junkies. Traditionally, the defense team takes a booth at one end and the prosecution at the other—though Aronofsky's enough of a pill to order his staff to stay in the office and miss all the fun. People play cards, drink way too much coffee, and (more to the point) stuff themselves with Mrs. Demetrios's moussaka, spanikorizo, skordalia, and avgolemono till they can barely move, then hope the clerk won't come in and roust them back to the courtroom just as they're tucking into their baklava.

The Shelley Freeman trial was a bust, culinarily speaking—the assembled masses barely had time to put away so much as a stuffed grape leaf. As I reported in the *Monitor* the next day, the five-woman, seven-man jury didn't just convict Shelley of second-degree murder; in a Walden County Courthouse record, they found her guilty in exactly one hour and twenty-seven minutes.

When things get slow in the newsroom, we've been known to hold contests to see who can come up with the best (or, rather, worst) journalistic clichés. *The plane crashed in a densely wooded area* is one; *the police declined to comment on the ongoing investigation* is another. And then there's this old faithful: *The defendant showed no emotion as the verdict was read.*

Such prose endures on the pages of newspapers everywhere because a lot of times it just happens to be true. Planes do tend to crash in the woods, and cops tend to keep their mouths shut. And as for the third one, well . . . Shelley Freeman was the exception that proved the rule.

To back up a bit: When the jurors first filed in, most of them looked her straight in the eye. Now, from what I hear, this is usually a good sign for the accused, as (generally speaking) is a speedy verdict. So when the forewoman said "guilty," everybody just about keeled over from the shock.

Shelley Freeman, in fact, did keel over. She also shrieked, and sobbed, and started screaming that the jurors—God damn them to hell for all eternity—were the biggest morons she'd ever seen. Even bigger, she yelled as two scary-looking deputies hauled her away, than her lousy, miserable, good-for-nothing husband.

～⊶⊷～

I stopped by Yanni's on my way back to the newsroom and, finding that Mrs. Demitrios's Verdict Watch discount was still in effect, picked up enough baklava for the cityside reporting staff. When I got upstairs with the honey-soaked box, I realized I'd once again demonstrated my talent for bad timing; the editorial meeting I'd been counting on missing was just getting started.

Too late to make good my escape, I laid the delectables at the altar of the city editor. Present and accounted for in Bill's office were three of the usual suspects: Lillian, the schools reporter and the kind of tough old bird you'd call a "steel magnolia" if she weren't from Maine; Marshall, the business reporter and a genuine son of Dixie; and Brad, the former intern who'd just been hired as a part-time towns reporter. (The latter, by the way, is both a newly minted Benson graduate and a genuine evolutionary throwback.)

Missing from this happy crew was one Jake Madison. Present—but, as far as I knew, unaccounted for—was a wiry, dark-haired guy who looked so much like my penultimate ex-boyfriend, I had to squelch the instinct to sprint out of Bill's office and hide under a desk.

"What the hell are you doing here?" asked Bill, who was running the meeting with his usual dulcet charm. "Alex. *Alex.* Aren't you supposed to be waiting on the verdict?"

"I . . . um . . . It already came in. They convicted her."

"Nice of you to mention it."

"Er . . . I was just about to."

Bill gave a disgusted sort of snort, then turned to Mr. Wiry

Stranger. "Well, Cal, it looks like you missed covering a murder trial by about half a day."

"Too bad," the guy said, and stopped smirking at me just long enough to stick out his hand. Then he started smirking again. "I'm Cal Ochoa, the new cops reporter. You must be Alex Bernier."

"Um, yeah." I was trying really hard to get my tongue unstuck from the roof of my mouth. "And you're . . . ?"

"Cal Ochoa."

"Right. Hi."

"Hi."

"You, uh, want some baklava?"

His smirk got even wider, and I was afraid he was going to laugh at me right there in front of God and everybody. But that honor went to Brad; Ochoa just said "thanks" and grabbed a pastry out of the box. Bill was right behind him, putting away the diamond-shaped chunk in one bite and proceeding to talk with his mouth full of phyllo. "Well, now that everybody's friends," he said, "why don't you sit the hell down and tell us what happened with Freeman?"

"Sure." I snagged a sweetmeat in the name of fortification. "They convicted her. In like an hour and change."

Now it was Ochoa's turn to snort. "That's totally loco," he said, and I caught just the faintest trace of a Mexican accent in his voice. "Juries never come in that fast, unless it's some evil son of a bitch who chopped up a cheerleader. You gotta be kidding me."

"Yeah, well, the jury hated her guts from day one. They couldn't wait to put her away. I mean, her lawyer gave a pretty decent close, but it didn't make a damn bit of difference."

"When's the sentencing?" Bill asked, taking a nibbling approach to baklava number two.

"Two weeks. And after the way she flipped out when she

heard the verdict, I'd be shocked if she didn't get the max. Judge Riegert was not impressed."

"Flipped out how?"

I told them. Bill started laughing so hard he spit baklava on me. "So when can you file?"

"Gimme two hours." I caught snarky glances from both Ochoa and Evil Brad, and tried to recover some dignity. "I mean an hour. I'll even throw in a sidebar on murder trials over the past twenty years."

"Of course you will," Bill said. "So what's everybody else got cooking? Lillian?"

"From what I understand," she said, "Gabriel High is firing its racist swine tomorrow morning. Apparently, no one expects him to go quietly."

"And you got this on the record?"

"Name withheld, of course, but yes it's on the—"

"*Alex.*" Bill made my name sound remarkably like a swear word.

"Yeah?"

"You're supposed to file in fifty-nine minutes."

"Right." I jumped up and grabbed another piece of baklava on my way out. "Hey, where's Mad?"

"AWOL. Now get typing."

I sprinted back to my terminal and banged out a twenty-inch story on Shelley's conviction, which was (naturally) running above the fold of the next day's front page and jumping to meet the sidebar on page four. I was just giving it a final read when Ochoa appeared over my shoulder. This time, I was too caught up in what I was doing to make an ass of myself.

"Yo," he said. "What's up?"

"Filing my mainbar."

He checked his watch. "Three minutes late."

"Thanks for noticing."

"Bill said I should help you out with the sidebar."

"Thanks, but it's hardly a two-man job."

"Maybe I can do it then. He said it'd be a good way for me to get into the cop files."

"In that case, be my guest." I took him over to one of the newsroom's umpteen filing cabinets and opened a drawer. "Here's all the active cop files—well, *reasonably* active anyway. Less current stuff's in the library. If it's really ancient, it's down in the morgue—like older than twenty-five years or so." I grabbed a folder labeled TRIALS–HOMICIDE and handed it to him. "Have fun."

He followed me back to my desk with his nose in the folder. "There's not much in here."

"Not a whole lot of murder trials lately. Most recent was before I got here—maybe five years ago. Bar fight gone hinky, from what I remember."

"Yeah, I see that one. Also one where a guy killed his wife for the insurance."

"There's more in the library." I waved toward a corner of the newsroom. "Down the hall on your left. Just past the men's john."

Twenty minutes later, as I was putting my Shelley Freeman file back in order and dreaming happy dreams of a Tanqueray and tonic, Ochoa asked me to take a look at his sidebar. I hopped over to his terminal—it's directly across from mine—and lurked over his shoulder. "You already finished it?"

"No sweat, *chica*."

"Bill's gonna love you."

"Hey, is there anyplace a guy can get a decent burrito around here?" He even rolled the *r*'s in *burrito*.

"Not really. Place at the end of the Green has its fans, but I think its pretty mediocre."

"I'm gonna *die* up here."

"According to my friend Gordon, there's no decent Chinese, either."

"You mean Gordon Band?"

"How'd you know?"

"His byline was all over the cop files."

"Oh, right."

"Listen, is there even any place a hungry man can get a sandwich in these parts?"

"Schultz's on the Green should be open another hour. Till seven."

"You want to show me the way? I'm buying."

I was about to say no—frankly, the resemblance to my ex was still creeping me out—when I remembered that my only other option for a dinner date involved my dog Shakespeare and a frozen vegetable pot pie, my impending move having temporarily derailed my cooking habit. So once Bill had signed off on the Freeman stories, Ochoa and I went over to the Green for a couple of Frau Schultz's sandwiches, which are three inches thick and have enough carbohydrates to calm a girl down even in the most tense of circumstances.

"So tell me about this Gordon Band," Ochoa said through a mouthful of turkey on rye. "His clips are damn good."

"Should be. He worked for the *Times* before and after he was at the *Monitor*."

"He went from the *Times* to a twenty-thousand-circulation paper? Bummer."

"Long story. Anyway, you'll meet him. He covers upstate news for them now."

"How long have you been without a cops guy?"

"Since last summer, if you can believe it. After Gordon, we got this kid named Franklin who only lasted like three weeks. Then Chester—he's the asshole publisher—he put a hiring freeze on the newsroom, and when he finally let up, Bill had a hard time finding somebody."

"You've been covering the beat on top of the city?"

"Sometimes. So has Mad—that's Jake Madison, the science guy. Plus whoever's weekend reporter has to deal with anything that goes down. The coverage has been kind of a mess, honestly."

He munched on his sandwich for a while, which gave me the chance to get a good look at him. The guy really did bear a rather horrifying resemblance to the last man who broke my heart but good. I mean, okay, that aforementioned male wasn't remotely Hispanic, and he didn't have Ochoa's caramelish skin, but the rest of it was all there—wavy black hair and intense dark eyes and teeth that could eat you in a Grimms' fairy tale.

Ochoa was damn cute; there was no arguing with that. In fact, he was just my type—or at least he used to be, before I decided lithe, muscular reporters with serious commitment-phobia weren't necessarily in a girl's best interest. I tried to concentrate on my food, but my stomach wasn't particularly happy.

Considering where my head was, what he said next was downright creepy.

"So who's Adam Ellroy? He was all over the clip files too."

Shit. "He, um, he was the cop reporter before Gordon."

"He off at the *Times* by now too?"

I put down my Swiss-cheese-and-mustard, which was suddenly not tasting so good. "Apparently, you didn't make it through the rest of the homicide files."

"Huh?"

"He's dead."

"No way." He waited for a punch line, and didn't get it. "For real? What happened?"

"He was killed two years ago. You can check out the clips for yourself."

"How about you fill me in?"

"Not my favorite topic." He looked like he wanted to push it, but didn't. "And just so you know in case people start acting weird around you . . . You sort of look like him a little."

"Son of a bitch."

"Welcome to Gabriel."

CHAPTER
3

College towns, as you probably know, have more transients than the San Francisco bus station. And though as a gainfully employed reporter I qualify as a townie, the fact is that (mostly due to circumstances beyond my control) I tend to move about once a year. Last time, it was because my law-student housemate met the man of his dreams and kicked me out on my pretty little ear; this time, it was because my room-mates had scattered to the four winds. One had fled vet school and gone home to her parents, another was presently interred in a Midwestern cemetery, and a third had just de-camped to the U.K. and broken Mad's heart.

That left me and Steve the Ornithologist, and — facing the prospect of splitting the rent on five bedrooms between the two of us or coming up with three decent housemates — we decided it was time to call it a day.

Luckily, my buddy Melissa (a *Monitor* photographer presently having a torrid affair with a Gabriel city planner) had gotten booted out of her apartment for harboring an ille-gal feline and was looking for new digs. With the semester ending and local landlords avoiding summer vacancies like the clap, we found a nifty little three-bedroom house exactly a block and a half from my old place.

That Saturday, therefore, I marshaled the troops for what wasn't so much a move as a bucket brigade. Mad, Marshall, Cody, and large, loud Irish sports editor Xavier O'Shaunessey stationed themselves at intervals and handed off my stuff in less time than it took the jury to convict Shelley Freeman. Melissa had to rent a truck to haul her earthly possessions from the other side of town, but we were still finished by five. Then, in observance of sacred tradition, we fed the muscle copious quantities of pizza and beer.

You never know what it's going to be like to live with somebody—not even somebody you've been friends with for three years—but I gotta say the first night with Melissa went swimmingly: She decamped to her boyfriend's place and left me and Cody to inaugurate the bedroom, chaperoned only by our respective dogs (his Zeke and my Shakespeare).

Come Monday, the mood in the newsroom was rather blue. The Freeman case, while a gigantic hassle a lot of the time, had been keeping our lives interesting since March. Now there were no more stories about screaming marital fights beneath the Gabriel Peace Pavilion, no more science pieces about gut-busting poisons, not even any lame follow-ups about local reaction to the guilty verdict. All we could do was go back to our little journalistic lives and wait for the appeal.

Meanwhile, I was plenty busy with the usual round of end-of-the-school-year stories. First came the standard fodder about graduates of Benson and its dopier, artier counterpart on the other hill, Bessler College. I wrote about the seventy-four-year-old guy who'd just earned his B.A., and the former welfare mother who pulled herself up by her bootstraps to get an Ivy League degree, and the pocket-protected nerds who'd sold their dot-com and made their first million before the ink was dry on their faux sheepskins.

Then it got worse. With Lillian off on the vacation she schedules every June to avoid such things, I got saddled with covering pre-commencement festivities at the three high schools. I attended the Socially Conscious Prom, where the kids blew off tuxes and limos and pledged the money to feed the hungry—though from what I could tell they'd felt perfectly free to smoke certain Third World crops to enhance their good time. I did a profile on a set of identical twin Mormons who'd deferred college to go on a missionary trip to Curaçao, and another on a native Gabrielite who'd gotten her G.E.D. by correspondence while touring as (get this) a professional dulcimer player, and yet another on a home-schooled Bible-thumper who'd gotten full scholarships to a grand total of twenty-two colleges, and was presently praying for guidance about which one he should attend.

Ochoa, for his part, was fitting into the newsroom nicely. This is more a journalistic compliment than a personal one; what I really mean is that he was as fundamentally insane as the rest of us. Work wise, he was sailing through the eight-week trial period during which new hires are advised to look both ways before they cross the road, since they don't have health insurance yet. And after hours, he was an enthusiastic patron of the Citizen Kane, where he not only proved himself to be an avid arguer but quite the tequila snob as well.

And then there was Mad, whose appearance at my moving party constituted his social event of the season. He showed up at the Citizen a few times to debate Ochoa on the relative merits of Centenario Plata versus El Tesoro de Don Felipe, but for the most part he kept to himself. He wrote his stories, sat through edit meetings (usually), ran his seven miles a day, went to the gym. As far as I could tell he wasn't drinking any more than usual—which admittedly is enough to put most people in a nice dark coffin.

But he was just, I don't know, *unplugged*. He didn't even get excited over a big conference on agricultural biotechnology they were holding up at Benson, which is normally the kind of thing he wouldn't shut up about. I made various and sundry attempts to get him to come clean about what was eating him, all of which culminated in him telling me to mind my own damn business. This would be followed by me reminding him that reporters are not generally good at minding their own business, at which point he'd tell me to go fuck myself.

It was also around this time that I got my first letter from Shelley Freeman, who was locked up in Bedford Hills—hell and gone from Gabriel in the context of upstate New York, but no sweat for the U.S. Postal Service. It came in a cheap, grayish envelope with warnings about its origins plastered all over it, lest some sneaky prisoner convince Miss Lonelyhearts he was writing from his villa in Capri.

The note was short, polite, and crafted in pretty Catholic school handwriting my dad would approve of. She apologized for bothering me, said she knew I was busy, but wanted to know if I'd be willing to come to the prison and interview her. It was understandable she'd address the letter to me— I'd covered her as much as anybody—but now the story belonged to the cop reporter. So, saying adieu to the AP award Ochoa was going to win instead of me, I passed the letter on to him.

The second one came a week later. And it—more than all the reporting I'd done so far or the interviews I'd have with her later—gave me an inkling of what it might have been like to be Lane Freeman.

The letter wasn't hysterical exactly, just really . . . strident. And the striking thing about it was that it was so different from the one before. Even the handwriting, though similar, seemed like it belonged to somebody else—maybe a slightly crazier member of Shelley's fourth-grade penmanship class.

It went like this:

Dear Alex,

    Perhaps I didn't make myself clear in my previous message and if that's the case then I apologize. However, I am astonished and somewhat angry that you took the liberty of passing off my story to another reporter—to a <u>male</u> reporter, for that matter. I just got a letter from this Cal Ochoa person today and, honestly, I'm utterly flabbergasted. How could you think for a minute that a <u>man</u> could possibly understand what I'm going through? How could you even <u>think</u> that? If you did think that you were wrong, and I hope that you never have the bad luck to be where I am today—helpless, frustrated, all alone, and completely <u>trapped.</u>

    Obviously when you read this you're going to think that I sound like I'm feeling sorry for myself. And you know something? I am feeling sorry for myself, and I damn well have a right to be.

    Let me get something straight from the beginning. <u>I did not kill my husband.</u> I'm sure you don't believe me, but you should, because if you're really the reporter you're cracked up to be you should always have your eyes open for the truth. And I swear to God that it's the truth. You also may not believe that I loved Lane but I did, and if the rest of the world doesn't get that or believe it either they can all go to hell. And all that aside, nobody who knows me could ever say I don't love my children, and if you think I'd put them through this <u>nightmare</u> of my own free will you're out of your mind.

I don't know what happened to Lane. I don't know if
he really died of what the police say he died of.
Everybody knows those people are a bunch of
incompetents who can barely even <u>read.</u> I don't
understand how they ever decided that I had this poison
in the backseat of my car—it's all been this nightmare
out of Kafka, you know? One day everything was
normal and the next Lane was dead and the next thing I
knew they were arresting me for it.

I'm praying that my appeal will go through and this
conviction will be overturned and I can get a new trial
that's better than that circus that Aronofsky ran and I
can find a lawyer who knows what he's doing. But at
this point I know better than to trust the legal system so
I'm not optimistic. My only hope is that public opinion
will be on my side and people in Gabriel will demand
that something be done about this miscarriage of
justice. And that's where you come in.

I don't want you to think it's just empty flattery when
I say that I've been reading your stories for a long time.
I honestly have. I've always thought you were the best
reporter at that paper. And I also know you're a woman
who's suffered like I've suffered and lost people you
care about. You can't go through something like that and
come out of it unscathed. It changes you. And that's
another reason I want to tell my story to you and not a
stranger.

There's another thing too. I saw you in the courtroom
during the trial, particularly when those son-of-a-bitch
lawyers did their closing arguments. I could tell by the
expression on your face that you thought they were full
of shit just like I did. And though this may come off as
inappropriate, I want you to know that it actually meant
something to me to have you in the courtroom—to have

a woman there who knew what it was like to get
screwed by the system. It made me feel somewhat less
alone, knowing you were there.

Is that crazy? Probably it is. But when you go
through what I've been through your sense of what's
right and wrong and decent goes right out the window. It
goes overboard because you know you're sinking and
it's all you can do to keep your head above water.

Please, please, please, Alex. Come out here and talk
with me for a few hours and you'll see I'm telling the
truth. Even if you don't want to do it for me
personally—and why should you except out of a basic
sense of sisterhood?—I think you know it would be a
great story for you to write and for your newspaper to
publish.

What do you say? Will you do it? I'll wait for your
answer, because nowadays waiting's all I can do—that's
all they let me do.

> Yours very truly,
> Shelley
> (Mrs. Lane Freeman)

I read through the thing three times before I brought it into
Bill's office. Then I got to sit there and wait while he read it
twice himself.

"The woman," he said finally, "is cracking up."

"You think?"

"Don't you?"

"Well, she's definitely under the gun. Wouldn't you be if
you were probably going to spend the next couple decades in
the clink?"

"Maybe she's getting her just desserts."

"She says not."

"And you believe her?"

"I don't know. I mean, like Cody says, every prison is jam-packed with innocent people, right? Everybody says he didn't do it."

"And Shelley's no different."

"So you're saying we shouldn't cover her?"

"Hell no. What do you make of it?"

"The letter? It kind of goes back and forth between reality and fantasy. Like this thing about making some connection with me in the courtroom? To tell you the truth, I didn't even know she noticed me there. We sure as hell never winked at each other or anything. And that part where she basically says we're soul sisters . . . It's kind of creepy. I mean, the idea that she's sitting in prison thinking about how I—"

"Do you want to write the story or don't you?"

"Who wouldn't?"

"Then let's get this over with." He barked for Ochoa, who came in, sat down, and put his feet on the edge of Bill's desk like he owned the place. "Alex got a love letter from Mrs. Freeman," Bill said, and handed it over to him.

He zipped through it, rolled his eyes, and tossed it on the desk. "Don't tell me you're falling for this."

I put my feet up on the desk too, a territorial gesture worthy of my dog—who, come to think of it, might just have peed on him. "What's that supposed to mean?"

"Are you really going to let the source dictate coverage?"

I rolled my eyes back at him. "And where, may I ask, did you pick up these high-and-mighty journalistic ethics?"

"The *North Lake Tahoe Bonanza*."

"Oh, *please*."

"Kids," Bill interjected, "though I'd like nothing better than to sit here and watch you two duke it out, you might as well remember it's not up to you. Thy editor is thy god."

I aimed a little head-bow in his direction. "Yes, Master."

Ochoa didn't seem inclined to get in on the joke. "It's my beat."

"You could look at it that way if you wanted to," Bill said.

"If you wanted to be an asshole," I offered.

"But," Bill continued, "there's also an argument that Alex is entitled to follow a story she started covering way before you got here."

I gave Ochoa a satisfied little smile. "It's an excellent argument."

He didn't smile back. "Why do you want this story so bad?"

"Why do you?"

"Because it's my beat." I opened my mouth to say something clever, but he kept talking. "And on top of that, it's the best damn thing that's come down since I got here. If I gotta do another prewrite on the goddamn D.A.R.E. campaign, I'm gonna—"

"Hey, it's not my fault Shelley doesn't want to talk to you."

"The woman's desperate for coverage. She'll talk to anybody we send out there."

"I wouldn't be so sure. You read the letter, didn't you? She wants to talk to me *personally*."

"Why do women reporters always try to hog all the good stories, like you've got to have ovaries to write a fucking personality piece—"

"You sexist prick—"

"Hey, I call them as I—"

"Goddamn Neanderthal—"

That was when Bill decided he'd had enough. "Just go interview her together." We shut up and stared at him. "You're both right. It's Alex's story, but it's Ochoa's beat. So just grow up and shake hands and cover the damn thing."

"Wait a minute," I said. "What makes you think Shelley'll go for it?"

"Why shouldn't she? She wants you; she's got you. And, like Ochoa said, she's desperate. She'll take what she can get."

Then it was Ochoa's turn to whine. "You really think the prison's gonna let us both in there?"

"How the hell do I know? Tell me if there's a problem. Now shut my door on the way out so I don't have to listen to you anymore."

"Jesus," I said as we commuted the ten feet to our respective desks, "you're one pushy son of a bitch."

"Takes one to know one."

"All I can say is you better not snore."

"What does that have to do with—"

"You really think this paper's got the budget for separate motel rooms?"

"You gotta be shitting me."

"I wish."

"My girlfriend's gonna kill me."

"My boyfriend," I said, "could kill you with his thumb."

CHAPTER
4

Apparently, you can't just waltz into a women's prison and start interviewing people. You have to make arrangements for these things with the Department of Corrections, which (from what I could tell) uses red tape for everything short of shackling its inmates. Ochoa and I had to file a request, Shelley Freeman had to file one of her own, and then all three of us had to sit around and wait until the bureaucrats gave the okay, which clearly wasn't going to happen anytime soon.

It probably didn't help that the *Monitor* is a rinky-dink paper in the geographic center of nowhere; I doubted the D.O.C. was processing our paperwork with the deliberate speed it'd give the *New York Times*. And then there was the fact that, if her tenure in the Walden County lockup was any indication, Shelley was as much of a headache behind bars as in front; the powers that be at Bedford Hills were obviously in no hurry to do her any favors.

So, with our road trip to the hoosegow on hold for the moment, I went back to covering the usual Gabriel city news — which, granted, was a hell of a lot more interesting than the D.O.C. probably gave us credit for. Gabriel may be five hours from a major metropolitan area, but we are in possession of the following: a genuine Ivy League research university, a working particle accelerator, the world's most famous vegetarian restaurant, several enormous gorges (providing ample opportunity for dramatic death, both intentional and accidental), a Tibetan Buddhist monastery founded by the Dalai Lama himself, and a remarkable congregation of some of the smartest, weirdest people on the planet.

On a Monday in early June, therefore, Mad and I went up to Benson to cover what would've been big news most places, but in Gabriel was just another day at the races: the kickoff of a week-long conference on agricultural biotechnology. That is, *he* was covering the conference—fortunate, since the last science course I took was high-school chemistry, and I got a C-minus.

No, I got drafted into doing a sidebar on the outdoor portion of the festivities, in which the predictable number of shaggy-haired protesters (say, a dozen) were going to troop around in front of the biotech building with signs warning of the sci-fi horrors of genetically engineered food, then repair to a local coffeehouse to drink Guatemalan Antigua and smoke cloves.

That's what I figured, anyway. But when we got up to campus, it turned out the local pierced-and-chanting set had invited several hundred of their closest friends to the party. Even Mad—a tall, well-exercised fellow who can usually part a crowd like the proverbial Red Sea—had a hell of a time trying to get through them and into the building. I never had a chance.

This didn't keep me from my appointed rounds, of course, as I was supposed to be covering the protest. What it did keep me from was the assorted croissants (and, more important, the almighty coffee) awaiting us at the registration table, which I had been counting on in lieu of breakfast. I was not starting the day off in a good mood.

I cursed Mad's stupid back as it disappeared through the double glass doors, then pulled out my notebook and resigned myself to covering the story hungry and decaffeinated.

Now, I don't mean to imply that I don't enjoy witnessing some civil disobedience now and again. Such a sentiment would be pointless anyway, since a *Monitor* reporter can avoid covering a protest like somebody from the *Detroit Free Press* can avoid writing about cars.

Because in Gabriel, you see, direct action is a spectator sport. Don't want a developer to tear down a historic theater? Shackle yourself to the front entrance. Want to keep the city from adopting a youth curfew? Get eighty teenagers together for a sit-in in the mayor's office. Upset that the Shop 'n Save won't sell BGH-free milk? Dress up like a cow and hand out flyers.

The upside of all this is that the Gabriel police are remarkably tolerant; you pretty much have to pelt the fire chief with monkey blood to get yourself arrested. But there's also a major drawback: In these parts, protest music is the official town soundtrack, so sometimes people don't pay much attention to it. More than once, I've solicited comments from passersby during a protest on the Green, and found they had no idea what today's fuss was all about—rather the opposite of what you'd want.

But there was zero doubt about the subject at hand this particular Monday, what with three hundred people besieging the entrance to the glossy white biotech building. I could tell right off these weren't just the usual suspects, either; on top of the sheer quantity, a lot of them had a more hardened look about them than you tend to see on the homegrown protest set, like they usually took their lattes and clipped their facial hair in a way-more-urban zip code.

I spent a fruitless fifteen minutes trying to figure out who was in charge, but nobody was in the mood to stop chanting long enough to answer me. After a while, somebody picked up a bullhorn and gave a rousing speech in which he did, indeed, warn us all of the sci-fi horrors of genetically engineered food. The guy seemed as likely a source as anybody, so (in sort of a mobile game of Where's Waldo?) I tried to keep track of him before he disappeared into the crowd. I eventually managed to make my way over to him, though not before I was elbowed soundly in the ribs by a girl whose blond dreadlocks were almost as tall as she was. When I caught up with my prey, I waved my press pass at him, and it had the desired effect.

Though he seemed perfectly content to do the interview amid all the shouting, I got him to go around the corner in the hope of actually hearing his quotes before I wrote them down. The first thing he did after we sat on the grass was express disappointment that I wasn't working for the *Times*. I didn't disagree with him. Then he pulled out a pack of American Spirits and lit up without offering me one.

"Do you think they're gonna show up?"

"Who?"

"The *Times*."

"Oh. I kind of doubt it."

I thought of Gordon, who enjoys protests like the Wicked Witch of the West enjoys a bubble bath. He'd only cover this thing if his job or his life depended on it—in that order.

"Why the fuck not?"

"Um . . . I'm not sure. You'd have to ask them."

He fingered his goatee, which hung two inches off his chin and looked very much like it belonged on an actual goat. "Who do you write for again?"

"The *Gabriel Monitor*. The local daily."

"Oh." He dismissed me, my paper, and my future offspring with one flick of ashes onto grass. "What's the circulation?"

"About twenty thousand."

"Oh." *Flick.*

"Listen, I just want to ask you a few questions about—"

"Is the AP coming at least?" *Flick, flick.*

"I have no idea."

"Son of a bitch." He sighed and leaned back onto one elbow. "Well, I guess you'll have to do."

"Lucky me." The D.O.C.'s foot-dragging over the Shelley Freeman thing had me feeling all defensive about the size of my paper, like I was coming up short in the journalistic locker room. I was on the point of telling him to kiss my French Canadian ass, but didn't. "So what's your name?"

"Tobias Kahan. That's *K-A-H-A-N.* Not Toby, *Tobias.* And don't go leaving out the second *a,* got it?"

"I'll do my best. So are you guys with any particular group?"

"You bet your ass we are. We're with the D.B.F.C." I could tell he was expecting something like awe, and my blank look didn't satisfy. "Haven't you even heard of us?"

"Can't say as I have."

"We're only, like, the biggest anti-G.M.O. group in the whole freakin' country."

"Anti-what?"

He took a long drag on his cigarette, like he needed something in his mouth to keep from spitting on me. "G.M.O. *Genetically Modified Organisms.* Jesus Fucking Christ, don't you even know what you're doing?"

"Um . . . Our science writer is inside covering the conference. I'm just doing a sidebar on the protest."

"*A sidebar?* What kind of pathetic—"

This marked the end of my good manners. "Hey, do you plan to be this much of an asshole when you talk to the *Times*? Because their upstate reporter's a buddy of mine, and I can tell you right now it's not gonna fly."

"Yeah, well, presumably the *Times* wouldn't send some-body who doesn't know her ass from her—"

"Look, obviously you think you're some pretty hot shit, though from where I'm sitting I have no idea why."

"Who the hell do you—"

"But let me give you some advice. If you really want to get your message out there, whatever the hell it is, you better fig-ure out that insulting a reporter you don't even know is a pretty lousy way to do it." He didn't say anything, just glared at me. I stood up. "Now, call me irresponsible, but I really don't give a shit if you get your name in the paper or you don't. I'm pretty sure somebody over there'll talk to me"—I aimed my pen in the direction of all the noise—"so I'm gonna get my story either way. Now you wanna play nice?"

More glaring, followed by a smoky sigh and a resigned snuffing-out of cigarette. "So what do you want to know?"

I sat back down. "What the hell is the D.B.F.C.?"

"It stands for 'Don't Break the Food Chain.'"

I was trying very hard not to snicker. "Are you serious?"

"Most people call it 'The Chain' for short. We've got over fifteen thousand members around the world, mostly in the U.S., Canada, and Western Europe—the countries most af-fected by scientific imperialism. Like I said, we're the biggest anti-G.M.O. group in the world." He finally held out the American Spirits. "You want a smoke?"

I did, but I was trying to be a good girl. "No thanks. So how many members do you have in Gabriel?"

"You mean people who live here," he said as he lit butt number two, "or how many are here now?"

"Both."

"There's about fifty members from the town, and a student chapter at Benson is getting together with a couple dozen, so I'd say . . . seventy-five or so. At today's action, we've got about two-fifty."

"You brought in people from out of town just for the protest?"

He looked at me like I was intensely dumb. "Of course. That's what we do."

"And are you staying all week? All two hundred fifty of you?"

He barked out an ugly laugh. "You ain't seen nothin' yet."

"Meaning?"

"Meaning they'll see."

"They'll see what?"

"No comment."

"Give me a break."

"Look, seriously, I couldn't tell you if I wanted to. All I can say is we're planning a major action. A *series* of major actions."

"Which means what exactly?"

"I'd just make sure your paper has enough reporters assigned to cover it. This is going to be a *major* international story. Trust me. This'll be the biggest thing you've ever covered, by a mile."

"I doubt that very much." He gave me a pitying look, like I had hay stuck in my teeth. I didn't bother to inform him that, interesting though it may be, his group had nothing on serial killers, eighty-year-old murders, and various other stories that had filled the *Monitor*'s pages of late. "So why is your group so against genetically engineered food, anyway?"

"How much time you got?"

"Plenty."

"Okay, first off, the bottom line is nobody knows shit about what could happen in the long run. The assholes in the lab coats'll tell you, 'Don't worry, it's all safe, nothing's gonna happen.' But they *don't know*. And that's a pretty stupid way to do things, don't you think? I mean, you don't release a drug until it's been tested for, like, ten years. But when it comes to G.M.O.'s, we *are* the experiment. *We're* the lab rats. Do you get it?"

"Um . . . no. You mean nobody tests this stuff?"

"Hardly. They say they do, but you gotta remember where the money is." He waited two seconds for me to answer, then gave up. "It's in international agribusiness. We're talking hundreds of billions of dollars a year. No way they're gonna let anybody fuck with that. So even when somebody does test this shit, most of the time it's the companies themselves who do the testing, and they get the results they want to get. But when you ask them the hard questions, they trip over their feet trying to make themselves out to be the good guys, like if you're not willing to eat their Frankenfoods, you're voting in favor of starvation in the Third World—"

"Look, you gotta give me a break here. Like I said, I don't usually cover this. I cover local government. My background in this stuff is pretty much zip. So can you try to explain this like you're talking to a second grader?"

He seemed about to say something uncharitable, then decided to light another cigarette instead. "Frankenfoods," he said when he'd sucked the butt to glowing. "You know what that means?" I shook my head. "It's like—"

"Yo, Tobias, there you are," said a voice from the direction of the mob. "I've been looking for you, like, everyplace. . . ."

The character approaching us might have been Tobias Junior—same slouch, same studiously unkempt wardrobe, same loathsome goatee, only about five years younger. He came over at a trot, crouched down next to us froggy-style, and started scratching at the back of his sweaty neck.

"Yo, Tobias, you seen the new banners?"

Kahan gave him a look that said he thought the kid was almost as stupid as I was; almost, but not quite. "Of course I've seen them," he said. "I *approved* them. Of course I've fucking seen them."

"Yeah, I know . . . I mean, of course you have. But I mean, like, have you seen them *lately?*"

"What the fuck happened to them? Did those pig bastards get their hands on—"

"No, I don't think that's—"

"Don't fucking *interrupt* me when I'm talking," Kahan said in a voice so nasty and condescending I wanted to punch him in the nose on the kid's behalf. "How many times have I told you when I'm talking you fucking *listen?*"

The kid didn't answer right away, just stared at the dirty toenails poking out of his Birkenstocks. His face was turning the color of your average pickled beet. Eventually, he mumbled, "Sorry."

"What?"

"I said . . . 'Sorry.'"

"Then don't fucking forget it again. You got it?" The kid nodded. "Now tell me what's going on with the banners."

"We, um . . . We can't find them."

"What?"

"I said, we can't—"

"I heard you. What do you mean you can't *find* them?"

"Lulu thought they were in the van, but they're not. We thought maybe you—"

"What are you, a bunch of *morons?*" Several veins looked like they might pop out of his cranium. "Telling me you can't find them is not fucking acceptable, do you get it?"

"Lulu thought—"

"I don't give a flying *fuck* what Lulu thought. Now get off your ass and go *find* them. *Now.*" The kid nodded, sprang up from his crouch, and fled. Kahan turned back to me with an astonishingly bland expression on his face, like he hadn't just reamed out one of his underlings right in front of a reporter. "You see the shit I have to deal with? Now where were we?"

"Um . . . Frankenfoods."

"Right. Like I was saying, these foods are the agricultural equivalent of Frankenstein's monster, get it? They're cobbled together from spare parts by people with egos so big they think they're gods, but the end result is something outside nature—something horrible that evolution never would have created, something man never *should* have created."

He was sounding both coherent *and* eloquent all of a sudden. Go figure. "And what you said about the Third World . . ."

"That's their Get Out of Jail Free card. It always has been. Whenever anybody objects to the use of this technology, or even just questions whether it should be put on the market without really being tested first, they turn around and accuse us of being spoiled First Worlders who have the luxury of eating organic potatoes. They talk about how G.M.O.'s are this miracle cure for feeding the hungry. And it would be great if it were true—or if it came without a huge price tag for the next generation. And you know what? We don't even know how high the price is going to be, or who's going to have to pay it. Don't you think that's scary?"

"But what kind of price are you talking about?"

"Like I said, we don't know. And in science, 'We don't know' isn't supposed to be a good enough answer before you sic something on the population at large, is it? But like I said, this isn't science we're talking about. It's business, pure and simple."

"I got that, but what specific things are you guys worried about?"

He flopped down on his back and recited a list like he was counting off Disney dwarfs. "Allergies. Antibiotic resistance. Genetic pollution. Superweeds. Field sterilization. More dependence on chemical farming. Species-wide kills that make *Silent Spring* look like a trip to summer camp. And that's just for starters."

"Allergies? What does that have to do with anything?"

"When you're messing with genes, you never know what the hell is going to happen. Like, one study found that a soybean modified with genes from a Brazil nut caused reactions in people allergic to the nuts. That one got stopped before it made it to the market, but how many others aren't, you know? Think about it this way: You know how sometimes you buy a box of, like, Gummi Bears and it warns you that they were packaged in a factory where they process nuts? That's because some people are so allergic that even that little contact could kill them, so they label for it. But nobody has to label G.M.O.'s. And the companies don't want to, because they know their sales would plummet. Nobody fucking wants genetically engineered cornflakes, right? Do you?"

"I never really thought about it."

"Well, think about it. Take antibiotic resistance. The whole scientific community is worried about the evolution of drug-resistant superbacteria. So they bitch and moan about antibacterial dish soap. But you know what's an even bigger problem? The fact that antibiotic genes are a key part of the genetic-engineering process—they're used to deliver the new gene to the host. And God only knows what that's going to mean in the long run. You want me to keep going?"

I was scribbling as fast as I could. "Sure."

"Genetic pollution. That's when pollen from a G.M.O. field drifts over and contaminates the organic farm down the road. Superweeds. You use enough Round Up, eventually weeds are going to evolve that are resistant to that and every other herbicide known to man, and the whole ecosystem is fucked. And plus, then the companies have got farmers even more hooked on their goddamn chemicals, right? Field sterilization is the idea that if you've got crops engineered to resist an herbicide you can douse the land with the stuff and kill everything else, but then there's nothing left for birds and insects to feed on—if they even survive."

"Huh?"

"Don't you know the story about the monarch butterflies? Come on, you've got to have heard about it. It happened right here at Benson."

It sounded vaguely familiar. "Was that the thing about the corn? I think Mad covered it."

"Pollen from corn engineered to repel pests by producing the *bacillus thurigenesis* toxin was put on milkweed and fed to butterfly larvae, and most of them died. It was an entomologist up at Benson who did the experiment. People jumped all over him for his methodology, but later studies showed he wasn't far off. Of course, he was denied tenure anyway. Don't kid yourself about where the Benson ag school gets most of its money."

"Then why are they hosting this conference? I mean, isn't this supposed to be a forum for all the different sides of the—"

"What a joke. If they were serious about it, anti-G.M.O. people would've gotten half of the speaking time instead of four lousy slots. They're just throwing us a bone, which is why The Chain told them to go to hell. We'd rather get our message out to the public than get co-opted by the fucking agribiz establishment. No way were we gonna help legitimize their bullshit conference. *No way.*"

"What about, you know, participating in dialogue? Wouldn't you have been more upset if they didn't even invite you?"

"Not inviting us would've been a lot more honest than inviting us just to try to marginalize us on their own turf."

"Sounds like you're saying they can't win."

He favored me with a creepy little smile, teeth blazing white against his black goatee. "I can tell you one thing. Winning is one thing those bastards are never going to do. Not in the long run. And nature," he said, "is all about the long run."

CHAPTER
5

The hour I spent on the soggy grass with Tobias Kahan, grand pooh-bah of Don't Break the Food Chain, taught me everything I ever wanted to know about genetically modified chow. Not that I learned all that much, mind you; it's just that—happy little consumer that I am—I was never that interested in it in the first place. After talking to him, though, it was hard not to look at every Twinkie and Ding Dong as an emissary of Satan.

Still, at the advanced age of twenty-seven, I'm not as easily swayed by dietary hyperbole as I used to be. A few years back, for instance, I did a story on a group dedicated to spreading the word about the evils of dairy. I was therefore inspired to go from vegetarian to vegan; this lasted all of a month, during which (my friends tell me) I became an intolerable bitch due to the lack of pizza in my life.

Despite Kahan's disdain for my place of employment, he told me some pretty damn interesting stuff. My sidebar on the protest metastasized to twenty-eight inches, which turned out to be seven inches longer than Mad's piece on the conference itself. I expected Bill to hack it in half, as was his privilege; imagine my surprise when I walked through the pressroom the next morning and discovered that Bill had flip-flopped them, with my story running above the fold and Mad's getting a lousy little billboard (COMPLETE CONFERENCE COVERAGE, PAGE 4) and running on the inside with the jump from my mainbar.

So I guess it was understandable that when he didn't show up for work on time a lot of people assumed he was just irked at getting kicked off page one. But I've known Mad a long time, and I didn't buy it; he's as competitive as the rest of us, and he's been known to have a temper, but I've never seen him throw a hissy fit for no good reason. By eleven-thirty I was starting to get worried, so I went over and knocked on his apartment door—it's just yards from the paper—but there was no answer. I tried the knob and found the door unlocked—not particularly alarming since Mad knows he has nothing worth stealing beyond some liquor and an ancient television.

Make that just the TV. When I first walked into the place, I thought it'd been tossed; then I realized it was just a god-awful mess, which was downright odd. Mad usually makes his bed with the anal retentiveness of a drill sergeant, but the blankets were thrown all over the place and the single pillow was on the floor. In the kitchen, the garbage can was overflowing with dirty paper coffee cups from the all-night deli across the street. There were empty take-out cartons and orange peels scattered all over the living room, and—this was the kicker—so many empty booze bottles it looked like somebody'd ransacked a liquor store. I counted something like a dozen magnums of Concha y Toro cabernet-merlot, a few Jack Daniel's empties, a plastic Gordon's Gin jug, and a fifth of Mezcal with the worm in the bottom—not to mention a few cases' worth of Old Milwaukee Light cans and a sad-looking bottle of Asti Spumante, which is something I'd have bet my life would never pass his lips.

The one thing I didn't see was a glass. Since he obviously hadn't cleaned anything up, I had a bad feeling that all the drinking had been done straight out of the bottle. Jesus Christ.

I sprinted back to the paper and grabbed O'Shaunessey just as he was getting to the sports desk.

"Have you seen Mad? He never showed up this morning. You been over to his place lately?"

"Yo, Bernier, slow down. . . ."

"Have you seen him?"

"Negatory."

"Well, I was just over there. His apartment looks like Sunday morning on skid row."

He raised a pair of prematurely graying eyebrows at me. "So?"

"So you know Mad. He misbehaves plenty, but he never does it in his own crib. And the place is a *dump*. Empties piled up to the ceiling. And this is the guy who gets pissed when you don't put a coaster under your salsa jar."

"He's been hitting the sauce pretty hard."

"No shit."

"What about his car?"

"Still behind his apartment. But you know he never drives anywhere anyway."

O'Shaunessey crumpled into his swivel chair with a sigh. "So where is he?"

"Damn good question."

"Maybe he got himself a date last night. Wouldn't be the first time, right? Mad never has a problem in that dep—"

"Yeah, but can you think of a single time he's been two hours late for work without calling in?"

He shook his head. "You want me to go call the hospital or something?"

"Jesus, I wasn't thinking anything *bad* happened to him. But come to think of it, I guess you might as well."

"And you might as well call your buddy Cody and see if Mad got himself locked up overnight. Ask me, that's your more likely scenario. Probably went another ten rounds with the cash machine on the Green."

"I'm pretty sure Cody'd have called me by now if something like that'd happened, but okay."

I headed straight for my desk but got intercepted by Bill, who called me into his office and—as if the morning weren't already melodramatic enough—had me shut the door. People were going to think *I* was the one in hot water.

"Anybody heard from Madison?"

"Not yet."

"Damn it. Where the hell is he?"

"I'm working on it."

"He better have a damn good excuse. The guy's got the page-three feature package for tomorrow—keynote speech of the genetic-engineering conference. What does he think I'm gonna do? Cover it myself?"

"So what are you going to—"

"It's at two. Have fun."

"Me? But I don't know anything about—"

"Do I have to remind you that you have a page-one story in today's paper on that very subject?"

"Yeah, but it wasn't about the science part. It was just about the protest."

"Which was all about the science. So go cover it."

"If you say so."

I was halfway out the door when he stopped me. "Hey, Alex, come back here a minute. What the hell do you think is going on with Madison?"

"Um . . . I don't know. He's just seemed a little distracted lately, I guess."

"A little distracted? He's all over the place. You know what it's about?"

"Maybe . . . Well, it's probably just some personal thing. Romance stuff or something."

"Madison?"

"He was, you know, dating one of my housemates for a while, and she just moved back to England. Far as I know they haven't spoken since. Maybe he's having a tough time."

"He actually told you this?"

I shook my head. "I asked him about it, but he told me to go to hell."

"Now *that* sounds like Madison."

"Can you, like, call today a sick day or something? Or maybe a personal day?"

Bill offered up something between a nod and a head shake. "I'll cover for him today, but he better not pull this again. Marilyn has a damn low tolerance for this crap."

"I'll talk to him."

"You gotta find him first."

I got Cody on the phone, and found out that as far as he knew Mad wasn't in the city lockup; he said he'd check for sure and call me back, which he did five minutes later. No Mad. According to O'Shaunessey, he was neither in the hospital nor the morgue. Good news, but not particularly helpful in getting me off the hook for covering a speech on gene splicing.

He still hadn't manifested himself by the time I had to leave, cursing him all the way up to Benson. I'd left plenty of time to drive around in search of a parking place, which was elusive enough on a normal day but near impossible due to the conference, the protest, and the attendant media frenzy. I finally found a spot on the hinterlands of campus and trudged back, whereupon I had the joy of busting through the chanting minions. I saw Tobias Kahan among them, but he didn't seem to recognize me, and I couldn't blame him; nobody's going to pay attention to a short brunette with a reporter's notebook when there's a cadre of guys parading about dressed as cartoon vegetables with big bloody fangs.

I made my way to the registration table and picked up the credentials that had been waiting for me the morning before. Officially dog-tagged, I made up for yesterday by snagging myself some coffee, a cheese Danish, an almond croissant, and a corn muffin and found a seat, where I consumed the muffin and half the croissant without giving a damn whether they'd been genetically altered or shot with a goddamn ray gun.

I flipped through the program while the rest of the conference-goers straggled in from lunch. The speech I was supposed to be covering was being given by somebody named Kate Barnett; according to the bio blurb, she was a professor of plant science at Benson and a world expert in the field of rice breeding. Thrilling.

The chairman of the conference took the podium at ten after but was immediately drowned out by the screech of a microphone gone mad. A techie rushed up to fix it, whereupon the chairman gave an interminable introduction comparing Professor Barnett to just about every saint in human history. As far as I was concerned, Mad deserved combat pay for sitting through this crap.

Then Kate Barnett started talking, and she was so damn eloquent I just about forgot my own name.

The woman had to be six feet, with a mane of gray-flecked black hair that flowed straight over her shoulders and disappeared behind the waist-high dais. She had big eyes—I couldn't tell what color from the back row—a mannish sort of nose, and a wide mouth with lines that looked like she frowned a lot, which is probably what you do when you're stuck thinking about rice all day long.

She had to be a big deal, because when she got to the podium she had to wait a good two minutes for all the applause to die down. She waved it off, but sort of halfheartedly, either because she didn't want to be rude or because she liked the sound of it—maybe she was a mere mortal after all.

When the clapping stopped, she breathed deep and took a long look around. I know it's impossible, but it honest-to-God felt like she looked at each of us individually, made some kind of connection or appeal. It reminded me of what people used to say about President Clinton—that he had this gift for making everybody feel like they were the only person in the room, or at least the only one who mattered.

"What," she asked finally, "do you hunger for?"

She let the question hang in the air for a while, then followed it up with more.

"Do you hunger for love? Do you hunger for . . . power?" Another long pause, and a little smile. "How about sex? We all want that, don't we? Do you hunger for companionship, for someone to tell you you're not alone in the world, that you matter? Do you wish you were more beautiful? How about fame? And fortune? World peace? Or maybe just a good long rest? Hmm? So tell me, what is it that you hunger for?"

Nobody answered, and I was reminded of Jim Collier's closing at the Shelley Freeman trial. They'd used pretty much the same tactic, but Kate Barnett was a way better speaker, with a deep voice that sounded like it came from a biblical mountaintop; maybe she could've actually gotten Shelley acquitted.

"The one thing you probably don't hunger for," Professor Barnett continued, "is food. Am I right? We all walked by that platter of treats as we walked in the door. It had"—she consulted a slip of paper—"coffee, both regular and decaffeinated; tea, not only regular and decaffeinated but also herbal; orange, tomato, apple, and cranberry juices; plain, almond, and chocolate croissants; apple, cherry, prune, and cheese Danish; corn, carrot, blueberry, bran, and chocolate-chip muffins; and a bowl of fruit containing apples, oranges, and pears.

"And that, ladies and gentlemen, was our afternoon snack." She paused a beat to let it sink in. "A *snack*. Enough calories to feed a village for a day, and we here in the developed world consider it a *snack*."

She made it sound like a four-letter word. I looked down at the crumbs clinging to the waxy muffin paper and had the good grace to feel a tad guilty.

"Now," she continued, "I have no interest in standing up here trying to make you feel guilty for not being hungry, or even for living lives of privilege." *Yeah, right.* "But when you bite into that perfect apple, or pull the top off that muffin and toss the rest aside, I just want you to remember that you're lucky. Not everyone in the world lives like this.

"Remember when you were little, and you didn't want to eat your brussels sprouts, and your mother would tell you . . . What?"

She looked out into the audience like a teacher seeking an answer from her class. Eventually, someone got the hint and called out something I couldn't make out.

"That's right," she said with another little smile. "Your mother would say, 'Eat your food, because there are starving children in Africa.' And I remember what I used to say. I'd say, 'Mom, if the African kids want the brussels sprouts so badly, why don't we just *send* them to them? They can *have* them.'"

Chuckles from the audience.

"But there's a serious side to this story, of course. The point I'd like to make is that there have been starving children in Africa for as long as we can remember. When we were children ourselves, we joked about sending the food we didn't want to the other side of the world. And now here we are—we're adults. But how many of those other children never grew up? How many never knew a life that wasn't marked by hunger, by drought and famine? How many perished from diseases that we'd cure with a trip to the drugstore? How many went blind for lack of vitamin A? How many saw their suffering compounded by war and corruption? How miserable were their lives, that when they starved to death or died of dysentery or malaria or cholera they actually *welcomed* it?"

She'd worked herself up into a minor frenzy and had to take a minute to get her composure back.

"The Green Revolution of the 1960s and '70s was a wonderful thing. But I'm here to tell you that *it wasn't enough.* There are still starving people in the world, millions upon millions of them. And now, at the start of the new millennium, they also face new enemies—not only diseases like AIDS and Ebola but a multiyear drought that could well be one of the most devastating in a century. The people of the developing world stand at the nexus between bad and worse, while those of us in developed countries enjoy prosperity the likes of which the Earth has never seen.

"But there is hope on the horizon. At the very moment when the problems of the developing world seem all but insurmountable, we find in our hands the tools to solve them.

"I'm speaking, of course, of genetic engineering. Now, we all know that some people consider this a technology to be feared. And do you know something? They're not entirely wrong. They understand that genetic engineering is a thing of awesome power. Like any technology, it can be used and it can be misused. Nuclear energy can fuel power plants or destroy whole civilizations. The same research that halts an epidemic can be rechanneled into biological warfare. A hammer can be used to build a house or kill a man.

"Genetic engineering, in other words, is neither good nor bad. No technology is; it's just a tool. How we use it is up to us. Now, I'm not advocating putting a fish gene into a tomato so it can have a longer shelf life. I'm not suggesting that this technology be used lightly, or frivolously, or without adequate testing. What I'm calling for is an end to the hysteria. Because the thing that scares me most is that out of ignorance and fear will come a regulatory climate like the one developing in Western Europe, where so-called 'Frankenfoods' are anathema, and where even the most beneficial research is seen as a step toward a 'brave new world.'

"And amid all this hysteria, it would behoove us to remember that humans have been genetically engineering their food for millennia. They've bred the bitterness and toxins out of wild potatoes until they became the staple food we know today. They've domesticated livestock to the point where most couldn't survive without human care. Before an Austrian monk named Gregor Mendel studied the peas in his garden and discovered dominant versus recessive traits, we didn't know exactly what it was we were manipulating. Now we know, and we can do it on a much faster timeline, but the principle is the same.

"I want to give you something." She nodded toward the back of the auditorium, and a pair of grad students started making their way up the center aisle with big wicker baskets, passing something around the room. Since I was in the back row, I was among the first to get the little Baggies, tied with curly gold ribbon and containing a few teaspoons' worth of shiny grains.

"What you're looking at," she said, "is called Golden Rice. It was developed in Europe by an international team including Dr. Benjamin Singer, who is here with us today."

She gestured toward a dapper-looking man a few rows in front of me, and he half-rose out of his chair in acknowledgment. "Take a good look at this rice, ladies and gentlemen. Isn't it beautiful? The first time I saw it, I thought it looked like something out of a fairy tale, like Jack's magic beans.

"But what this rice can do is entirely real. It's been engineered to contain vitamin A and other micronutrients to save the sight and otherwise improve the health of undernourished children. Right here on campus, Dr. Shep Robinson"—she waved a hand in his direction—"has designed a banana that contains a hepatitis B vaccine. Dr. Jack Cerretani is working on a potato containing a vaccine against a form of diarrhea that costs untold lives each year. Imagine what that will mean—the ability to inoculate millions without needles or perishable vaccines.

"Those are just a few of the projects under way in this field right now. If we are indeed on the brink of a 'brave new world'—and I mean it in the best Shakespearean sense of the phrase—then many of the people in this room will be its leaders.

"But we can't just be scientists. An essential part of our jobs will be communication, teaching people—not just the average citizen but those people chanting and carrying signs out front—that we're not villains. All we want is to make Earth a better place, to alleviate suffering, to raise the rest of the world up to something approaching the standard of living that we take for granted.

"And that," she said with a da Vinci smile, "is what I hunger for. What about you?"

CHAPTER
6

Mad still hadn't manifested himself by the time I filed my story and drove out of the *Monitor* parking lot in my beloved red Beetle. I made two stops on my way over to Cody's: one to leave a note on Mad's door informing him that I was worried as hell and he'd better call me at Cody's ASAP *or else,* the other to change into something moderately sexy and pick up Shakespeare and Zeke, who'd been spending his days at my house for canine companionship.

I got to Cody's apartment before he did and let myself in with my key; this always makes me feel sort of giddy, since up to now I've never had a relationship long enough (or, indeed, normal enough) to warrant access to each other's stuff. I picked up the mail off the floor before the dogs could trample it, and found myself nose to nose with a rather official-looking letter from the Boston Police Department.

Now, I swear I wasn't trying to snoop. I had no intention of steaming the damn thing open or anything. I wouldn't have read it even if it *hadn't* been sealed up but good—at least I'm pretty sure I wouldn't. As it was, I just piled the rest of the bills and junk mail on top of the (disturbingly heavy) manila envelope, put it all on the dining room table, and tried not to think about it. I channeled my emotional energy into dinner.

In case you're wondering what prompted these mental gymnastics: Cody used to work for the Boston P.D. He only came to Gabriel because his twice-widowed mom lives here, and—more to the point—because his now ex-wife was, as he has so eloquently put it, "banging anything with a shield." Since he got to our sleepy little burgh, however, he's done some damn good police work, and lately I've been having conniptions over the very real possibility that his old bosses are going to offer him detective first grade or some damn thing. Then the only guy worth dating in this entire ZIP code is going to migrate several hundred miles east, mere months after swapping *I-love-yous* with yours truly.

It's not a subject about which I'm particularly rational.

Cody and I get along famously for several reasons, not the least of which is that I like to cook and he likes to eat. Also, in the infamous words of Jake Madison, the two of us have so little in common that—perversely enough—it's been hard for us to find anything to fight about. Cody is a real Boy Scout law-and-order type, though he's rarely an asshole about it; I'm one of those bleeding-heart, anti-death-penalty, save-the-seals sorts of people. My parents, who've been known to host large Republican fund-raisers, think he's pretty much the best idea I've ever had. From my standpoint, it doesn't hurt that the sex has been fabulous from the get-go.

The gentleman in question walked in around seven-thirty, put his gun away so I didn't have to look at it, and flopped down next to me on the couch.

"Busy day?"

He shook his head. "Paperwork."

"Story of my life."

"How about you? Busy day?"

"Bill made me cover the story Mad was supposed to do. Big speech up at that biotech conference on campus."

"You were up at that zoo?" He pecked me on the lips. "Poor baby."

"You catch it on Nine News?"

"Nah, I was up there for a while. Benson cops asked us to back them up, so we sent some uniforms."

"Then what were you doing there?" He gave me my least-favorite look. "Yes, this is off the record. Jesus Christ."

"Sorry."

"So what's up?"

"Apparently, the powers that be at Benson are worried that the protesters are up to something."

"You mean something other than the obvious? Like something criminal?"

"Yeah."

"Really? How criminal? You mean actually *violent?*"

"They're not sure. The main thing at this point is to take all the precautions they can without looking like they're quashing the protest. Seems they don't want to be accused of 'undermining the free exchange of ideas'—at least I think that's how they put it."

"Colleges are weird that way. You can't just go water-cannoning them. Gotta be diplomatic."

"Which makes life a whole lot easier for the bad guys. Frankly, if I had my way, I'd stop-and-frisk the lot of them."

"Just because they're out there carrying signs and dressing up like—"

"No, because of the threats."

"What threats?"

"Nothing specific. Not enough to constitute probable cause, anyway. There's just been some bragging about how the conference is going to be a major forum for the . . . What's the group called?"

"Don't Break the Food Chain."

"*Right.* For them to really make a name for themselves as a force to be reckoned with."

"I wrote as much in my story that ran on today's page one."

"Which the Benson cops have blown up and pasted on the wall of their squad room."

"Thanks . . . I think. So what do you suppose The Chain folks are up to, anyway?"

"My guess is some flagrant act of civil disobedience—at least I hope that's all it is. Like, apparently they have a new tactic where they take pieces of P.V.C. piping and run chains through it and all around themselves so it's just about impossible to cut them apart. Makes collaring them a nightmare."

"And you think they're gonna . . . What? Play ring-around-the-biotech-building?"

"That would be the good news. Bad news is they try to blow something up."

"*No way.* You really think that's likely? Jeepers, I've spent the better part of the past two days up there. . . ."

"Are you going back up tomorrow?"

"I guess that depends on Mad."

"You know, I'd just as soon you didn't."

"Yeah, and I'd just as soon nobody on the reporting staff gets dead this week."

"Alex—"

"If you really think it's so all-fired dangerous, how come they're not shutting down the conference?"

"Because, like I said, there's nothing definite. There hasn't been a bomb threat or anything even close to it. I've just got a bad feeling about it. These Don't Break the Food Chain people are an unknown quantity, and what I see, I don't much like. I never dealt with anything like this in

Boston, and since I've been here, I've seen plenty, but this is different. These guys are pros."

"Yeah, I noticed that too. They make our homegrown agitators seem kinda quaint, don't they?"

"I'll say."

"So what are you guys gonna do about it?"

"Lots of manpower, for one thing—both Benson cops and G.P.D. Not so many that it'll feel like a siege, but enough so they know we're ready to deal with whatever they dish out. What you might call a polite show of force. Plus, we've got some of the younger guys out of uniform, dressed like students so they can blend in and get a look around. Also, since the group is headquartered in Seattle, we've got their P.D. sending us everything they've got on them."

"Sounds like you're locked and loaded."

"Have I mentioned how sexy it is when you talk like a cop?"

"Often."

"Kitchen smells good, by the way. What are we eating again?"

"Lasagna with goat cheese and pesto."

"Right. Did I pick everything up for it I was supposed to?"

"Yep."

"And how long until we eat?"

"Hour. You thinking about dragging me over to the bedroom and ravishing me?"

"Baby, I'm *always* thinking about dragging you over to the bedroom and ravishing you. But at the moment I was also thinking about asking you about Tobias Kahan."

"I must be losing my charm. So what do you want to know?"

"Impressions. I mean, you're one hell of an interrogator—"

"Interviewer."

"Chief Hill might argue that point. Anyhow, you're damn good at getting people to talk."

"But Kahan didn't tell me anything he wouldn't tell anybody with a notebook."

"Right, but the other thing I was going to say is that you're pretty good at sizing up what makes people tick."

"Thanks."

"You're welcome," he said. "So what was your impression of him?"

"Have you met him?"

"Only briefly."

"And what was *your* impression?"

"That he needs a shave."

"No kidding. Do guys really think chicks go for that Fu Manchu thing? *Yuck*. Anyway, my impression of him was, number one, that he's an arrogant jerk."

"I noticed that myself."

"But he's also one smart little bastard. He was reeling off facts and figures and scientific mumbo jumbo like a pro."

"You know what his background is?"

I nodded and started playing with Cody's hair, which is extremely red and always smells clean even when he's sweaty. "Didn't wind up having room for it in the story, but I asked just in case. I guess he grew up in some posh suburb down in Westchester County—which, by the way, is something he obviously didn't feel like admitting. Got a B.A. in poli sci from SUNY something-or-other. Moved out to Washington for what he called 'personal reasons,' which I took to mean some girl. He got into the anti-G.M.O. thing out there. That's all I know."

"That jibes with what we got."

"I assume you ran his name. He got a rap sheet?" He gave me that damn look again, and I went from stroking his hair to smacking him upside the head. "Door swings both ways, Cody. You gotta play fair."

"Sorry again. There was nothing big. Just your usual trespass and nuisance tickets—typical protest stuff. Nothing violent. Not even resisting."

"But you're not sure about this guy?"

"Yeah, I'm sure about him. I'm sure he's trouble. Only question is, what *kind* of trouble."

"Well, he's definitely a fanatic. I don't mean like he'd go blowing up a bus or anything, just that he's totally convinced of his beliefs. Didn't seem like there was a whole lot of room for compromise. Lady on the inside seemed a lot more reasonable."

"What lady was that?"

"Professor Kate Barnett. The speech I covered today. Going on page three tomorrow."

"What was it about?"

I told him. "Now she's *definitely* a crusader. But her whole shtick is trying to get people to understand that the whole genetic-engineering thing can be—what did she call it?—'used and misused.' Anyway, I got some quotes from the audience after the speech, and I guess she's some kind of poster girl for curing world hunger. I overheard some people talking about how she's tough as nails and a big pain in the ass sometimes, but even they seemed to think she walks on water. She's an impressive lady. Smart as hell, obviously, but charismatic too."

"Hmm. Maybe I better meet her."

"Do I have to watch my back? You into older chicks now?"

He blushed, which comes so easily I don't even try anymore; it's not enough of a challenge. "What I meant was that if she's a major player, she could also be a target for whatever the protesters have up their sleeves."

"Yikes. You mean you think they'd try to hurt her?"

"I doubt it. I've been reading up—there's rarely been any violence associated with these guys. I think it's more likely they'd try to hurt some*thing,* not some*body.* Like, if her lab is here on campus, they might try to do some damage."

"So why are you so worried?"

"Because you never know who's going to get hurt in the cross fire."

"Creepy thought."

"That's what they pay me for. Did you get a chance to meet this lady personally?"

"No, but I think Mad has. Plus, Bill liked my speech story so much he said he's gonna assign him a big profile of her."

"Speaking of which, has he turned up yet?"

"Nope. I left him a message to call me here when he gets home."

"What do you think is going on with him, anyway?"

"You know, you're about the twelfth person today who's asked me that. But I gotta tell you, I just don't know. I mean, Mad and I have been friends for a long time, but he's never been one to share the soft and squishy stuff."

"But you've got to have an idea."

"Yeah, which is still that it's all about Emma. He was way more whipped on her than I've ever seen him be on anybody, but he's never been known to take such things too seriously."

"Maybe the bigger they are, the harder they fall?"

"Something like that."

"Hey, I almost forgot to tell you. Actually, I probably shouldn't even be telling you, this being official business and all. . . ."

God damn the Boston Police Department. "Um, yeah?"

"Chief got a call about you from corrections."

"What?"

"Something to do with a request you filed to set up an interview with Shelley Freeman. Apparently they wanted to know how much of a pain in the neck you are. Also your friend Ochoa."

"Can they do that? I mean, is that kosher? Don't they just have to process the paperwork and do it by the book or something?"

"Don't kid yourself."

"Oh, man . . . So what did he tell them?"

"He didn't. I did."

"What? Since when do you mix business with—"

"Seemed a minor matter."

"So what the hell did you tell them?"

"I told them," he said, "that I've always found my dealings with you to be—"

"Oh, God, don't say it. . . ."

"*Entirely* pleasurable."

⁂

I stopped by Mad's on my way into the newsroom the next morning, but there was nobody home. But there had been; that much was obvious. My note was gone, and when I tried the door, it was locked. If the sight of his place hadn't freaked me out so badly the day before, I probably would've left it at that. But since it did—and since I know that he hides a spare key under a loose corner of carpet in the hallway—I let myself in.

The place was back to normal. All the empties were gone, and the bed was made; good news, I guess, but a little weird just the same. I locked up, stuck the key back under the carpet, and went to work. And there was Mad, sitting at his terminal, typing away with two fingers.

"What the hell happened to you yesterday?"

He looked up at me for half a second, then back down at the keyboard. "Just playing hooky. No big deal."

"Playing hooky, my ass."

"Lighten up, Bernier. What's it to you?"

"What's it to me? I'm your *friend* for chrissake. I was worried sick about you. So were O'Shaunessey and Bill and Cody and—"

"Why did you have to go dragging them into it?"

"Dragging—"

"Look, I got a lotta work to do, so if you don't mind . . ."

I took two steps toward my desk, then stopped. "You're having lunch with me."

"I can't, Bernier. I'm—"

"You're having lunch with me and I'm buying you a grilled chicken pita and you're gonna tell me what the hell is going on with you."

"Listen, I really can't. I've got an interview with Barnett at noon for this profile Bill wants."

"But I thought that wasn't running till next week, what with all the conference stuff on the budget. . . ."

"Yeah, well, she's a busy lady. When I called her this morning, she said she was all booked up for weeks but her lunch date today got canceled. So it's now or never. Works for me, anyway. I gotta be up there to cover the afternoon session. Today's when the loonies come out."

"Huh?"

"The anti-G.M.O. angle's up this afternoon."

"I thought The Chain told them to go to hell."

"They did, but they're not the only group, just the one with the most loudmouths."

"So who's speaking?"

"What do you care?"

"Hey, you know, I did get dragged into covering this stuff *twice,* thanks to you."

"If you really care who's speaking, it's one of the members of the co-op that runs the Ecstatic Eggplant, the tall one with the beard."

"Rich Krikstein? That chef guy who writes the whole-foods column for us?"

"Right. Also some woman from that lobbying group for organic farmers, Nature's Way. I'm not sure who else."

"Have fun." I was on the point of telling him to watch out for guys with goatees pelting Molotov cocktails. Then I remembered I wasn't supposed to blab about the cop stuff Cody tells me in the privacy of our love shack. Damn.

"Good job on the Barnett thing, by the way."

"Thanks," I said. "I'll be interested to hear what you get out of your big interview. She seemed like a pretty amazing lady."

"Talk about a one-track mind."

"All about the starving kids?"

"I'll say. Should make for an entertaining hour and a half. Over *lunch* no less."

"There's your color right there."

"No shit."

I raised my voice a couple of octaves. " 'I want to help the hungry children of the world,' she said, biting into her organic veggie burger with a side of curried tabouli. . . ."

"You got it."

"So you wanna come over for dinner tonight? Cody's seeing his mom, and I'm pretty sure Melissa'll be on a booty call at Drew's place. . . ."

"You feeding me so I'll tell you all about Barnett and her starving kids or me and my fucked-up life?"

"Oh, hell. Whatever you want."

"Come to think of it," he said, "it's hard to decide which one is less appealing."

CHAPTER
7

The biotech conference ended Friday. The circus, however, stayed in town a whole lot longer.

On Saturday, the man-sized veggie monsters commuted down the hill to the Green, where they proceeded to scare the crap out of several dozen children shopping with their parents. The protesters wandered around the pedestrian mall dressed like very angry broccoli and tomatoes and carrots and ears of corn, handing out literature about how genetically altered food was going to send us all to hell in the proverbial handbasket. Since I was weekend reporter—something each of us gets stuck with once a month or so—I had the joy of interviewing these irate vegetables. The turnip turned out to be Tobias Kahan.

I asked him what the so-called "action coordinator" of the group was doing dressed like a rutabaga. He said that no general should ask his troops to do something he wasn't willing to do himself, and that he'd garnered this tidbit from no less a source than George Washington. Then he proceeded to compare the members of Don't Break the Food Chain to the Sons of Liberty, and himself to Nathan Hale (and yes, as the daughter of an American history professor, I *was* tempted to point out that Hale wound up swinging from the end of a rope, thank you very much).

The conference had come and gone without anybody getting hurt—unless you counted the protester who somehow managed to sprain both wrists while participating in the chaining trick Cody had mentioned. But Cody's relief didn't last long; Saturday, while holding forth on the imminent invasion of herbicide-resistant superweeds, Kahan announced that his group had chosen Gabriel as its new East Coast headquarters. He handed out yet another flyer on this very topic. Here's part of what it said:

> Gabriel has welcomed The Chain with open arms. We have felt a sense of belonging here like no other place we've ever worked. It is home to countless organic growers and whole-food stores, one of the most vibrant farmer's markets in any small city in America, and of course the world-famous Ecstatic Eggplant Vegetarian Restaurant, whose cookbooks have spread the message of socially conscious eating to millions.
>
> Gabriel is a place where the progressive attitudes we share exist in close proximity to the irresponsible research we despise. It is a place where selflessness and selfishness live side by side—the perfect expression of a Utopia residing beside a Brave New World. In short, Gabriel and The Chain are truly a *natural* fit.

Who writes this stuff?

Style issues aside, I wasn't sure who was going to be less thrilled—Cody, Chief Hill, or the president of the Walden County Tourist Board, who's sick to death of having Gabriel cast as the stomping grounds of the lunatic fringe. And as for me: If I had to hear the phrase "brave new world" one more time, I was gonna blow a gasket.

The flyer announced that The Chain had formed an alliance with the university's student environmental group, Keep Benson Green. (What they didn't mention was that its members have a reputation for being so militant that everybody swaps their initials and calls them the K.G.B.) For now, they'd be operating out of the K.G.B.'s office, which has been located downtown ever since their guerrilla tactics got them kicked off campus.

I wrote up a short piece for Monday's paper about The Chain setting up housekeeping in Gabriel. One thing they'd told me is that they planned to have an information table on the Green every weekend, staffed with members and likeminded scientists to answer questions about the evils of genetic engineering. So on Sunday, I trooped back there to check out the first day of their "Sanity Kiosk." And there they were, engaging in earnest conversation with anyone who'd give them the time of day.

But there was another table set up at the opposite end of the Green. And this one was manned by Professor Kate Barnett herself.

She wasn't alone—there were four students with her—but she was doing most of the talking. My notebook and I made haste in her direction.

"Hi, I'm Alex Bernier from the *Monitor.* I was wondering if I could ask you a few—"

"You covered my most recent speech." Not a question.

"Um, that's right."

"Your story was quite good." She fixed me with a pair of intense brown eyes. "It was unusually human."

"Oh. Thanks."

"And are you also planning on writing something about this"—she gestured toward the contra-dancing veggies at the other end of the Green—"*spectacle* for tomorrow's paper?"

I wasn't sure what answer she was looking for, so I stuck to the truth. "Er . . . yes."

"Then it's a good thing we came." She turned to one of her students. "Cynthia, would you get some information together for Ms. Bernier?"

An Asian girl in pale green overalls started pulling together sheets from the various stacks of propaganda. I felt like I was walking in a trench as we commuted to a nearby bench; the woman topped me by a good ten inches, which did indeed put her a tad over six feet.

We sat down, and I finally got a good look at her. Up close she wasn't what you'd call pretty, but the podium photo that ran in the *Monitor* hadn't really done her justice, either. She was wearing a dark blue silk blouse tucked into tailored khakis—no jewelry, no makeup except maybe a swipe of Chap Stick. Her hair was brushed straight over the back of her head and cinched in a barrette at the base of her skull; the waist-length salt-and-pepper mane was the closest thing to girlie about her. In short, she was one of countless Gabriel women—many of them Benson professors like her—who think far too many great thoughts to waste time on their looks.

As for me: I have fifty-seven different kinds of lipstick on my dresser.

"What do you think of those people?" she asked, jerking her head toward the spectacle at the other end of the Green.

"No offense, but it really doesn't matter what I think. The question is, what do *you* think of them?"

She laughed, a brief rumble in the throat. "The quintessential reporter's answer. Apparently, you've been in the business longer than I'd assumed."

"I'm older than I look."

"And how old are you?"

"Twenty-seven."

"What's your background? Academically?"

"Double major in French and Spanish from Vassar."

"You're not trained as a science writer, then."

"Not even a little. I only covered your speech because the regular reporter was . . . out sick. And I'm only covering this today because I'm on weekend duty."

"I see. It's not surprising, then."

"Huh?"

"Not surprising that your piece on my speech came out as it did. Science writers generally spend a great deal of time on the science. Your story concentrated on the human issues."

"Well . . . it seemed to me that was what you were talking about."

"So it was." She looked up at the sky, either because she was thinking some of those great thoughts or because Gabriel sees a cloudless day roughly twice a year.

"What do you think of them?" I asked, jabbing a pen toward the protesters.

She didn't answer for a minute, just kept staring up at the sky. I was starting to wonder if maybe she hadn't heard me when she finally spoke.

"I think," she said, "that those people have never been hungry."

"Meaning?"

"Neither have they seen hunger—not real hunger, anyway. Oh, perhaps they've volunteered at a soup kitchen during Christmas, but that isn't hunger. *Believe me,* it isn't."

"Then what is?"

"Once you've seen people starve, it changes you. You'll never look at the world the same way again. The privilege of contemporary American life just seems . . . unreal—that it would be impossible for human beings to live in such diametrically opposed conditions in the same time. On one side of the planet, a good portion of the population is morbidly obese and the desire to lose weight funds a billion-dollar industry. And on the other, suffering and deprivation exist on a scale you couldn't imagine if you hadn't seen it with your own eyes."

"But do you think . . . I mean, can you understand why some people are upset at the idea of genetically engineering food?"

"Of course I can understand. Fear and ignorance are nothing new."

"But to play devil's advo—"

"Do you know anything about the history of pasteurization?"

"What? Um . . . no."

"When pasteurization was first introduced in the nineteenth century, many people were horrified. They thought it was an intrusion of science into nature, something to be resisted, while the unadulterated products were seen as wholesome. In other words, they reacted exactly the way the anti-G.M.O. forces are now. But today, we know that it's *un*pasteurized foods that are dangerous. Don't you see? It's all a question of fearing the unknown. And as I said in my speech, it's up to the scientific community to teach the public that the benefits to humanity will far, *far* outweigh the costs."

"But what about all the issues the protesters are raising?" I hunted my brain for the facts. "About the superweeds and the antibiotic resistance—"

"I've never said that we don't have to be vigilant. We do. But that does *not* mean abandoning a technology that will be enormously beneficial to mankind."

It sounded eminently reasonable, the way she put it. It didn't hurt that Barnett came off as the opposite of a fanatic—she didn't raise her voice or bug her eyes out or rain spit on me. She just sounded like . . . well, like she meant what she said, and since she knew she was right there was no point in getting all huffy about it.

Then the human vegetables showed up. I'd caught them lurking out of the corner of my eye, but I was hoping they'd keep their distance. No such luck. Though, frankly, if I was going to be all journalistic about it, I'd have to admit that what happened next made for a hell of a better story.

There we were, sitting on a bench on the Green talking about starving children and pasteurization and genetic engineering, and the next thing I know we're surrounded by the Fruit of the Loom guys.

That's what they looked like, anyway—except the underwear folks always seemed so jolly, and these particular veggies were really pissed off. The six of them formed a semicircle around the front of the bench, so the only way we could've escaped them was to leap over the back. Professor Barnett didn't seem inclined to go anywhere, though, so I stayed put myself.

At first, they just stood there. I had a flashback to the time my parents took me to Disney World when I was six and the guy dressed as Tigger was so perky he scared me and I panicked and yanked his tail *clean off*. I recovered my wits and turned my attention to Professor Barnett, who was eyeing them up and down like she'd never seen anything so tedious.

"Excuse me," she said finally, "but if you don't mind, we're doing an interview here."

The carrot took it badly. "Don't break the food chain!" said a muffled voice from within. It took about a millisecond for the broccoli, tomato, corn, eggplant, and turnip to join in, and pretty soon they were all chanting, "Don't break the food chain! Don't break the food chain!" and pointing their green-gloved fingers at her. Barnett looked like she was getting a migraine.

"If you people would stop shouting and calm down, I'd be

more than happy to discuss the subject with you in a rational manner."

No dice; they actually got louder. She turned to me with a beleaguered expression. "Perhaps we should continue this conversation somewhere else."

We stood up and Barnett tried to go, but the carrot wouldn't get out of her way. She tried to sidestep him (it?), but the broccoli was too fast for her. The next thing we knew they'd joined hands around us and the bench — six angry veggies playing a stationary game of ring-around-the-rosy, with us in the middle.

I'm fairly sure this would satisfy the dictionary definition of *surreal.*

"Tobias," I said, directing my attention to the turnip, "would you please cut the crap?"

No response. I considered asking him if he'd pull this kind of stunt with somebody from the *Times*, and decided he damn well would.

"Do you people really think you're furthering your cause with this kind of behavior?" This from Barnett, who'd obviously gone ten rounds with a rutabaga on previous occasions.

I, for one, was more than willing to knee one of them in the groin, but the suits were so well-padded I doubted they'd even feel it. "Have you assholes ever heard of unlawful imprisonment?" I said, to no effect whatsoever.

The professor and I swapped glances. She looked even more beleaguered than before, but also sort of resigned; at any rate, she was nowhere near as annoyed as I was. At some point, our tormentors switched their chant to "Organic forever! G.M.O. never!" It must have worked for them because they stuck with it for a while. They'd just moved on to a rousing chorus of "Down with Frankenfoods!" when the cops finally showed up.

They shouted something at the protesters, but I couldn't

make it out over the chanting. One of the four cops talked into a radio Velcroed to his shoulder and a minute or so later eight more showed up. Half of them appeared to have jogged the two blocks from the cop shop on Spring Street, while the rest had zoomed down the pedestrian mall in two squad cars. That made twelve uniforms all together—which, considering the size of the Gabriel force, probably accounted for the entire duty shift; the city's criminal masterminds could feel free to run amok. The cops paired off, grabbed each vegetable by the arm, and our horticultural nightmare was over.

Freed from that particular circle of hell, I noticed we'd become quite the center of attention. There were several dozen people enjoying the show, which presently consisted of the cops trying to cuff the protesters, and being stymied by the fact that the costumes were so bulky their wrists couldn't come within two feet of each other.

I thought I heard a camera snap amid the din and sure enough there was Melissa, taking the picture that would dominate the next day's front page: Val, a veteran officer who'd clearly spent much of his youth shopping for pants in the husky boy's department, trying very hard to arrest a giant broccoli.

In a line out of Civil Disobedience 101, the protester had gone all flaccid and uncooperative. Val and another cop started to drag him bodily across the pavement, and since the outfit was made of canvas, it slid quite nicely. The other policemen followed suit, and the next thing you knew, there was a conga line of cops and protesters dragging and gliding their way toward the station.

"You know," said Professor Barnett, who was still standing next to me, "I really did think I'd seen it all."

"Gabriel," I said, "has a way of surprising you."

CHAPTER
8

Cody's kind words must've paid off, because the day after the fiasco on the Green, Ochoa and I got permission for a three-hour interview with Shelley Freeman. Bedford Hills is a good two hundred miles from Gabriel, so while I drove us in my super-fabulous Volkswagen Beetle, Ochoa had plenty of time to remind me that by all that's holy the story should have been his. I, in turn, had ample opportunity to reply that if it weren't for my womanly charms we wouldn't have gotten the interview in the first place, and anyway even kindergartners know the virtues of sharing. He remained unconvinced.

I'm not sure how I'd expected Bedford Hills to be, but considering the name and the fact that it was a women's facility, I guess I'd imagined some sort of extremely strict boarding school. And, frankly, that's kind of what it looked like—small buildings spread out like dorms, only a twelve-foot fence to keep the ladies in, and nary a sniper rifle in sight. Inside, though, the atmosphere felt a whole lot like a prison, except that a few of the fixtures had been painted a sickening shade of magenta. After umpteen searches and much clanging of doors, Ochoa and I were escorted into a spare little room where all the furniture had been welded to the floor. Charming.

We cooled our heels in there, locked up like a couple of felons, until Shelley Freeman was finally brought in by a surprisingly pretty corrections officer with French-braided blond hair; so much for my image of Nurse Ratched with a nightstick. The woman was no marshmallow, though. When Shelley caught sight of us, she was so psyched she actually seemed about to hug me, but the C.O. grabbed her by the elbow and stopped her short.

"Here's the rules," she said in a Long Islandish accent. "No physical contact. You stay on one side of the table. They stay on the other. I watch through the window. Got it?"

Shelley nodded, looking like she'd love to spit in her eye. But she sat down where she was supposed to, and Ochoa and I did the same. Pissing off the people who could lock us up and throw away the key was not high on my to-do list.

"What a *bitch*," Shelley said, jutting her chin toward the square window at the end of the room. Then she turned back to us with an alarmed look on her face. "Jesus Christ. *Please* don't quote me. You won't, will you?"

"Of course not," I said. Ochoa stomped my foot under the table and I whacked him in the shin by way of reply. "You know, I thought Bedford wasn't supposed to be that restrictive—I mean, compared to other prisons, anyway. Can't you even touch the people who visit you?"

"Off the record?"

"Sure." Another whack from Ochoa.

"Officially, we can, in the visiting room. But the first thing you learn in here is that the C.O.'s do whatever they feel like doing on any particular day. It's like a game to them, seeing how they can mess with our minds. Policy doesn't seem to matter very much. Like, the visiting hours are pretty good, but if a C.O. feels like it, she could say you can't have your visit because you're not dressed properly, even if you're wearing exactly the same thing you wore last time. Like I said, for them it's just a game. Something to pass the time."

"Couldn't you, you know, complain?" She looked at me like I was a fourteen-karat moron. "Um, well . . . Shelley, meet Cal Ochoa. Like I said in my letter, Cal's our new police reporter."

"Hey," said Ochoa, flashing her a way-too-friendly smile. She eyed him doubtfully, but just said, "Hello."

"And like I also wrote you, our editor thought it would be best for us both to come out here and talk to you."

Shelley took another long look at Ochoa. "Do *you* want him here?"

"Me?" I grinned at Ochoa, who'd clearly expended his smile quota for the day. "Not particularly."

This made Ochoa scowl and Shelley laugh, which was fine with me. "Then let's talk," she said.

I pulled out my pen and notebook—which had been thoroughly inspected for firearms, hand grenades, and all other manner of contraband—and waited for her to pour out her sad tale. Ochoa clicked on his tape recorder. She didn't say a word.

"So," I said, "um . . . What did you want to talk to us about?"

She'd been gazing down at her fingernails, and when she looked back up at us, her eyes were all teary.

"I . . . ," she started, but the syllable just degenerated into a moan. Tears started flowing down her cheeks, and she swatted at them like they pissed her off. "I . . . Oh, *shit*. It's just that I . . . I've been thinking about this for so long, rehearsing what I wanted to say to you if I ever got the chance, and now I don't even know where to start. . . ."

Ochoa—who has a thing or two to learn about how to conduct a sob-sister interview—gave a disgusted chuckle. I was halfway to patting her on the hand when I remembered Angie Dickinson on the other side of the window.

"It's okay," I said, trying hard to sound soothing enough for the both of us. "Would it be easier for you if I started off with a few questions?" She nodded, pulled a piece of toilet paper out of her left sleeve, and blew her nose. "All right, um . . . How are you doing?"

She looked equal parts annoyed and disappointed. "Jesus, how the hell do you think I'm doing? I'm in *jail,* for chrissake. How would *you* be doing if you were me?"

"Sorry. Stupid question." I decided to go the honesty route and see how it flew. "Listen, I've never been in a prison before. I'm kind of freaked out, honestly."

"So am I." Her voice was so small as to be unrecognizable all of a sudden. "And I've never been in a prison before, either, you know."

"Then I guess we're in the same boat, huh?"

"I didn't kill him," she said. "Do you believe me?"

The question blindsided me, which is probably just how she'd meant it. "Well, I . . . A jury thought you did."

"You didn't answer me. Do you believe me or don't you?"

"I don't know. I've only been talking to you five minutes."

"You were at the trial."

"Not much of it."

"Fair enough."

"Then let's talk about—"

"I'm going to ask you again, though."

"What?"

"Later, at the end of the interview, I'm going to ask you again if you think I killed Lane. Will you tell me the truth?"

"All right." What the hell was I supposed to say?

"Then let's get on with it. What do you want to know?"

"Well, first off . . . What was Lane like?"

She didn't answer, just looked down at her fingernails. They were clean, long, and perfectly manicured, and it occurred to me that maybe it was important to her to keep them that way, even in here. *Especially* in here.

This inspired me to take a critical look at the whole Shelley package, at least from the waist up. She was wearing a powder blue blouse that was badly cut and looked to be made of polyester. I hadn't seen any of her fellow inmates on the way in, so I didn't know if this was prison-issue or what, but I couldn't imagine it was her idea of a fashion statement. She didn't have any makeup on, but she'd given her hair the same attention as her nails, her black curls parted smartly on one side and brushed over the top. Problem was, the color stopped an inch short of her skull. I wondered if maybe they didn't let you dye your hair in prison—and decided the threat of going gray was enough to keep me on the straight and narrow, thank you very much.

"You know," she said finally, "no one's asked me that— not for years. I mean, when we first started dating at Benson, my girlfriends from high school would ask, 'What's he like?' But no one ever asks you what your husband's like, do they? They might ask what he does for a living. Or your friends will say, 'How are things going between you two?' But no one ever asks, 'What kind of *person* is he?' And even during . . . this whole nightmare, they tried to ask me every question under the sun, not that Collier let me answer. . . . But nobody ever asked me that. Not once."

"Is it something you feel like talking about?"

She nodded slowly, staring at a spot in the middle of the dull gray table. "Lane was . . . I guess I'd have to say he was my soul mate."

"You're *kidding*." I should've kept my mouth shut, but I couldn't help myself. Shelley just laughed, not a pretty sound.

"I know what you think of us," she said. "I know what *everyone* thought of us. But nobody had any right to judge. No one ever really knows what a relationship is like except the people in it. And sometimes *they* don't even get it, do they?"

Totally against my will, I found myself thinking about Adam Ellroy, whom I loved and who probably loved me back—only we were both so busy playing it cool we never figured it out. And then somebody killed him.

I tried to think about something fun, like prison.

"No," I said. "Sometimes they don't."

"I know you're not married. Do you have a boyfriend?"

"Yeah."

"Who is he?"

"Listen, Shelley, this interview isn't about—"

"So I'm supposed to sit here and tell you anything you want to know about me, but you won't answer one simple question? That's not fair."

"Look, no offense, but you're the one who wanted me here in the first place."

"That's true. I do want you here. But why does it have to be so one-sided? I think it's only fair if there's some give-and-take, don't you?"

"Rule number one is the writer keeps herself out of it. I'm not the story. You are."

"So you're never supposed to tell the people you interview anything about yourself? Nothing at all?"

Actually, sharing a few personal tidbits is par for the course if it helps butter up the source, make them think you feel their pain. And, frankly, that was precisely why I didn't want to spill the beans about my love life, which was guaranteed to have the opposite effect on Shelley. I looked at Ochoa, who knew the score and had no interest in bailing me out—his revenge for me hogging the interview.

"No, that's not it," I said when the silence had gotten good and weird. "There's nothing wrong with telling you something about myself, but the truth is . . . My boyfriend helped put you here. He works for the Gabriel police."

"*What?* You're joking."

"Nope."

"Who?"

"Brian Cody. He's a detective."

"I know damn well who he is. He's the worst of the worst."

"Come on, he was just doing his—"

"I have to say I'm surprised at you, Alex. I would've expected better."

"What's that supposed to mean?"

"As I told you in my letter, I've followed what's happened to you over the past few years. You've been through a lot. I would never have expected you to be involved with someone so . . . *prosaic.* So . . . dull and uptight and narrow-minded. And *stupid.*"

The loyal-girlfriend thing made me want to argue with her, but under the circumstances it would've been just plain dumb. "Sorry to disappoint you."

"Now don't be like that. I'm trying to give you a compliment. All I'm saying is that a strong, intelligent woman like yourself shouldn't be dating a dictatorial jerk like Brian Cody."

Thanks a *lot.* "Look, let's just get back on track here, okay?"

She gave me a look that said *you're very disappointing.* Then she whipped around to face Ochoa. "And what about you, Cal? Do you have a girlfriend?"

He didn't even blink, either because he'd expected the question or because he felt like showing me up. Probably both. "Sure. She's a master's student at Benson—at least she will be in the fall. She hasn't moved out here yet."

"From where?"

"Tahoe."

"And what's her field?"

"Environmental conservation."

"See?" Shelley said, smiling at Ochoa before turning another disapproving look on me. "That didn't hurt a bit, did it?"

The interview was getting more unpleasant by the minute. I was starting to wonder why Lane hadn't been the one to off *her*. "Do you feel like answering some questions now?"

"You mean about Lane?" The memory seemed to deflate her in a *whoosh*. "Of course I do. Why else would I ask you here?"

"So what was he like?"

"You asked me that already. But I never really answered you, did I?"

"You said he was your soul mate."

She started tearing up again. "He was. Do you think that's absurd?"

"Why would I?"

"Because I know what people thought of us. They called us 'the Fighting Freemans.' But what nobody understood was that it was just our way. It always was, ever since we were in college. We fought; we made up; we fought some more. It was just our way. Why should that be anybody's business?"

"Um, maybe because your relationship became so . . . public sometimes."

"What do you mean?"

"You had screaming fights in the supermarket."

She smiled at the memory. I'm not kidding. "We did, didn't we?"

This time, the expression on her face said *those were the*

days. Then she came back to the present with a thud, looking around at the captive furniture and the bulletproof glass and the braided-haired matron like she couldn't believe she was where she was.

"It wasn't your typical relationship," she said. "I'll give you that. But you have to believe me when I tell you that I loved him more than anything. More than my own life. Even—look, can we go off the record again?" I stuck my pen through the spiral top of my reporter's notebook and dropped them both on the table. Ochoa clicked off the recorder with a scowl. "I don't want you to print this, because it's probably horrible. I would never want my kids to hear this. But the truth is . . . Even though you're always supposed to put your children first . . . I just never did. If my whole family was falling off a cliff and I could only save one of them, I would've saved Lane. I swear to God. Do you think that's terrible?"

I glanced over at Ochoa, who was trying very hard not to look horrified. "No," I said.

"I'm not a bad mother. Ask anybody. I love my children. I just . . . I just loved Lane more. I loved him *first*. Do you understand?"

"Of course I do."

She exhaled, long and deep. "I had a feeling you would."

"Let's go back on the record, okay?"

She nodded. "I still haven't answered you about Lane, have I? Well, the truth is Lane was a real handful. He was moody and judgmental and pigheaded. And he was vain— going bald drove him *insane*. He tried Rogaine the minute it came out, but it never did him any good. He hated being overweight, but he hated dieting even more. Lane was . . . He was one of those people who'd always refuse the first table he was offered in a restaurant, just to show that he could. He'd send food back to the kitchen for the least little thing, like the lettuce in his salad had a drop of water on it. And now my daughter Samantha — she's the oldest — she does it too. She's *just* like her father. . . ." The thought made her smile again. Then she shook her head, like she had to force her brain back on track. "Lane *hated* his job, which is why he worked so hard to do well at it."

"Huh?"

"He had a very strong work ethic. And I think he felt as though, since his heart wasn't in what he was doing, he owed it to them to be that much more productive — like what he lacked in enthusiasm he should make up for in sweat. Do you see?"

"I think so."

"He never really wanted to work for the news service, you know. He only did it because it was the only way he could make decent money in Gabriel in something even close to his field. You must know he worked at the *Monitor* when we first graduated. . . ."

"I heard that, yeah."

"If it'd been up to him, he would've stayed in newspapers. But you can't raise five kids on a reporter's salary, can you?"

"No," I said.

"Hell no," said Ochoa.

"So he worked for the university. And he was good at it. I think that bothered him more than anything, the fact that he was good at something he didn't admire. You reporters don't like to think you could ever end up working as . . . What's the word?"

"Flacks." This from me and Ochoa simultaneously. We looked at each other and laughed, and the room suddenly felt a lot less chilly.

"That's it," she said. "Admitting that he was one . . . wasn't easy for him. But he did it for me and the kids. Lane was that kind of guy — an old-fashioned family man. A Ward

Cleaver type. That probably sounds strange to you considering all the fights we had, but it was true. Lane left work at six every night and he came straight home. He helped the kids with their homework and he cleaned up the house and he cooked a lot too, especially outdoors. He *loved* his barbecue grill. It's huge and it has a pipe that's connected right to the gas line. He liked to watch basketball on TV and he hated it when anybody interrupted him. He wouldn't even come to the phone if somebody called. He did something on the Internet with his friends, where you'd invent a fantasy team. . . . What do you call that?"

She looked at Ochoa for the answer—which I found particularly amusing after the aspersions she'd just cast on my feminism. Unfortunately, though, I had no damn idea what she was talking about.

"A rotisserie league," Ochoa said.

"That's it," she said. "But this is all just silly stuff, isn't it? It's probably not the kind of thing you want to hear about. . . ."

"Actually, it is," I said. "Details are what makes a person come alive."

"What I'm trying to say is . . . Lane loved our house. It was the focus of his life. Our family was the most important thing in the world to him, and to me too. Maybe that's why we fought as much as we did—because it was so *important*. Neither one of us could ever let anything drop. We always had to see it through to the end. And now it's over. Lane is dead, and it's over for good, isn't it?"

Ochoa was staring holes through her, a funky expression on his face. Finally, he leaned across the table and put his hand on hers; I expected the lady C.O. to come bounding in and whack him over the head with her nightstick, but apparently it wasn't an egregious enough offense.

"You really didn't kill him, did you?" he said.

"No." Long pause. "No, Cal, I damn well did not."

"So what do you think really happened?"

"How would I know?"

"Don't give me that," he said. "You were closer to Lane Freeman than anyone in the world. You've been cooped up for weeks with nothing to do *but* think. If you didn't kill him, you've got to be sitting here asking yourself who did."

"How do I even know he didn't really die of a heart attack? The idiots at the medical examiner's and the police and the district attorney . . . Who's to say they didn't screw everything up from day one and I'm rotting in here so they don't have to admit their mistakes?"

I spoke up then, either to be the voice of sanity or to defend my extremely cute boyfriend. "Come on, Shelley, don't you think that's a little far-fetched?"

"Far-fetched, my ass. Look, they stood up there in court and swore I had poison all over the backseat of my car and I *didn't*. Why shouldn't all the rest of it be every bit as much of a lie?"

"Wait a minute," I said. "Hasn't it occurred to you that maybe the cops really found what they said they found, even if you weren't the one who put it there?"

"You mean somebody tried to *frame* me? That's ridiculous."

"Why?"

"Because like I've been saying all along, nobody would have wanted to kill Lane in the first place. Nobody except . . ."

"Except . . . ?"

"Except *me*. What I mean to say is, nobody else felt that passionately about him. And like I already told you a hundred times, I never wanted him dead. I mouthed off about it and so did he, but it wasn't true. Just the opposite—I'd do anything to have him back. *Anything*."

Ochoa glanced toward the window and let go of Shelley's hand. "So you can't think of anyone who would've wanted to hurt him?"

"Aren't you listening? I already told you no."

"Then can you think of anyone who'd want to hurt *you?*"

Her eyes widened and I could see the whites above and below the iris. "You mean, like, it was really intended for me, but they poisoned Lane by accident or something? That's crazy...."

"It could be that," he said, sounding like his brain was already halfway back to Gabriel, "but I was thinking more along the lines of exactly what happened."

"I don't understand."

"He's dead. You're in prison. God knows what's going to happen to your kids. As revenge goes, it's pretty—"

"That's *absurd.*"

"Is it?"

"Look, I'm not saying I'm everybody's best friend, but there's no way in hell anyone would hate me enough to ... Really, it's completely absurd." She sat there chewing on it for a while. Then the expression on her face turned nasty. "But ..."

"But what?"

"But if that were true ... If someone really killed Lane, and tried to fix it so I got the blame, and now I'm rotting in here and my kids are destroyed and my whole life is ruined ... If that were true, and I ever found out who did it ... I swear to God, that would be one homicide I *was* guilty of."

CHAPTER
9

The fact that Shelley Freeman was most likely innocent was one of two things I learned that particular day in mid-June; the other was that Cal Ochoa did indeed snore, and like a freight train.

We spent the night in a double room at a Super Eight half an hour from the prison, to the joy of the *Gabriel Monitor* bean counters and the great consternation of Ochoa's absent ladyfriend. I wasn't sure if she was just the jealous type or if (I'd bet on this second one) Ochoa had taken his love to town on previous occasions. Either way, though—resemblance to Adam Ellroy be damned—she had nothing to worry about from me.

Cody, for his part, is of the opinion that if you have to obsess about the possibility that your girl's cheating on you, you probably shouldn't be with her in the first place. Admittedly, this attitude didn't do him a lot of good when he was married to a serial adulteress.

And Shelley called him narrow-minded. Go figure.

The drive back was considerably more congenial than the drive there, the Freeman interview having served as quite the bonding experience. Ochoa told me all about the aforementioned babe, whose name turned out to be Elena. She was spending the summer at some park-ranger thing before joining him in Gabriel, though he was actually the trailing spouse. He'd applied for the *Monitor* job because she was starting her master's program at Benson in the fall, and when he got it he had to hightail it east on three weeks' notice. Now he was residing in that particular circle of hell reserved for long-distance relationships: He had a lease on a two-bedroom apartment, a phone bill in the triple digits, and a nightly confab with the girlfriend equivalent of the Spanish Inquisition.

He, in turn, asked me all about Cody—and I've got to admit I was something less than forthcoming. Ochoa was the cop reporter after all, meaning that Cody was part of his beat. I doubted very much he'd appreciate having the guy who was sticking a tape recorder in his face know all about his love life, thank you very much.

This, of course, made Ochoa even more curious; he kept up the third degree for a good fifty miles.

"What the hell is he doing in Gabriel, anyway?" he said as we passed through the outskirts of lovely downtown Binghamton. "It's obvious the man is completely overqualified."

"I told you, he came here to be near his mom. She's a widow twice over."

"Yeah, but why didn't he just move her to Boston? Didn't he grow up there?"

"I guess his mom likes it here."

"Nobody gives up a job as a big-city detective to chase drunk college kids around West Nowhere just to keep their *mom* company."

"What can I say? He's a good and faithful son."

"Come on, give me the scoop. What, did he get into some shit back there? Internal Affairs or something?"

"Would you give it up?"

"I'm thinking police brutality, right? I mean, he *is* a scary-looking son of a bitch. . . ."

"Are we talking about the same person?"

"Guy can't be sticking around here for long, can he? Like, *nobody* sticks around here for long, do they?"

"You know, for about ten seconds I was starting to think you were a human being."

"Come on, Alex, lighten up. All I'm saying is, this town's like some giant halfway house, you know? Everybody's on their way to someplace else."

It was damn perceptive. It was also just about the last thing I wanted to hear. "Some of us like it here, you know."

"Like who?"

"Like me, for one. And O'Shaunessey's been sports editor for like ten years. And Mad—"

"O'Shaunessey's the kind of guy who was put on this earth to cover high-school football at a twenty-thousand-circulation paper for his entire life, and that's not much of a compliment. I mean, don't get me wrong, I like the guy. But he's not what you'd call ambitious. And Madison . . . He's a damn good reporter, but he's a drunk and everybody knows it. What I can't understand is you."

"What the hell does that mean?"

"You could go anyplace you want. Well, maybe not the *Times* right away. Nobody makes that kind of jump. But you could get a job at a midsize metro. So what are you still doing here?"

"Like I said, I like it here."

"So what? So you're gonna stay here covering the goddamn Gabriel common council for the rest of your life?"

"I . . . How the hell do I know? And what do you care, anyway?"

"I don't. I'm just curious is all."

"And anyway, if Gabriel sucks so bad, what are *you* doing here? Huh?"

"Hey, I'm not saying it isn't an okay place to spend a year or two. Don't get me wrong."

"God forbid."

"But I'm only here as long as Elena's here. Besides, the *Monitor*'s got a rep as a good launching pad, you know? Some interesting shit goes on down here, despite the size of the place, so I figure I can get some decent clips over the next couple of years and make a pretty good jump after that. Deal is, I followed her here, so next time she goes where I go."

"So you two are pretty serious?"

"Claro que sí."

"¿Estas completamente enamorado?"

"Since when do you speak Spanish?"

"Since I got a degree in it in college."

"Your accent's pretty good."

"Thanks. Unfortunately, my vocabulary sucks. My French is pretty fluent, though."

"You've got to get out of this town."

"So answer the question. Are you madly in love with her or what?"

"Sure. She's a hell of a girl."

"Any woman who'd put up with your bullshit has gotta be a *saint*."

"Hey, she's nuts about me. Putty in my hands."

"I bet."

"Mexican men are masters in the art of love."

"Oh, *please*."

"You don't know what you're missing, baby."

"I'm taken, thanks very much."

"So you're pretty whipped on that cop of yours?"

"Totally."

"Yeah, well, he must be bucking for sainthood himself."

"Thanks a lot. You want to talk about Shelley Freeman now?"

"Sure. Shoot."

"How do you want to hit the story?"

"You mean I actually have a say?"

"Don't be a jerk."

"I was figuring on 'Shelley Freeman pleads innocence in jailhouse interview.' What else is there?"

"I guess that's the one."

"Hey, wait a minute," he said. "Isn't this a conflict of interest?"

"For whom?"

"For you. Like you told Shelley, your boyfriend put her there."

I stared at him for so long I nearly rear-ended a minivan. *"Shit.* You know, you're not gonna believe this, but it never occurred to me."

"Well, maybe it should have."

"Give me a break. Bill never thought of it, either. Or you, for that matter."

"Hey, I'm not the one who's—"

"I mean, I never really covered the cops part of the Freeman story, just some of the court stuff. And as for the thing yesterday . . . Well, I guess I never expected to *believe* her. I just thought of it as a human-interest story—how she was appealing the conviction, dealing with life in the clink, that sort of thing. I didn't know I was gonna come out of it thinking the G.P.D. had actually nailed the wrong person."

"So what do you want to do about it?"

"Same as before, I guess. I cover Shelley; you cover the cops."

"So you're willing to admit it's a damn good thing I'm on this?"

"Don't gloat."

"Hey, when I'm right, I'm right."

"Oh, hell."

"Come on, it's not that bad. Like you said, we split the coverage and nobody gets hurt."

"I sure as hell hope not."

"Meaning what?"

"Meaning that the whole situation is not going to further the cause of domestic bliss. Specifically, mine."

⤜⥈⤛

I was probably overreacting, but I was in a genuinely foul mood by the time we got to the paper around one-thirty. The news we got at the top of the stairs didn't help.

Mad was AWOL again. He'd been incommunicado since he filed at seven the night before, hadn't come to work, was answering neither the phone nor the door at his (locked) apartment. He'd been budgeted to do a profile of a Benson microbiologist who'd just announced some study of how many *E. coli* are lurking on your average pay phone, but he never showed; we knew because the guy had called the newsroom looking for him.

Considering his previous performance, nobody was worried enough to call around looking for him this time. But sure enough, when I checked my voice mail, there were three messages from Cody. They varied in exasperation, but the substance was essentially the same: Mad, like Shelley Freeman, was in the slammer.

The cop shop is a five-minute walk from the paper; I jogged it in two. Gabriel is a small town (particularly if you don't count the fifteen thousand or so students) and the G.P.D. is equally provincial when it comes to everybody nosing into everybody else's business; the guy at the glassed-in reception desk knew both who I was *and* why I was there.

Within a minute, Cody appeared, and in the very vestibule where we'd met almost exactly a year before.

I was so freaked out I didn't even kiss him. "What the hell happened?"

"Madison screwed up bad."

"What did he do?"

"Let's take a walk." We went around to the back of the building and sat on a bench with a view of a garbage-strewn stretch of Mohawk Inlet. "First off, Madison's okay. He's in trouble, but not as much as he should be. And physically, all he's got is bruises. The uniforms had him checked out at the E.R."

"Oh, my God. What went down last night?"

"He had a load on at the Lakesider, and—"

"The Lakesider? *No way.* That place is too much of a dive even for him. It's practically a biker bar."

"I'm thinking he went there looking for trouble. Anyway, he found it."

"What'd he do?"

"He picked a fight with the wrong guy. The wrong *three* guys, more like. He got himself beat up pretty good."

"So why's he locked up?"

"Because the bartender said he threw the first punch."

"But come on, there're fights at that place every night of the week."

"True, but this one got out of hand damage-wise, and the barkeep called the cops. That would've been bad enough, but Madison decided to take a swing at the arresting officer."

"No way. Who?"

"Pete Donner."

"Oh, shit." Donner was, with the exception of Cody, the sweetest guy on the force. "Did he get hurt?"

"Madison was pretty loaded. Lucky for him, he didn't connect."

"So is he gonna get charged with . . . Jesus Christ, assaulting an officer or something?"

Cody shook his head. "Donner said he'd write it up as Drunk and Disorderly. As a favor to you."

"I better bake the man some banana bread."

"Yeah. He called me last night after he collared him. I tried you on your cell, but I couldn't get through."

"Damn. I turned it off for the interview. Guess I forgot to turn in on again."

"How did that go, anyway?"

"Long story. But wait—I don't get it. How come Mad's still in the lockup? Couldn't somebody've bailed him out?"

"Sure, but he wouldn't call. Said he'd just as soon serve the three days."

"So can I bail him out now? How much is it?"

"A hundred bucks. But you can't get him out if he doesn't want to go."

"Can I see him?"

"I can get you in there, but I doubt he'll go for it. He'd barely talk to me."

"Let me at him."

We went back inside, and Cody took me into a part of the station you don't ever want to see—not because it's inhumane or anything, but because unless you're on some official tour with the Rotary Club your very presence means you're in deep, at least temporarily. Apparently, it wasn't the busy season for miscreants, because there was exactly one person behind bars. To wit: my best friend.

He looked like hell. His face was all stubbly, which was pretty disturbing in and of itself because Mad is a twice-a-day shaving fanatic. The front of his blue oxford was speckled with a variety of substances that appeared to be blood, beer, vomit, and God only knows what else. Good thing he had a dozen others just like it in his closet, because this one was beyond cleaning. His pretty face wasn't going on the cover of *GQ* anytime soon. And the gray metal bars made him look like some sorry animal on display at a cut-rate zoo. I had competing urges to laugh, cry, and strangle him.

"Are you all right?"

"Get lost, Bernier."

"Thanks a lot."

"Cody, do me a favor and get her out of here, will you?"

I turned to the cop in question. "Do you guys have a cattle prod I could borrow?"

"Bernier," Mad said with a growl, "would you just—"

"For chrissake, what the fuck is wrong with you?"

"Don't worry about me. I'm fine."

"Yeah, I can see that from the way half your face is purple."

"Look, would you just—"

"Do you want to get yourself fired?" That shut him up, for the moment anyway. "Do you realize you totally blew off work today? Some prof up at Benson's been calling the newsroom all goddamn day wondering where the hell you are."

"So what?"

"So you really think Bill and Marilyn are gonna let you spend the next two days in here without spiking your ass? And what about Chester?" I invoked the name of our much-despised publisher. "You know his obsession with the whole 'community newspaper' thing. You think *he's* gonna like the idea of one of his reporters spending three days in the can? Well, do you?"

"I don't give a flying fuck what he likes and what he doesn't."

"Yeah, well, neither do I. But he's the boss."

"Come on, Marilyn wouldn't—"

"Can some joker who missed one day of work on a bender and another one getting his ass arrested in a goddamn bar fight? Oh, yeah, perish the thought."

"Will you cut the melodrama? There's no way they're gonna fire me for missing two lousy days of work. I've been there too damn long."

"Okay, fine, maybe you're right. Maybe they wouldn't actually *can* you yet. But they sure as hell might send you someplace to dry out."

He'd been on the point of offering another snarky retort, but that shut him up good.

"Come on, Mad," I said, trying to sound considerably less furious at him than I was. "Just let me pay the bail and get you out of here."

He looked up at me from the ugly metal bench, Nordic jaw tight. "No."

"Why the hell not?"

"'Cause you're just gonna bug me with a bunch of stupid questions."

"No, I'm not."

"Yes, you are."

"Okay, you're right. I probably am. But for chrissake, Mad, I'm a reporter. What the hell else am I supposed to do?"

He chewed on that for a while. "You, um . . . You really think maybe I've still got a job?"

"If you get yourself cleaned up and file something within the next five hours, yeah."

"And you don't think . . . You don't think they're gonna try to make me go to . . ." He dragged out the next few words like the syllables hurt his tongue. "Fucking . . . Betty . . . Fucking . . . Ford?"

"Like you said, so far you've only missed two days."

"Then get me the hell out of here."

Cody escorted me to the counter where they deal with bail—possibly the only place in the free world where you can swap five twenties for a live human being. I only had forty bucks in my wallet, but Cody spotted me the rest.

"You're a nice guy, you know." Nobody was looking, so I kissed him smack on the lips. "I'll pay you back tomorrow."

"Don't worry about it. Just try to knock some sense into Madison, okay? I've got a bad feeling about him. I've seen this kind of thing happen before, with guys on the job. He's at a point where things could go either way for him."

"How do you mean?"

"All this could just be him taking a bonehead detour from his normal life, or he could be on his way down a serious slide. Getting liquored up in a place like the Lakesider is a habit you don't want to get into."

"No kidding."

"He's lucky to have you in his corner, you know."

"Thanks. I'm pretty damn lucky to have you in mine."

He gave my hand a quick squeeze. "Feeling's mutual."

"Then forget tomorrow," I said. "I have a plan for paying you back tonight."

CHAPTER
10

Jake Madison has been accused of a lot, but doing things halfway isn't one of them.

The morning after I liberated him from the hoosegow, he came into work an hour early clad in a crisp blue oxford and a pair of khakis so sharply creased you could slice a finger on them. He filed two stories by deadline, and even managed to squeeze in some research on his Kate Barnett profile. He also covered a car wreck when Ochoa was out on something else, was the first in Bill's office for the daily editorial meeting, and actually refilled the newsroom coffeepot. *Twice.*

He was on the straight and narrow for the whole rest of the week and well into the one after. Every day he'd work his nonexistent ass off; every night he'd go for his usual seven-mile run, lift weights at the gym, slam down some pasta, and meet us at the bar with his hair still damp from the shower. He showed up at Café Bernier for the regular Thursday-night newsroom food orgy armed with four loaves of garlic bread and a positively peppy demeanor. At the Citizen he drank only beer, which he ordered by the mug rather than the pitcher—behavior that wouldn't earn any A.A. chips but for him was tantamount to checking into rehab.

His profile of Professor Barnett ran on a Saturday, when the paper has its highest circulation—not so much because of the feature packages Marilyn loves to saddle us with but because that's the day the coupons come out; you can make your fifty cents back with one pack of Charmin. The story started on page one with a color portrait of Barnett standing among willowy plants in one of the Benson greenhouses—the hammer head said RICE DREAMS—and jumped to take up most of page six. There was a sidebar on the history of rice (more interesting than I would've thought, frankly), another on criticism of her work by the Don't Break the Food Chain people, and a box, courtesy of the paper's graphic artist, illustrating the process of genetic engineering so simply a kindergartner (or I) could understand it.

The mainbar, which stretched to forty inches, felt less like a Jake Madison byline than, well, an Alex Bernier one—a fact that a number of our colleagues took particular glee in pointing out. Sure, it had copious quantities of the usual migraine-inducing science, but it was also surprisingly touchy-feely; I was starting to wonder if whatever he'd been going through had put him, at the advanced age of thirty-five, in touch with his feminine side.

For one thing, the piece didn't lead with a bunch of five-syllable words but with a revealing little personal detail: the fact that none of Barnett's grad-school friends called her Kate. Her nickname was "Yaitza," which sounds girlie but is apparently the Russian equivalent of *cojones*—a moniker she picked up by telling the Soviet powers-that-were to screw themselves during some Siberian human-rights mission she'd gone on in the late seventies.

The mainbar went on to tell the story of Yaitza Barnett's life, starting with an unremarkable childhood as an Iowa farm girl with a zillion 4-H badges and a knack for science. She'd gotten a full scholarship to the state university in

Ames, where she'd also picked up a Ph.D. in plant breeding. Her humanitarian work started during her undergrad years, when she spent summers in various foreign hellholes as a volunteer for the Red Cross, and it never stopped. Ethiopia, Eritrea, Somalia, and just about every other place I never cared to visit—you name it, she'd been there.

Her combination of scientific smarts and social do-gooding paid off, and not only altruistically: Kate Barnett was a very big deal, in rice-breeding circles anyway. Side-tracked by all the relief work, she'd taken longer than most people to concentrate on the publish-or-perish thing, but once she buckled down she turned out to be damn good at it. She won one of the first MacArthur genius grants in the early eighties, and after that, dozens of colleges were wooing her like jocks after the prom queen. Benson won out, apparently, by offering her all kinds of fancy facilities, a minimal teaching load, and carte blanche to go careening around the world whenever she damn well felt like it. And when she was in town, she did some local do-gooding as well: She served on the boards of both the Gabriel battered women's shelter and the Walden County food bank.

None of that was particularly surprising, of course. But the personal stuff was. For some reason, it'd never occurred to me that Kate Barnett could be married, and she wasn't— but she had been, briefly; her ex-husband was a professor at the Benson med school.

And as for kids? Barnett didn't have any biological ones because—get this—she'd had herself sterilized at twenty-six as a statement against overpopulation. After her divorce, she'd adopted brother-and-sister orphans from a Somalian refugee camp. And, as though the whole story wasn't melo-dramatic enough, the girl had died in a car accident at seven-teen, four years ago; the boy, now nearly twenty, was taking time off from school to see the world.

Professor Barnett kept pictures of both of them on her desk, a tidbit that Mad noted in his piece, to the further astonishment of the newsroom at large. And since we *Monitor*ites have both an inherently snarky sense of humor and access to a variety of typesetting gizmos, it was only a matter of time until somebody churned out a mocked-up version of the story. It appeared first thing Monday morning, with the portrait of Barnett replaced by a blowup of Mad's mug shot from his weekly technology column; instead of RICE DREAMS: BENSON PROFESSOR KATE BARNETT & THE QUEST TO END HUNGER, it said I AM WOMAN: MONITOR REPORTER JAKE MADISON & THE QUEST FOR HIS INNER CHICK.

As for the continuing saga of Shelley Freeman: My—okay, *our*—package on her was slated to run the following Saturday. And, fabulous clip that it might prove to be, I had to admit that I had mixed feelings about the whole thing. On the one hand, I was pretty damn certain that she hadn't killed Lane, so I felt sorry for her; on the other, I could see exactly why she'd been convicted of it in an hour and change.

The woman was a rather spectacular pain in the ass: equal parts whiny and demanding, with a liberal sprinkling of righteous indignation thrown in for good measure. And although she had a hell of a good excuse for being a cast-iron bitch—God knows how I'd behave if I got railroaded into Bedford Hills—it didn't make her any more fun to deal with.

When you've been in journalism for a while, you get so you can tell pretty early on in the research process who's going to be a pest and who isn't. Some sources are pretty laissez-faire, while others try like hell to get you to let them read your story before it runs (they can't). Some insist you check all your facts and quotes with them, while others bury you in way more information than you either want or need.

Shelley Freeman was in the latter category. Every day since the interview, we'd gotten a letter from her filled with all sorts of things we absolutely, positively couldn't leave out of the story—from her kids' middle names to the time she volunteered to help build an interactive playground at the science museum.

Neither was the creative process going especially smoothly. On the Monday before the story was supposed to run, Ochoa and I were squished together at his terminal, arguing for the tenth time about what the lead should be, when the police scanner delivered what will very probably go down as the weirdest alert in newsroom history.

Emergency control to Gabriel monitors. Report of a . . . of a . . . giant pile of potatoes at the intersection of Route 13 and VanCampen Street. G.P.D. is requested to respond with traffic control and . . . um . . . City sanitation will report to the scene with collection crews and a garbage truck. With, er, two garbage trucks . . .

Ochoa and I stopped jockeying for the keyboard and stared at each other.

"Alex?"

"Yes, Cal?"

"Did you just hear what I just heard?"

"Did you just hear that there's a giant pile of potatoes in the middle of Route 13?"

"*Sí.*"

"Then I just heard what you just heard."

He jumped up and grabbed a notebook. "I gotta go."

"Hold up. I am *not* missing this."

I stuck my head in the darkroom on the way out; two minutes later, there were three of us—Ochoa, myself, and one extremely psyched girl photographer—speeding down Van-Campen in my Beetle. The street gets a fair amount of traffic, and sure enough the cars were already backed up six blocks from the hideous commercial strip that is Route 13. We decided to park and hoof it.

Now, Gabriel is not what you'd call a honking town; it isn't the kind of place where people lay on their horns if you take more than a nanosecond to go through a green light. And sure enough, some of the trapped motorists were sitting patiently, reading copies of the weekly *Gabriel Advocate* or sipping their (no doubt) organic herbal tea. Every thirty seconds or so, one of them would realize the futility of it and cut over to a side street, but VanCampen is one-way, so the poor bastards stuck between the last intersection and Route 13 were out of luck.

The intersection itself was, well . . . You sort of had to see it to believe it. The phrase "giant pile of potatoes," while seemingly quite descriptive, still failed to capture the magnitude of the object.

It was a very, very large pile of potatoes.

The thing stretched across all four lanes of Route 13 (which was backed up way worse than the cross street) and had to be at least fifteen feet high. Upon closer inspection, you could see that it wasn't really one big pile but four smaller ones, as though they'd been plopped there by a quartet of dump trucks—which eyewitnesses later confirmed to be the case. I tried to calculate how long such a pile could satisfy my french fry habit, but gave up when the math got too hard. Then I started thinking how much fun it would be to lob a few of them at Ochoa. The concept was amusing but unwise; God forbid Cody should have to bail me out on a charge of Assault with a Deadly Spud.

The mood at the scene wasn't nearly as jolly as you might think, considering the absurdity of it all. The cops, who'd had to jog most of the way there, weren't inclined to savor the moment. One of them was barking into a walkie-talkie to get some cruisers into position to divert the crush of lunchtime traffic around Mount Tater, while another was in the midst of a screaming argument with an orange-jumpsuited garbage guy.

"So how the hell are we supposed to get our trucks in here?"

"Like I said, just drive down here against traffic. Nobody's going anywhere in that lane anytime soon."

"I wanna drive on the wrong side of the freakin' road, I gotta clear it with my supervisor. Union contract says—"

"Screw your contract. I got half a ton of potatoes blocking the goddamn highway. . . ."

It went on like that for a while, until the garbageman finally gave in—possibly because, unlike the cop, he did not have a gun strapped to his hip.

Melissa, very much in her element, was flitting about the intersection and snapping photos of stranded motorists—some of whom had decided they might as well get something for their trouble. A few had left their cars and wandered into the nearby fast-food joints for lunch, but others were busy collecting potatoes in empty grocery bags, backpacks, or (in one case) the voluminous folds of a peasant-style skirt. At first, the cops tried to stop them on the grounds that it was "evidence." Eventually, they just gave up.

"What do you make of this?" Ochoa said, handing me a potato on his way back from interviewing one of the uniforms.

"Looks like an Idaho."

"Very funny."

"I think our friends at Don't Break the Food Chain have been busy little beavers."

"Yeah?"

"Didn't you see the signs?"

"What signs?"

I took him over to the far corner of the potato pile, where the cops had stacked them up. "Somebody said these were out in front of the B.K. and McDonald's." I waved toward the two restaurants, sitting catty-corner across the intersection from each other. "I guess the workers pulled them down. Not the first time these places've had trouble. The Meat Is Murder people have sit-ins here every once in a while, bless their hearts."

" 'Down with Frankenspuds,' " Ochoa read aloud, kicking the sign aside so he could see the one beneath it. " 'Fast food kills you quick.' "

"That one seems kind of gratuitous, huh? Check this one out." I pointed the toe of my Joseph Seibel clog at a drawing of an icky-looking monster; the slogan read YOU ARE WHAT YOU EAT.

"Those guys are gonna be in a shitload of trouble."

"Yeah, if the cops can prove anything. I'd imagine they at least *tried* to cover their tracks."

"Don't you think they'll want to, you know, claim responsibility for this?"

"Hmm . . . I kind of doubt it. If they did, they'd probably be out here handing out flyers, but there's not a walking rutabaga to be seen, thank God."

I picked up a falafel pita with extra tahini on the way back to the newsroom. After washing it down with a vast quantity of diet Pepsi, I called Tobias Kahan. As predicted, he was in no hurry to admit that his group had anything to do with the mess on Route 13—though he did call it, quote, "a heroic action."

"What's so heroic about dumping a bunch of potatoes in the middle of the street?" I asked, just to be ornery.

"You wouldn't understand."

"Try me."

Silence, while he considered whether I was worth the oxygen. "Well," he said finally, "not that I'm saying I have any *concrete* knowledge about what took place."

"Of course not."

"But I'd imagine that such an action would require a certain level of personal risk, not to mention organizational acumen."

"Huh?"

He favored me with an exasperated snarl. "First you'd have to get yourself a large quantity of transgenic potatoes without having them traced to you—"

"What makes you think the potatoes are transgenic?"

"What else would they be?"

"Oh. Right."

"Then you'd have to plan a way to drop them off on a busy street in the middle of the day without being caught or identified. Furthermore, after you did that, you'd have to get away."

"I see."

"That's all I have to say on the subject."

"There's a shocker."

The question of who was going to write the story—me because I'd been covering the G.M.O. thing or Ochoa because he was the cop reporter—was bound to be a point of discussion at our afternoon editorial meeting. But by then, I no longer gave a damn.

Why? Because Mad, who'd had a perfectly normal morning and then gone home for lunch, showed up to the meeting twenty minutes late.

And drunk off his ass.

I'd seen Mad that sloshed before, plenty of times. But never, *ever* at the office. And, frankly—in kind of a reverse of the Prince Hal scenario from *Henry IV*—his recent virtue made his behavior seem even worse than it was, which was pretty bad to begin with.

It didn't help that each and every drunken stereotype was present and accounted for: He was slurring his words, couldn't focus on anything, practically missed the chair when he sat down, and stank like an explosion at the Jack Daniel's factory.

"Madison," Bill said finally, sounding as pissed off as I'd ever heard him, "I think you better get the hell out of my newsroom."

"Hey, come on, what's your problem . . . ?"

"You're drunk."

"No, I'm not."

"Come on, Mad," I said, "let's you and me get—"

"Shut the fuck up," he said—so meanly I nearly started sniffling right there in front of everybody. "Keep your goddamn nosy nose out of my goddamn business for once in your goddamn life, will ya?"

I stared at the floor. So did everybody else.

"Madison," Bill said again, "I think you better get the hell out of my newsroom."

"Why?" He was sufficiently loaded as to be genuinely confused. "Why the hell . . . Why?"

"Because you're drunk. And because I said so, and I'm your goddamn boss. So get out. *Now.*"

Mad stood up, and for a second, I thought he was actually going to leave. But he just glared at Bill for a while. Then he said, *"Fuck you."*

Bill didn't take it well. *"Nobody* comes into my newsroom drunk, Madison, not even you. Now if you don't get out of here in the next ten seconds, you're out of a job."

Mad glared at him some more, tottering so much on his feet that I thought he might actually keel over.

And then, because he was completely snockered and in the grip of what demons I could only suspect, he said something so stupidly predictable his sober self would've been downright mortified.

"You can't fire me," he said. "I quit."

CHAPTER
11

Reporters can joke about practically anything, from dead babies to natural disasters. But Mad's departure was an eight-hundred-pound gorilla; the circumstances of it were so weird and awful—and he'd been a newsroom stalwart for so long—that nobody seemed to be able to talk about it, much less crack wise.

Bill, who was no more in the mood to discuss it than the rest of us, only mentioned it to the extent he had to, i.e., doling out Mad's stories and reassigning his weekend cop duty. Predictably, I got stuck with the biotech thing—which is why when a certain letter came addressed to him I was the one who read it.

It was two pages long, unsigned, postmarked L.A.

Dear Mr. Madison,

I'm writing because I've just finished reading your story about Prof. Kate Barnett, which was mailed to me by a friend. What I want to say is that although obviously there are many reasons why she deserves praise, there are other reasons why she doesn't. Your article made her out to be perfect and that's just not the case.

I don't want you to think that I'm one of those anti-genetic-engineering people. I'm not. In fact, I got a master's in plant science at Benson a few years ago. (I'd planned to get a Ph.D., but it didn't work out.) I'm not interested in slinging mud at Prof. Barnett and even if I were I'm *really* not interested in being sued for libel even though the stuff I'd tell you is absolutely true. My case should have come up in front of the academic conduct committee, but people like Kate never have to face the music, do they? She's too big and everybody loves her, and nobody would ever have believed the word of a lowly grad student over a tenured professor anyway, so I doubt a lawsuit would ever go anywhere even though it should.

I also don't want you to think that I'm accusing her of something really *terrible.* I mean, it was bad enough for me, but what it really comes down to is a case of abuse of power. I would have thought that someone like her would have been more considerate of a fellow woman scientist but obviously that wasn't the case. I won't say anything more, not only for the reasons I mentioned but because I gave my word that I wouldn't, and to me that means something.

So that's all I wanted to write to you. I'm not going to sign my name because the academic world is too small and I can't afford to lose my teaching job. It just really bothered me to see her portrayed as some kind of paragon of virtue, and I had to get it out of my system.

> Yours truly,
> A concerned former student

It wasn't exactly a poison-pen letter; frankly, I didn't know what to make of it. It was obviously not for publication, so there was no passing it off to the editorial page editor—an eccentric fellow named Benjamin who appears to have been born not with a silver spoon in his mouth but a pipe clenched in his teeth.

I would've liked to run it by Mad, but obviously he was incommunicado. I had a feeling I knew what he'd say, though, which is that anonymous notes are damned unimpressive; it's easy to talk trash about somebody when you don't have to take the heat for it. The *Monitor,* like most papers, rarely runs unsigned letters, and only when the circumstances warrant it—say, a rape victim writing to complain about how she was treated at the hospital. The general attitude is, our bylines are on everything we write, so you can damn well put your name behind whatever you have to say.

I mention all this by way of explaining why I stuck the thing in my Kate Barnett bio file and forgot about it.

Until three days later, when somebody tried to kill her.

At least that's what everyone figured the perpetrators were trying to do—that and a whole lot more. And seeing as the very place where she was supposed to be got blown to smithereens, it struck me as a pretty reasonable guess.

I found out about this in the wee hours of an otherwise enjoyable Thursday morning; Cody and I were snuggled up in my bed with our respective dogs when his pager woke us up. I was dimly aware of him looking for the cordless phone when it rang, and although I was still mostly unconscious, his highly refined SEAL instincts allowed him to triangulate its location. He handed it off to me, pulled on his boxers, and went downstairs to call the station on his cell.

It turned out to be Bill.

"You gotta go up to campus and cover a bombing."

"Wha . . . ?"

"Wake the hell up and get dressed and get your butt up to Benson."

"Wh . . . Where's Ochoa?"

"His line's busy. I've been redialing every ten seconds but no go. If the little bastard doesn't get call waiting, he's fired."

"What time is it?"

"Three-thirty. Now get up and go."

"Where?"

"You can't miss it," he said, and hung up.

I'd taken out my contacts to go to sleep, so I was hunting for my glasses when Cody came back. Apparently, it was a fairly amusing sight.

"Give me a break," I said. "I'm blind."

"You're blind *and* naked."

"Oh."

"If I didn't have to go, I might not mind so much."

He found my glasses, which turned out to be two feet away from me on the nightstand. Putting them on vastly improved my ability to locate my underwear.

"You going up to Benson?" I asked as we pulled on our jeans.

"Yeah. You?"

"That was Bill on the phone. He said something about a bomb. What the hell is going on?"

"You know what I know."

"Where was it?"

"One of the agriculture buildings."

"Did anybody get hurt?"

"They're not sure. Scene's a mess."

"You want to go up there together?"

"Probably wouldn't look good."

"Yeah," I said. "It probably wouldn't."

So he got into his Camry and I got into my Beetle, and half an hour later we were standing within twenty yards of each other—the time lag being due not to the drive (five minutes) but to the fact that he got to go straight to the scene, while I was diverted to the hinterlands of campus.

By the time I hoofed it back to the far corner of the ag quad, he was deep in conversation with the usual suspects: Wilfred Hill, chief of police, Bernie Belding, fire chief, and Phil Herzog, Benson's vice president of university relations. He's also their resident master of spin control. I wondered how he was going to craft a bombing as a "challenging but valuable learning experience."

None of them looked like they had any idea it was four in the morning. They were wide-awake and (unlike me) their hair was neat. They all looked pretty grim, though—not surprising since they were standing in front of a scene that resembled Beirut circa 1979. Or, come to think of it, maybe it looked more like something out of a Japanese monster movie, like Godzilla had taken a whopping bite out of the corner of the plant-science building, then promptly thrown it up all over the ag quad. The chunks of brick ranged in size from pebble to minivan, and shards of glass littered the grass, sparkling under the fire department's emergency floodlights like some weird winter wonderland.

As I sidled up to the four men with my notebook at the ready, there were several things I was trying very hard not to think about. One was what it would've felt like to be standing there when the bomb went off, how your body would be blown to pieces in an instant. Another was the question of just who the hell would want to do something so insanely destructive. And a third, unrelated though it may be, was that one of the men I was about to annoy had very recently bonked my brains out.

I took a deep breath and advanced. For the record, none of them were particularly excited to see me: Cody, because of the uncomfortable mixture of business and pleasure that had defined our relationship from day one; Belding, because he's always considered me an enormous pain in the patoote; Herzog, because it's my job to make his life harder; and Chief

Hill, because he knew I was going to ask him questions to which he had no answers.

I was about to displease all four of them when Herzog decided the best defense was, well, to be offensive.

"What are you doing here, Miss Bernier?"

It was a simple question, if entirely pointless, but I knew there was a trap in there somewhere. Unfortunately, I couldn't figure it out on two hours' sleep. "Um, covering . . ."—I waved my notebook toward the missing corner of the building—". . . this."

"I mean, how did you find out about it so quickly?"

He turned his beady eyes toward Cody, and I got his drift in a jiffy. *Jerk.*

"Well," I said, "I was fucking Detective Cody here when his pager went off, so he spilled his guts about the whole thing and here I am."

Actually, I didn't say that. My id kind of wanted me to, but instead I just told him that my editor called me. Herzog obviously didn't buy it, though why he was pushing the issue was beyond me.

"You mean to tell me he listens to the police scanner at all hours of the night?"

"He's been known to. He's what you might call an insomniac workaholic."

"You can rest assured, Miss Bernier, that I plan to speak to your publisher about the level of professionalism at—"

"I gotta get back to work," the fire chief said, and left. Lucky bastard.

". . . at your newspaper. Clearly, no one has taught you people the first thing about journalistic standards. And as for common decency—"

Chief Hill, who enjoys Herzog's company about as much as I do, decided he'd had enough.

"What I can tell you right now," he said, "is that at ap-

proximately three A.M. there was some type of explosion in
one of the greenhouses attached to the plant-science building. Whether that explosion was accidental or not, I wouldn't
want to speculate, so don't bother asking. The blast destroyed the greenhouse and a portion of the building itself.
As far as we know, no one was injured, but we don't know
for sure since it's the middle of the damn night and there's no
way to account for everybody. We've called in a K-9 unit
based in Syracuse that specializes in finding victims in these
types of situations, and they're en route to the scene. Hopefully, if there's anyone under there, God forbid, we can get
them out."

"Has anyone claimed responsibility?"

"Not as of yet, no."

"What kind of bomb was it?"

"Give me a break, Alex. It only happened an hour ago.
And that's all you're getting."

It was Hill's code for *Asking more questions will accomplish nothing beyond ticking me off.* I knew better than to
push it. "Press conference tomorrow?"

"Undoubtedly." He took a few steps away from me, then
offered a parting shot over his shoulder. "Press conference,"
he said. "I just can't wait."

He stalked off toward the rubble. Cody paused long
enough to give me a quick little salute when he was sure no
one was looking, then jogged to keep up with his boss.

That left just me and Herzog. Lovely.

"I'm not finished," he said.

"That makes one of us."

"You're quite rude, you know."

"So they tell me."

He fiddled with his tie, like his loathing of me just might
choke him. It was four o'clock in the morning, and the guy
was wearing a pin-striped suit. It was, however, an ill-fitting

one; as always, his paunch strained against the buttons of his jacket. Herzog looked very much like the Benson-linebacker-gone-to-seed that he was—and though he may have been staring at his glory days in the rearview mirror, apparently he didn't want to admit it by buying up a couple of sizes.

"I assume," he said finally, "that you intend to make this incident as melodramatic as possible."

"Somebody blew up the plant-science building. How much more melodramatic can you get?"

"That's precisely what I'm talking about. No one 'blew up' the plant-science building. There was an explosion in a greenhouse. As far as we know, it could have been an accident."

"Oh, please."

"It could very well have been an accident." He was liking the idea, so he stuck with it. "It could have been some sort of . . . some sort of fertilizer accident. So it would clearly be irresponsible of you people to call it a bombing. I'm sure your publisher would agree."

And I'm sure you can kiss my ass, Mr. Herzog.

"I have no intention of misrepresenting the facts, and you know it," I said, instead of punching him in his bulbous snout. "If the chief says they haven't figured out whether or not it's a bomb, that's what I'm going to report."

He didn't look the least bit satisfied. In fact, I think he would've liked it better if I'd said I was going to write that the bomb had been planted by the C.I.A. to blow up Elvis, just so he could keep yelling at me. Herzog has pulled some hissy fits in his day, but this was a new level of prickishness. I wondered whether it was inspired by the hour or my charming company.

"I'm sure that you'll find a way to make more of this than there is," he said. "As far as I can see, that's always been your principal talent."

Favoring me with a dirty look, Herzog turned his back on me and headed toward the center of the action. I was debating whether to bother getting some color quotes from the bleary-eyed student spectators when everything went to hell.

If I had a religious bone in my body, I'd say it sounded like the apocalypse; suffice it to say, it was the loudest thing you can possibly imagine. In terms of destruction, the second blast made the first one seem like a goddamn firecracker— it took out the entire front of the plant-science building.

It also did a fair amount of human damage. I was relatively far away and I had my back to it, which was incredibly lucky. Some of the others will be carrying around the scars as long as they live. One girl lost her sight; a seventeen-year-old boy lost a hand.

And they didn't get the worst of it.

CHAPTER
12

I only found all that out later, of course. For the first few minutes after the blast I was busy with other things — specifically, with lying flat on my stomach on the ag quad, which is where I'd landed after the force of it threw me ten feet in the air.

My first coherent memory of what happened afterward was somebody yelling my name and sounding really, really upset that I wasn't answering. Whoever it was touched my back, which hurt like hell — I felt as though I'd gotten stung by a hundred very sadistic bees. I woke up enough to start coughing into the damp grass, and I heard this somebody say, *"Thank God."*

He continued, *"Alex.* Alex, baby, are you okay? Hold on, baby, the ambulance is on the way. . . ."

I rolled over enough to squint up at him, my glasses having flown somewhere far from my nose. "Cody?"

"Shh . . . Don't talk. You're gonna be okay. Just don't move."

I moved anyway. *"Shit.* My back's killing me. And my legs feel like—"

"Don't move. You could make it worse."

I squinted at him some more and sat up. "I'm . . . I'm fine."

Actually, I wasn't; every inch of the back of me ached, and most of the front too. Plus, my butt hurt like hell.

"Jesus," I said, "where's all the blood coming from?"

"You got cut. Flying glass."

He'd been kneeling next to me, so we were nose to nose. I expected him to yell at me for moving, but he didn't—just ran his hand down the side of my face like he couldn't quite believe I still had a head.

"When I saw you lying there, I . . ." He cleared his throat. "I thought . . ."

"Something very bad."

"Yeah."

"I'm okay."

"You're going to the emergency room."

"I'm not gonna argue."

"I love you."

"I love you back."

"Jesus, baby, I was . . . I was so . . ." He gave up and kissed me, which was just what the doctor ordered.

It was about then that I started to notice we were in the middle of a disaster area. People were crying and screaming and yelling for help, and some very freaked-out cops and firemen were running around trying to do something about it. "What the hell happened?"

"Bait and switch."

"What?"

His face tightened up. "That's probably not the right word for it. It's an ugly tactic, whatever you call it. Lure people to the scene with a little bomb, then kill them with a big one."

"Are you serious?"

"That's my first guess. I hope I'm wrong."

An EMT came by, and Cody flagged him down and tried

to get him to treat me. Apparently, though, having a zillion cuts on my back still put me way at the bottom of the triage list. The guy kept going.

"Are some people hurt really bad?"

"I'm not sure. When I heard the explosion, all I could think about was you."

It was officially the nicest thing a guy had ever said to me. Too bad it'd been prompted by so damn much carnage.

"Thanks," I said, because I couldn't think of anything else.

"Can you walk?"

"Yeah. I think."

"I'm taking you to the hospital myself. I'd carry you, but I'm afraid it'd hurt you more."

"Don't you have to stay here?"

"There's not much for me to do until it's light out."

"Yeah, right. Come on, what'll the chief say if you just take off?"

"That he doesn't need a man messing up his crime scene because he's too worried about his girlfriend to think straight. Besides, right now the arson and bomb-squad guys have to do their thing, and I'm just gonna be in the way."

"Nice try, but I know you too damn well. I can tell just by looking at you—the idea of blowing off your—"

"Fine, you're right. I know I should stay at the scene, but I'm taking you to the hospital anyway. Got it?"

"But—"

"Listen, I'll be up to my neck in it soon enough. So let's just worry about you, okay?"

I couldn't think of anything else to say—and the pain in my backside was getting worse by the second. "Okay."

"I'll be back in a minute."

He was, and looking twice as grim.

"What's going on?"

"Can you stand up?" He pulled me to my feet, slowly. "How's that? You think you can walk?"

I took a step, wobbled, but didn't fall over. "Yeah."

"Be careful. There's glass and concrete all over the place."

"I can't see too well. My glasses must've landed someplace else. And my notebook . . . I must've dropped it when—"

"Don't worry about it."

"I gotta find it. And my backpack . . . I left it on the ground someplace when I was talking to Herzog. My wallet's in there, and my car keys. . . ."

He started to argue with me, then just shook his head. "Stay here. I'll go find them."

"I really, *really* need the notebook. There's a bunch of other stuff in there, stuff for other stories . . . *please?*"

Being a detective, he detected. Luckily, nobody stopped to ask why the hell he was looking around for his girlfriend's purse while people were bleeding all over the place. He found everything but the glasses, and was apparently still too pleased that I wasn't dead to give me shit for it.

We got to his car, and when I went to sit down, it hurt so much I just about fainted. Cody had me lie across the backseat on my stomach.

"What happened?" I asked as he drove me down the hill that Benson's on and toward the opposite one, where the hospital is.

"We're not going to know for sure until the crime-scene guys get going, figure out the chemical analysis of the bombs. I wouldn't be surprised if somebody takes credit for it, though."

"I meant before, when you went to talk to the chief. What'd you find out?"

"Don't worry about it right now."

"Come on, just tell me."

I heard him sigh, and I could practically see the wheels turning in his brain as he tried to calculate whether it would be worse to give me the bad news — whatever it was — or let my curiosity go postal on its own.

Another sigh. "You really want to know?"

"Just tell me."

"Phil Herzog is dead."

"Holy shit."

"Yeah. And it wasn't . . . nice to look at."

"Did anybody else get . . . ?"

I twisted my neck so I could see his eyes in the rearview mirror. Even without my glasses I could tell they were very green and very, very sad.

"So far he's the only one," he said. "So far."

Four hours, two dozen stitches, some pain pills, and a tetanus shot later, Cody brought me home. We went straight upstairs, and the first thing I did was call Bill and tell him what was up. Then I tossed my bloody clothes in the garbage.

I stretched out on the bed on my stomach, and when I closed my eyes, I had an elaborate vision of what Bill Herzog might have looked like with most of his limbs blown off.

I decided to open them again.

Cody was lying there, staring at me. He still looked more than a little grim.

"Why do you think it is," he said, "that you're always the one who gets hurt?"

"A strangely philosophic question."

"It was on my mind while I was waiting for you in the E.R."

"Oh."

"So why do you think it is?"

"You know, I seem to recall you almost dying once upon a time."

"Feels like that was ages ago."

"It was last summer."

"So it was." He ran his finger around the circular scar on my left shoulder. "Bullet wound's fading."

"But it'll never go away."

"Not completely, no."

"For some reason, I don't give a damn. It's not like I'd ever forget."

"Ah." He surveyed my more recent injuries. "How's your back feel?"

"Better. It just kind of aches all over, all those little cuts. Doctor said the front part's not gonna be too gorgeous, either, once the bruises come out."

"Yeah, well, you're always gorgeous to me."

I slid across the sheets to put my head on his shoulder. He reached out to stroke my hair, and the next thing I knew we were kissing like mad—my brush with death having acted as quite the turn-on for both of us. Go figure.

The next half hour was downright amazing and, considering the state of my injuries, had not a single thing in common with something a missionary might do. We fell asleep for a while, and those who know me will be profoundly unsurprised that when I woke up my first coherent thought involved food.

There are many charms to living in a college town, and not least among them is the ability to score a pizza at ten o'clock in the morning. I phoned, Cody took a shower, and by the time I was finished with my sponge bath, breakfast had arrived.

I fell asleep again with a gut full of pizza—probably not a good idea, dietarily speaking—and when I woke up, he was gone. He'd left a note saying he had to get back to work, that he'd left Zeke, and that he'd stop by that night to see how I was doing.

How I was doing was a matter of some debate. My back hurt like hell; rolling over on it was what had woken me up in the first place. Bill had told me to take a sick day (*duh*) when I called him from the E.R., but for some reason I couldn't sit still. I kept thinking about what might've happened to all those kids who'd been standing around, gawking at the destruction in their pj's. And then there was Phil Herzog, a guy I'd mentally tossed to the bottom of the gorge more than once. Now he was dead, presumably in pieces all over the ag quad's lawn.

I lay there on my stomach, a pillow over my head and a dog on either side of me, wondering what I would've done if I'd known what was coming. Sadly, I had zero success in concocting some heroic vision of myself; the idea of me leaping between Phil Herzog and the blast was, frankly, comical. And . . . if I was going to cop to the God's honest truth, one of my chief emotions at the moment was abject relief that if one of us had to get blown to bits, it turned out to be him.

It's not nice, but there it is.

After half an hour of that, I figured I'd better get out of the house, as my brain was proving an unappealing companion. I rooted around my bedroom for something reasonably loose-fitting to wear to work, and came up with a pair of faded khakis and a cotton sweater. When I got out to my car, though, it occurred to me that driving would require me to sit down. I decided to walk the fifteen minutes instead, and the fresh air made me feel a little more like a human being.

I stopped for a gigantic cup of coffee at the big all-night deli across from Mad's apartment. And since I was very much in a no-bullshit, life's-too-short kind of mood, I stomped (gingerly) up the dingy staircase to his door and knocked. No answer. I looked under the carpet for his key, and it was gone.

When I got to the newsroom, the mood was downright jolly. If you've got this vision of a bunch of people hanging their heads in shame because they have the unwelcome duty of reporting tragic news to a suffering public—well, as our downstate comrades would say, *fuhgeddaboudit*. Nothing gets the blood flowing like a good disaster; just as cops like working a homicide a whole lot better than nailing turnstile jumpers, reporters would much rather write about a four-alarm fire than the goddamn Rotary bake sale.

And blowing up a building at Benson University was big news—not just in Gabriel, but everywhere. The anti-G.M.O. thing was, obviously, an international story, and TV crews were descending from all over the place. Bill had assigned a big chunk of our staff to cover it.

Marilyn, the managing editor and one very tough babe, was directing the whole scene with the competent glee of a general who knew the battle was all but in the bag. These were her reporters, covering her town—and the guys from Reuters could go to hell.

"*Alexandra Bernier,*" she said, sounding a whole lot like my mother. "What the hell are you doing here?"

"Cabin fever."

"You're turning out to be no damn good for the company health insurance."

"Sorry."

"What'd the E.R. doc say?"

"That it's gonna hurt like hell to sit down for a while. I took a bunch of shrapnel in the rear area."

"You're starting to talk like that soldier boy of yours. How's he doing, by the way?"

"Okay. He was on the other side of the building when the second bomb went off. Herzog and I were at the front."

"Nasty business."

"Yeah. Give me something to do."

"How you gonna write? You can't even sit down."

"I was planning on kneeling."

"Fine. Go type up your notes from last night and we'll figure it out from there."

"I could maybe help Marshall with the Herzog obit. I mean, I covered the guy more than anybody."

"Good. Do it."

"You know," I said on my way out, "I'm pretty sure the last thing Phil Herzog ever heard was me bitching at him."

"And I'm pretty sure I'd feel sorry for the guy," she said, "if he hadna been such a prick."

After the bombings, things up at Benson got tense, to say the least. A fair number of high-school kids were pulled out of the college-prep program by their parents, who apparently weren't interested in having their little darlings blown to bits. The university's regular summer classes were even suspended for two days before the president—a shrimpy Brit who's starting to look more and more like an elderly vampire—declared that he wasn't going to have his university, quote, "taken hostage by the forces of fear."

Classes resumed the following Monday, though all those in the ag school were jammed into other buildings on the arts, hotel, and engineering campuses. By then it seemed like the death toll was going to stay at one; nobody had been found in the wreckage, and the other victims looked like they were going to make it.

Cody's suspicions, however, turned out to be right: Peo-

ple were indeed lining up to take credit for the night's festivities. For days, the newsroom fax spouted melodramatic
claims like nutritional wheatgrass, and their level of coher-
ence varied considerably. One particularly charming one referred to Herzog and the other victims as "casualties of war";
another indicated that the authorities ain't seen nothin' yet.
Still another, from a group calling itself the OATs (for "Organic Activist Tribe," if you can believe it) sent a detailed
statement about why it had blown up the building, but swore
up and down that it hadn't planted the first bomb—and that
the other perpetrators were obviously just trying to make
them look bad.

The reasons they cited, of course, were all about Kate
Barnett. The OATs people didn't name her specifically, but
when they talked about "stopping Benson's own Typhoid
Mary, the chief spokesperson in favor of the agricultural
holocaust," everybody knew who they meant. The authorities were also clued in by the fact that Professor Barnett—
the same sort of insomniac workaholic as my boss—was
scheduled to be in that very greenhouse at the time of the explosion. She owed her life to luck and an excess of e-mail;
she'd gotten bogged down at the computer in her other office
in the biotech building, lost track of time, and never even
heard the blasts.

The Monday morning after the bombing, the "Typhoid
Mary" in question held a press conference in front of the rubble. The whole building was still cordoned off with yellow
crime-scene tape, and Benson workers were in the process of
putting up a chain-link construction fence around it. There
was no intro or anything, just one tall, broad-shouldered
woman standing before a dozen or so reporters.

"I'd like to make a statement," she said, looking tired and
drawn and generally beat-up. "It will be brief, and then I'll
take a few questions, if you'd like." She looked down at an

index card, cleared her throat, and looked back up again. "I don't usually use notes, but I'm feeling . . . somewhat distracted right now by all that's happened.

"What I'd like to say is that these people are not going to win. In fact, to my mind what they've done here only reinforces the fact that they will *never* win, because the world can see how ill-conceived and hypocritical their actions are. They claim to want to protect lives, and instead they've taken one. They claim to want to safeguard human health, and instead they've maimed innocent people.

"I understand that I was their target, and I can honestly stand here before you and say that I wish it *had* been me rather than Philip Herzog. If I'm going to be required to die for my principles, then so be it. Nothing worth doing ever comes without sacrifice. But the problem with terrorists is that they're more than willing to get what they want by sacrificing everyone around them as well.

"Well, it isn't going to work. These selfish, senseless, violent acts are not going to accomplish what their perpetrators set out to do. We scientists will not stop our research, work that will be enormously beneficial to humanity, simply because it might put us in the line of fire."

It was a pretty speech, and as far as I could see, it accomplished two things. One, it made me feel like a moral wasteland by comparison. And two, it practically dared whoever'd blown up the building to have another go at her.

CHAPTER
13

I was writing up my story on the press conference Monday afternoon when I ran across that anonymous letter in my Kate Barnett file. Marilyn, who'd previously been as unmoved by it as I was, now agreed that it wouldn't be a bad idea to show it to the cops—both to do our civic duty and (more to the point) sow the seeds of future cooperation. She pushed the CHIEF HILL button on her speed dial, and fifteen minutes later Detective Brian Cody was in the newsroom.

He read it, copied it, thanked us, told us it probably had nothing to do with the bombings, took the original, winked at me, and left.

Be still, my beating heart.

He looked great as always, but also pooped—not only because he'd been working eighteen-hour days but because the F.B.I. had shown up on Friday, and the Feds always gave him a headache.

It was also Monday that the G.P.D. announced that the arson investigators had found traces of fertilizer and gasoline, that infamous Oklahoma City concoction.

The bombing, of course, had been front-page news every day since it happened. Now we were working on your classic follow-up stories: profiles of the various groups who'd claimed responsibility, a piece on how Benson was beefing up security, another on how the scientists who'd worked in plant science were grumbling about not being let into the intact two-thirds of the building to retrieve their stuff. I also did some in-depth profiles of the victims—and if the story didn't already have enough pathos, the sophomore who lost his hand turned out to be an aspiring concert pianist.

And I think I've got problems.

It was the science piece Ochoa pulled together for Tuesday's paper on the chemistry of fertilizer bombs that made me realize that Mad's disappearing act had gone on long enough. I tried calling every ten minutes for the rest of the afternoon. I went over there and pounded on his door. No dice.

I considered calling in the marines—or, to be perfectly accurate, the goddamn navy SEALs—and decided there was no use dragging Cody away from a major investigation just because my (usually faulty) woman's intuition had gone into overdrive. Neither were there any manly types immediately available in the newsroom. So I went back over to Mad's, determined to break the door down myself—a rather amusing concept since I'm all of five feet three inches.

But when I got there, it was ajar. Not wide open, just cracked a little. I went in without even knocking, since the politeness bit had gotten me nowhere. What I found pretty much conformed to my worst fears—well, my second worst, anyway.

Mad was facedown on the couch, legs splayed diagonally onto the floor. For a second, I just stood there, gaping and terrified; the man sure as hell looked dead to me. Then I got off my ass and called 911.

"This is bad," O'Shaunessey was saying as we drove up West Hill toward the hospital. "This is *bad*. This is *really, really bad*. What the fuck was he thinking?"

"I wish I knew."

"I mean, the booze is one thing. But pills? Since when does Madison take—"

"Since when does he come to work drunk off his ass? Since when does he get himself fired?"

"Yeah, but are you sure he—"

"Christ, O, I already *told* you. The EMTs took one look at him and they knew he was on something. They made me toss the place and I found the goddamn bottle under his bed, okay? And I've got no more fucking idea of why he did it than you do. So can we just drop it?"

We got to the hospital around four, and stayed there until well after midnight—first in the E.R. waiting room, then upstairs in I.C.U. As the EMTs had so eloquently told me, it didn't look good. Mad was on life support. At one point, his heart had stopped beating and they'd had to shock it. Brain damage was an open question. So was whether or not he'd ever wake up.

The nurses kept wanting to know about his next of kin, which scared the hell out of me. Finally, I asked one of them if their point was finding somebody with the authority to pull the plug, and she just stared at her chunky orthopedic shoes and told me, well, there were a lot of issues to be dealt with, and he needed his family around him.

Clearly, she hadn't met his family.

Mad's parents are both dead, but he has two sisters. One is a born-again Christian who's always sending him long letters about how he's going straight to hell, and backing it up with lots of quotes from Revelation. The other is slightly more to his liking, except that she's married to a guy who thinks Mad's an unwholesome influence on their three kids and won't allow him in the house.

I would've called them anyway—I knew I *had* to call them sooner or later—but frankly I had no idea how to find them. I didn't know their married names, and as far as I knew, Mad didn't keep an address book. All *Monitor* reporters have an in-case-of-emergency number in their employee files, but Mad's contact person was me.

By the time we finally left the hospital, I was feeling like I might have to check in there myself. My various wounds were still killing me, and now I had a blazing headache from the fluorescent lights, plus an upset stomach from eating egg-salad sandwiches out of the vending machine for dinner. I went home, hoping Melissa the Invisible Roommate had fed and walked the dogs, and found Brian Cody in my living room. Thank God.

I sat down next to him on the couch and cried like a baby, which is something I seem to do around him far too often.

"What did the doctors say?" he asked once I'd stopped sobbing all over his Red Sox T-shirt.

"They used every cliché you can think of. 'It's touch and go. We'll have to wait and see. Take it one day at a time. The next twenty-four hours are critical.' Son of a *bitch*."

"Shh . . . It's gonna be okay."

"It damn well is *not*."

"There's nothing you can do for him right now. You've just got to take care of yourself."

"More clichés."

"Sorry. Do you think you can get some sleep?"

"Not a chance."

"Then let's just sit here for a while."

"Don't *you* need to get some sleep?"

"Yeah, but don't worry about it. Do you want a drink?"

"Oh, God, yes."

He went into the kitchen and came back with a glass of red wine for me and a Guinness for him; apparently, he'd restocked his private stash.

"I've got to track down his sisters," I said. "The hospital . . . needs his next of kin."

"And you don't know where they are?"

"I don't even know their names. I know one of them—the one he doesn't totally hate—she lives in Pittsburgh. Her husband works for some insurance company or something."

"Tell me what you know later, and I'll track them down."

"You don't have to do that."

"Actually, yes, I do. When somebody . . . has an accident, finding their next of kin is the cops' job in the first place. I'll do it first thing in the morning."

"Thanks."

"No problem."

"Let's talk about something else, okay?"

"Like what?"

"Like, what's up with the investigation?"

"That's gonna cheer you up?"

"Perversely, yeah. So how's it going?"

He shut his eyes and gave a low groan. "Not good. Or maybe too good, depending on how you look at it."

"Huh?"

"We've got suspects coming out our ears. Everybody and his brother seems to want to take credit for it, which is unbelievable. I'd have thought that since someone got killed, all these groups would be running for cover."

"So why aren't they?"

"The Feds—by the way, they know everything about everything, just ask them. We've got A.T.F., F.B.I. . . . There are so many guys running around in navy windbreakers with yellow letters on the back, you wouldn't even believe it.

Anyway, they say it's fairly typical for a bunch of obscure groups to try to make their bones off somebody else's job."

"You mean, they just want to get their name in the paper?"

"You got it."

"So if they cop to it, that means they actually *didn't* do it?"

"Something like that. Only . . ."

"Only what?"

"You want to go upstairs?"

"Are you just trying to distract me from—"

"No, I'd just really like to lie down. I've been riding a desk all day and my back is killing me."

"That makes two of us."

We went upstairs and stretched out on the bed in the company of our faithful canines. Cody was on his back; I was on my front, with my head on his chest and his arm around me. The day was finally improving.

"The thing is," he said after a while, "I've been looking into these OATs people, and I don't like it one damn bit."

"Hmm . . . ?" That part about me not being able to sleep was turning out to be a big lie. I was totally wiped.

"I think they're dangerous."

"Yeah?"

"They're like . . . Well, I think they're like a snake with lots of heads. That's probably a dumb way to put it; you're the writer, not me. But what I mean to say is, they're everywhere and there's no way to catch them—at least no way the F.B.I. has found so far. They work in individual cells, and they're set up so nobody has a bird's-eye view of the whole operation. No one will even admit to being a member. If there's a leadership structure to it, the Feds have no idea what it is. They've just got this spokesman, a guy named Richard Krikstein who sends their—"

That woke me up. "You mean from the Ecstatic Eggplant?"

"That's the name, yeah. What is it exactly?"

"God, you are such a *carnivore*. The Eggplant is this incredibly famous vegetarian restaurant downtown, the one with all the cookbooks and everything. You know, in the mall that used to be a junior high? The big brick building?" Nothing. "I'm taking you this week. Call it research."

"I'm not gonna eat seaweed."

"Me neither. Anyway, Krikstein is a member of their collective. He writes a whole-foods column for the *Monitor* every other Saturday."

"What the heck's a collective?"

"Think of it as the food-service version of a commune. They share the work; they share the profits."

"Oh. How well do you know the guy?"

"Not well at all. I've run into him in the newsroom when he's dropping off his column. And Mad said . . . Oh, shit."

"What?"

"Mad. I forgot about it for thirty seconds."

He rubbed my neck a little. "Tell me about Krikstein."

"Oh . . . It's nothing really. I was just going to say that Mad told me he spoke at that genetic-engineering conference. The Don't Break the Food Chain people wouldn't have anything to do with it, but he was one of the guys who gave the anti-G.M.O. side. I could get you a copy of Mad's story if you want."

"That'd be good, thanks."

"So how's Krikstein involved in this? I don't think I let you finish that part."

"He's their spokesman. Claims he has no direct contact with any bona fide OATs members, just relays messages he gets over e-mail. And according to the Feds, they're always routed in such a way that you can't trace it to the sender."

"And what's so evil about—"

"Nothing. It's what they've been up to that worries me.

They and another group called the Secret Gardeners have been targeting farms that grow genetic crops—ripping up plants, setting fires, destroying equipment, that type of thing. They've done a fair amount of damage and the cops have never even come close to nailing them for it."

"Just property damage?"

"That's the thing. It looks like they're escalating. One person barely escaped from a barn after they set a silo on fire and it spread. And last month a night watchman almost died after somebody hit him over the head and knocked him out."

"And how do they know the OATs are responsible?"

"Because they take credit. They spray-paint their initials somewhere, or fax a statement to the media, or Krikstein calls the cops."

"How come I haven't heard about this before?"

"They're just hitting their stride. I also get the feeling Krikstein just got involved, so probably there wasn't a local connection until now."

"Are you arresting him?"

"On what charges? So far, no one can prove he's involved beyond being their mouthpiece, and that's not against the law. The F.B.I.'ve questioned him, tossed his place and confiscated his computer, but they haven't found any links to who the OATs really are."

"And you think they're the ones that blew up the building?"

"Far as I'm concerned, they're leading the pack."

"But I thought you said that the people who *claimed* to've done it probably didn't do it at all."

"Maybe that's what they want us to think."

"You really believe these OATs guys lured people to the scene on purpose and then set that other bomb so they could kill everybody? That's not what you'd call environmentally conscious, now is it?"

"That's the odd thing. They specifically said they set the second bomb, but they wouldn't cop to the first."

"Can you blame them? It was the combination of the two that actually got people killed."

"So why take credit for either one of them, particularly the big one?"

"Come on," I said, "don't tell me you think it's possible that two different groups just *happened* to set two separate bombs in the same place on the same night."

"Yeah, I know. It's absurd. Forget I said it."

"Except that lately," I said, "absurd is the goddamn campus motto."

CHAPTER
14

The bombing of the Benson plant-science building accomplished one thing, at least: To the (presumably) great satisfaction of Don't Break the Food Chain hotshot Tobias Kahan, the *New York Times* finally came calling.

The paper had the usual first-day, page-one coverage of the bombing itself, of course, and a rather portentous editorial about the need to be on guard against domestic terrorism. Then the powers that be at "the Gray Lady" started formulating a giant package on the whole genetic-engineering thing and its basis in Gabriel—something I found out about days before it ran because the reporter in question was one Gordon Band, the *Monitor*'s former cop guy and my (sometime) pal.

Gordon had worked at the paper during an oh-so-brief hiatus from the *Times*, mostly to keep his health insurance while he tried to grovel his way back to the big city after having punched his editor in the face. His official title is upstate correspondent, which is quite a hoot; as far as Gordon is concerned, the great state of New York might as well end fifteen minutes north of Westchester. But he does what he must in the furtherance of his quest to cover One Police Plaza (or whatever the hell he's aspiring to), and in a field filled with tenacious bastards, Gordon Band is the bulldog at the head of the pack.

But don't get me wrong. Gordon has his rough edges, but he's a fundamentally decent sort—although if you accused him of decency, he'd turn all red and deny it. He, Mad, and I had worked on what remains the single biggest story of our collective careers, and it was quite the bonding experience. Even though he's done me the occasionally shitty turn in the intervening two years, in other words, I'd probably still take a bullet for the guy.

The first time I ran into him during the G.M.O. thing was at Chief Hill's third press conference on the bombing, the one where the cops basically just said that they were still on the case.

Stop the presses!

Gordon hadn't heard about Mad, so I filled him in. He was pretty upset, but when I suggested that we go see him, Gordon's already-buggy eyes bugged out even farther. He declined, on the basis that hospitals gave him "the heebie-jeebies." We went out for drinks instead, with Gordon trying to make himself feel more manly by mumbling about how Mad would've wanted it that way, after all, didn't I think so?

"What the hell," he said once we'd settled into the window seat at the Citizen Kane and he was sufficiently lubricated to start picking on me, "is a chocolate martini?"

"Godiva liqueur and Stoli vanilla, shaken with ice. Utterly yummy."

"Yuck."

"Bold talk from a man drinking fermented hops."

"So . . . What's your cop loverboy got to say about the building going boom?"

"Jesus, Gordon, nothing like getting right to the point."

"And?"

"And nothing. He's telling me nothing."

"Lying little shiksa."

"Fine," I said, "He's telling me nothing I'm gonna tell *you.*"

"Now *that's* honesty."

"Piss off."

He smirked at me over the lime in his Corona. "Miss me?"

"Every single day."

"Right." The green glow of the Rolling Rock sign was reflecting off his extremely pale skin, making him look like a Jewish zombie with eyeglasses. "How's the great romance going, anyhow?"

"Good. Weird. Weird but good."

"Sounds like haiku. Waddaya mean weird?"

"Same-old, same-old. Trying to make sure being a good girlfriend doesn't turn me into a sucky reporter. You remember the drill."

"Me, I'd screw the girlfriend stuff and concentrate on the reporting."

"Which is why you have such a rich and fulfilling personal life."

"Shut up and drink your Hershey bar."

"Hey, how big is this story of yours gonna be, anyway?"

"Pretty damn big, I hope. Front page of Metro and jumping inside, at least. Maybe billboarded off page one. Depends on how much ass I kick, which I plan to be considerable."

"Who you talked to so far?"

"Huh. Like I'm gonna tell *you.*"

"Don't be a jerk. What difference does it make?"

"You buying me another beer?"

"Sure, whatever."

"Tit for tat." I handed him a ten and he went for another round. "Let's see," he said when he got back, "I talked to Professor Kate Barnett, o'course, and the guy who heads Don't Break the Food Chain. Speaking of which, have you ever heard a more moronic name for an organization in your whole miserable life?"

"You forgetting the Benson Animal Anarchists?"

"Yeah, okay, you win. Anyway, I talked to that D.B.F.C. guy. . . ."

"Tobias Kahan. Ego the size of the ag quad."

"Yeah? I kind of liked him."

"What a shocker. Anyway, I bet he was a whole lot nicer to you, being from New York and all. I'm just a yokel who fell off the turnip truck, don't you know."

"Hmm . . . Who else . . . ? A couple of scientists in Barnett's department . . . Cerretani and Robinson. A scruffy person from that disgusting restaurant—"

"You might wanna keep your voice down. Ragging on the Ecstatic Eggplant in these parts will get your ass kicked but good."

"Who knew you vegetarians were so hostile?"

"Only when provoked."

"Oy. What's his name again . . . ?"

"Rich Krikstein."

"The man smelled like yeast."

"That's *nutritional* yeast. Very healthful."

He wrinkled his nose. "So's corned beef."

"He tell you anything about the OATs?"

"Party line only. But interesting."

"And if he told you anything more, you wouldn't tell me anyway."

"Correct."

"What'd you think of Barnett?"

"I think she could break me in half."

"So could I. What else?"

"Smart," he said amid a waggle of eyebrow. "*Scary* smart. Intense. Stares lasers through you to make sure you're getting whatever she's saying."

"I guess she sort of does. Anyway, I'm doing another interview with her first thing in the morning. Way too bloody early, in fact. She's a busy lady, saving the world and all."

"What're you seeing her for?"

"Another follow on the bomb—how her team is soldiering on in the face of adversity, yadda-yadda."

"Better you than me. Honestly, the woman gave me the creeps. Way too *on*. Do-gooder to the hilt."

"Hmm. I kind of liked her."

"Like you said, *there's* a shocker."

"What do you think it means," I said, "that you like the arrogant people and I like the smart ones?"

He stuck his tongue out at me. "As Madison would say, you chicks sure do stick together."

For the second time in two days, the mere mention of Mad blew my mood in a big way. "Jesus, Gordon, I . . . I'm not sure he's gonna be okay."

"Sure he is."

"Since when are you so optimistic? Come to think of it, since when are you the *least bit* optimistic?"

"I'm not. I just know Madison, and he's a tough son of a bitch."

"A tough son of a bitch who fucking OD's himself on vodka and Percodan?"

"Is that what he took?"

"Yeah."

"*Asshole.*"

"Yeah."

Gordon stared out the window for a while, taking in the usual cast of characters that congregates on the Green at all hours. "Hey, Alex . . . Would you ever?"

"Would I what? Try to off myself?" He nodded, still gazing at the disaffected youth playing Hacky Sack in the fading light of early summer. "Are you kidding? *No way.*"

"How can you be so sure?"

"I guess because it just seems so . . . I don't know, so *pointless*. I mean, it's not as if you aren't gonna die sooner or later. Why rush it?"

"Presumably, because you think life isn't worth living."

"Look, I'm not some fucking Pollyanna or anything. But, you know, I think there'd always be *something* I wanted to do—a movie I wanted to go to, like, or maybe a hot-fudge sundae I wanted to eat. . . ."

"That's either poetic or pathetic," he said. "I'm just not sure which."

"Yeah, well, it may not be much, but it'd be enough to keep me from jumping in the goddamn gorge, okay?"

"In Madison's case, I would've thought the same thing."

"Me too. Except about the gym and expensive tequila."

"Right."

"But you should've seen him, Gordon. For the past month or so, he just wasn't the same old Mad. I think the Emma thing really got to him."

"Hard to picture. But I guess it goes to show you, even when you think you know somebody . . ." His voice trailed off, and he turned his attention back to the Hacky Sackers.

"Hey, Gordon . . . You telling me you would?"

"Rub myself out? Nah. I'm a cynical bastard, remember?"

"What does that have to do with it?"

"I don't expect much out of life."

"So?"

"So," he said, "I'm rarely disappointed."

～≈◈≈～

The subject of death was still very much on my brain when I hauled myself out of bed at six-thirty the next morning to make it to Kate Barnett's lab by the obscene hour of seven.

Thanks to the plant-science bombers (whoever they were), I'd had no Brian Cody in my bed the night before. The lack of which may well have contributed to the nightmare I had involving the posthumous distribution of Mad's worldly goods—a process that took about three minutes, including his TV.

But let's face it: When I walked into the biotech building, I was thinking about the abstract kind of death. Two minutes later, it turned into something a hell of a lot more concrete.

Because there, on the floor of her lab and surrounded by a pool of blood the size of my living-room couch, was Professor Kate Barnett.

When I saw her, the first thing that occurred to me was that it was an excellent time to scream my head off. I did this for a while, but if I thought somebody might come save me from having to look at her anymore, I was sorely disappointed.

The building was mostly empty. The door had closed behind me. Because of the various experiments conducted there, the biotech building is built like a freaking *bunker*. So if anybody was even on the same floor, they didn't hear me.

In horror movies, you always see characters—okay, mostly women—frozen in place by the sight of something really grisly. And at the risk of turning myself into yet another stereotype, I gotta admit that's exactly what I did.

It was a rubbernecking, don't-want-to-watch-but-can't-look-away kind of moment: me with my reporter's notebook in one hand and a big take-out coffee in the other, and Kate Barnett lying there on her stomach, her long strands of gray-black hair splaying out into the blood like an octopus in the Red Sea.

Or something like that. I don't know. I was a little delirious.

Head wounds bleed a lot, I thought, though I couldn't tell you why I thought it.

And speaking of heads, she didn't really have one any-more. It was so bashed in, there wasn't much left but a red-dish purple mess, and it occurred to me that I was looking at the woman's brain. Or chunks of it, anyway.

When I finally stopped gaping at the body, I noticed there was a very bloody length of pipe beside her. Then I noticed the walls were as red as the floor, and the reason why was re-ally nasty. First off, there was an insane amount of blood splattered all over one wall, a Jackson Pollock painting via Count Dracula. I wondered how much force you'd have to use to accomplish that, and decided I didn't really want to know.

But there was something else—something even worse, if you can believe it. Using a paintbrush that was still sitting on one of the counters, somebody had written some creepy graf-fiti in three-foot-high letters, with Barnett's blood as their artistic medium.

DEATH TO DR. FRANKENFOOD! it said. TIME TO SOW OUR OATS.

⸂⸝⸜⸀

Most people, admittedly, do not have the phone number of a homicide detective programmed into their speed dial. I do.

The first thing I remember doing after I (sort of) came to my senses is putting my coffee down on the slate countertop so I could dig my cell phone out of my backpack.

The goddamn cup fell over.

I wasn't paying attention, and I'd set it half off the edge. It exploded onto the ground, soaking not only my pants and clogs but also a large portion of the industrial tile floor. I briefly considered cleaning it up, then figured it wasn't par-ticularly wise to tamper with a crime scene.

I pushed the right button on my bat phone, and he answered on his own cell. I didn't even say hello, just "Where are you?"

"At the house." For some cop reason I have yet to fathom, this means the police station.

"Please come here right now."

"Are you okay? You don't sound like yourself. Where are you?"

"I'm in Kate Barnett's lab at the Benson biotech building. She's dead."

"What? I don't think I heard you right. I thought you just said—"

"She's dead. Somebody beat her to death. It's *awful*. There's blood everyplace, and somebody—"

"I'll be right there."

"Cody?"

"Yeah?"

"I spilled coffee."

"What?"

"I spilled—"

"Calm down, baby. I'll be right there."

"Can't you stay on the phone with me?"

I'm not proud of it, but that's what I said. All this happy-couple stuff was making me damn codependent.

"Sure," he said. "Just hold on a second, okay?"

He sounded like a TV cop trying to placate a tongue-lolling ledge jumper. I heard him say something vaguely commanding to somebody else; then he was back on the line.

"Where are you?"

"I told you, I'm in Kate Barnett's lab. She's on the floor, and—"

"You're still in there?"

"Um, yeah. . . ."

"Listen to me, okay? I want you to walk out the . . . Wait. Is the door closed?"

"Uh-huh."

"Can you get out of there without touching the handle?"

"Huh?"

"It would be good if you didn't ruin any—"

"Fingerprints. Oh."

"That's right. Can you?"

Your girlfriend's eyeballing a dead rice breeder, and you're worrying about the . . . Oh, hell.

"Yeah, I guess."

"Good girl."

I stretched my right sleeve down over my hand, used it to push the door handle down from three o'clock to six, and got the hell out of there. It wasn't until I made it to the hallway that I realized I'd tracked reddish footprints behind me. I'd been standing in her blood, and I hadn't even noticed. Jesus Christ.

"Okay," I said. "I'm out."

"What floor are you on?"

"The fourth, all the way down at the end of the hall. Her lab is the whole corner of the building. Where are you?"

"On my way out to the car. Benson cops'll be there any second. They're gonna secure the scene."

"How about you drive fast?"

"Are you all right?"

"Yeah. I mean, no. . . . I mean . . ."

"Talk to me. Just keep talking."

"I . . . I mean, I've seen stuff before, lots of stuff, but I've never seen anything so . . . *vicious*. I mean, how could somebody . . ."

"It's gonna be okay."

"Christ, Cody, all she ever tried to do is help people. She didn't deserve to . . . Oh, God, it's so awful. . . . There's blood everyplace, and her head . . . It's practically not even *there*. . . ."

"Alex, baby, try to calm down. You're hyperventilating. I can hear it in your voice. Just breathe, okay? I'm on my way."

For some reason—why, I couldn't tell you—the memory of Barnett's body was even worse than the sight itself. And trust me, it was pretty damn bad to begin with.

"You don't understand," I said. "There's so much blood. And I spilled coffee. . . ."

"Alex, honey, I really need you to calm down. I'll be there in five minutes, okay? And Benson security's on its way."

"Oh, Christ, I'm so pathetic. . . ."

"No, you're not."

"I am so. . . ."

By then I was crying, which is how the two Benson cops found me—a blubbering mess on the doorstep of an even bigger, nastier mess. Humiliating.

"We've got her," one of them said into a radio. "She's okay."

For some reason—sanity not being high on my list of things to do at the moment—this made me absolutely *furious*. I pictured Cody putting the Benson cops on alert for a hysterical female, telling them to pat me on the head and give me a cookie if I promised not to spill anything else all over his crime scene.

Like I said, I was less than rational.

"Of course I'm okay," I said. "I'm *clearly* okay. Who said I wasn't okay?"

They eyed each other like they were each hoping the other had remembered to bring the straitjacket.

"Look, miss," the older one said, "how about if you come down the hall with me and sit down? You look like you might—"

"I do *not*."

For the record, I had no idea what he was going to say, but I contradicted him anyway.

I was still making an ass of myself when Cody and the rest of the Gabriel Light Infantry arrived a few minutes later. He put a hand on my shoulder, which was as close to PDA as he'd ever get in the midst of a homicide.

And . . . among the morning's embarrassments, I have to report that the sight of him actually calmed me down rather efficiently.

Later, long after the crime-scene guys had finished and the cops had confiscated my shoes and Kate Barnett's body had been removed to the morgue, Cody called me at home to tell me not to feel bad about turning into a simpering idiot.

By then, though, I was halfway into stiff drink number three. And although I should've had a hell of a lot on my mind—the fact that I'd spent the morning within spitting distance of a genuine martyrdom; my best friend was very likely going to die; sooner or later, Cody was going to leave town and forget all about me—the happy truth is that by the time the phone rang I was no longer capable of thinking about very much at all.

CHAPTER
15

My drunken vision of Kate Barnett as a martyr didn't turn out to be far off. The avalanche of grief that followed her murder was, well, practically biblical. Her colleagues at Benson and beyond lamented her death at the top of their lungs, eulogizing her as (and this is a quote) "agriculture's own Mother Teresa." Her murder, they said, was the quintessential sacrifice of science to hysteria, and the greatest insult to the advance of human knowledge since the Inquisition tortured Galileo into saying his idea about the sun being the center of the universe was really just a fraternity prank.

But, truth be told, not everybody was sorry. The genetic-engineering debate being what it is, Barnett's death was roughly equivalent to the assassination of a doctor who performs abortions: A lot of people were outraged, a few were terrified, and a vocal minority were damn glad. No . . . make that downright gleeful, like they were watching the villain get his just desserts at the end of a James Bond flick.

And the press attention was *unbelievable*. Gabriel has been the source of a fair number of national datelines in its day, but this was the first time it really went global and stayed there. Barnett was, after all, a prominent scientist working on issues affecting the Third World even more than the First. Around here, that became a story in and of itself: In what probably amounts to classic media navel-gazing, Marilyn had Brad do a piece on the international coverage, which he researched up at the Benson library. My favorite headline (among many) came from Addis Ababa and said MOTHER-ANGEL OF FAMINE RELIEF GONE FOREVER.

The campus, not to mention the town in general, was veritably crawling with reporters. You'd think locals like me would still have the home-court advantage, but it didn't happen that way—and from what I hear it never does. In case you're interested, the pathology goes like this: First everybody gets goggle-eyed that the *London Times* actually gives a damn what they have to say; then they get sick to death of having tape recorders and microphones shoved in their faces; then they tell us all to piss off.

Which is pretty much what occurred.

The more angles a story has, the longer its legs—and the Kate Barnett murder was a goddamn giraffe. There was her biography, with all the scientific genius and the activism and the adopted Somalian waifs. And then there was the whole G.M.O. thing, which had the world agog to begin with. And the sheer grisliness of the crime—not to mention the fact that it came right on the heels of a double bombing.

And then, of course, there was the burning question of just who the hell killed her. Fortunately or unfortunately, there were enough suspects to fill the Benson football stadium.

Based on the extremely icky graffiti at the crime scene, the cops had busted into the Ecstatic Eggplant during the lunchtime rush and dragged Krikstein—who was in the midst of making the restaurant's famous chopped salad with beets, roasted sesame seeds, and organic mesclun—out by the scruff of his neck. But although plenty of people were willing to believe that the OATs had beaten Barnett to death with their own vegan hands, others argued that it was just garden-variety misdirection; maybe a rival group had taken the opportunity to get rid of her and blame it on somebody else. Then there was a backlash that figured that the OATs would be wily enough to anticipate that, so taking credit for the crime was tantamount to concocting an alibi. This was followed by a backlash to the backlash and . . . Well, you get the idea.

The Don't Break the Food Chain people were also guests of the local constabulary, and they loved every minute of it. Most sane human beings wouldn't be flattered to be considered capable of beating a middle-aged woman to death, but apparently the D.B.F.C. considered it evidence of their entrée into the activist major leagues.

It was barely seven hours after I found Barnett's body that the OATs confessed to her murder via fax.

Two hours later, they turned around and denied it.

The next morning, they took credit for it again.

By then, nobody had any idea which way was up. Either they were implementing some fiendish plan, or the Organic Activist Tribe was even more disorganized than the *Gabriel Monitor* newsroom.

The paper, by the way, was a madhouse. With Mad down for the count, I was so busy I barely had time to maintain my reputation as a regular consumer of fattening sandwiches. It was a good thing I was so swamped, though, because I also didn't have time to slide into the hideous depression that was lurking at the margins of my brain.

Mad had been vegetating for days, and the doctors were telling his sisters to prepare themselves for, quote, "the worst"—inspiring the older one to fill his hospital room with a stunning variety of devotional objects. The sight of him lying there had been horrible enough; the plug-in Jesus (complete with glowing red stigmata) pushed me over the edge.

Bad friend though it made me, I couldn't bear to go in there anymore. Guilt got piled on top of anxiety—which was already piled atop plenty of residual guilt for not stopping him from taking the Percodan in the first place.

The memory of Kate Barnett's body, too, was always waiting to bite me on the ass. I saw it every time I closed my eyes, which didn't make for restful sleep.

And what's worse, I was sleeping alone—and it looked like I would be for the foreseeable future. The Feds, who clearly know way too much for their own good, had come down hard on Chief Hill for letting his lead detective fraternize with the local media in the midst of two gigantically sensitive cases. Hill had told Cody (not unkindly, granted) to do him a favor and cool it for a while.

This, despite plenty of phone conversations and a few sneaky late-night booty calls, gave me a taste of what life would be like without him. I didn't like it.

With Gordon firmly in the enemy camp—running around like a happy mental patient, scooping the rest of us right and left—that left me pretty much on my own. Which is how I ended up spending so damn much time with Cal Ochoa.

As the cop reporter, he well and truly was entitled to cover the Barnett murder. And although Ochoa was obviously a territorial animal, he was fine with having me feed him some background—as long as he was in charge and nobody tried to foist a joint byline on him.

We'd taken to closing the Citizen Kane every night, sitting in the window seat and talking and drinking until they kicked us out at one-thirty. And although I'm sure Ochoa is a perfectly decent human being, I would've given just about anything to be there with an independently breathing Jake Madison instead.

Apparently, I wasn't as successful at hiding this opinion as I might have liked.

"Yo, Alex," he was saying one night around midnight, "where's your head right now?"

"Huh?"

"You're looking at me like you wish I were an empty chair."

"Oh. Sorry. I'm just spacing. What were you saying?"

"Kate Barnett."

"Of course, Kate Barnett. What about her?"

"She's still dead."

"Don't be a jerk."

"Then pay attention, *chica.*"

"You know, you've been rather vehemently Mexican the past couple of days."

"That's why my name's *Caliente.*"

My drink stopped in mid-swill. "It is *not.*"

"It's on my birth certificate."

"You've got to be kidding me."

"Es verdad."

"Oh, my God. I'm going to try very hard to forget that. So what about Barnett again?"

"Hey, if you're not interested . . ."

"Give me a break. I feel like six different kinds of lousy."

"You kinda look it. Any news on Madison?"

"No change. Now can we please not talk about it?"

He sipped his tequila, which he had previously explained indicated not a lack of manliness but an appreciation for fine liquor. "I was telling you about the list of suspects."

"Again."

"Hey, you got someplace better to be?"

"No. And neither do you, so there."

"Touché," he said. "See? I speak French too."

"I better watch my back."

"Especially once I crack this case. Give me that and a big pair of *tetas* and I'm Alex Bernier."

"Shut up."

He didn't; actually, he chuckled at his joke for a while. "Suspects," he said once he was done. "You got your members of Don't Break the Food Chain, who I think are a bunch of pussies. Then you've got the OATs—"

"Probably not pussies."

"Probably not. Anyway, they're sneaky little bastards. Even the G-men don't know who they are, right?"

"Right."

"Then you've got—"

"Are you serious?"

"Serious about what?"

"What you just said."

"Hey, come on, you know as well as I do you've got a huge pair of—"

"I meant about cracking the case."

"Sure, why not?"

"Because you're not a cop. In fact, you're a reporter whose previous job was at the goddamn Tahoe *Bonanza*."

"Hey, you've figured out some shit in your time."

"Is that what this is about? Competition?"

"Look, this is the coolest thing I've ever come across, okay? You can't blame a guy for wanting to have a little fun. My girlfriend's not getting here for another—"

"Cal, for chrissake, Kate Barnett got her brains bashed in. Believe me, it wasn't a pretty sight."

"So what are you saying? You want to figure it out for yourself? Finders keepers?"

"No, I do not fucking well want to figure it out for myself. I'd just as soon let the police deal with this one, thank you very much."

"That's pretty lame, if you ask me."

"Good thing nobody asked you."

"What's your problem? I'd have thought you'd be way into this."

"Well, I'm not."

"So can I bounce some stuff off you, or are you gonna totally lame out on me?"

"*Arrgh.* All I'm saying is, for once in my life I'm in no mood to play Nancy Drew. I'm totally exhausted, okay?"

"Okay." If he gave a damn, he was concealing it extremely well. "So like I was saying, the OATs are a bunch of sneaky bastards. Nobody seems to know who belongs and who doesn't. Krikstein's the closest they have to a mouthpiece, and he's so hot right now he's gotta be outta the loop, don't you think?"

"I'd imagine the cops have tapped his every orifice."

"Right. So how do we infiltrate?"

"How do we *what?*"

"I was thinking, maybe I could go undercover somehow—"

"Man, you are just licking your chops."

"Come on, this is *cool.*"

"Okay, fine. How the hell are you gonna go undercover in an organization when you have absolutely no clue who the other members are?"

"I haven't figured that part out yet. You got any ideas?"

"Nothing leaps to mind at the moment."

"So, come on, how would you do it? Solving the murder, I mean. What did you and Madison and Band do on that Adam Ellroy thing?"

I stared at him. "How the hell do you know about that?"

"You, um, you told me the guy was murdered. . . ."

"I sure as hell didn't tell you the rest."

He had the good grace to look abashed, but just a little. "Madison and I were in here one night, and he . . . kind of mentioned it."

"Well," I said, "I kind of don't feel like talking about it."

"Just come on, you know, give me someplace to start."

"Other than telling you to kiss my *gringa* ass?"

"Look, I'm sorry, okay? I shouldn't have brought that up. It was out of line."

"You bet it was. And anyway . . . Honest to God, I don't really know what we did. We kind of just stumbled through. We had to do it, so we did."

"Oh."

Rather than throttle him, I decided to concentrate on my gin and tonic, which was damn good; the single positive thing that had happened to me all week was Mack, the bartender, finally giving in to my pleas to lay in a supply of Junipero.

"Well," I said after a while, "I guess what we did a lot was sit around and ask each other questions. We kind of figured out what we needed to answer and then we tried to answer it."

"Sounds good. So let's do it."

"Now?"

"Like I said before, you got anything better to do?"

"Fine. Suit yourself."

He pulled his reporter's notebook out of his jacket pocket with a flourish. On second thought, throttling him was starting to look like a good idea.

"Okay," he said, "here we go. First off, who capped Professor Barnett?"

"You know, maybe you oughta go over to the cop shop and offer your services. They could use a clever lad such as yourself."

"Bitch, bitch, bitch. You want another drink?"

"Yeah."

"Then go get one. Get me another one too while you're at it."

I might have taken offense at this, if he hadn't been

pulling out his wallet while he said it. But when he proffered cash, I grabbed the wallet instead, and before he could snatch it back, I was nose to nose with his driver's license.

"You are so full of shit," I said, laughing so hard I decided to sit back down lest I fall over. " '*Caliente,*' my ass. . . ."

"Give me that."

"*Calvin?* Your real name is *Calvin?*"

"Would you please shut up?"

"Mister macho Mexican is named *Calvin?*"

He grabbed the wallet back. "It was in my mom's family, okay?"

"Okay, *Calvin.*"

"I swear, if you tell anybody, I'm gonna—"

"So I take it your mom's Anglo, huh?"

He seemed totally disinclined to answer, but for some reason he did anyway. "She's from Connecticut."

"Oh, yeah? Where?"

"Cos Cob."

"You gotta be kidding me. Do you realize how goddamn preppy—"

"Are you gonna get us some drinks or aren't you?"

"And lemme guess. Your dad's a corporate lawyer."

"He's a brain surgeon, okay? And they live in Mexico City. Now will you please get me a drink?"

When I came back, he was hunched over his notebook like it was the centerfold of *Hustler.* He looked up at me warily, but when I didn't recommence the ribbing, he took his tequila without a snarky comment.

"Okay," he said, "you wanna hear what I got?"

"You're buying, guess I'm listening."

He looked up from his notebook and squinted at me. "Jesus, Alex, what the hell is wrong with you tonight? You're not usually this much of a wench."

"Maybe this is the real me. Maybe I've just been on my best behavior up till now."

"Yeah, right. Seriously, are you okay?"

"Seriously, no. I'm worried as hell about Mad, for one thing, and this Barnett thing has me totally freaked out. Plus, in case you missed it, I practically got blown to hell along with Phil Herzog last week. And although it's none of your business, on top of all that, I haven't seen Cody in like *forever*. I'm in what they call a foul humor."

"I'll say."

"So cut me some slack, *muchacho*."

"Hey, I can be a nice guy, just ask Elena. Far as I'm concerned, you ladies can have your moods if you gotta have 'em."

"How enlightened of you."

"It's the lack of curiosity I don't get. About Barnett, I mean."

I thought about it for a minute. "I don't get it, either, really. It's not my style. I'm just in a funk is all."

"So snap out of it."

"Thanks."

"Next question: the motive. Who got something out of Barnett's death? And speaking of which, what was it they got?"

"Hating her and everything she stands for doesn't cover it?"

He looked back down at the page, which was covered in a mighty scribble. "I thought about that. In that case, I'd say they killed her to stop her from doing her work. Logical, see?"

"Truly, the mind boggles."

"Damn, I'm *good*. Okay, next. Is the person who killed Barnett the same person who blew up the plant-science building? And what was the motive for blowing it up, anyway? Was it really just to kill her? And if it was, why bother with the second bomb? To cover your tracks? Or because you really want to knock off as many people as you can? And, hey, what kind of sick fuck wants to do that kind of thing in the first place?"

"Good questions."

"I've got more. You wanna hear them or what?"

"Yeah."

"A sign of life," he said. *"Que bueno."*

CHAPTER
16

Don't ask me how it happened: I went from being the girl-friend of a cop to the girl Friday of a cop *reporter* in all of five seconds. Not that my lust for Cody was on the wane, mind you; if anything, absence was making my heart (not to mention several other organs) grow a whole lot fonder. But after that long, boozy night in the Citizen Kane, Cal Ochoa had me hooked on the Kate Barnett story right along with him. Whatever he asked me to do on it, I did—and then some.

If I felt like analyzing why I got so into it (which, frankly, I don't), I might say something about how I was inspired to seek justice for poor, pipe-bludgeoned Kate Barnett. This would be a big lie.

So I went to work, and I covered Common Council, and I came home and walked Shakespeare around the block.

I wrote stories about recycling—which, in an ecologi-cally obsessed place like Gabriel, is big news even in the wake of a high-profile homicide.

I went to the junior high and gave a career-day talk about journalistic ethics, and managed to keep a straight face.

I did a news obit on a longtime county legislator who (in

merciful contrast to Kate Barnett) died in his sleep at the ripe old age of ninety-four, after ingesting a church supper that would choke a pig.

I talked to Cody and worried the F.B.I. was checking our phone records.

I thought about holding a Thursday-night dinner for the sake of newsroom morale, and decided I was too damn tired.

I took up smoking again, just a little, even though Cody and I had pledged to quit once and for all.

I felt guilty and gave the pack away to a guy collecting cans on the Gabriel Green. Then I went out and bought another one.

My life, as you can doubtless tell from the preceding laundry list, felt choppy, disjointed, out of whack. I managed to put one foot in front of the other, do what I was supposed to do roughly when I was supposed to do it, but the only thing I halfway cared about was figuring out who had murdered Kate Barnett. I suppose the truth is that the weird, lonely rut I'd fallen into—minus Mad, minus Cody, minus my city-planner-shagging roommate—had somehow made me feel closer to her. Even though I'd barely known her, I was starting to think of her as a friend; in other words, I was starting to take her murder personally.

Which is how, on a mild day in late June, I found myself in the ag-school coffee shop with three genetic engineers. The so-called Alfalfa Room is located in the basement of the oldest building on the quad. It has broad wooden tables, cider direct from the university orchard, and muffins as big as your whole head.

So there I was, drinking coffee and nibbling on a cappuccino-and-chocolate-chip affair that, admittedly, was managing to rouse me from my dietary doldrums. The ostensible purpose of the interview was a soft feature on how Barnett's team was doing without her—carrying on her dream of feeding the world despite their grief, yadda-yadda-yadda. In actual fact, I'd sold Bill on the story so I could get another perspective on Barnett herself, the getting-to-know-the-victim thing being something I'd heard Cody preach on numerous occasions.

I'd brought my tape recorder, which I rarely use. Although some journalists swear by them, they just tend to make me sloppy: When I go to write the story, there's a great temptation to use a bunch of mediocre quotes just because I've got them, while taking notes forces me to jot down just what's important and genuinely quotable. (And besides, transcribing a whole interview can be a huge waste of time, which daily news reporters don't have.) But Ochoa had insisted on hearing the interview for himself, so I taped it.

Occupying the other chairs were three members of Barnett's department: doctors of philosophy Jack Cerretani, Shep Robinson, and Lindsay McDaniel. To describe them a bit:

Cerretani is fiftyish, burly, Italian looking, with a thick head of graying black hair and a sea captain's beard. Big nose with visible hairs protruding, thick lines across his forehead like he raises his eyebrows a lot, not what you'd call a heartbreaker. Wears a thick turquoise wedding ring and silver neck chain with some sort of Native American symbol on it. Wouldn't stop calling me "Miss Bernier."

Robinson is black, maybe thirty-five, clearly a gym-goer, cute little wire-rimmed glasses, dark blue oxford over a white T-shirt and well-fitting jeans, probably gay. (Mental note: Find out more for possible introduction to Steve the Ornithologist as palliative for recent heartbreak.) My favorite of the three.

McDaniel, aged early thirty-something, your classic grown-up girl-nerd. Zero makeup, bad posture, unfortunate eyewear, in serious need of a haircut. Wearing a diamond engagement ring the size of a jawbreaker, however, so somebody must think she's babelicious. Plus, she's clearly smart as hell. You go, girl.

We sat there for an hour, with them singing the praises of the late, lamented Professor Barnett and me eating not one but two of the aforementioned muffins. But when I say "singing the praises," I don't mean it was a particularly catchy tune—at least not at first. The three of them are scientists, not P.R. people, and all the press attendant to the bombing and Barnett's murder clearly had, to varying degrees, freaked them out.

Sample conversation, straight off the tape:

ME: "So, in retrospect, what would you say were her greatest strengths?"

[Insert yet another awkward silence.]

McDANIEL: "Well, I . . . um would have to say . . . everything. She was good at everything."

ME: "Could you be a little more specific?"

McDANIEL: "Well, you know . . . dealing with people. She was really good with people. Better than I am, that's for sure." [Chuckle, chuckle.] "She always knew the right thing to say. She could . . . She could convince people . . . She could get them to . . . get them to see the—"

CERRETANI: "Miss Bernier, did you by any chance happen to hear Professor Barnett's keynote speech at the G.M.O. symposium?"

ME: "Yes, I did."

CERRETANI: "Then you can appreciate what Lindsay's describing. Dr. Barnett was a talented individual. She was not only an extremely gifted scientist, she was also a genuine humanitarian. That's a rare combination, you know. Kate Barnett was a very special woman."

ROBINSON: "That's what I was going to say—that Kate was a very unusual person."

[More silence here.]

ME: "How so?"

ROBINSON: "I suppose I'd . . . I say, just look around this table. At the risk of putting too fine a point on it or kowtowing to stereotypes, well . . ." [Chuckle.] ". . . I'll do just that. Look at the three of us. Lindsay is an amazing scientist, a crackerjack hands-on researcher. In the lab, she's *fierce*." [McDaniel looks down at her bear claw, blushes, pushes up her glasses even though they don't need it.] "Jack here is a leader, chair of the plant-science department. This man definitely knows how to shake the funding tree."

CERRETANI: "No pun intended." [Belly laugh.]

ROBINSON: "And as for me . . ." [Broad smile, self-effacing wink.] ". . . I've got *personality*. I'm not a genius like Lindsay, and I'm probably never going to be the chair of anything—"

CERRETANI: "Shep's being modest. You don't get on the tenure track in plant science at Benson without being one hell of a scientist."

ROBINSON: "Thanks, Jack. What I mean to say is, yes, I'm a solid scientist, but more important than that, I can do something most of us can't: I can work a room. I can go in front of a lot of strangers or on PBS or whatever and I can make them understand why we do what we do—*usually*, anyway." [Big chuckle.] "So that's what we three bring to the table. And what I'm trying to say is, Kate had all of that wrapped up in one person."

[Looks of relief, like they fell off the hook en masse.]

CERRETANI: "I couldn't have put it better myself."

ME: "What about you, Dr. McDaniel? Did you want to add anything?"

[Look of deer in headlights.]

McDANIEL: "Just that Professor Barnett was . . . was a very special person."

ME: [Concealing desire to throttle tongue-tied source.] "Special how?"

McDANIEL: "Like . . . like Shep said."

ME: "Meaning?"

McDANIEL: "She was . . . really well-rounded. She was a very special person."

ME: [Swearing under breath and asking next question out of pure, old-fashioned journalistic cussedness.] "So . . . do you think Professor Barnett's tendency to be outspoken may have contributed to her death?"

[Horrified stares all around.]

CERRETANI: "What could you possibly mean by that, Miss Bernier?"

ME: "Professor Barnett was extremely vocal in her support of genetic engineering of food crops, right? And at one of her last press appearances, she practically dared whoever blew up the plant-science building to come after her."

CERRETANI: [Forehead lines deepening like the Mariana Trench.] "That's your opinion."

ME: "A minute ago, you referred to the speech she gave at the symposium. . . ."

CERRETANI: "Yes . . . ?"

ME: "Well, obviously, Professor Barnett was a fantastic speaker. She really got her passion across. I'm just wondering if you think that passion got someone angry enough to kill her."

CERRETANI: "That's a ridiculous question."

ME: "Why is that?"

CERRETANI: "Because what you're doing is blaming the victim."

ME: "I didn't mean it that way. What I'm wondering is, do you think Professor Barnett was murdered to stop the actual work she was doing, or to silence the beliefs she represented?"

CERRETANI: "What difference does it make?"

ME: [Behaving like a weasel.] "I'm not saying it makes any difference per se. I was just wondering your opinion, that's all."

CERRETANI: "To be honest, I have no idea what could have been in the minds of the people who did this terrible thing to Kate. And frankly, Miss Bernier, I'd just as soon not think about it. Those people are monsters. Small-minded monsters."

ME: "Dr. McDaniel?"

McDANIEL: "I . . . I don't have anything to add. I agree with Professor Cerretani. Why they did it is too horrible even to think about."

ME: "Professor Robinson?"

ROBINSON: "Obviously, it was both. Kate was what you might call one-stop shopping." [Appalled looks from the other two.] "Oh, come on, she knew she was a target. She was just too dedicated to care. Or, more to the point, she . . . Can you turn off your tape recorder for a moment?"

I did. Ochoa was not going to be happy.

"Look," he said, "this is off the record, all right?" I nodded. Cerretani and McDaniel looked damn uncomfortable, but Robinson didn't seem to notice. "I don't see any reason to waffle about this, since I don't believe it really reflects badly on Kate in any way—to the contrary, actually."

McDaniel took a passionate interest in her tea bag. Cerretani's caterpillar eyebrows threatened to meet his hairline. "The truth is," Robinson went on, "she knew she was likely standing in the path of an oncoming train, and she just didn't care. In fact, she probably loved it."

"What makes you say that?"

"This is going to sound like a tangent, but . . . Have you ever heard of Vavilov's seed bank?" I shook my head. "Niko-lai Vavilov, a pioneer in plant genetics. One of the first people to take Darwinian principles and apply them to agriculture. He not only developed a theory about the evolutionary origins of food crops, he also went all over the world collecting seeds to try to protect their genetic diversity." He took a sip of his coffee. "You know about the siege of Leningrad, right?"

"You mean World War Two?"

He nodded. "It was the winter of forty-one through forty-two. The Germans had locked down the city. Conditions were desperate—no food, no heat, constant shelling. Right?"

"Right."

"So, at the time, Vavilov's seed bank was stored in the basement of the Leningrad plant institute. And after a while, word started to spread around the city that there was food to eat there, so the scientists decided to barricade themselves inside to protect the collection. Nearly a dozen of them died."

"You mean people killed them to get the food?"

"No. They starved to death."

"What?"

"That's right. They just sat there, amid piles of potatoes and rice and wheat and corn and peas, and let themselves starve rather than eat Vavilov's seed bank."

"Jesus Christ. And Vavilov wanted it that way?"

Robinson shrugged. "He didn't have much say in the matter. He was rotting in jail on a trumped-up espionage charge."

"How come?"

"He debunked an ally of Stalin's as a pseudoscientist. It's not a happy story."

"I'll say."

"My point is, Kate knew the Vavilov story. She knew it very well—in fact, she cited it constantly, particularly something Vavilov said before they arrested him. He said, 'They can send us to the fire, burn us, but we won't recant our principles.'"

Cerretani and McDaniel had joined in halfway through the sentence. It was a little creepy, actually.

"As you can see," Robinson said, "Kate taught us well. Now, none of us could forget Vavilov if we wanted to. To her, he and those dozen scientists were like Joan of Arc at the stake. Good, old-fashioned martyrs."

"And you think that's also how she saw herself?"

"I think she saw the willingness to sacrifice all for your cause as a very romantic notion. A noble act."

Cerretani scratched his beard and shook his head. "Shep here has a taste for melodrama. It was something he and Kate had in common."

Robinson turned to him. "You disagree?"

"Kate was a grown woman. She was also a scientist, and she was a mother as well. She didn't want to die any more than you or I."

"I never said she wanted to die," Robinson said. "I said I think she liked the *idea* of sacrificing yourself for the greater good. The reality of it . . . obviously, that's not so pleasant. I doubt even Saint Joan had much fun being burned alive, now did she?"

"'Saint Kate,'" McDaniel said in a tiny voice, and the rest of us stared at her. "Is there one, do you think?"

Cerretani raised a hand. "There was Saint Catherine of Siena, of course. And as the product of a parochial education, I can tell you that she was way out of even Kate's league. To my knowledge, our Dr. Barnett neither levitated nor had the stigmata."

The conversation was getting weirder by the second. Too bad I wasn't allowed to use any of it, damn it all.

"If she had," Robinson said, "I'm sure she would've been more than happy to use it as a fund-raising gimmick. Anything to keep the work going, right? Anything to feed the hungry . . ."

The other two nodded. "'They can send us to the fire, burn us, but we won't recant our principles,'" Cerretani said. "If they still put epitaphs on tombstones, that would have been hers."

"Not," Robinson offered, "that Kate ever would have done something so ecologically selfish as interment. She was for cremation all the way, just like the rest of us. And that's on the record."

I reached for the tape recorder, pondering the headline possibilities: PLANT SCIENTISTS FAVOR IMMOLATION. "Do you mind if I turn this back on?"

"Fine with me," Robinson said. The other two nodded.

"So let me ask you this," I said. "Of the anti-G.M.O. groups you know of, which one do you think would be most likely to do something like this? Or do you think the OATs are really responsible, like the . . . the writing said?"

All I got was a trio of blank stares.

"You understand," McDaniel said finally, "we really don't know those people. We'd be the last ones who'd know them, you see? They consider us the enemy."

"Have you gotten any threats yourselves?"

McDaniel looked back down at her pastry. Robinson gave a low whistle. That left Cerretani to take the question. "Nothing we ever took seriously," he said, "until now."

"Meaning . . . ?"

"Meaning we got the average, uninformed rants about how what we're doing is wrong and"—he lowered his voice to sound like a cartoon thug—"They're '*gonna stop us.*' Nothing specific."

"And is there anyone in particular you know of who might have held a grudge against Professor Barnett?" Silence.

"Look, I'm not trying to spread gossip or anything. I'm just trying to get an idea of what the situation was."

"You know," Robinson said, "you sound more like a cop than a reporter."

Busted.

"Yeah, I get that a lot." I was trying to sound cool. I rarely pull it off. "I guess it's all the probing questions."

"'Probing,' eh? Some might just call them 'inappropriate.'"

"Hey, I just ask them." I tried to summon up a lighthearted chuckle, which came out more like a whinny. "I don't apply the thumbscrews or anything."

"You asked about grudges," Cerretani said. "And if you had to ask that, you obviously don't know very much about academia."

"How do you mean?"

"The groves of academe can be a nasty little place, Miss Bernier. We've got all sorts of ideals about worshiping at the altar of knowledge, but the truth is that everybody and his brother wants to get ahead, just like in the rest of the world."

"And?"

"And when you're at the top of the heap, like Kate was, there are plenty of people more than willing to knock you down a peg so they can take your place. Kate was a star, Miss Bernier. She achieved success young and she kept on achieving. And although she was often gracious and helpful to others, she was also one tough cookie. She didn't brook stupidity or sloppiness. In fact, I don't think it would be unfair to say that she took every mistake someone made in her field as tantamount to taking food out of the mouths of starving children. That's a damn high standard to maintain. And she did it, but few others could. That kind of drive can win you a Nobel, but it doesn't necessarily win popularity contests. Do you see?"

"I think so. She sometimes stepped on toes."

"That's a gentle way of putting it, yes. And now if you'll excuse us . . . I think we all need to get back to work."

They stood up, and we migrated to the corner of the room to put our plates and coffee cups into a rubber dishpan.

"Look," I said to Robinson, "I know that part of the interview was off the record, but is it okay with you if I use the Vavilov thing in the story?"

Robinson shrugged. "I don't see why not. I suppose it's an inspirational little anecdote, isn't it?"

"Yeah, it is. Whatever happened to him, anyway?"

"Vavilov? He spent three years in prison. Died there in 1943."

"They executed him?"

"Actually," he said, "he died of hunger."

CHAPTER
17

That night, hoping his sisters would be out eating a wholesome dinner, I finally went back to see Mad.

The good news is that they indeed weren't there. The bad news is that I felt like I'd dropped into a goddamn TV soap.

There I was, sitting at his bedside while the machinery all around him went *beep-beep* and *whoosh-whoosh-whoosh*. I was on the edge of one of those massively uncomfortable institutional chairs, the molded plastic kind that seem designed to (a) anesthetize your butt and (b) make sure you leave as soon as possible.

And as for Mad: He looked like . . . well, like *death*. His skin was waxy and gray, as though some overzealous mortician had sneaked in and given him a premature embalming. Come to think of it, he looked worse than death; my mémère Bernier, professionally made up and lying in her satin-lined casket, had seemed comparatively spry.

Mad's sisters had told me that the doctors were encouraging them to sit there and talk to him, as though a familiar voice might somehow get through to him. This seemed to me the height of stupid melodrama, but hey—who was I to argue with somebody who'd actually passed chemistry?

So I sat there, drinking a liter of diet Pepsi as my backside went slowly numb, and poured my little heart out. At least, I tried to; I got interrupted so many times I was starting to wonder whether we should put one of those deli-counter dispensers on his door and have everybody take a number.

First Melissa stopped by, bearing a framed black-and-white photo of all of us she'd taken at the Citizen one night last winter. We were all scrunched in around a bunch of two-seater tables jammed together—me, Mad, O'Shaunessey, a slumming Gordon Band, Marshall and his wife, a couple of radio reporters, my friend Maggie from the local TV news, and a bucktoothed Benson flack. To sum it up: We looked happy, relatively carefree, and more than a little drunk.

What Melissa thought she was going to accomplish by putting a picture on the nightstand of a guy who was the very definition of *out cold* was beyond me, but I appreciated the sentiment. She stayed for half an hour or so, mumbled something about being late to meet Drew, and took off.

Next came O'Shaunessey, on his dinner break from the four-to-deadline shift. He had, in fact, brought said dinner with him—a gigantic bratwurst from Schultz's, smothered in mustard and sauerkraut, with a big pickle and a side of oily potato salad. This was a calculated move; Mad has always been a fanatic about his fat intake, but every once in a while he'll slip and ingest something really disgusting for the pure sinful joy of it—and Schultz's bratwurst is about as venal as it gets. Clearly, O was hoping that the mere scent of the thing would make Mad bolt upright and take a bite. No go.

O'Shaunessey was just tucking away the last rounded nub of the thing when Marilyn arrived, clad in sweats and with a vee of perspiration down her front. It was the first time she'd seen him, and it obviously got to her. Mad has been one of her pet misfits for the better part of a decade, and firing him had been tough enough; seeing him like this practically brought her to tears, which as far as I know would've been a first.

She and O'Shaunessey left together about ten minutes later, so I was finally all by myself. Well, okay—Mad was there, but he was considerably less talkative than the heart monitor.

"Hey, Mad," I said once the silence had gotten good and creepy. "How ya doin'?"

This conversational gem inspired me to spend some quality time feeling like a moron. It took me a while to get up the nerve to say something else. But when it finally came out, it probably wasn't what the doctor ordered. Neither was it going to win me any awards for eloquence.

"Jesus Christ, Mad," I said. "What the fuck were you thinking? I mean, you've pulled some bonehead moves in your time, but this is the mother of them all, you know? I could fucking *kill* you."

No response. I kept talking.

"I mean, forget about what you did to yourself, to that precious body of yours—to that precious, run-fifty-miles, work-out-all-night, three-showers-a-day body of yours. Like, way to go, okay? You spend five fucking years complaining about the fat in my pesto sauce and yelling at me for eating too much MSG and then you go and pull the goddamn most assholic stunt of the century.

"And forget about you for a minute, all right? Don't you even care how you screwed the rest of us over? Did that not even *occur* to you—that maybe, just maybe, your friends might actually be upset if you go and off yourself? Well, did it? Huh?"

Berating him was surprisingly cathartic. I kept going.

"And how about the *why*? Let's look at that, shall we? Do you realize that all this shit is over a goddamn *girl*? I mean, how many times have you read me the riot act for getting all freaked out over some worthless guy? And now you go popping fucking Percodan over some British twit who goes running back to her asshole drunk of an ex-husband? Like, how stupid can you be? If I ever pulled something like this, you'd kick my ass and you know it.

"But you know what I can't believe? That you'd let your goddamn love life get in the way of your job—make you *lose* your job, for chrissake. You loved your beat—science writer covering this huge research university. You told me one time they'd carry you out of the paper on your back, remember? And come to think of it, they practically had to, you *numskull.*

"And don't go blaming the rest of us, okay? We tried to help you, and you wouldn't let us. How many times did I go knocking on your goddamn door and calling you and trying to get you to open up for half a second and actually tell me what was eating you? But no, you had to be all macho and screw around with this strong-and-silent-type bullshit, right? God forbid you should express an emotion like a normal human being. I tried to help you. I fucking *tried,* you know. . . ."

At this point, I was on the verge of a genuine tizzy. Whether I was more likely to cry hysterically or slap Mad across his gunmetal-gray face was very much an open question. Luckily, though, some nurse chose that moment to come fiddle with his IV, so I had to get a grip and stop making an ass of myself. By the time she was done, the sisters had shown up, and I decided to get the hell out of there.

I sat behind the wheel of my Beetle for a long time, key in the ignition but going nowhere. Although my level of Cody-related dependency was really starting to bug me, I knew there was exactly one person on the planet who could make me feel better.

So I called him. He was home, and he could tell right off

this was no time to bow to the whims of the F.B.I. He told me to come over, and I did—though an attack of mommy guilt made me swing by the house and pick up Shakespeare.

He offered me some leftover spaghetti, but I wasn't hungry. He asked if I felt like a drink, but for once alcohol didn't appeal. All I wanted was for him to hold me and tell me I wasn't a monumental fuckup—a bad friend who lets her buddy OD, a bad reporter who can't concentrate on her beat, a bad girlfriend who wants to keep her guy around at all costs, his dreams be damned.

I wasn't crying on his shoulder exactly; come to think of it, I wasn't crying at all. I was just a 120-pound lump of raw nerves, sitting on an overstuffed couch with two dogs and a nice guy who happens to carry a gun to work.

"I really feel like I let him down," I said after a while. "Like I failed him somehow."

"Look, baby, I'm no philosopher. But I'd be more inclined to say that he failed himself."

"But I—"

"He's a grown man, Alex. You're not responsible for him."

"But maybe if I'd realized sooner that he was—"

"*Stop.*"

I opened my mouth to keep arguing, then changed my mind and flopped against the couch. "You know," I said, "love is nuts."

"Sometimes it's the only thing that makes sense."

"But other times," I said, "it makes you certifiable."

We sat there on the couch for a while, not saying anything. After about five minutes of this bliss, and for no good reason, my big mouth got the better of me.

"Cody," I said, "are you moving back to Boston?"

"What?"

"Um . . . nothing."

"Obviously, it's not nothing. What made you ask?"

"I don't know."

"Sure you do."

"Okay . . . Look, I wasn't trying to snoop, but I was in here one time and I noticed there was this big envelope from the Boston P.D. So I thought maybe—"

"I was trying to get back there without even telling you?"

"Hey, I know it's none of my business. . . ."

"If you really think that, you're not nearly as smart as I thought you were. And to answer your question, the envelope was a benefits thing, just some paperwork. I wish you'd just asked me instead of worrying about it."

"I guess I'm asking you now."

"Look, I admit, I miss the city. But my mom's still here, and you're here, and at the moment, I can't say my job isn't interesting. Moving back . . . I suppose I haven't really thought about it."

"Oh."

"And if I did transfer, I wouldn't do it behind your back."

"Thanks."

"Jesus, Alex," he said, "did you really think I would?"

CHAPTER
18

You may have noticed that I appear to have forgotten all about Shelley Freeman.

It's true; I more or less did. There she was, rotting in a cell in Bedford Hills for a crime she very likely didn't commit, and her journalistic champions got totally distracted by shiny objects. To wit: a pair of bombings and a violent murder, not to mention Mad's imminent demise.

But although we may have put Shelley on the back burner, she sure as hell hadn't forgotten about us. Her letters—beautifully penned, hysterically paced—arrived nearly every other day; clearly, she had somehow fixated on, of all things, the idea that Ochoa and I were way more likely to get her out of the hoosegow than her new lawyer was.

So, with the Shelley guilt stacked atop the Mad guilt, I tried to focus on her predicament. I also tried to get Ochoa psyched about it, but it was no use; the Kate Barnett thing had him hooked, and on that point at least he was entirely monogamous.

I thought about trying to talk to Cody about Shelley, but chucked the idea immediately. With all the stress I'd been under, I'd been sucking on our couplehood like it was a goddamn scuba tank—and I'd therefore never had the *cojones* to disrupt our domestic bliss by suggesting that he may have helped put an innocent woman in prison. Now that we were in touch only sporadically, needless to say, the prospect of dragging him into it seemed even less appealing.

That left me pretty much on my own, or so I thought— until I recalled the existence of one particularly aggressive newshound.

But drafting Gordon Band onto Shelley's virtual defense team was, of course, an iffy proposition; there was always the likelihood that he'd go commando on me and hijack the story. This inspired me to try to figure out just what it was I was trying to accomplish. Was it to get myself a Pulitzer (always a goal)? Or was it something more humanitarian—like figuring out whether Shelley really and truly deserved to be locked up like a pooch at the pound?

My id said the former; my superego said the latter. My ego didn't seem to have an opinion.

I decided to flip for it. The superego won, so I put the quarter back in my change purse and called Gordon on his cell.

The guy doesn't actually have an office, though he could've had one if he'd wanted to: The *Times* powers that be said he could choose among Buffalo, Rochester, Binghamton, and Syracuse for his homebase. Gordon found them all equally nauseating and opted for his car, which is actually a Volkswagen Vanagon.

Don't tell him I told you this, but . . . he also sleeps in it.

Gordon answered the phone with his usual flair.

"Band. Whaddaya want?"

"Hey, Gordon, it's Alex. Where are you?"

"Elmira."

"You having fun over there?"

"I'd rather get pistol-whipped in Alphabet City."

"Seriously, what are you covering?"

"Seriously, nothing that doesn't suck."

"Well, can you finish it up and get to Gabriel by dinner-time?"

"That depends. What's up?"

"I've got a proposition for you."

"Oh, yeah? And of what nature might *that* be?"

"Hey, you don't have to sound so annoyed."

"I spent the last hour talking to some local-history moron about goddamn Mark Twain's goddamn birthplace. Don't tell me how to sound."

"Poor baby. Listen, I—"

"I hate my fucking editor."

"What else is new?"

"Why are you bothering me again?"

"Listen, I promise, this is more than worth your while. I swear."

"Specifics."

"It's a story. A potential story, anyway."

Even over the shaky cell connection, I could hear him snort at me. Twice.

"Now, why the hell would *you* give *me* a story? I work for the competition, remember?"

"Gee, Gordon, you saying that the *Gabriel Monitor* is actually competition for the *New York Times* may just be the nicest thing you've ever said to me."

"I was speaking in loose terms. In *very* loose terms."

"Oh, hell, of course you were."

"So are you gonna tell me what's going on already? I've gotta account for my cell phone bill, you know."

"Okay, listen. I—"

"Wait. Let me guess. You've got something brewing, some story you think could be really big, and you're willing to let me in on it because you need my help. But if I sign on for it, I can't use it until and unless you say so."

"Um, well . . ."

"Am I right or am I right? Or am I right?"

"Yeah, I guess that just about covers it."

"Piss off, sweetheart."

"Does your mother know you talk to girls that way?"

"My mother *taught* me to talk to girls that way. Why do you think I get my head shrunk three times a week?"

"Right. So you up for this or not?"

"Not."

"You haven't even heard what it's all about yet."

"That's because you haven't bothered to tell me."

"So meet me for dinner. I'll take you to that Chinese-buffet place you like. I'm even buying."

"I never said I *liked* it. I said it was comparatively edible."

"A ringing endorsement. Be there at seven."

"Fine. I don't know why I'm bothering, but fine."

"Hey, when have I ever steered you wrong?"

"You want it in alphabetical or chronological order?"

"Keep up that kind of talk and I won't let you stay in my guest room tonight. Doesn't that sound better than the back of your minivan?"

"It's not a mini—"

"Whatever," I said. "See you at seven."

Gordon was on time as always, and in between our usual orgiastic consumption of lo mein, egg foo young, veggie spring rolls, and eggplant with garlic sauce, we talked about Shelley Freeman.

"You telling me you really think she didn't do it?" he said, picking a cellophane noodle off his tie. It had a black-and-red geometric print on it; for Gordon, who usually favors flow-ered neckwear, this was a walk on the fashionista wild side. I wondered if he'd gotten it from some dame, then decided I didn't actually give a damn.

"Yeah," I said. "I gotta admit I kind of do. Not for any

concrete reason, just a gut instinct. I mean, the woman is clearly a gigantic pain in the ass, but I just don't think she offed him. I'd lay odds that she didn't, anyway."

"And the cop reporter agrees with you?"

"Definitely."

"So what the hell do you need me for again?"

"Weren't you even listening? I told you, he's gone off half-cocked trying to solve the Barnett murder."

"And you haven't? Rather out of character, don't you think?"

"Yeah, okay, I have too. But I also feel like I've got this Shelley thing hanging over my head—"

"So you decided it might be nice to hang it over mine too. Thanks a ton."

"Hey, you don't have to join up if you don't want."

"And come to think of it, what's this Ochoa person inclined to think about you letting me in on the gag?"

"Um, he's probably gonna garrote me. I'll deal with it later. So are you up for this or what?"

"*Oy vavoy*. You've got me hooked and you know it."

"You're nothing if not predictable, Gordon."

"And how do you propose we deal with the coverage if and when the story breaks?"

"I don't know. I guess I haven't thought that far ahead."

"Well, think about it. It could get messy."

"Messy how?"

"Messy," he said, "because I have been known to be one ruthless and competitive son of a bitch."

"You? Perish the thought."

"You're cute when you're stupid."

"Okay, well . . . What if we maybe agreed to embargo each other? Like, whenever the story breaks, we break it the same day. And we could credit each other, like . . . like the

Times and the *Post* both publishing the Unabomber's Manifesto. Right?"

"My, but don't we have delusions of grandeur. . . ."

"Hey, you gotta aim high."

He gave me a look like I had a big wad of Chinese cabbage hanging out the side of my mouth, which I was fairly sure I didn't. "And tell me again why it is you need me? I mean, I think I'm the shit and all, but we both know my main talent involves shuffling through big stacks of papers everybody forgot about—and that doesn't seem to apply here. The people thing isn't exactly my forte, so—"

"Hey, don't sell yourself short. I've seen you schmooze the best of them."

"Thanks, but I still don't see what you want me for."

"I'm lonely."

"You're *what?*"

"You heard me. I just don't feel like doing this on my own, okay?"

"Okay . . . Let me get this straight. Just to get yourself some company, you'd share this story—which as far as I can tell you had on an exclusive—with a potentially disloyal reporter from the biggest damn newspaper in the country?"

"Something like that, yeah."

"Like I told you recently on a vastly different topic," he said. "That's either poetic or pathetic. I'm just not sure which."

"Wonderful. So are you in?"

"I'm in. Let's talk turkey. What's the game plan?"

"Well, I'd imagine that Shelley's lawyers are working on an appeal based on whatever you base appeals on, so let's not worry about that part of it. We don't know anything about the legal procedural stuff anyway. I say we dig for some exculpatory evidence. We prove she didn't do it; Shelley gets sprung; we get the story. Everybody's happy, right?"

"Except the guilty party."

"Except him, yeah."

"All that's easier said than done, my little chickadee. So where do we start?"

"Might I suggest consulting the gods?"

I handed him a fortune cookie, and he cracked it open.

" 'You will know success in all endeevor.' Doesn't anybody copyedit these things? And besides, my inevitable success is hardly news. What's yours say?"

" 'Today is not good day for chance-taking.' Not exactly auspicious. Now where were we?"

"The gods were going to tell us who killed Lane Freeman. And as usual, the gods let us down."

"But it still brings us to the same basic question."

"Which is?"

"Which is, if Shelley didn't kill her husband, who did?"

"Or on the other hand," Gordon said, "did anybody kill him at all? You told me Shelley thought the cops might have been full of it from the get-go."

"I seriously doubt they'd screw up that bad. And besides, I refuse to believe that if they did they'd want to cover it up so bad they'd let an innocent woman rot behind bars."

"Hmm . . . What was that you said a while ago about how being a good girlfriend was going to turn you into a crappy reporter?"

"Shut up, okay? Can we just go on the assumption that he was really and truly murdered? I mean, it seems more reasonable to think that he was actually poisoned, and somebody besides Shelley did it, than that the G.P.D. and everybody screwed up that massively, right?"

"Fine."

"Aren't *we* turning into Grumpy dwarf all of a sudden?"

"Who?"

"You know, the Disney . . ." No response. "Are you sure you're American?"

"I try not to let it show."

"So where was I? Right. If Shelley didn't off him, who did? And just as important, why?"

"Boy, I am having major déjà vu here, aren't you? I mean, all we need is Madison and . . . Oh. Sorry."

"Never mind," I said. "Just answer the question, okay?"

"Okay, let's see. . . . It's either personal, or it's professional, or it's random. What other choices are there?"

"And if it's random, we're pretty much screwed."

"Correct."

"But if it's personal, and Shelley didn't do it, then it's gotta be somebody he pissed off somehow—"

"Hey," he said, "maybe this is your classic love triangle. Maybe there's some guy out there in love with Shelley who wanted to get Lane out of the way so he could have her for him—"

"Majorly doubtful. Trust me. You've haven't met the woman."

"*O-kay* . . . Next idea. If the guy was really as annoying as you said he was, maybe—"

"Nah, she's the one who's kinda annoying. He was more of a sad sack."

"Well, maybe the sad sack did something to really piss somebody off—a neighbor or somebody like that."

"Who got so pissed he killed Lane and went to the trouble of framing Shelley for it? That's some major-league agita."

"How about some family thing? I mean, it's a miracle nobody in the Band *mishpoche* has ever killed anybody else, frankly. Like this one time, my uncle Ikey just about—"

"Good point. Family stuff can get damn nasty. I'll ask Shelley about it. Hopefully she'll be straight with me."

"Which brings us to the professional."

"The man was a flack."

"I see your point," he said. "Hardly worth the powder it'd take to blow him to hell, huh?"

"Something like that."

"What did he cover again?"

"Science. That is, hard science—not psych or sociology or anything like that. He covered stuff like physics, chemistry, biology, genetics, the Benson med school, plus all that ag-school shit. . . ."

My voice trailed off. He stared at me. I stared back. If I hadn't already swallowed my fortune cookie, I would've choked on it.

"Gordon . . . Are you thinking what I'm thinking?"

"That there's been a lot of shit going down at the ag school. A *whole* lot of shit."

"Oh, my *God.*"

"So it could be that maybe—"

"You know, I just thought of something Shelley told me in jail. She said that because Lane hated his job, he worked his ass off at it."

"Meaning?"

"Meaning maybe he was determined to be better than your average bear at the flackery business. Maybe he even decided to act like a reporter again for five minutes."

"And?"

"And maybe he dug up something somebody didn't want him to dig up."

"So somebody killed him to shut him up?"

"It's been known to happen. You and I know that as well as anybody."

"It damn well has," he said. "So he found out whatever he found out, and somebody offed him and pinned it on Shelley. Is that what you're proposing?"

"Why not? As frame-ups go, it's perfect—everybody

knew about the Fighting Freemans, right? All you'd have to do is pour that *Abrus*-whatever all over the backseat of the car, which you could do in half a second as long as it was open, and nobody locks up around here anyway. . . ."

"So what do you think it could've been? The motive, I mean."

"Well . . . let me think for a minute. On the one hand, there's so much going on up at Benson—I mean at the ag school alone, not to mention the rest of his so-called beat— it's hard to know where to start. But . . . my gut tells me that if it was something worth killing Lane over, it had to be something big. And we know damn well there's been a whole hell of a lot of big news up there lately, don't we?"

"Keep going."

"So I'm thinking, what if he stumbled onto something connected to all the shit that was brewing for later—the bombings and the Barnett murder and everything else?"

"You mean, you think he somehow figured out what the OATs or Don't Break the Food Chain or whoever else was up to?"

"It's a possibility," I said. "I mean, think about it. It's not only connected to Freeman's beat, it's actually worth killing over. If he found out about it, not only would you want to get him out of the way so he didn't spoil your plans, you'd also want to get rid of a potential witness against you. Conspiracy to do all that shit is a felony in and of itself, even if the crime never actually goes down, right?"

He started scratching his scalp, his signature nervous habit. "My head hurts."

"Have some more tea. It's good for the digestion."

"I said my *head* hurts, not my—"

"So what do you think he might have found out?"

"How the hell do I know?"

"Come on, be a sport," I said. "Free-associate with me."

"I've never been a sport in my whole miserable life."

"A point that I concede wholeheartedly. Now play nice."

"Okay . . . Let me think about this for a minute. So Freeman is covering campus, right? He's not likely to be nosing around with the fringe groups, is he?"

"Probably not. Nearly everything in every press release that pain-in-the-neck news service churns out quotes Benson sources exclusively. Sometimes there's an exception, like they'll cite some NASA administrator on a space story, but it doesn't happen very often."

"So the odds are that whatever he found out, he found out from somebody on campus."

"That's the most likely thing," I said. "But we don't know for sure, so assuming that much is probably not a good idea."

"Duly noted."

"Holy *shit.*"

"What?"

"Do you realize the theoretical corner we just backed ourselves into?"

"Well . . . I can't say as I do."

"Think about it."

"I'm thinking," he said. "I'm just not coming up with anything."

"Oh, for chrissake . . . We just said that more likely than not, whatever Lane found had something to do with what's been going on at the ag school."

"Right. So?"

"And we also said that—again not for sure but more likely than not—whoever he picked it up from was somebody from Benson itself. Not from the outside, but from within the university."

"Yeah. What's your point?"

"My point," I said, "is that what's gone down may damn well turn out to be an inside job."

CHAPTER
19

Gordon was right: He knows how to schmooze live human beings, but he's even better at digging through documents. So while I tried to come up with a way for him to contribute to the Shelley Freeman thing, I wandered up to the Benson news service to buttonhole one of Lane's colleagues.

The university's flackery machine, which is both an occasionally useful thing and a frequently nauseating one, is housed in a long, low building where they used to do veterinary surgery; in the summer, if all the windows are closed, you can still smell the cows. When I got to campus, I went straight to one of the traffic booths to get a media parking pass, in an attempt to avoid another ticket. Then, miracle of miracles, I found a legal spot outside the livestock-showing pavilion, just yards from my prey.

News-service writers aren't *always* sitting on their asses at their desks; just most of the time. So it was a good bet that Lenny Peterson, the fourteen-karat nerd who took over Lane's beat after his untimely demise, would be there.

Lenny is yet another Benson grad who never left town. He majored in communication, did some student reporting for the *Bugle,* interned at a P.R. firm, and spent like ten years in the press office of a factory on South Hill that made (get this) plumbing parts. When the company hightailed it to Mexico post-NAFTA, Lenny got laid off; he then landed a clerical job at the news service, where he sent out press releases and followed up on them with the rabid zeal of a telemarketer on commission.

Lenny eventually worked his way up to a part-time writing job covering some campus arts stuff, then went full time on the soft-science beat. When Lane died, he was drafted to take over the hard-science coverage; he did it, albeit reluctantly. Apparently, Lenny had the self-awareness to know when he was dog-paddling out of his depth.

I knew all this because Shelley had sketched a lot of it out in a letter; also, Lenny had told me plenty of it himself over ginger ale at the Citizen Kane—where, as a teetotaler, he was subject to the frequent derision of one Jacob Ebenezer Madison.

So why was I seeking out Lenny in particular, of the dozen or so news-service drones? Two reasons: One, Lane was his idol. Don't ask me why, but he was.

And, secondly, well . . . Lenny has had a rather massive crush on me for quite a while. I was fairly sure that if I showed some cleavage, batted my eyelashes, and bought him an ice-cream cone, he'd tell me whatever I wanted to know, and keep his mouth shut about it afterward.

All right, so it wasn't nice. It was also very probably antifeminist. But like my grandma always told me, sometimes a girl has to shake her booty for the greater good.

So, clad in a V-necked minidress and sandals, I wandered into the bovine-scented news-service office and asked for Lenny. The receptionist buzzed him, and two seconds later he was tripping over his Hush Puppies to greet me. *Excellent.*

Now, all the local media know that there's one tangible benefit to visiting the Benson News Service: It's three doors down from the Benson Dairy Bar, which makes its own ice cream using amazingly fresh ingredients and milk from the university herd. And on top of the high-quality sweetmeats, the place has got *character.* Every year they celebrate Christmas with the traditional lighting of the rooftop cows, and they're always coming up with funky new flavors with names like Publish or Perish Peppermint and Rocky Road to Tenure. Don't laugh; low-fat it's not, but it's damn good.

I, therefore, had the opportunity to meet a trio of needs at once: satisfying my eternal lust for frosty treats, bribing a potential witness, and finding a reasonably private place to talk. So I went to the counter and purchased a double-chocolate malted and a giant mocha-chip cookie (for him) and a two-scoop dish of Pistachio Pedagogy with rainbow sprinkles (for me), and we settled in at a red-topped corner table.

Lenny was wearing a blue checked shirt, which looked to be one of those no-iron cotton-poly blends you can get at your finer Kmarts. He had a maroon tie around his neck, because Phil Herzog is (or, rather, was) sufficiently uptight to require it. His tan pants were extremely wrinkled, he'd missed two shirt buttons, and he had major-league bedhead. The whole picture reminded you of Pig Pen from "Peanuts" —except that, according to a woman who dumped him after four dates, he spends *hours* in the mirror trying to get the look just right; call it studiously schlumpy.

"You look nice," he said after a long slurp of his shake. "You always look nice, anyway."

Have I mentioned Lenny Peterson is a very smart man?

"How you doin', Lenny?"

"Okay, I guess. How are you?"

"Not bad."

"So . . . what's this for?"

"What's what for?"

"You coming by the office and taking me out to the

B.D.B. and buying me a milk shake," he said. "What's it for?"

"Why does it have to be *for* anything?"

He cocked an eyebrow at me. "Isn't it?"

"Yeah, actually, it is."

"So . . . what?"

"Lane Freeman."

"Lane? What about him?"

"Listen, Lenny, can this be just between the two of us? As kind of, you know, a favor?"

"A favor to you?"

"Yeah, but maybe also . . . Maybe also a favor to Lane. And possibly Shelley too."

"Fuck Shelley."

"So . . . I take it that means you think she did it."

"Course she did it. She got convicted, didn't she?"

"Yeah," I said, "but convictions can be wrong. It's been known to happen, hasn't it?"

His mouth was half open, and his gap-toothed overbite was even more pronounced than usual. "Are you saying you think she didn't?"

"I don't know. I'm just entertaining the possibility is all."

"Why?"

"Because she asked me to."

"And?"

"And if she got the shaft, it could make one hell of a story."

His pale eyes said I'd let him down. Well, fine; it wasn't the first time.

"Of course that's what it's about," he said. "All you news-people ever care about is—"

"Okay, so I know a good story when I see it. So sue me. But it's not just about that, all right? I want to make sure that if she's doing the time she actually did the crime. What's wrong with that?"

He started chewing on his lower lip, which made him look very much like the Easter Bunny. "Nothing, I guess."

"So will you help me?"

"Help you how?"

"Well, for starters, you could tell me if Lane was acting weird at all in the week or so before he died."

"Weird? What do you mean weird?"

"Oh, hell, I don't know. . . . Did he mention he was covering anything out of the ordinary?"

"Not that I can remember."

"Well, what was he covering, anyway?"

He fiddled with his straw for a while. Then he broke the salad-plate-size cookie in half, broke one half in two, shoved the whole quarter into his mouth, and proceeded to talk through it.

"Umm . . . Well, it was around the beginning of the semester, so things were pretty slow around here, you know? I think . . . I think there were some N.A.S. awards announced around then, so Lane did profiles on the guys who won them."

"And who were they?"

"I don't remember. I'd have to go look it up. It's on our Web site, anyway, so you could find it yourself if you wanted."

"Okay, what else?"

"Oh, I don't know. . . . Why don't you just look at his press releases on the Web? They're all organized by month, you know."

"I will. I was just wondering if you knew about anything that might not be there."

"Why would I?"

Warning: shameless attempt at flattery ahead.

"Because," I said, "you two were really close, right? You probably helped him out a lot. I know he really relied on your judgment, and—"

"He did?"

"Sure he did. Shelley told me so."

"Really?"

Actually, what she said was that you're a big doofus. But that's not going to get the job done, now is it?

"Absolutely," I said. "She told me you two were tighter than tight. She also said you were his favorite person at the whole news service. By a *mile*."

"Wow, I . . . I didn't know that. He never told me. That's . . . That's really nice to hear."

For a minute I thought he was actually going to get all sniffly on me. And yeah, I felt like a heel. But it wasn't the first time for that, either, so I got over it pretty quick.

"So, Lenny . . . Can you maybe think of anything else Lane might've been working on?"

"What?" Oh, um . . . Well, it's probably not that big a deal, but that was right around the time we were announcing plans for the big biotech conference, the one that was held in . . . Hey, Alex, are you—"

"Yeah, I . . . It's nothing. Go on."

"Well, there's nothing else really. Just that Lane was helping put the whole thing together—all the P.R. stuff anyway. That's why there was such a big turnout, you know. Lane did a really great job of getting people from all over the world to show up."

"And how do you think he did that?"

"Um, I guess he just, you know, tried to emphasize what was going to be interesting about it."

"Like what?"

"Like, you know, all the people who were going to be speaking, and how we'd be giving tours of the Benson research facilities, and how the gene gun was invented here—that's the technology that allowed gene-splicing in the first place, right?"

"If you say so."

"Yeah, it's really amazing. Did you know the prototype used actual gunpowder to shoot the—"

"Listen, do you think Lane ever imagined the anti-G.M.O. protesters would show up? That there'd be so many of them, I mean?"

He looked back down at his cookie. This time, he broke off a little piece and started using it to jump imaginary checkers on the red-and-white paper plate.

"Lenny . . ." He didn't look up. "Is there something you're not telling me?"

"Um, no . . ."

"No offense, but you're a really bad liar."

"Oh."

"So come on, what's up?"

Long pause, big sigh, more jumping checkers. When he finally spoke, it was still to the cookie. "Lane, well . . . You knew Lane, right? You know the main thing he was always looking for was . . ."

"Publicity. For Benson."

"Yeah."

"So what are you saying exactly?"

"Do you promise you won't think badly of him?"

"Sure."

"Well . . . You know, my desk and his desk were right next to each other, right? So this one time I heard him make this phone call, and when I asked him about it later, he admitted it to me. Actually, he was kind of proud of it."

The desire to pummel him was strong. And growing stronger. "Proud of what?" Nothing. "Come on, Lenny, just tell me what went down, okay?"

"He . . . um . . . He helped."

"Helped do what?"

"Helped the D.B.F.C."

"Helped them how?"

"He helped them plan their strategy, I mean for all the protesting. He spent a lot of time on the phone with some guy, Tony somebody. . . ."

"You mean Tobias? Tobias Kahan?"

"Yeah, that's the one, at least I think so."

"I don't *believe* it. That is so . . . Man, I don't even know what this is. Phil Herzog would've blown his top."

Which is pretty much what happened to him, I thought, then tried in vain to get the image out of my head.

"Please, Alex," he was saying, "don't think badly of Lane, okay? He just knew that if all these protesters showed up, the story would be that much bigger. And it was, wasn't it?"

"Did Lane ever contact anybody else from The Chain? Or maybe one of the other groups — the OATs, say, or some people who called themselves the Secret Gardeners?"

"Not that I know of. What difference does it make?"

"One more question. Do you know if he ever channeled any of this through anybody at Benson?"

"You mean, was somebody on campus helping out the protesters?" I nodded. "Well, like I said, I don't know of anybody else Lane talked to specifically. But sure, there were people on campus who got into all that. There were a couple dozen students, for one thing. They started a Chain club here, you know, so they—"

"Anybody besides students?"

"Sure, I think there were a couple faculty from arts who got into—"

"Anybody from ag?"

"Yeah, you know, there's Debbie Newman, who's got the chair in organic farming—"

"Anybody from plant science?"

Again with the visible overbite. "Are you kidding?"

"I'm just wondering, that's all. I take it the answer's no."

"Definitely no."

"Fair enough," I said, and stood up to go.

"Hey, no offense," he said, "but that's gotta be the stupidest thing you ever asked me."

"Come on, you know the expression," I said. "There are no stupid questions. Just stupid reporters."

❧❧❧

My next move took me from Lane Freeman to Kate Barnett—not to mention directly from fats to carbohydrates.

I left the Dairy Bar and commuted to the Alfalfa Room, where I was scheduled to meet a plant-science grad student named Cynthia Chu. She was waiting for me when I got there, drinking coffee with soy milk and wearing the same pale green overalls she'd had on the day I'd met her on the Green, in the company of Kate Barnett and the very angry veggies. Which, come to think of it, kind of sounds like a Gabriel-based girl band.

I'd told Cynthia I wanted to talk to her for yet another follow-up feature on Professor Barnett. In actual fact, I was on a good old-fashioned fishing expedition. And since fishing takes energy, I decided to fortify myself with a big coffee (with real milk from a real cow, thank you very much) and another one of those cappuccino muffins. Clearly, my dietary excesses were swinging to the opposite extreme.

Cynthia Chu is probably twenty-three years old, but she could pass for fifteen. She's about four-eleven, and she wears her hair in a pair of braids with a geometrically perfect part down the middle. Unlike most of her female colleagues,

however, she seems to understand the concept of lipstick—
cotton-candy-pink lipstick, as a matter of fact.

"Thanks for meeting me," I said once I'd joined her at the
same wide wooden table where I'd interviewed the Three
Gene-Splicing Musketeers two days before. "I know you're
probably really busy. . . ."

"Actually," she said, "the truth is, things in the lab are
kind of on hold since . . . since . . ."

"Since the murder."

She nodded, but barely. "You can't imagine how awful it's
been."

"I know."

"So what can I help you with? You said you were doing
another story on Kate. . . ."

"Yeah, something like that. It's actually more like research
for something bigger that might run later, like when—"

"Like when they catch the creep who did this to her?"

"Yeah."

"Then I'll help you any way I can."

"Thanks. For starters, let me ask you this: Did you ever
feel like you were in any kind of danger working in her lab?
I mean, obviously, before the bombing. . . ."

"That depends on what you mean by danger. I'd have to
say . . . Before the bombing, we'd always gotten threats from
the anti-G.M.O. people. But it always seemed basically abstract, you understand? So I wouldn't say I was ever *scared*
per se. But my parents weren't thrilled about it. That is to say,
they want me to get my Ph.D., and they were really proud to
have me working under Kate, but once . . . I made the mistake of telling them about a flyer everyone in the department
got in our mail cubbies—typical Frankenfoods propaganda,
but more aggressive. My mom was pretty worried for me
after that."

"Okay. Can you tell me about the other people in your department?"

"What would you want to know about them for? I thought this was about Kate."

I cast about for something that might satisfy her. "It is," I said, "but I also need to figure out who else to talk to for the piece. If I can get an idea of who else is around, and what they're like, it might save me some time."

"Oh. Well, to start at the top, there's Professor Cerretani, who's the chair of the department. . . ."

"What do you think of him? I mean, personally?" A wary look commuted across her face. "Don't worry, I'm not going to print any of this. I'm just trying to get the lay of the land."

"In that case, I'd have to say that he's kind of . . . I suppose I'd have to describe him as an alpha male. He likes to be in charge, or perhaps I should say he likes people to *know* that he's in charge. But he's really good politically, so I'd guess he's the right man for the job, you know?"

"Who else?"

"Hmm . . . Well, there's a number of emeritus profs I don't really know, so I don't think I can help you there."

"What about the tenured faculty?"

"There's Arnie Kim, who also does rice. He's Korean—I mean born there, not Korean American. He's single, and I hear he's kind of a party animal. There's Jeff Leeming, who's been doing a lot of work out at the ag experiment station on the papaya ring-spot virus. He's nice, really quiet. Lisa Archer's heavily into integrated pest management—she works a lot with entomology. But she just had a baby, so she's on leave right now. Cy Doebler is on sabbatical in China looking for apple germ-plasm, I think. I don't know him very well—he's off at the ag station a lot too, or out at the orchard. That's everybody with tenure. It's a relatively small department."

"What about the rest?"

"Well, there's Shep Robinson, who's working on enriching bananas with various things. He's kind of a character, but I like him. Martin Lee is on Cerretani's potato team. He's got little kids, so he tries to get out of here by six every night. Jim Adler works on . . . Come to think of it, I don't know what he works on. I'd say of everybody he's the most involved in teaching undergrads—the most excited about it. He's nice too. Lindsay McDaniel is a serious brain. I'd have to say she's the smartest out of all of them, honestly. She's contributed to a lot of those projects I mentioned, particularly the rice and the bananas. Oh, and the potatoes too, I guess. Melvin Tighe is kind of dabbling right now, which isn't likely to get him on the tenure track. Kate used to hold him up as an example of what I shouldn't do if I wanted to play the academic game. He's an oddball, but I like him too."

"An oddball how?"

"He does that . . . What do you call it? The people who dress up as though it's medieval times, and everyone pretends to be a different person. . . ."

"Creative anachronism."

"That's it. Calls himself 'Sir Morgan of Tyre,' or something like that. Alan Frantz is into . . . Scratch that. He's gone now. He was denied tenure, so he left at the end of the semester."

"And was he upset about it?"

"Of course. You put in seven years and then you get denied. Who wouldn't be upset?"

"Good point. Is that everybody?"

"Yeah, I think. There's one opening, to fill Frantz's slot. They're supposed to announce any day now, but I'm not sure when. As I said, it's a small department. There are a number of people who have joint appointments with other departments, but plant science isn't their main focus and they don't have offices here, just a mailbox. There are also about a half-dozen lecturers, but I don't really know any of them."

"What about the grad students?"

"There are about ten of us. Do you really want to hear about all of them?"

"If you don't mind."

I could tell she sort of did, but she told me anyway. I wrote down their names and the descriptions Cynthia gave me, and wondered for the hundredth time if any of this was going to do me any good.

"Out of all of those," I asked when she was done, "which ones were particularly close with Professor Barnett?"

"Well . . . I'd have to say that, out of all of them, probably I worked with her most. I was on her rice-research team, and she was the chair of my thesis committee. After me, probably Ellie Gilbert and Ron Bozier—they're the couple I told you about. The ones who met in the department and now they're engaged."

"Right. Listen, Cynthia, how long have you been around here again?"

"Seven years, if you can believe it. I did my undergrad at Benson, but I majored in A.B.E.N.—that's agricultural and biological engineering. It's a split department between ag and engineering. So I've been on campus for a while, but not in plant science until three years ago."

"Listen, this may sound out of left field, but I was wondering if you might be able to help me track somebody down. It's a woman who used to be a grad student here. I think she got her master's in plant science a few years back. She might live in L.A. now."

"What's her name?"

"That's the problem. I don't know."

"So what do you need to find her for?"

"It's related to another story I'm working on. It's not that important."

"And you're not sure when she was here?"

"Well, I think she did a master's a few years ago. She was supposed to get a Ph.D. but didn't finish. I think maybe she might have had some sort of personality conflict with Professor Barnett—"

"Jeepers, why is everybody so interested in—" She clapped her hand over her mouth. After five seconds, she removed it but left it dangling in midair. "Um . . . Never mind."

"What were you about to say?"

"Nothing. Never mind."

"Come on, Cynthia; obviously, it's not nothing."

"I'm sorry, but I really can't tell you, okay?"

"Why not?"

"Because, well . . . The police said I shouldn't."

"What?"

"Um . . . well . . . After the explosion, the police asked me essentially the same question you just did. And afterward they said, 'Thank you very much, and it would be best if you didn't talk about this with anyone else.'"

"They always say that, but trust me, nobody ever cares."

"Really?"

"Yeah. So can you please tell me what's up?"

"I . . . You know, I probably shouldn't even be talking about this. It's not really fair of me, because I didn't know this person very well."

"Who was she?"

"Look, I'm sorry, but I really don't feel comfortable naming names, okay?"

"All right. What do you feel like you can tell me?"

"Just that . . . Okay, there was this grad student. She was working on Kate's rice team, same as I am. I'm not really sure what happened, but I guess Kate told her she couldn't support her research anymore. I guess she didn't like the way she was performing."

"That was it?"

"Yeah," she said, practically burying her snout in her coffee cup. "I think so."

Two lousy liars in one day. Wonderful.

"Come on, Cynthia. Do me a favor and tell me the truth."

There was nothing I could do to make her talk, of course. But the human psyche is a beautiful thing: The fact is that fundamentally honest people usually can't stomach out-and-out lies. Sure, they can fudge the truth a little, but blatant tongue-forking makes them feel bad.

To my great convenience, Cynthia Chu was a fundamentally honest person.

"Well," she said, "it was just a rumor. And I know it's not true, so there's probably no harm in telling you."

As logic goes, it was fairly perverse. But I decided not to point that out to her.

"That's right," I said. "Go on."

"Around the time this girl left, there was talk. Just talk, mind you. But apparently she made some accusations."

"What kind of accusations?"

"Listen, like I told you before, it's not true. There's no way Kate would have ever done anything like that."

"Like what?"

She sighed, long and deep. Then she picked at the edge of her paper cup for a while. It occurred to me that perhaps I should set her up with Lenny Peterson, since they were starting to look like two peas out of precisely the same pod.

"Come on, Cynthia," I said. "What kind of accusations?"

"There were rumors . . . not very nice ones. People said she'd accused Kate of stealing a research idea she had, and then drumming her out of school to cover it all up."

"And you think it wasn't true?"

"No way. Absolutely no way. Kate wasn't like that."

"You're sure?"

"I'm . . ." Her eyes wandered past me to the doorway. "Hey, Ellie, can you come over here for a second?"

I twisted around to see a girl about Cynthia's age with close-cropped dirty-blond hair and a pair of seriously unfashionable glasses, carrying a book bag that looked like it weighed more than she did. "Yeah?" she said, sidling up to the table but not sitting down.

"This is Ellie Gilbert, one of the other grad students I was telling you about," Cynthia told me, then turned to her. "This is Alex Bernier from the Gabriel newspaper. We were just talking about Kate, and I thought maybe she should hear the same thing from you."

The strap of her book bag was slipping, and she shoved it up onto her shoulder. "What same thing?"

"We were just talking about, um . . . Kate's ethics and all, and I was just telling Alex that there's no way she was the kind of person who'd pass off someone else's work as her own. Right?"

"What?" She ran her left hand over the top of her head so the fine strands feathered, and I noticed that on the third finger was a diamond ring so teeny the stone didn't even catch the light. "You shouldn't ask questions like that," Ellie said. "It's not nice."

"Look, I was just—"

"Can't you get into trouble for that? Isn't that . . . you know, libel?"

"Libel's something you write down," I said, giving her Journalism 101 for no particular reason. "Slander's something you say. And anyway, there's nothing slanderous about asking a question. I'm not saying she did it. I'm just asking if you thought she might."

"I think it's awful," she said, and left without buying anything.

"See?" Cynthia said. "I told you it was ridiculous. Kate would never do anything like that. She'd never."

"Look, no offense, but how can you be so certain?"

"Because she just wouldn't," she said. "Just ask anybody, and they'll tell you. Kate Barnett was a very special person."

CHAPTER
20

Kate Barnett was a very special person.

It was starting to sound like some sort of weird mantra. Or, come to think of it, like that line out of *The Manchurian Candidate:* "Raymond Shaw is the kindest, gentlest, most honorable man I've ever known." Most of the characters say it, but none of them mean it; truth is, they've been brainwashed by the Commies.

I doubted the Commies had scrubbed the noggins of the entire Benson plant-science department. But I was starting to get the feeling that something funky was going on.

Still, said impending funkiness didn't liberate me from my normal reporterly duties. In fact, the reason I'd been able to spend the day nosing around campus was that I had to cover a night meeting—a public hearing during which a large number of people went plumb crazy over plans to build a gigantic shopping center within spitting distance of a small-but-spectacular state park on the edge of town. The thing started at seven-thirty and went until almost eleven, at which point I had to hightail it to the paper to bang out my fourteen inches before deadline.

Afterward, I went straight home; although there would

undoubtedly be plenty of carousing going on over at the Citizen, for some reason I just wasn't in the mood. I'd only had hummus on a bagel for dinner, so I microwaved some leftover pasta and ate it on the couch with Shakespeare. She seemed kind of down in the snout—though, it must be said, not so depressed that she wouldn't eat tortellini off my fork—and I chalked up her malaise to the fact that she hadn't seen Zeke in nearly a week. I knew the feeling.

There I lay, with a shocking disinterest in cable TV and Cody's "know thy victim" credo echoing in my head. Or should I say "victims"—there was, after all, the Lane Freeman thing to deal with as well. But for the moment, stretched out on the couch with the bowl on my stomach and the dog on my legs, I found myself fixating on Kate Barnett. I'd gotten to know her, but only briefly (and, admittedly, superficially). So what was she really like?

One thing was for sure: She was incredibly dedicated to her work; the feeding-the-hungry thing was her whole raison d'être. Her principles seemed to rule her life in a big way— hence having her tubes tied at the tender age of twenty-something. Robinson (or maybe it was McDaniel?) had said that she held everyone in her field to an incredibly high standard. So could someone like that really do what this mysterious grad student had accused her of—rip off a protégée's research, then kick her out of school to cover her tracks?

It didn't make sense, and it sure as hell didn't sound like the Kate Barnett I'd met.

But did any of that really matter? Would a postmortem understanding of "the real Kate" help us figure out who killed her? Assuming she'd been done in by somebody from one of the anti-G.M.O. groups, it probably didn't make any difference; they would've killed her whether she was a nice rice-breeder or a nasty one.

But what if there were some other motive behind her

death—somebody jealous of her, or just plain furious—and the Frankenfoods thing was simply a dodge? I mean, it wouldn't be the first time, right? Hadn't there been some marine back in the seventies who killed his wife and kids, then covered it up by writing crazy hippie slogans on the walls in their blood?

Okay, I realize these were pretty nasty thoughts for a Tuesday night on the living-room couch. I debated turning on the Food Network to get my mind off it for a while, then decided I didn't really want to; zoning out while some crazy Cajun made jambalaya was just going to make me more depressed.

Which, in case you didn't notice, means that I was happier pondering a brutal murder than my own miserable life. This was probably not a good sign. So . . . In the glorious tradition of Scarlett O'Hara, I decided not to think about it.

Back to Kate Barnett. How was I possibly going to figure out what really made her tick? I could talk to everybody in her department—but I wasn't particularly optimistic that I'd wind up with anything more than I'd gotten out of Cerretani et al. Plus, there was always the risk that they'd realize I was getting way nosier than any reporter they'd ever met, and clam up. Frankly, I was starting to wonder why any of them had talked to me at all, since it already sounded like they'd been instructed to spout the party line—whether implicitly or explicitly, I wasn't sure.

"Kate Barnett was a very special person." What the hell was *that* all about?

That set me to wondering just whom I might contact to get the straight scoop about Kate. Maybe some of the grad students would be more forthcoming than the faculty. Or, come to think of it—academic hierarchies being what they are—they might be even more skittish.

So who else?

There was Barnett's ex-husband, who taught at the Benson med school. But what were the odds he'd talk to a reporter about his erstwhile spouse, even off the record? Maybe I'd have better luck with her adopted son, who'd been traveling cross-country but would presumably be back in town for the memorial service, which was being held in the Benson Concert Hall the following Saturday. I wasn't sure who Barnett's friends had been — or, frankly, whether her work had left her enough time to have any. I made a mental note to try to find out, since making a physical note would require me to get my lazy ass off the couch.

And then there was the anonymous grad student, whoever she was. Now, *she* might offer a unique perspective on Professor Barnett; she'd felt strongly enough about her to send a letter to the paper long after leaving campus, hadn't she? In her note, she specifically mentioned that she'd promised not to talk about whatever problems she had with Kate — but she'd sent the letter anyway. Interesting.

Finding out her real name didn't seem like that much of a hassle; even if no one would straight-out tell me, I'd just have to figure out who'd bailed on their Ph.D. in plant science over the past couple of years. Tracking her down to wherever she was teaching didn't seem that hard, either.

But . . . okay, all right, time to consider the flip side.

What if we were just wasting our time going off on tangents? What about the more logical scenario, that Barnett was bludgeoned to death to stop her from twiddling with rice DNA? The Don't Break the Food Chain people (not to mention the OATs and the Secret Gardeners and the rest of their ilk) definitely seemed to hate her guts. Tobias Kahan, for his part, had one hell of a temper; the memory of how he'd gone off on his poor, goateed underling — and seemed way more proud of it than ashamed — still gave me the creeps.

The thought of Tobias reminded me of the whole Lane Freeman thing, which was starting to feel more and more sordid. I mean, offing your much-despised husband is a tried-and-true motive for homicide; it's not nice, but you can get your mind around it with no problem.

But what had Lane actually been into? Clearly, if he'd been working with Kahan to turn the G.M.O. conference into a goddamn zoo, he wasn't exactly the gutless news-service drone we'd all thought, now was he? And if he'd really been up to those sorts of shenanigans, was there any way Shelley didn't know about it? In other words, was she holding out on us big time? And what else wasn't she telling us? She'd sworn up and down neither one of their families could possibly be involved. Was she on the level?

There was, in other words, quite a miserable whirlwind of homicidal concepts swirling around my brain as I lay there on the couch with my dog. Eventually, my poor cranium must've had enough, because I fell asleep. The next thing I knew, it was three A.M.: The pasta bowl was empty, the dog looked guilty, and the phone was ringing.

Still half conscious, I whacked about the coffee table for the cordless, managing only to knock over my empty diet Dr Pepper can. By the time I found it, the machine was already spouting Melissa's all-too-perky message.

Hi, you've reached Alex and Melissa and Shakespeare the Wonder Dog and Fabulous Marmalade Kitty. None of us can get to the phone, but we really want you to leave us a message, okay? So do it at the beep!

"Yo, Alex, it's me." O'Shaunessey's voice sounded tinny coming through the machine's crappy speaker, but I could still make out the hysteria. "Are you there? Listen, you gotta pick up. Are you there? Yo, Alex, are you there? If you're there, you gotta—"

I finally found the phone. "Oh, my God. Tell me it's not Mad."

"It's Mad."

"Oh, God, no. . . ."

Thus began the hysterical sobbing.

"Alex? Yo, Alex, can you hear me?"

"I can't . . . I just can't believe . . ."

More hysterical sobbing.

"Jesus Christ, Alex, listen to me—"

"I can't . . . Oh, God—"

"Will you calm down a minute and just listen? He's *awake*."

I hyperventilated some more before the message actually got through. "He's . . . He's what?"

"Madison's not dead. He's awake."

"That's . . . That's great." More sniffles, the relieved kind this time. "How . . . How did you . . ."

"I was there. I mean, I'm *here* . . ."

"You're at the hospital? How come?"

"I've been, um, hanging out here some nights. After deadline sometimes, after the Citizen closes . . ."

"God, that's so *sweet*."

"Yeah, well, don't go telling him, *capice?*"

"God, I'm so . . . How did he look? Did he say anything?"

"I didn't get a chance to see him or anything. I was just out in that lounge-place down the hall from his room reading the *Sporting News* when one of the night nurses started to go apeshit. At first I thought, you know, that it was something really *bad,* so I kinda grabbed her and made her tell me what was going down. That was just like ten minutes ago."

"I'm on my way."

"Nah, I wouldn't bother right now. There's no way they're letting anybody in there who isn't family, and maybe not even them, either."

"Well, when *can* we see him?"

"I dunno. She wouldn't say. Listen, do you think somebody better call his sisters or something?"

"Yeah, I'll do it. Probably the hospital will anyway, but I'll do it just in case."

I heard him take a deep breath. "Alex, man," he said, *"shit."*

"Yeah," I replied through yet more sniffles. "You said it."

⤜⤛⧉⤜⤛

I didn't get to see Mad that day, or the whole next one, either. Although the medical powers that be had been happy for his friends to commune with his lifeless form, once he was conscious they apparently had to guard against us tiring him out, or some such thing. His sisters got to visit him, though—if only for a few minutes—and I was willing to bet their presence wasn't exactly palliative.

In fact, they seemed to enjoy it as little as he did. When I stopped by his apartment Wednesday night to get the scoop, they both looked rather shaken. "Jakey's just not himself" is how they put it, and though I tried to get them to elaborate, it was no use; they were either too upset to talk about it or plain didn't trust me.

I finally got a chance to see for myself the following Thursday afternoon, on what happened to be the Fourth of July. The short version is, he wasn't pretty. Or, for that matter, particularly coherent.

Mad looked liked he'd lost fifteen pounds off his already-lean frame. He was downright gaunt, his sharp Nordic cheekbones threatening to pop right through the skin. He was dozing when I got there, so I lingered inside the door for a while. I tried to picture this body lifting something heavier than a soup can, and couldn't.

Sure enough, when he finally opened his eyes, it seemed to take a lot of effort.

"Hey . . . Bernier . . ."

"Hi," I said, trying like hell to sound casual. "How you doin'?"

"Okay."

"Yeah?"

"Top . . . o' the world, Ma."

He smiled a little, but it only lasted for a second, and it seemed to tire him out too. Tough chick that I am, I promptly started tearing up. I'd been on my way to the chair by his bed, but I detoured to snatch a Kleenex box off the dresser before I sat down.

"That's good," I said. "You, um, you look good. . . ."

"You sound like my goddamn sisters." His voice was gravelly, strained, totally un-Mad-like. "Don't bullshit me, okay? Just don't. . . ."

"Huh?"

"I said"—he had to stop and cough—"don't bullshit me like them. I know what I look like."

"Yeah, well, you look pretty damn good to me."

"Yeah?"

"I thought you . . . It didn't look good for a while."

"I guess." *Cough, cough.* "It's all kind of mixed up."

"What?"

"I said I don't remember too much."

"Lucky for you."

"Huh?"

"Nothing. So how do you feel, anyway? No bullshit."

"Like I got pummeled by Frazier *and* Ali."

"Yeah?"

"Throat hurts, getting fed through my arm, and I got a tube up my pisshole."

"Ouch. Well, at least you're starting to sound like your old self."

"You look like shit, Bernier."

"*Me?* You're the one who's in a hospital gown."

"What's wrong with you?"

"What's *wrong* with me? I thought you were gonna die, you asshole. I haven't been sleeping too well." I was practically yelling at him, which probably wouldn't please the nurses. I forced myself to tone it down a notch. "Look, I've been worried as hell about you, okay? The last time I saw you outside a hospital was when you were keeled over on your couch."

"Oh."

"Yeah, *oh.*"

"How did I . . . What happened, anyway?"

"You mean how did you get here?" He nodded. "You disappeared. I got worried. I went to your place, and there you were. I called an ambulance and they dragged your ass over here. That was almost two weeks ago."

"Crazy."

"No shit."

"Who . . . had to drag my sisters into this?"

"Hospital needed next of kin. Cody tracked them down."

He lifted one arm off the bed to form a feeble wave, and it must have felt heavy because he dropped it almost immediately. The IV line wiggled like a see-through snake. "Do me a favor. . . . Get this out of here."

"You mean all the Jesus crap? Sure."

"I mean *now.* Please?"

I got up and started shoving the various devotional objects into the closet, hoping this wasn't going to get me a one-way ticket to hell.

"Those two are . . ." His voice trailed off. He looked exhausted.

"They were just trying to help," I said. "I think maybe they needed something to take their minds off things." I decided now was not the time to tell him about the froufrou job they'd done on his apartment, which might very well send him into cardiac arrest. "You know, they were pretty upset after they saw you yesterday."

"They kept talking shit."

"Bible-thumping shit?"

He shook his head, also feebly. "Spouting crap about how I need help. Did you know they're actually going to send a *shrink* in here?"

"Imagine that."

"What's that"—*cough, cough*—"supposed to mean?"

"Never mind."

"Don't do that, Bernier. Be straight."

"I don't think now's the right time."

"Stop that shit."

"Look, you just woke up. We can deal with it later."

"Now." He was coughing harder, and I was afraid he might bust a lung. "You want to help me out, be straight with me."

That did it. "Be *straight* with you? Give me a fucking break. First you start missing work; then you get into a stupid bar fight and get yourself arrested; then you come into the newsroom drunk off your ass and get yourself fired; then you fucking OD yourself into the hospital. . . . Don't go telling me *I'm* the one who's got to be straight, you moron."

"What do you mean?"

"You know damn well what I mean."

"What do you mean I *OD'd* myself?"

I stared at him. "You mean you really don't remember?"

"Remember what?"

"Remember chasing a bunch of Percodan with a whole bottle of vodka."

"Jesus Christ, is *that* what they were talking about?"

"Huh?"

"My sisters . . . They kept saying 'How could you? How could you?' That must be what they meant."

"It's a pretty good guess."

"But I *didn't.*"

"You mean you didn't really want to kill yourself? It was all just—what do they call it?—'a cry for help'? That's *classic.*"

"No, I mean I *didn't.*" His voice was so raw as to be almost unintelligible. "I didn't take any drugs. . . . For fuck's sake, you know me better than that."

"Jesus, Mad, I don't think I know you at all anymore. Listen to me: The doctors found it in your system, and I found the damn bottle in your bedroom, so there's no point in lying about it."

"But I didn't. You gotta believe me, Bernier. I didn't."

"I think you're in what they call denial."

"Fuck denial," he croaked at me. "I'm telling you I didn't take any drugs. Do you believe me or don't you?"

"Look, if you say you didn't take it, I—"

"Don't motherfucking patronize me."

"Mad, would you just—"

A nurse came in then, correctly ascertained that I was not enhancing Mad's calm, and kicked me out on my ear.

"Wait a second," he said as the door was closing behind me. "Please . . . I have to ask you one thing. Does Emma know?"

"That you OD'd?"

"About any of it."

"I don't think so. I haven't talked to her, anyway."

"Then don't tell her," he said. "Don't you fucking tell her. Give me your word."

"All right."

"And listen, Bernier . . . I really didn't take that shit. You gotta believe me."

"We can talk about it later."

"Okay, but you gotta promise me something else."

"What?"

"Do me a favor," he said, "and get my sisters the hell out of town."

CHAPTER
21

That wasn't the only favor Mad asked of me. The other one, considerably less delicate, was for a bratwurst with all the trimmings. And no, he didn't have some metaphysical memory of O'Shaunessey's bedside visit; he was just sick of hospital food. I therefore went straight to Schultz's to procure the object of his desire—and who did I find all cozy at a corner booth but Cal Ochoa and Gordon Band.

At first, I thought of turning tail and running, lest Ochoa rip me into my constituent parts for letting Gordon in on the Shelley Freeman story. But they saw me two seconds later, so there went that idea.

I shuffled over to their table, said hi, and awaited my fate. It only took me maybe two more seconds to realize that Ochoa had no idea of what we'd been up to; whatever the two of them were talking about, it wasn't me and my big mouth. Still, Ochoa didn't appear particularly glad to see me.

"Hey," I said, "what are you guys doing here? I didn't even know you two knew each other."

"You don't know everything," Ochoa said, a shade too snarkily for my taste.

Gordon started to shove over. "Wanna sit down?"

"She's probably busy," Ochoa said. I sat down anyway.

"I just came from Mad," I said. "The bozos at the hospital finally let me see him."

Gordon took a giant bite of his (equally giant) pickle. "Hey, how's he doing?"

"Okay. Really tired, obviously. But pretty good, I guess, considering. He wanted me to get him a bratwurst."

"You're kidding."

"Nope. I'm sacrificing my vegetarian principles in the name of friendship."

"The doctors really gonna let him eat that?"

"I seriously doubt he gives a damn."

Ochoa chuckled at that, gave me a mildly dirty look for no good reason I could discern, and turned his attention back to his grilled ham-and-cheese. Frau Schultz came over then, and I ordered two sandwiches to go: Mad's guilty treat plus egg salad on rye with mustard for me.

"So," I said, "what're you guys up to?"

Zip from Ochoa by way of reply; Gordon was busy polishing off the first of his two knishes and washing it down with homemade root beer.

"Hey," I said, "what's the big secret?"

"None of your business," Ochoa said, and went back to his sandwich.

Gordon gave me a look that said he didn't get what Ochoa's damage was. That made two of us. "Nothing much," he said. "Cal here called and wanted to know a few things about the *Times*, that's all."

"Networking, huh? You applying for a job there or something?"

"Give me a break," he said. "You know I'm nowhere near there yet. I just wanted to know how the place works, okay? Like it's any of your business . . ."

I turned to Gordon. "Since when are you into career counseling, anyway?"

"Hey, I'm always into making new friends."

"Yeah, *right.*"

"And besides," he said, "Cal's buying. Least I can do is answer a few questions."

He grinned at Ochoa, who didn't return it—just turned to me and said, "Don't you have to be someplace?"

"I'm waiting for my food. What's your problem?"

He muttered something in Spanish under his breath, then shook his head. "Nothing," he said to his sandwich. "Not a goddamn thing."

I walked out of there ten minutes later and, on the ride back to the hospital, replayed the scene in my head half a dozen times. What the hell was wrong with Ochoa? Our interchange had been astonishingly unpleasant—although, it must be said, not nearly as unpleasant as Kate Barnett's memorial service the following Saturday.

It was held in the creaky old Benson concert hall, the largest-capacity venue on campus after the gigantic ROTC building, and the place was still stuffed to the gills. There was a whole passel of dignitaries; I know who they were because, at the insistence of our execrable publisher, I compiled a who's-who for a sidebar that ran with my story on the service. The list included Gabriel's own Mayor Marty; our local congressman, surprisingly sober for two in the afternoon; the president of Benson (of course); a teary V.P. from Iowa State; a very cute special-assistant to the U.S. agriculture secretary; some UNICEF bigwig in a bad suit and an expensive watch; and plenty of eminent scientists and assorted academic pooh-bahs.

But to me, what was even more interesting was who *wasn't* there: The section down front reserved for the family was just about empty. Barnett's parents came, but only one brother out of three; her son didn't show, and neither did her ex-husband.

Of course, those folks could've sat somewhere else—maybe to avoid some family angst or something—but if so, they didn't play any part in the memorial, which was conducted by Cerretani. A women's a cappella group sang some sad songs, a bagpiper blew a soul-busting lament, and half a dozen colleagues (including Cerretani himself) gave testimonials about Kate and her dedication to making the world a better place.

It was all very moving, and plenty of people cried. But for some reason, all those empty chairs in the family row really got to me.

I asked around as people were filing out, but nobody could tell me what was up with the Barnett clan. Cynthia Chu, eyes all puffy and nose red from blowing, said she'd never met the professor's son—but she thought maybe somebody named Chuck Dwyer had, since he'd been in the grad program longer. She tracked him down a couple of aisles away and dragged him over, but although he knew the kid, he hadn't seen him there, either.

"And besides," said Chuck, a very skinny fellow maybe three years younger and ten inches taller than me, "you shouldn't be bothering him at a time like this anyway."

"What makes you think I was planning on bothering him?"

"Because you media people are all alike."

"And how is that, exactly?"

"Like vultures sniffing around roadkill."

"Thanks. That's a really lovely image."

"What do you want with Koigi, anyway?" He pronounced it *ko-EE-gee*.

"I'm doing a story on the memorial service," I said. "I need to say who was there."

"Well, I'm sure he's around here someplace," Chuck said, rubbing at a prematurely balding spot atop his skull. "I mean, he'd have to be, right?"

"You'd think. What's he like, anyway?"

His gray eyes narrowed, and he looked at my notebook like it might sprout teeth and bite him on the nose.

"Look," I said, "this isn't for publication or anything. I was just wondering."

"What do you care?"

"I interviewed Professor Barnett a bunch of times, and I thought she was a pretty amazing lady. One of the amazing things about her was saving these kids from a refugee camp. I was just wondering what her son was like, that's all."

He looked a bit less wary. But not much. "I don't really know him. I only met him once or twice, and it was only in passing."

"And what did you think of him?"

He eyed my notebook again. I shoved it into my backpack, but it didn't inspire him to answer. Instead, he flopped all six-something of himself down onto one of the wooden seats and said, "Can you *believe* those people out there?"

"What people?" I sat down next to him. "Oh . . . You mean the protesters?"

"Of course the protesters. I mean, don't those people have any respect? One of them *killed* her, for chrissake. How they can have the gall to show their faces here is beyond me."

"There's only about a dozen of them. Just the hard-core ones, I guess."

"It's appalling."

"Professor Barnett might have taken it as a compliment."

I caught the sound of sobbing from about twenty yards away and saw Cynthia with her arms wrapped around another girl, both of them rocking side to side, comforting each other. At the other end of the hall, another bunch of stragglers were laughing and crying and chatting all at once, clearly reminiscing about Barnett. Filing down the aisle past me was Ellie Gilbert, looking shell-shocked but stoic, holding hands with a clean-cut guy in a too-large sportcoat.

When I turned back to Chuck, I found he'd twisted his neck to look me up and down, and way too assessingly for comfort.

"You know," he said once he'd finished his visual pat-down, "you may be right about that."

"About . . . ?"

"About Professor Barnett taking the protesters as a compliment. She was an amazing lady."

"Yeah, she was—" I caught myself before I said *she was a very special person.* Yikes, maybe I was halfway to brainwashed myself. "She was really interesting."

"And you're really not trying to do a hatchet job on her? You swear?"

"Why would I?"

"Look, I worked on the student paper at Penn. I know a few things about the news cycle."

"What does that have to do with anything?"

"You know how it goes. First you tell the world how great Professor Barnett was. Then that's not news anymore, so you tear her down—you trash the idol you built up yourself. Everything's about making a story."

He was right, but I decided that pointing this out was not in my best interest. "Look," I said, "all I wanted to do was find out if her son showed up to the service. There's no hidden agenda here, okay? What's the big deal?"

He rubbed his bald spot again for a while. "Are you just trying to—what do they call it?—*massage* me?"

Yes. "No."

"And this is really off the record? Honestly?"

"I swear."

"All right . . . But I'm only telling you because it's really nothing."

He then proceeded not to say anything at all. I considered nudging him, and figured it might make him clam up instead. A minute later my rare display of patience paid off.

"Okay," he said, "it's just that . . . Well, the truth is, I wouldn't be surprised if he wasn't here after all—Kate's son, I mean."

"Yeah?"

"And when you asked about him—about Koigi—I figured you were trying to make her out to be a bad mother, you know? And she really wasn't. It wasn't her fault the kid turned out as screwed up as he was. From what I figured he was plenty screwed up when she got ahold of him."

"Screwed up how?"

"He had a really bad temper, for one thing. A couple of times when I was waiting outside her office to talk to her . . . I'd hear them fighting. He'd say things you shouldn't say to your mom."

"Like what?"

"Nothing I can remember, not specifically. He was just a really angry person. But you can hardly blame him, you know?"

"How come?"

"Well, just think about the hand he got dealt."

"You mean his background? Coming from the refugee camp?"

He nodded. "They say . . . Well, I've done a little reading, because it's sort of related to my dissertation, and they say there's all sorts of problems you can have from childhood malnutrition. You can lag behind your peers forever, not only physically but mentally too."

"And Koigi did?"

"Um . . . He was really small for his age, and his head was

kind of out of proportion, you know, so I think he had some stunted growth. And I don't know if he was learning disabled or what, but I heard he had a really hard time in school—he got held back several times, I think, and Professor Barnett finally put him in that private school up on West Hill, but it didn't do much good."

"The Griffin Academy?"

"Yeah, that's it. And maybe his school problems weren't the reason he was so messed up, but I got the idea he was mad at the whole world—his mom most of all."

"But she was the one who got him out of the camp, right? She probably saved his life."

"Look, I told you I barely knew the kid. I'm just telling you my impressions so you don't go blaming Kate. And besides, this stuff I'm telling you, it goes back a ways—like three or four years. Maybe he's got his act together by now. Anyway, he hasn't been around for a while, at least I haven't seen him."

"Do you think he was violent?"

"I don't think so. I mean, once I heard he smashed a coffee mug against her office wall, but I don't think he'd really do anything . . . Oh, God. You're not suggesting he—"

"I'm not suggesting anything. I was just wondering, that's all."

He stood up. "I think I'm done talking to you now."

"Wait, I just want to ask you one more thing. Do you know a girl who left a while ago with a master's degree instead of—"

He started to walk off, then stopped. "Don't forget, this was all off the record," he said. "If my name ends up in print, my dad's lawyer's gonna sue your ass off."

With those genteel words ringing in my ears, I went back to the paper and wrote up my story on the memorial, which—short of unforeseen mayhem—was running on

Monday's page one. When I was finished, I went out to the Green and rewarded myself with a falafel pita (extra tahini, natch) and a diet raspberry Snapple. I consumed these sitting on one of the Green's artsy concrete-block benches, soaking up the afternoon rays and wondering what the hell was up with Kate Barnett's son.

She'd told Mad he was traveling around the country between high school and college. From what Skinny Chuck had just told me, that sounded like a crock.

Okay, maybe he really had gotten his act together and was taking some kind of gap-year trip—but would that really keep him from his own mother's memorial service? Was it possible that he hadn't even heard about her death? Considering all the media coverage of her murder, that seemed like a long shot, right?

And anyway . . . Did it really matter?

I wasn't sure, but for some reason the whole thing had me fascinated—and sitting there watching two prepubescent girls braid friendship bracelets, it finally occurred to me why. Like a con man falling for his mark, I'd committed a basic journalistic faux pas: I'd started rooting for one side over the other. Kate had been a damn sight more appealing than the angry-vegetable crowd, and I liked her a lot. Plus, she'd keyed right into my postfeminist, Gen-X obsession with women who somehow mange to have it all—okay, her marriage flunked, but she was still a scientist, a humanitarian, a crusader for battered women, and an orphan-rescuing mom to boot.

Now, with the news about her messed-up son piled on top of the allegations by the mysterious grad student, my vision of her as some sort of *übermensch* was starting to sag under its own weight. Damn.

Either because I needed to understand the real Kate or (more likely) I desperately wanted to have this less appealing version contradicted, I went back to the paper and looked up Lillian's home number. I let it ring like twenty times, because — as she herself once typed up and taped to the newsroom wall — six rings equals about fifteen seconds, and expecting somebody to snap to it that fast is downright rude.

"Hey, Lillian," I said, "it's Alex. You got a minute?"

"Certainly."

"How's your ankle doing, anyway?"

"Nearly fine. And I do hope that question isn't leading up to a request that I cover for—"

"Hey, I know you don't do weekends anymore — one of the perks of being senior reporter, right?"

"The only one, actually."

"Anyway, I was just calling to ask if you could send me toward somebody at the Griffin Academy."

"Whatever for?"

"I want to get the dirt on a former student. Big screwup, from what I hear. I just wanted to hear how bad."

"On the record or off?"

"Way off. I'm just sort of curious about him."

"Do you mind if I ask why?"

"It's Kate Barnett's son. She made him out to be a solid citizen, but now I'm not so sure. Anyway, he didn't show up to her memorial."

She made a noise that actually sounded like *tsk-tsk,* followed by a patented Lillian sigh — the most disapproving sound you can imagine. "I'd suggest Jeanne Dodd," she said, "but I know for a fact she's out of town. It is summer, you know. Teachers go away."

"Right. Anybody else?"

"Hmm . . . There's Bob Laughton — he's the sports coach, and he gets to know all the students quite well."

"Great."

"But you can't call him. He wouldn't talk to you."

"Only to you?"

"I'm afraid so."

"A lot of your sources seem to be like that."

"Education people can be skittish. Nowadays they're always afraid of being sued for one thing or another."

"So can you call him for me? Like right now?"

"It's—"

"I know it's Saturday. Please?"

"I was going to say, it's probably not a good time to reach him. He coaches a weekend soccer league. But I'll try him later."

"You're an angel."

"And you're a pest. But you're a good reporter, so I'll forgive you your trespasses."

"Hey, I'm touched."

"What's this child's name?"

"Koigi Barnett."

"All right. I'll let you know."

"Before you go, can you tell me something else? What's the deal with the Griffin Academy, anyway?"

"Aren't you familiar with it? You were schools reporter for a while."

"Yeah, but I was a really bad one."

Another disapproving sigh, this one aimed at me. I got a feeling I'd just been demoted to pest again.

"It was founded about twenty-five years ago by Edwina Griffin," she said. "She had a philosophy that some adolescents could thrive if they had certain unfettered freedoms within the context of strictly enforced rules. It's a bit hard to explain, to tell the truth. People tend to love it or hate it."

"What kinds of kids go there?"

"A lot of them are what you'd call second-chancers, students who were expelled from somewhere else. And they don't live in a dormitory. They board with local Griffin families, who act *in loco parentis*. As I said, it's an unusual place."

"Would you send a kid there?"

"Heavens no."

"Oh. Let me bounce something else off you, okay? Hey, am I keeping you from something?"

"I was quilting," she said, sounding like she'd been interrupted from Middle East peace talks.

"I'll make it fast, I promise. I was just wondering how you might hit a particular angle. I mean, when it comes to getting people to cough it up, you're the *queen*."

"There's no need to flatter."

"Okay, well . . . How would you get a guy to spill his guts about his dead ex-wife?"

"Oh, my."

"Yeah."

"Was it an acrimonious divorce?"

"I have no idea."

"How long ago did it occur?"

"I think at least fifteen years."

"And this is for publication?"

"No way."

"Goodness, Alex, you seem to be spending a great deal of time on things that aren't going to end up in print."

"Tell me about it."

"To answer your question . . . I'm afraid I don't have any words of wisdom. If the divorce was that long ago, the element of revenge would be low, don't you think? You couldn't get him to talk just to do her a bad turn. Did they have children?"

"No."

"That's better, then—no one to protect by keeping quiet."

"True."

"I'd just hit it head-on, I suppose. Tell him you want to

know her better and he's in a position to fill in the blanks. He'll either talk or he won't. I'm sorry, but I can't think of anything better than that."

"There's nothing like a frontal assault. You taught me that."

"If you come up with something clever, let me know," she said. "Even at my age, I'm always quite pleased to add to my repertoire."

❧

Mad came home from the hospital the next day, which seemed astonishingly speedy. But the state of managed care being what it is, the minute the good doctors decided he wasn't going to croak on his way out of the parking lot they showed him the door.

As per his orders, I'd had a heart-to-heart with his sisters during which I'd essentially told them that their presence was doing him more harm than good. I tried to spin it as him feeling guilty that they were away from their families on his account, but I could tell it didn't fly. They left in a huff, but not before confronting a still-bedridden Mad about whether what *this person* (me) said was true. Did he really, really want them to leave?

He said he did. So they left, taking their plastic Jesus with them.

I spent the morning of his homecoming trying to restore his apartment to its former squalor. His sisters had been staying there to avoid a motel bill—and, unsurprisingly, everything about the place horrified them. So, between a human urge to do *something* (which I shared) and a more-specifically-girlie urge to decorate (which I did not), they'd concocted a scheme to "fix the place up for Jakey." And they'd done it, in spades.

Setting it right proved to be difficult, because they'd chucked a fair amount of his stuff. There were no ratty bath towels to put back up once I'd torn down the Laura Ashley curtains (complete with balloon valance) they'd installed in the bedroom, no half-crushed wicker TV stand to replace the new baby-blue wooden one, decorated with yellow daffodils. I did the best I could.

I picked him up from the hospital and delivered him to his digs. He got out of breath just going up the narrow staircase to the first floor, and the sight of him so damn diminished just about brought me to tears. He took in the decorative changes with one sour glance, said nothing, and sat down on the couch—which, luckily, I'd been able to return to its state of dinginess simply by ripping off the pink-and-white polka-dot cover.

"I need a drink," he said.

"Come on, Mad, you just got out of the—"

"I gotta get back to normal. I just want to get back to normal, okay?"

"So you want a drink at three o'clock in the afternoon?"

"Pretty normal for me."

I couldn't argue with him.

"Sorry, but there's no booze in the house." He gave me a look loaded with equal parts suspicion and ire. "Hey," I said, "don't get all pissy with me. I didn't go cleaning it out or anything."

"My goddamn sisters—"

"They didn't, either. By the time I found you here, there was nothing left. Your sisters just threw away the empties."

"Oh."

"Yeah."

"I still need a drink. Be a good girl and go across the street to the—"

"Kiss my ass."

He favored me with the same evil look he'd just given the TV stand. "So it's like that, is it?"

"Apparently."

"I don't know what I did to deserve having you turn into the bitch of the century."

"Are you out of your *mind?* You try to kill yourself with booze and pills and you wonder why I don't feel like helping you take another crack at it?"

"I *told* you, Bernier. I didn't take any goddamn pills."

"Give me a break, okay?"

"Believe me or don't. I don't give a shit anymore."

"Mad, I found the bottle under your bed. The doctors found the drugs in your system. So just give it up, all right?"

"Christ, Bernier. How long have we known each other? Five years? When have I ever lied to you? Huh?"

"Including now?"

"Fuck you."

"Look, I'm just worried about you, you know. I hate to see you going into this—"

"If you say 'denial' again, I'll wring your neck, I swear."

"In the state you're in, I doubt you could manage it."

It was a cheap shot, but it worked—maybe too well. He closed his eyes and slumped down on the couch, feet up on the new coffee table. It had a glass top, and the sides were decorated with wrought-iron hearts. "That goddamn shrink they sent in, that's all she said, fucking over and over and over. 'Denial, you're in denial, don't go being in denial.' Made me want to yak."

"Imagine that."

"Look, I'm going to say it once and for all. I didn't take any pills. I drank a shitload of booze, yeah. So sue me. It wasn't the first time. But I didn't take drugs. I wouldn't know where to get them even if I wanted to. And I sure as hell didn't want to kill myself. I can't believe you'd think I would. *You,* of all fucking people."

"Come on, after everything that happened—Emma leaving, and getting fired from the paper . . ."

"Screw all that. I mean, yeah, it all sucks. It sucks like a son of a bitch. But I can't believe you'd think I'd ever do that to you."

"To *me?* What the hell is that supposed to mean?"

"After . . . you know, after what happened with Adam—how at first everybody thought he'd . . . done it. I know what that did to you. You tried like hell not to show it, Bernier, but I could tell. Everybody could. And even if I was totally gonzo, I'd never . . . I'd just never, that's all. Come on, Jesus Christ, don't cry. . . ."

"I can't help it."

He sat up and put an arm around me. "Come on, it's gonna be okay. . . ."

"I bring you home from the hospital, where you practically *died,* and you're the one telling me it's gonna be okay. What the hell is that?"

"Don't worry about it. Here, take that handkerchief off the goddamn end table and blow your nose."

"It's a doily. I must've missed it before."

"Huh?"

"Never mind."

"Christ, Bernier, maybe you're the one who needs a drink."

"Citizen should be opening any minute."

"You serious? You'd really go have a drink with me?"

"Yeah."

"How come?"

"Because even though it's totally nuts," I said, "I think I'm starting to believe you."

CHAPTER 22

Mad's return to the Citizen Kane was celebrated with all due ceremony; if Mack'd had a fatted calf behind the bar, I feel sure he would've roasted it over the pool table. You'd think that most decent folk would be appalled to see Mad back at the trough after what had happened, but they weren't—probably because they were so relieved to see him someplace, *anyplace,* other than in an open casket at Sand's Funeral Home.

The parade of well-wishers finally got so intense we moved from the window seat to a booth in the back, which is dark enough so a person doesn't have to get recognized if he doesn't want to. Either out of deference for me or because the whole OD experience had really hit him hard (mentally, physically, or both), Mad was still nursing his first beer. I, on the other hand, was on my third pony bottle of Chianti.

The topic of conversation, once we'd relocated to the booth and could talk uninterrupted, was everything Mad had missed during his field trip to dreamland. He knew a lot of it already because—against the express wishes of his sisters—O'Shaunessey had brought him a stack of *Monitor*s going back to the day he got canned. Mad had been so desperate for stimulation he'd read them cover to cover, including the comics and the syndicated bridge column.

But there'd been a lot that didn't make it into print, of course, and I filled him in on all of it—bringing Gordon in on the Shelley Freeman thing, and finding out Lane had been in cahoots with the Don't Break the Food Chain people, and the interviews I'd done with Kate Barnett's colleagues and students. He took it all in, slamming back two bowls of honey-roasted cashews from Mack's private stash but still mostly ignoring the alcohol he'd so longed for.

"What the hell," he said when I'd run out of news, "could possibly have possessed you to drag Band into this?"

"I was lonely."

"You were *what?*"

"You were out cold, Cody was mostly incommunicado, Melissa's always off getting laid, and Ochoa totally bailed. I was lonely."

"So you handed a potentially huge motherfucker of a story to *Band?*"

"He was plenty astonished himself, trust me."

"You females never fail to astound."

"I'm glad the world didn't change too radically while you were off in la-la land."

"You know," he said, "I've had a lot of time to think, over the past few days, since I woke up in that goddamn hospital. One of the main things on my mind was how to convince you I didn't OD on purpose. And the—"

"You did a good job of it," I said. "The Adam thing, I mean."

"It's the truth, Alex. I'd never put you through that crap again. I swear I wouldn't."

"You know . . . I've been thinking about him a lot lately—more than I have in years, since right after it happened."

"Why do you think that is?"

"Isn't it obvious?" Blank stare. "How could I not? Ochoa's practically a dead ringer for him."

"You've gotta be kidding me."

My stare was even blanker than his. "Huh?"

"Alex, Cal Ochoa doesn't look a single thing like Ellroy."

"Sure he does."

"Yeah, he's got two arms and two legs and a head, but the similarity pretty much ends there."

"Are you out of your mind?"

"Contrary to popular opinion, no. Are you out of yours?"

"Come on, it hit me the minute I laid eyes on him. He's got the same . . . the same . . . Hell, I don't know how to describe it."

"Sure, because it's all in your head."

"But come on, Mad, he's so much *like* him—same kind of attitude, the whole don't-pin-me-down, devil-may-care thing, the huge competitive streak. He even gets the same look in his eyes when he talks about reporting. Are you seriously telling me you don't see it?"

"Hey, don't take my word for it. Ask Melissa. Ask anybody."

"Oh, *please*." I slammed back the rest of my wine, which wasn't bad for something that came in a screw top. "It is not all in my head. It is *not*."

"Anyway, like I was saying, when I was stuck in that hospital, I was thinking about a lot of shit, when my sisters weren't driving me up the wall. And the main one was, since I know damn well I didn't take the Percodan on purpose, how the hell did it get in me?"

"Are you sure you want to talk about this now?"

"Hell yes."

"Okay, well . . . Could you've taken it by accident?"

"Jesus, I don't see how. You know I don't even take

Tylenol, for chrissake. And the empty bottle under the bed . . . I know damn well I didn't put it there."

"So . . . What? You think somebody poisoned you on purpose?"

"What the hell else am I supposed to think? I know you're gonna think it's crazy. . . ."

"Hey, do you hear me contradicting you? I've heard crazier, and you know it. The question is, who? Not to mention why."

"That's what I've been wondering, believe me."

"You know anybody who's ever taken the stuff? Somebody who had it handy?"

"I . . . I dated this chick a year or so ago. She'd screwed her knee up in a skiing accident, and the pain was real bad— that's what one of the nurses told me you take Percodan for. It's a serious painkiller. Packs a big punch."

"Right. And this girl took it?"

"I think so."

"And did you break up on, you know, negative terms?"

He concentrated on swishing the remaining cashews around the bowl with his finger. "Um . . . She was 'the Serial Luncher.' "

"The one who baked you all those yummy cookies?"

"No, not her—that chick was relatively normal. This girl was the one who'd leave those five-course meals outside my apartment door. I'd just trash 'em, 'cause I figured God knows what she'd put in there."

"How long did she keep them coming?"

"Maybe three months. Seemed like a long time."

"And this was how long ago?"

"About a year and a half. Right before I hooked up with Emma."

"And you think maybe she'd still be pissed enough to do you in?"

"Nah, I don't know . . . I haven't heard from her since. You just asked if I knew anybody who took Percodan, and she's the only one I can think of. She was definitely a wacko, though."

"So how come you got together with her in the first place?"

"She was a wacko with really great tits."

"God, you're such a throwback sometimes."

He raised his mug to me and took a sip. "And ain't it a beautiful thing?"

"You're seeming relatively chipper all of a sudden."

He put down his drink, and when he looked up, his expression was serious again. "Look, Alex, I don't want to go all gay on you or anything, but I gotta tell you. . . . It means a lot that you believe me."

He sounded so earnest I didn't even call him on the homophobia bit. "Yeah?"

"If you really thought I could do something like that . . . I just couldn't stand it, okay?"

"I appreciate that."

"Then enough said." He grabbed up the rest of the nuts and started shaking them in his fist, like he was about to throw craps. "You want to hear the other thing I was thinking in the hospital?"

"Sure."

"I've been thinking," he said, "that there's something funny going on in plant science."

"Yeah," I said. "The building blew up, for one thing."

"Besides that. I mean, *before* that."

"I'm listening."

"Look, there's something I haven't told you yet. I think it might be important."

Long pause.

"So spill."

"First off . . . I kind of want to, you know, apologize for the way I acted before. Around the time I got canned . . ."

"You *kind* of want to ap—"

"Okay, I apologize, all right? I acted like a horse's ass. And don't go asking me why, 'cause I still don't want to talk about it. Just take my word for it that it didn't have a damn thing to do with you personally. Okay?"

"Okay."

"Thanks. So after I got myself fired, things got worse— big shock, right? I had all this time on my hands, and plenty of money in the bank to drink with, so I did. But the whole time I could only think about one thing."

"Emma?"

"Okay, two things. Her, and trying to get my job back."

"Really?"

"I got what you might call obsessed with it—with getting my beat back. And I never looked at the paper, I guess 'cause it pissed me off to think it could go on just fine without me. I thought about you or Brad or Ochoa or whoever covering my beat in some half-assed way and it drove me nuts. And then I thought maybe you weren't covering it half-assed, maybe you were doing a damn fine job of it, and that drove me even *more* nuts. You follow?"

"I think."

"So I got this idea in my head."

He picked up my empty wine bottle and started tapping the bottom edge on the table, *rat-tat-tat,* and refusing to look me in the eye.

He was embarrassed. Jake Madison was actually blushing. There is, apparently, a first time for everything.

"Okay," I said, once I'd started to despair of him ever actually saying anything, "what idea was that?"

"Um . . . I thought that if . . . You know, if I really hit one out of the park, Bill and Marilyn'd have to take me back. I figured I'd show them nobody could cover the beat better than me, and if I cleaned up my act and promised to be good from now on, they'd give me another shot."

"You mean you wrote a story?"

"I started to . . . I mean, I tried."

"But it didn't go so well?"

"No, that wasn't it. It was going pretty good. But just when it started to get going, I woke up in a hospital room feeling like something Melissa's goddamn cat dragged in, and everybody's yelling at me about suicide."

"And the story was about plant science."

"Right. Specifically, it was going to be this in-depth piece about Barnett and her lab and everybody in it, something way bigger than that Saturday profile I did before—hardcore science stuff, but with lots of personality crap and everything. I was gonna interview a bunch of the protesters, and maybe even try to track down somebody from the OATs, and get in touch with somebody from the Rice Institute in the Philippines so it'd have this whole international angle. I had it all outlined—a five-thousand-word feature with a shitload of sidebars, the kind of thing you'd kick off with a double-truck and run over maybe three Saturdays. I was gonna kick ass and take names. And I figured once I did, I'd drop it on Marilyn's desk and she'd read it and I'd be back in clover."

"So what happened?"

"I told you, I was just getting into it when I got knocked on my ass."

"And you think maybe somebody connected to the story put you there?"

"What else could it be?"

"You mean, besides every woman you've ever screwed over?"

"Besides them, yeah. And I really don't think my personal life has a damn thing to do with this."

"Neither do I, actually."

"Oh, yeah? How come you're giving me so much credit all of a sudden?"

"Because compared to what's been going on at that ag school, the body count in your love life is comparatively low."

"Meaning?"

"Meaning somebody poisoned Lane Freeman—and for the record, I definitely don't think it was his wife. Somebody *tried* to poison you. And somebody beat Kate Barnett to death. Not to mention the fact that somebody blew Phil Herzog's head off, although that was obviously more a question of being in the wrong place at the wrong time."

"And you think the same person did all of it?"

"No . . . I don't know. I mean, the motivations are all so screwed up. It's giving me a headache just thinking about it."

"That makes two of us. My head's been killing me ever since I came back from the dead."

"That's not funny."

"But it's true. I know damn well what a close call it was. You saved my ass, Bernier."

"You barely even have an ass, so how is anybody supposed to save it?"

"Seriously, I owe you one."

"Seriously, don't worry about it. Listen, about the story you were working on . . . Did you find out anything that somebody might not want in the paper? I mean, if somebody really did try to get rid of you, there'd have to be a reason, right? Something other than your tendency to be a generalized pain in the ass?"

"I've been thinking about that too, but I just don't know. I was just starting to set up a bunch of interviews, getting people on Barnett's team to send me their academic papers, trying to get permission to shadow a couple of them for the day, meet with the Food Chain idiots, that kind of thing. I didn't stumble into some deep dark secret or anything, if that's what you're getting at."

"Honestly, Mad, I don't know what I'm getting at."

"Like I said before, that makes two of us."

"And what about Lane? Why do we think somebody wanted to get rid of him too?"

"Besides the fact he was a flack?"

"Be serious."

"Right. Well, plant science was obviously in his beat, so there's that connection again. And then there's the stuff you just told me about him being in cahoots with Tobias Kahan, which would obviously piss off plenty of people. I mean, if it ever got out that somebody from Benson was helping instigate all the protests just to raise the university's profile . . . Man, that would be a *huge* scandal. And you know how the grant givers are—when it comes to scandals, they're damn allergic. Shit like that could cost Benson a lot of money. And come to think of it, losing the funding could cost a lot of people their jobs."

"Plus, it'd be a blotch on the university escutcheon."

"You and your damn Vassar vocabulary."

"I mean, it'd make Benson look bad."

"Then why the hell didn't you just say that?"

"Because I have style," I said. "Okay, so if the Lane thing came out, whose head would be on the chopping block?"

"Now that Herzog's dead, probably nobody's."

"But if he weren't, do you think he would've gotten the shaft over the whole thing? Enough to make him get rid of Lane to make sure it didn't come out?"

"Nah . . . I mean, I guess there's an off chance the Benson prez would've made him resign over it, but I kind of doubt it. The university doesn't really work that way. And even if it did, Herzog wasn't the type. He liked to be a pain, but I always thought he was really just a big pussy. He wouldn't have the balls to kill anybody."

"You know, I think that's the only nice thing I've ever heard anybody say about him."

"May he rest in pieces."

"That was *awful*."

"Hey, even half dead I've still got it."

"And here's another question," I said. "If somebody really slipped you a Mickey, how did they do it?"

"I've been thinking about that one too, obviously. And I guess I'd have to say it wouldn't have been that hard."

"Yeah?"

"Look, that whole couple of weeks is kind of a blur. I had my load on but good most of the time, except when I was trying to cover that story. Sometimes I locked my door, but most of the time I couldn't even find my keys. I had half-empty booze bottles all over the place, and I can't say I noticed how any of it tasted. If I'd wanted to poison me, I would've just waltzed in there, dumped some chopped-up pills in one of the bottles, and been out of there in thirty seconds."

"But are you sure you wouldn't have noticed . . . I don't know, the residue or something?"

"Bernier, in the state I was in, I didn't notice much of anything."

"But how would somebody know that?"

"Good question. That's one thing I hadn't thought about."

"Well," I said, "come to think of it, I guess a certain amount of stuff happened in public, like the bar fight. Plus, reporters aren't particularly good at keeping our mouths shut, so maybe somebody at the paper told somebody who told somebody else—"

"Which means it might as well have been on the fucking AP wire. You've got a point there."

"Sorry."

"What does Ochoa think of all this?"

"About what?"

"About the Barnett thing. You said he was on a one-hombre crusade to crack the case."

"Yeah, he is. Last thing I heard he was trying to infiltrate the anti-G.M.O. protest groups. He was hanging out drinking absinthe with Tobias Kahan at some sissy bar in College-town."

"Absinthe is illegal."

"Armagnac. Whatever."

"And is he getting anyplace?"

"Not that I know of."

"Hey, wasn't he going off all half-cocked over Shelley Freeman before? And what makes you guys so sure she didn't do it, anyway?"

"For me, the bottom line is I really don't think she wanted him dead—I think she much preferred to have him alive and kicking right back at her. Ochoa'll tell you he looked deep into her soul or some damn thing, but if you ask me, he wanted to believe her all along."

"How come?"

"Because once she got convicted, if she's not guilty it makes for a better story—innocent woman unjustly ac-cused." I thought of Skinny Chuck's damning words about the fundamentally slimy nature of my profession, and winced. "But then once Barnett got killed, it blew that story out of the water. And besides, as long as she's rotting in jail, the Freeman story is evergreen."

"What about Gordon?"

"He was supposed to be helping me with Shelley. But once I dragged him into it, I couldn't really think of anything specific for him to do, and anyway now he's off to Niagara Falls on some story about power plants. I assume he's suit-ably miserable."

"Isn't he always?"

"That's our Gordon."

"And how's Cody doing?"

"My, you are the social animal today."

"Hey, I'm just wondering."

"He's okay, I guess."

"Jesus, Bernier, don't tell me there's trouble in paradise."

In another context, Mad could've said precisely the same thing and meant it sarcastically. This time, he was actually concerned.

"No, not like that. It's just that the Feds don't want him fraternizing with a reporter at the moment. We're probably not going to get to see much of each other until the investigation's over, that's all."

"Can't be easy."

"No kidding."

"Hard to be apart from someone you love."

"A thoroughly un-Mad-like statement."

He cocked an eyebrow at me, picked up his mug, and took the longest swallow of the night. "Am I really that much of a hard-hearted son of a bitch most of the time?"

"Yeah, you are."

"I try," he said. "I surely do try."

CHAPTER
23

As anticipated, the top headline on Monday's page one was BARNETT CELEBRATED IN CAMPUS MEMORIAL. But below the fold was something considerably more surprising, and which I'd been pulled out of the Citizen Kane to cover in a state of semi-inebriation. The head, which ran over a two-column story that jumped to page four, said this: E. EGGPLANT UNDER FIRE.

Now, elsewhere this might cause confusion. It did here too, but not because people didn't get that we were talking about a restaurant and not a beleaguered foodstuff. The misunderstanding came because people who blew right by the subhead (DOZENS PICKET EATERY AS "SELL-OUT") thought there'd actually been gunplay at the old watering hole. There hadn't, but just barely.

When I got the call, Mad and I had been on the way out the door to the Chinese buffet, with the intention of helping him regain his strength through the ingestion of several thousand calories' worth of egg foo young and spicy bean curd. Instead, he went home and I attended the Eggplant's Sunday Supper—its busiest meal of the week and a Gabriel tradition since the early seventies—where I proceeded to go hungry and get beaten up.

I'd gotten to the restaurant mere moments after the thing had started. One of the diners was a buddy of Bill's and had called him on his cell phone to tell him he *had* to get somebody to cover this; Bill found me at the Citizen and I was there two minutes later. Lucky me.

The gist of the thing was that somebody had apparently tipped off the Don't Break the Food Chain people that the Eggplant was cutting corners by using some nonorganic produce—meaning it could potentially have some genetically modified grub on its battered butcher-block tables. Now, the Eggplant has never claimed to be exclusively organic, just entirely vegetarian and (if you ask me) frequently bland as a middle-aged missionary. But the knowledge—or at least the rumor—that this storied bastion of conscientious cuisine might have tried to save a buck a pound by serving nonorganic arugula had sparked a minor jihad.

It didn't help that plenty of people were already beginning to think the Eggplant was getting too big for its britches, what with all the cookbooks and bottled dressings and purple aprons with the bright green logo. The Eggplant used to be counterculture; now it was starting to look like The Man.

So there were the regulars and the tourists, sitting side by side at the long wooden tables, wolfing down their twelve-dollar plates of summer-vegetable stew over herbed couscous, when the picketers arrived and blocked the view out the plate-glass window. Some of them even had the *cojones* to conduct an impromptu sit-in on the floor of the dining room, yelling "SELL OUT, SELL OUT, SELL OUT" until one lady from Biloxi (literally) dumped a bowl of ginger-miso soup on somebody's head.

The irony, of course, was that the members of the Eggplant Collective are about as crunchy as you can get, sandals and pierced noses being the de facto waiters' uniform. The Chain people weren't just preaching to the choir, in other words, they were shanghaiing the entire church. Truly, the restaurant staff looked like they didn't know whether to call the cops or drop their aprons and start chanting.

I need to pause here to admit something: I am sick to death of protests. It would probably cost me my job if it ever got back to Bill, but I mean it; if I have to cover another sit-in, be-in, bed-in, love-in, march, candlelight vigil, act of civil disobedience, or goddamn direct action, I am going to kill someone. I don't care if it's Gandhi's ghost practicing *satyagraha* on the steps of the Christian Science Reading Room; I am well and truly going to commit murder.

And to think, I used to find all that stuff sort of charming. For the life of me, I can't remember why.

Speaking of which . . . There's something else I can't quite fathom. This would be whatever possessed me to mouth off to Tobias Kahan, and very nearly get my ass kicked.

Okay, maybe I do have some idea; it may be related to the four (relatively teeny) bottles of wine I'd just consumed on an empty stomach.

Kahan had been chief among the protesters, chin hair waggling back and forth as he shouted "SELL OUT, SELL OUT" in a rain of spit. At one point, he gave a speech condemning the Eggplant for obvious capitalistic practices, and when the manager tried to respond in the name of "open dialogue"—she still hadn't had the heart to call the G.P.D.—the crowd shouted her down. Lovely.

He noticed me and, probably figuring there was zero chance the *Times* was going to show up for this one, flagged me down. In what felt like déjà vu all over again, we went around the building to do the interview away from the shouting. There, I dutifully wrote down his comments on how the

Eggplant should have the highest standards, its leadership role in the whole-foods community, blah-blah-blah. Not to belabor the point, but if Bill ever found out how wildly uninterested I was in the whole thing, I'd very likely be out on my ear.

"But hold on," I said in an effort to do my job. "Are you telling me you don't actually have any concrete evidence the Eggplant is serving genetically modified produce?"

"I told you, we got an anonymous tip. Aren't you listening to me?"

As little as possible. "Yeah, I'm listening. But a tip and actual evidence aren't the same thing, are they?"

"Just the *appearance* of wrongdoing is enough to shake the community's faith. The Ecstatic Eggplant should be above reproach."

"What is this, the Salem witch trials? Do you really mean to tell me you stormed the place on the strength of one person's say-so?"

"It was a very reliable source."

"If it was anonymous, how the hell do you know if it was reliable or not? And what are you saying—that the restaurant is guilty until proven innocent? Who *are* you people?"

"We're the conscience of an entire—"

"Oh, *please*." His face was starting to get red, but this barely registered in my slightly clouded brain. "Do you actually have nothing better to do than bust into someplace where ninety-nine percent of the people actually agree with you? Why don't you just stick to Burger King, for chrissake?"

"You wouldn't understand."

"There's an original argument."

Quick intake of breath, like he couldn't believe anybody would have the gall to talk to him in such a disrespectful manner. "If you think I give a fuck what some nobody reporter from the middle of nowhere has to say about me, my cause, or anything else on the goddamn planet, you're very much mistaken. Got it?"

"Middle of nowhere, eh?" I said, smarmy as all get-out. "I thought Gabriel was the heart and soul of your East Coast operations. Now we're just some hick town, huh? I'll bet the locals'd be interested in *that.*"

"Look, you stupid little small-town bitch. You better not fuck with me. *Do not fuck with me.*"

This inspired me to start digging my own grave with a very large shovel.

"And that's not the only thing they might be interested in," I said. "There's also the little sweetheart deal you made with Lane Freeman."

"The *what?*" He said it without an ounce of incredulity, but bucketloads of fury.

"You know exactly what I'm talking about, you big hypocrite."

"I'm sure I do *not.*"

"Lane helped you organize the protests during the G.M.O. conference to get more publicity for the university. You know it and I know it, so don't even bother—"

"You better shut your mouth," he said in a growl. "Or somebody just might shut it for you."

It was about then that I realized I was acting like a reckless moron. I also realized how entirely alone we were, standing in the corner of the back lot, the big brick building stretching out on either side and a Dumpster blocking us from the parked cars.

"What's that supposed to mean?" I said, trying to sound as *macha* as I had before I figured out I was behaving like a dolt.

"Don't play games with me, or I swear to God you'll be sorry." He grabbed me by my upper arms and squeezed, hard. And as if that didn't hurt enough, he shoved me against the building so my head snapped back and connected with the brick. "Are you listening, you stupid little bitch?"

"Get your hands off me."

"You know, I could snap your neck right now if I wanted to."

"Get your fucking hands off me *now.*"

"I could erase you right here and now, and nobody would ever know I did it."

"Except the hundred people who just saw us leave together." I was sounding increasingly desperate, and I knew it. "There are plenty of witnesses, so you better just—"

He pulled me toward him, so close I could smell the peppermint Altoids on his breath. "*Don't—ever—call—me—a—hypocrite,*" he spat out, slamming me against the building again for emphasis.

I was starting to sober up fast.

"Get your hands off me," I said again, for lack of anything else. I struggled to wrench my arms free, but it was no use; the wiry son of a bitch was stronger than he looked. He was also in a frothing fury, which seemed to give him the muscle power of a junkie on angel dust. "Let me go *right now* or you're gonna get arrested."

"Oh, yeah? Who's gonna do that?"

"My boyfriend's a cop. Now get your fucking hands off me."

Instead, he leaned in again, using his whole weight to press me against the building. I was wearing the T-shirt and shorts I'd put on to pick up Mad from the hospital, and I could feel the rough bricks scrape me through the cotton. I tried to scream, but he was too fast for me. He clamped a rock-solid hand over my mouth, and pinned the other arm across my collarbone to keep me trapped.

"Your boyfriend's a cop," he said, sounding (if such a thing is possible) even more creepy than before. "Isn't that just *too cute.* And where is he right now, I wonder? *Not* here. So I can't see how he matters one . . . single . . . bit."

We were nose to nose, and for a second, I thought he was actually going to pull his hand off my mouth and kiss me. Don't ask me why; it was just a freaky impression. Maybe it was because his voice had turned from anger to something scarier, like he was going to teach me a lesson I had no desire to learn. His body was against me, his legs surrounding mine on either side, and that disgusting goatee was scraping against my face.

"Now who's in charge, Alex?" he whispered. "Now who's in charge?"

I kneed him in the nuts. And I mean I kneed him *hard.* It worked like a charm too—he'd had his legs spread to pinion me, so his groin was thoroughly unprotected. He grabbed his stomach and doubled over, and at the behest of a very satisfying surge of adrenaline, I kneed him in his hairy chin and his head snapped back. Then I stomped him on the foot with the heel of my chunky sandal (I'd learned this when I covered a women's self-defense class for my college paper), gave him a shove, and he hit the pavement.

Honestly, I felt like one of Charlie's Angels. Cody would've been damn proud.

I felt considerably less heroic when I took off at a run, breath ragged as I tried desperately to get someplace public before Kahan caught up to me. I cut across Summer Street to the Green, and like a swallow returning to Capistrano, I was back in the Citizen Kane. Mack took one look at me and said I could have one on the house, but I wasn't in the mood; I did, however, indulge in a calming dose of nicotine provided by the guy at the next barstool.

I sat there and puffed on the Marlboro Menthol (yes, I was that desperate), wondering what the hell had just gone down. Unfortunately, all the fear, adrenaline, alcohol, and bravado had conspired to make the memory kind of hazy all of a sudden; the details sort of mushed together. I was fairly sure, however, that I had been stupid enough to inform Tobias Kahan that I knew he'd been in cahoots with Lane Freeman. The ramifications of this were anything but clear, but even with my overactive imagination and a nifty dose of nicotine, I couldn't concoct a world in which this was a good thing.

Smelling like an ashtray, I walked to the paper, eyes darting back and forth as I scanned the street for a professional protester with a bad goatee and a worse temper. I made it to the newsroom unscathed, sat down to write the story, and realized my notebook and backpack were back at the Eggplant.

And what's worse . . . Although my pack was hopefully in the corner of the restaurant where I'd left it, the last time I'd seen my notebook was when I'd dropped it during the tussle. *No way* was I going back there by myself.

A tour of the newsroom found O'Shaunessey in the far corner, where we keep the sportswriters so their mess doesn't spill over and infect the rest of us. He was slotting (also known as "driving the bus"), which means he was coordinating all the scores and stories as they came in. I got him to leave long enough to chaperone me to the Eggplant, where I retrieved my backpack; my notebook was nowhere to be found. Damn.

This meant that Kahan probably had my notes on the Eggplant debacle, which was a drag—but he also had access to whatever else I'd scribbled in there. I wasn't exactly sure, but I had a bad feeling it had a lot to do with Kate Barnett. The good news was that my handwriting is essentially illegible to anybody but me, so he probably couldn't make sense of it anyway. I hoped.

In any event, I was obviously going to have to reconstruct the Eggplant story from memory—never a good idea, now a damn poor one considering the state of my brain. I muddled through, but the thing was half as long (not to mention half as good) as it would've been otherwise.

My duty thus discharged, I didn't know what to do with myself. I could go home, but Melissa was probably you-know-where, and I definitely didn't feel like being alone. I thought about tracking down Cody for post-Kahan consolation, but for some reason I didn't want to; I guess I'd had enough of blubbering on his shoulder for a while. Obviously, at that point I wasn't really considering Kahan to be much of an actual threat. Despite the way he'd manhandled me—and despite my revulsion at going back to the scene of the crime—something about him made me think his bark was way worse than his bite. At least, um . . . I hoped.

I decided to go check on Mad, to see how he was doing alone in his pad for the first time since he got out of the hospital.

Answer: Just fine, thank you.

When I walked in, he was watching a documentary about diving for old World War II plane wrecks in Truk Lagoon, lying on the couch and eating microwave popcorn out of the bag and drinking a neon-orange Gatorade. If it hadn't been for the flowery TV stand and the new coffee table—plus the fact that until his sisters' redecoration he hadn't actually owned a microwave—the whole OD thing might never have happened.

"God, give me some of that," I said, reaching for the popcorn as I flopped down into his battered easy chair. "I'm starved."

He handed it over. "So what went down at hippieland?"

I told him. He was not pleased.

"Son of a bitch," he growled through the popcorn. "That guy comes near you again, I'll clean his clock for him."

I was on the point of reminding him he was presently as

weak as a New Hampshire Democrat, but I decided it might not be good for morale. "Thanks."

"You calling the cops?"

"You mean the cops or the Cody?"

"Either. Both."

"Jesus, I don't know. You think I should?"

"Tell Cody? Yeah. File charges? Up to you. Might not be bad to show that mo-fo the inside of a jail cell. It's not as much fun in there as you'd think."

"Yeah, well, you should know."

"*Ha.*"

"Man, Mad, I don't know what to do. . . . It was just so weird."

"What the hell is wrong with you, Bernier? This guy practically assaulted you."

"Yeah, I know. It just seems so funky in retrospect, you know? One minute, I was mouthing off at him, and the next thing I know, he's got me pinned against a building and he's threatening to wring my neck. That man's got one hell of a temper, I'll tell you that."

"But you still don't think he'd follow through?"

"Oh, hell . . . I don't know. He's a crazy son of a bitch."

"Then why the fuck aren't you calling the cops?"

"I don't . . . Wait, okay, maybe I do. Truth is, I think I'd be more inclined to report it if it weren't for Cody."

"Huh?"

"I guess, well, I'm perfectly happy having the cops cart his ass off to the slam. I just don't want Cody to find out about it, that's all."

"Why the hell not?"

"Because I'm sick of crying on his shoulder and I'm sick of having him worry about me."

"So you think it'd be better if you let this guy get off scot-free so he can come around and mess you up some other time? Jesus, Alex, *now* which one of us is acting like a self-destructive fool?"

"Come on, lighten up. And he didn't actually hit me or anything. He just kind of . . . manhandled me a lot. Besides, if I press charges, the whole thing's gonna be in the paper, and goddamn Ochoa's gonna hafta write a story about it."

"So?"

"So I'm sick of being *in* the news instead of just writing about it, okay?"

"Too bad. You're telling Cody and that's that."

"Who elected you my fairy godfather, anyway?"

"You saved my life. That means I'm responsible for you from now on."

"You moron. It's the other way around—*I'm* responsible for *you* from now on."

"Then you have to do what I say."

"Aren't you listening? I'm responsible *for* you, not *to* you."

"Whatever," he said. "Sounds like the same thing to me."

CHAPTER
24

I told Cody. It was inevitable, of course; Mad just made me do it faster. I called him on his cell, spilled the whole thing, and got exactly the reaction I'd been afraid of. He was furious, determined to make me press charges, and more than happy to separate the guy's head from the rest of his body with his own two hands.

"I think the department frowns on that sort of thing," I said.

"I'll make it look like he tripped," he said.

I knew he was joking—mostly joking, at least—but it took considerable verbal gymnastics to calm him down. In the end, I agreed to make a complaint without necessarily pressing charges; that way, Cody could have some uniforms shake him up without landing me on the *Monitor*'s page three.

He asked if I wanted him to come over, but I told him I was okay—the instinct to preserve my dignity (for once in my life) more powerful than my desire to be cuddled. I therefore slept badly and reported for work the next day with some startlingly attractive bags under my eyes. I was groping for coffee and trying to remember what I was supposed to cover when Lillian appeared at my elbow.

"I was mistaken," she said.

"Huh?"

"I'd thought Coach Laughton wouldn't speak to you directly, but apparently he'd like to."

"Who?"

"Off the record."

"What are you . . . *Oh*. The Griffin Academy."

"He's expecting you in his office at noon. The school hosts a summer day camp, but he has a break then."

"Okay," I said, gulping so fast I got a noseful of powdered creamer. "What'd you tell him?"

"That you were asking after this Koigi Barnett."

"That's all?"

"That's all."

"And now he wants to talk to me?"

"I was surprised as well," she said as we walked back to the cityside desks. "I gathered the boy was a favorite of his. Or perhaps he was a thorn in his side—either way, Coach Laughton isn't neutral on the subject. That much I could tell."

"I owe you one."

"As a matter of fact . . . I was wondering if you might care to purchase some raffle tickets for the quilting guild."

"What do I win?"

"An Amish wedding blanket."

"Just what I need." I reached for my wallet. "How much are we talking?"

"A dollar each," she said. "But a book of six just costs five. Isn't that a bargain?"

My assignment for the day proved to be a profile of the new city attorney who, like just about every lawyer in town, was both a graduate of the Benson law school and a card-carrying member of the A.C.L.U. I could've written it in my sleep, which was a lucky thing considering my relative state of (un)consciousness. I scheduled a lunch interview with her for one o'clock, spent the morning cleaning the gigantic pile of press releases off my desk and churning out city briefs, and made it to the Griffin Academy at twelve.

The school is perched on the west side of the lake, and it looks like a castle—one of three castles, in fact, since all the buildings were once part of an enormous estate that everyone in town collectively refers to as "Xanadu." On the left is a paleontology museum; on the right is a massage school; the Griffin Academy is in the middle.

I found my way to the coach's office. It looked a whole lot like a coach's office, with various balls and sticks and clipboards piled about, and smelling like the oil you use on a catcher's mitt. The man himself was behind a desk that was way too small for him, eating chicken salad on a croissant with a big wad of sprouts snaking out the sides. He was maybe forty, African-American, and burly enough to outweigh Brian Cody. He sported a goatee—a neatly clipped one—and the very sight of it made me want to scream *Would you guys please shave already?*

"Coach Laughton?"

"Ms. Bernier?"

"Yeah."

"You write those movie reviews."

"'Alex on the Aisle.' Yeah."

"I very seldom agree with you."

"Neither do most people."

"Sit down." I did. In fact, his voice was so commanding I probably would've rolled over and played dead if he'd told me to. "Ms. Comstock said you wanted to talk about Kenny Barnett."

"Who? You mean Koigi?"

"Koigi was his birth name. Kenny was his American name. He prefers it—at least he used to. I don't know about now."

"I didn't know that."

"What *do* you know?"

"About Koigi—I mean Kenny? Not much." I decided to stick with the truth, albeit an edited version. "I was just doing a story about his mom's memorial service and he didn't show up, or I don't think he did anyway. I was just wondering why."

He took a bite of his sandwich and a long swig of apple juice. "I expect he probably didn't. Even if he could, I don't think he'd be inclined to."

"Could? Why couldn't he? Is he still traveling?"

"Traveling?" He laughed, but he neither looked nor sounded amused. "Where did you hear that?"

"That's what Professor Barnett told one of our reporters."

"I see. Well, Kenny wasn't traveling, at least not the last I heard. He was in jail."

"What?"

"I should say he was in juvenile detention. The D.A. wanted to try him as an adult, but Kenny's mother convinced the judge to treat him as a youthful offender."

"For what?"

He smiled, more genuinely this time. "You mean what did he do, or what did he get caught for?"

"Both, I guess."

He sighed, pushed back the empty take-out clamshell, and put his feet up on the desk. "Kenny was a very troubled young man. Life didn't exactly give him a fair shake."

"But he got rescued from that—"

"He lost his parents, he was subjected to war and starvation, and he was pulled from his home to a place utterly foreign to him. And that was all by the age of eleven."

"Yeah, but——"

"Think about it, Ms. Bernier. How must a Gabriel winter have felt to a boy who'd known nothing but hundred-degree heat? How did he deal with cars, or school——or even a can opener, for Pete's sake? How do you think he managed to make sense of it all?"

"I, um . . . Didn't his mother help him?"

"His mother didn't take the time out from her research to bother with him. Or with his sister, either, for that matter."

"But why would she bring them here if she was just going to——"

"Adopting them was a symbol," he said. "A political act."

"Are you saying he would've been better off if she left him there?"

"That's a loaded question. All I'm saying is, he didn't have it easy. The only thing he had in the world was his older sister, and then he lost her too. She died in a car accident when he was fifteen."

"I heard that. What happened?"

Laughton gave a deep sigh and shifted in his chair, like his back hurt. "Rainy night. She was driving; he was in the passenger seat; neither one of them had a seat belt on. Off the road, into a tree, and that was it——for all intents and purposes he was alone in the world. She was only two years older."

"Jesus."

"So that's the story."

"Wait a minute. You never told me what he did to wind up in jail. Plus whatever it was he didn't get caught for."

Another sigh. "First, before he came to G.A., he was picked up locally for shoplifting quite a few times. He didn't officially get kicked out of Gabriel High, but if his mother hadn't transferred him, he would've been expelled. He'd gotten into some scrapes with other kids——he had a very short fuse, that's for sure."

"Like what?"

"Once, another student at Griffin made fun of his name, his African name, and Kenny vandalized his bike—bashed it up nearly beyond recognition. His mother paid for a new one, a better one, and that was the end of it. And he had trouble in school—of course, academically he was already way behind when he started school in the States, and he kept being held back. . . . Even though he was small for his age, he still stuck out like a sore thumb, which was the worst thing in the world to him."

"How do you mean?"

"All Kenny wanted was to fit in. That's why he went by his American name—he just wanted to be another American kid. But his mom insisted on Koigi; she said he had to stay in touch with his African heritage. She seemed to consider it a character flaw that he didn't want to wear kente cloth over his school uniform."

"I take it you didn't like her very much."

"I barely spent more than five minutes with the woman, not that I didn't try. She just never had time to meet with me about her son. In my book, *that's* a character flaw."

"Even if the reason she was so busy was because she was trying to end world hunger?"

He cocked an eyebrow at me. "You know the expression in the mosaic on the bridge over the inlet?"

"'Think globally, act locally'?"

He nodded. "That woman was so worried about the fates of children she'd never met, she barely thought about the ones under her own roof."

"So how did he end up in jail? And where did he go, anyway?"

"To Spofford. Ah—I see from the expression on your face that you've heard of it."

"Not a nice place. The kiddie Attica."

"More or less. As to what he did . . . It was basically just more of the same, only worse. One day, he took the bus to Elmira to see a minor-league baseball game, and he got into an argument at the park over something—probably some perceived slight. Kenny was small, but . . . It sounds funny, but I always thought of him as a piranha. He was fast, and he could inflict a lot of damage in the blink of an eye. Anyway, as I say, I don't know what they argued about, but the other boy lost some teeth and needed thirty stitches, nearly went blind in one eye. Kenny was charged with assault, and I'm fairly sure Professor Barnett made some sort of monetary settlement with the victim's family to hush it up. At any rate, I never saw anything about it in the *Monitor*."

"There's nothing in our files. I looked him up, and we don't have anything on him personally. There's a story about his mother adopting him and his sister back when it happened, but that was filed under his mother's name."

"And doesn't that just say it all?"

"Um . . . Do you know when he got out of jail?"

"I imagine on his eighteenth birthday, whenever that was."

"But he'd be out now?"

"Unless he did something else to get put back in."

"Coach, let me ask you something. . . . Do you think he's dangerous?"

"I think I just explained to you that he is. Or at least he was. But as I said, I think all of it was based on anger at what his life was like. He took it out on the whole world."

"Do you think he would've wanted to hurt his mother?"

If I was expecting the same horrified look I'd gotten from Skinny Chuck, I was disappointed. I barely got a raised eyebrow.

"Are you asking me if I think he killed her?"

"I guess I'm asking you if you think he's capable of it."

"Kate Barnett was murdered by anti-genetic-engineering protesters. Everyone knows that."

"Yeah, I know everyone does. I was just trying to get a picture of Kenny, that's all."

"I know people, Ms. Bernier, and I'm not sure I believe you."

"Look, I've never met the guy. I'm just wondering what he's like, what he could or couldn't do."

"And I'm really not comfortable speculating."

"Fair enough." I got up to go, then sat down again. "There's something else I'm wondering about. How come you're even talking to me? Lillian told me you're usually not much for the press."

"Good question. I happen to have a good answer."

"Yeah?"

"All the time I knew him, I wished somebody would take an interest in Kenny Barnett," he said. "And out of the blue, you did. How in the world could I say no?"

∽✦∼

I drove down the hill from Xanadu feeling increasingly glum, the image of Kate Barnett as an absentee mom making my stomach hurt. Truth be told, I liked the image of her as a martyr a whole lot better—bashed-in cranium and all.

A political act. That's how Laughton had described Barnett's motivation for adopting the two Somalian children. He'd meant it as an insult, but hey . . . Why does anybody have kids in the first place?

Is it vanity? Replacement value? The burning desire to pass on your DNA? To make sure there'll be somebody around to sign the papers and put you in a home?

Okay, I'll cop to it: The concept of motherhood terrifies me. Never mind how cute and conservative my mom thinks the potential Bernier-Cody offspring might turn out; the very idea of a job that high-maintenance, from which you never get a vacation and you can't resign, gives me the heebie-jeebies in a big way.

"But you have a dog," says my mother, the aspiring grandma and veteran litigator. "*That's* a big responsibility, isn't it?"

"Yeah," I say, "but you can tie the dog out back all day, and nobody calls the cops."

I mention this by way of explaining why I wasn't anywhere near ready to write off Kate Barnett. I mean, so what if she wasn't Carol Brady? The woman was busy trying to save the world, for chrissake. You can't expect her to have time for bake sales and the P.T.A., now can you?

Not for the first time, I wondered just why I was so obsessed with understanding the real Kate. It wasn't just the know-thy-victim thing; I kept coming back to the idea that she'd satisfied some sort of cockeyed ideal: the poster girl for self-actualized womanhood. And damn it—she was letting me down.

I cheered myself up with a cheesy comestible from Schultz's, where I'd arranged to meet the new city attorney for our lunch interview. The chat was as straightforward as I'd predicted, and I had the story filed by three-thirty. I then proceeded to try and look as busy as possible, lest Bill foist another assignment on me. I was sitting there doing my civil servant impression—to wit, moving papers from one pile to the other and back again—when I was seized by an urge to annoy my bosses. I shot up and marched into Marilyn's office before I lost my nerve.

"You should hire Mad back," I said.

"Since when are you the goddamn publisher?" she said.

The conversation degenerated from there. I believe I did some top-quality whining, however.

"Get out of my office," she said five minutes later. "You're giving me a headache."

"Come on, you gotta give him another chance. He was here for, like, ten years."

"His job didn't seem to matter to him," she said, thumping a baseball from palm to palm. "Why the hell should it matter to me?"

"Because he's a good reporter. He's a *great* reporter. With his science clips, he could've gone just about anywhere."

"So let him."

"But—"

"And with the booze problem he's got, he's not fit for a metro and you know it."

"Are you serious? I'd think it'd make him singularly qualified."

"*Ha.* Okay, Alex, that was a good one."

"Will you at least think about it?"

"*Jee-zus,* will you quit already?"

"He's cleaned up his act." She gave me the patented Marilyn fish-eye. "Really, he has. I swear."

"Cleaned it up how?"

"He's hardly drinking at all."

"Tell him to call me when he goes cold turkey."

"Come on, he'll never go cold turkey. But he's got it under control."

"Alex, the man tried to kill himself. He needs professional help."

"No, he didn't."

"Excuse me?"

"Mad says he didn't take the pills on purpose, and I think he's telling the truth."

"That's cuckoo-bananas."

"Hey, you know damn well crazier stuff than that's gone down around here."

"Okay, that much I can't deny. . . . But are you honestly telling me Madison says somebody poisoned him?"

"Yeah."

She barked out a laugh and shook her head. "Man, I always *knew* one of those women of his was going to turn out to be trouble."

I didn't see the point in contradicting her. "So will you think about it?"

"What makes you think he'd want back in anyway?"

"Are you kidding? He'd kill to come back. He told me . . . Look, I probably shouldn't say anything, but he told me that before he, er, got sick . . . he was planning to put together some big story package so he could drop it on your desk and convince you to take him back."

That got her. "Really? You're not just bullshitting me?"

"Yeah. I mean, no—I'm totally serious. So will you think about it? Please?"

"Madison's a head case."

"Come on, boss, who around here isn't?"

"You've got a point. Tell him to call me."

"You're gonna give him another chance?"

"Eventually, probably, yeah," she said with another canine chuckle. "But first I'm gonna have me a good old time watching him grovel."

CHAPTER
25

That night, Cody and I went on a date like a couple of secret agents. This involved going to the multiplex separately, where he picked up the free pass I left for him at the counter and we rendezvoused in the darkened theater.

What this actually accomplished, I couldn't tell you. But it was a lot of fun, even without the trench coats.

The movie was some testosterone-laden action flick with lots of exploding helicopters. I was reviewing it for my column, which was unfortunate since (truth be told) I spent less time watching the film than necking with my escort.

Afterward we went back to his place, where Zeke practically knocked me over with kisses. Then his owner did the same. Things were looking up.

"Not that I want to break the mood," he said when we'd segued to the snuggling, "but I thought you might want to know we picked up Tobias Kahan. He wasn't happy."

I kissed him on the neck. "What happened?"

"He denied the whole thing. Said you were . . . Well, never mind what he said."

"Come on, tell me." He didn't. "Hey, you gotta tell me."

"He said . . . He claimed it was the other way around. Said you were, er, all over him."

"You mean he said *I* assaulted *him?*"

"Sort of."

"No *way*. He said I . . . what? I hit on him or something?"

"Basically."

"Oh, my God. What did you say? *Please* tell me you resorted to police brutality."

"I wasn't there. Kind of a conflict of interest, you know."

"So who was?"

"Pete Donner and his partner."

"Swell."

"I thought you'd be relieved Pete was taking care of it."

"Yeah, but the idea of him hearing about me throwing myself at that *troll* is no fun whatsoever."

"He didn't buy it, don't worry."

"So now what? It's his word against mine?"

"You've got the bruises on your side."

"Oh, hell, he'll probably just say he acted in self-defense."

"Yeah, he did."

"Oh, *hell*. What happens now?"

"You want to press charges?"

"Not particularly."

"Then there's not much. I'd been hoping the uniforms would put the fear of God into him, but apparently he's had more than his share of run-ins with the cops. Didn't even faze him."

"Can't you, you know . . . dump him on the other side of the county line or something?"

"Wish I could oblige, little lady. Unfortunately, the man's got what you bleeding hearts call civil liberties."

"Rats." I wriggled my chin against his neck. "So what's going on with the case? I mean, the *cases* . . ."

"You know," he said, tightening an arm around me, "I'm

pretty sure this is what the F.B.I. was talking about when they said 'fraternization.'"

I lifted my head to survey the territory. "You lying here naked with a reporter while she pumps you for information about two highly sensitive"—I ran my hand down his stomach—"investigations?"

"Er . . . yeah. What you said."

"This mean you're not gonna tell me zip? Even though I've been a very good girl about keeping it in the boudoir the whole past year?"

"Yes . . . and no."

"Meaning?"

"No, I'm not going to tell you about the Barnett case, because there's not a damn thing to tell. We've interviewed dozens and dozens of people, and we're no closer to closing it than the day you found her."

"Shit."

"Yeah."

"What did . . . ? Never mind."

"What?"

"Nothing. I was going to ask you something, but I'm not. Mad's on it anyway. Let's just not mix business with pleasure, okay?"

"Hey, you're the one who asked me what was up with the case."

"So I'm the queen of inconsistency. I know for a fact it just makes me more alluring." He snorted, which did not sound like a compliment. "You men know so little."

"That's a fact."

"Was that the yes or the no?"

"Huh?"

"When I asked if you were going to tell me, you said 'yes and no.' Which was it?"

"Ah. That was . . . Well, I'm not sure which one it was.

But as I said, there's nothing new on the Barnett case. The bombing is something else again."

"Oh, yeah?"

"We're about to make an arrest."

"You're kidding. Who?"

"That, I can't say. In the name of not mixing business with pleasure, of course."

"I take it back."

"Look, I really can't tell you. I promised Chief Hill. I said if we did happen to run into each other, we'd steer clear of that kind of talk. I gave him my word."

"So why did you tell me about the arrest?"

"Consider it a tip. No different from what any other cop would give to a reporter he was favorably inclined to."

"When?"

"The arrest? I'm betting within the next few days."

"No way. Really? You're that close?"

"Hey, don't look at me. I'm just the local muscle. We owe it all to the F.B.I. and the A.T.F."

"What does the A.T.F. have to do with it?"

"Good question. From what the Bureau guys tell me, soon as anything blows up, the A.T.F. likes to come sniffing around claiming jurisdiction. Makes 'em feel good. Anyway, I'd expect some big press junket in the afternoon. Around three."

I groaned into his shoulder. "Just in time for the evening news to scoop our ass but good."

"Yeah, but I don't think that's on purpose. These guys just think TV, that's all."

"Is that why you're giving me the heads up?"

"Seems only fair to level the playing field."

"Awfully sporting of you."

"I aim to please," he said, and kissed me for a while.

"Hey, what'd you think of the movie, anyway?"

"You mean the part we actually saw?" I poked him in the ribs. "Dumb but fun, I suppose," he said. "If I ever see a realistic cop character in one of those action movies, I'll be a monkey's uncle."

"You mean you don't usually shoot the bad guys with two guns at once?"

"Only on national holidays."

I kissed him some more. "Damn, Cody, it's good to see you."

"You too."

"Yeah?"

"Yeah," he said, "and it's good to see you smile like that. Seems like it's been a long time."

" 'I have of late, though wherefore I know not, lost all my mirth.' My dog wrote that."

"Hey, you just made a joke. Nice to see that again too."

"Jesus, have I really been that much of a downer lately?"

"Uh-huh."

"Oh. Well, I've had a lot on my mind."

"I know."

"You don't know the half of it."

He rolled over on his side to face me. "Then tell me."

"What would you say," I said, "if I told you Mad was poisoned?"

∽∾∾∾

I wasn't faking when I said Mad was "on it"—meaning the search for the elusive grad student, which was turning out to be a lot harder than I'd expected.

When I'd told him Marilyn was thinking about taking him back, he'd gotten all happy and hyper and started pacing around his apartment demanding something to keep him occupied. I'd suggested perhaps he might like to figure out just who the hell had slipped him the near-fatal Mickey—not only to catch the son of a bitch but to prevent him (or her) from giving it another try.

Mad, however, had surprised me: He copped to his limitations. "It's too damn soon, Bernier," he'd said. "I'll deal with it—I gotta deal with it—but not when I'm so far off my game."

So I'd sicced him on tracking down whoever had sent him the letter. That, of course, had been the question I'd been about to ask Cody; if they'd interviewed dozens of witnesses, surely they'd spoken to her. After all, I knew for a fact that Cynthia Chu had given them her name over a week ago. But in terms of relationship maintenance, digging for specifics had seemed a very bad idea all of a sudden. And sure enough, Cody had promised the chief he'd keep his mouth shut. Maybe there was hope for us after all.

"Okay," Mad was saying over hot-and-sour soup at the Chinese buffet, where he was cashing in the rain check from a few days before. "I've got it narrowed down to three people." He consulted his soup-flecked notebook. "Ann Tucker, Rebecca Slack, and Christina Downs. It's gotta be one of them."

"Why so many?"

"I went up to campus and did a bunch of digging through student directories, trying to figure out who left plant science a couple of years back but was here for a couple of years before that."

"But we know she was on Barnett's team, right? So can't you just go ask the—"

He shook his head. "The department has really battened down the hatches. Nobody's saying diddly to the press."

"Are you serious? I did a bunch of interviews just a few—"

"Well, you must've grilled them over a spit, because they

ain't talkin' to nobody nohow. Somebody must've put the kibosh on media stuff even the least bit connected to the bombings and Barnett, because everything's getting referred to the
news service."

"Huh. No wonder Ochoa's been looking so glum."

"Yeah, and get this: I was up there looking through the department scrapbooks they keep in the main office, trying to
see if there maybe was a group picture of Barnett's grad students, and the secretary bounced me out on my ear. That's
why I had to go through all the student directories in the library."

"No *way*. And those three people you mentioned all left
around the same time?"

"Yeah. So it could be any one of them. I'll just have to
keep digging."

"We know she was supposed to get a Ph.D. but only
wound up getting a master's. Does that help?"

Again with the head shake. "Plant science is a damn rig-
orous department—Barnett's program doubly so. Bailing
with just a master's isn't that uncommon."

"Damn. So we don't know for sure if any of those three
was on Barnett's team?"

"Nope."

"What are you going to do now?"

"I've got some ideas up my sleeve. I'll keep you posted."

"Look," I said a little while later, once he'd gotten good
and logy on MSG and was less likely to kill me, "I kind of
told Cody about you and the poison thing."

" 'The poison thing'?"

"What else do you want me to call it? Anyway, we were
sort of having, you know, an intimate moment, and it kind of
slipped out."

"What did you tell him?"

"That you told me you didn't take the Percodan, and I believe you."

"Good."

"Good?"

"What are you, surprised?"

"You usually aren't so hot on other people knowing your business."

"Sure 'nough. But in this case, I like it a hell of a lot better than the alternative. I'd just as soon not have Cody think I tried to make a rush for the exit, you know?"

"Ah. You care what he thinks of you."

"He's a guy I respect. One of about five."

"High praise."

"What'd he say when you told him?"

"At first, he didn't buy it. Told me he admired my loyalty but thought you were selling me a bill of goods."

"But you convinced him?"

"Eventually."

"How?"

"Same way you convinced me. I told him you'd never do that to your friends."

"And once he bought it . . . ?"

"You mean is he gonna rush out and try to bust somebody? Hardly seems practical at the moment. But he's worried about you. He said if somebody really tried to off you, dollars to doughnuts they'd try again."

"He actually said 'dollars to doughnuts'?"

"He's a cop. They're very partial to doughnuts."

"Har-har."

"Seriously, he said come talk to him. Like, soon."

"I will, I guess. I dunno, Bernier, I still can't believe this really went down."

"Used to thinking of yourself as indestructible, eh?"

"Give me a break with your psychobabble shit, will ya?

What I meant was, I can't believe somebody out there would want me dead bad enough to pull a stunt like that. It's creeping me out, I'll tell you."

"Hey, welcome to my world."

"You've been on the receiving end of your fair share of ill will, I'll give you that."

"Yeah. And at this point, I'm getting plenty of it from in-house."

"You mean Brad?"

"Him, yeah—the usual muckraking, misogynist bullshit. But I was thinking more of Ochoa."

"I thought you two were working together on the Barnett thing. The Shelley Freeman one too, right?"

I groaned and tossed my chopsticks onto my plate. "We *were,* yeah. But like I told you, once Barnett got killed, he pretty much bailed on Shelley. And since he got going on it, he's been playing the lone gunman act to the hilt."

"Doesn't want to share the wealth?"

"I guess. I don't know. There's something weird going on with him. Everytime he sees me coming, he runs the other way. I mean, I knew the man was allergic to joint bylines, but this is ridiculous."

"You call him on it?"

"I would if I could get him alone for five seconds."

"Whew. So now what?"

"Good question," I said. "When it comes to the Barnett thing, I say screw Ochoa—if he's gonna go all commando on us, there's nothing we can do about it. See what you can do to track down that grad student pronto. I've got a feeling she can tell us a hell of a lot somehow. Hey, I've been meaning to ask you—you ever heard of a guy named Alan Frantz?"

"Broccoli guy. Yeah."

"Huh?"

"He was working on this project to design a broccoli re-sistant to—"

"Whatever. What do you know about him?"

"I was just telling you, he's a prof up in plant science. What about him?"

"He got denied tenure."

"Oh, right, I heard that. Bummer."

"You think that makes him a suspect?"

"You mean, do I think the guy got so pissed he bashed Barnett's head in real hard?"

"I guess so, yeah."

"Um, no."

"You sure?"

"Bernier, this guy Frantz was not what you'd call a he-man."

"It doesn't take that much muscle to whack somebody over the head if they're looking the other way."

"True, but Frantz doesn't have it in him. Trust me. Be-sides, I think he's off teaching someplace else by now. Ten-nessee, maybe."

"Hell, wouldn't getting shafted to Tennessee make you mad enough to kill somebody?"

"You've got a point there. But I still think you're barking up the wrong tree."

"Okay, riddle me this. Do you know who Barnett's friends were?"

"Hmm . . . Not off the top of my head. There's a bunch of lady professors who get together for this power-lunch thing every other week during the semester, but I'm not sure if she was part of it or not."

"You mean those profs who got Hillary Clinton to eat with them that one time? When she was up here stumping?" He nodded. "I did something on that, remember? They wouldn't

let me cover it, but I talked to one of the members later. . . .
Mehta-somebody . . ."

"Reena Mehta. Big deal in nanofab. Chick loves me."

"You wanna talk to her and see if she knew Barnett?
Seems as good a start as any."

"What do you want to know?"

"The usual. You know, what Barnett was like, who she
was close to. The woman still totally eludes me. It's driving
me kind of nuts, actually."

"Gee, I didn't notice."

"You ever met her ex?"

"The med-school prof? A couple times, yeah. I did a
package on him a while back. Before you got here."

"What's his name, anyway?"

"Kravitz. First name Oren."

"What's he like?"

"Big muckety-muck in in vitro fertilization. You know,
Benson runs this clinic down in New York that has the highest success rate in the—"

"You have *got* to be kidding me."

"What?"

"Barnett is this huge advocate for population control, so
much so that she goes and has her goddamn tubes tied, and
you're telling me her ex-husband is a *fertility* doctor?"

"Yeah."

"Don't you think it's just a tad ironic?"

"Guess I never really thought about it. They've been split
up a long time."

"Is he remarried?"

"Yeah, and three kids. Real active in the conservative syn-
agogue—at least he was when I did the piece. I don't usually deal with a lot of personal crap, but he made a point of
it."

"Interesting."

He speared a pork dumpling with a single chopstick and popped it into his mouth. "Talked to Marilyn today."

"Yeah?"

"She said she'd think about it."

"That's good, huh?"

"I gotta find something pretty soon. I'm running out of cash. And, man, if I didn't have the health insurance from the severance thing, I'd be in big trouble. You don't wanna hear about the hospital bill."

"So what are you gonna do?"

"Mack said he'd give me some shifts at the Citizen, but I don't know. . . ."

"Didn't you used to bartend in college?"

He shrugged. "Might be kinda weird. I dunno. Sammy up at the liquor store in Collegetown said he could use somebody for late nights. I might do that instead. Probably wouldn't run into anybody I know that way."

"I'm noticing a disturbing pattern to your career options."

"Hey," he said, "you gotta stick with what you know."

CHAPTER
26

The press release came via fax the next morning. If brevity is indeed the soul of wit, the grainy page was a real gut-grabber. "Press conference, Gabriel Criminal Justice Building [this being the fancy new name for the old, distinctly unfancy police station], 3 P.M." was all it said—not even any mention of what the press conference was going to be about.

It was, in fact, a miracle that I even saw the thing. Ochoa grabbed it off the fax machine so fast he practically got ink on his fingers. He'd known it was coming, of course—I'd told Bill and Bill had told him—but for some reason he felt the need to be a pig about it. For the millionth time, I considered asking him just what the hell was going on, and for the millionth time, I figured all I'd get for my trouble was a resounding *go-screw-yourself.*

So imagine his delight when Bill assigned us both to cover the press conference. Why he opted for the double-team approach, I wasn't quite sure—though I suspected it had a lot to do with teaching Ochoa a lesson, Bill having a short fuse for the prima donna act. We walked over there together, or rather I tailed him as he broke the land-speed record from the *Monitor* to the cop shop. If I thought this was going to be a golden opportunity to make nice, I was sorely disappointed.

"Lovely weather we're having," I said.

"Whatever."

"Not a cloud in the sky."

No answer. Truth be told, he started walking even faster. My attempt to attract flies with honey was summarily chucked.

"Jesus, Ochoa, what the hell is wrong with you? You've been acting like a total freak the past few weeks."

"I'm doing my job. Get off my back."

"Doing your job, my ass. You won't even talk to me about the Barnett thing, and you've totally given Shelley Freeman the heave-ho after you were all hot and bothered to bust her out of prison. What gives?"

"None of your goddamn business."

"Gee, thanks. That really explains a lot."

He stopped so suddenly I passed him and had to retreat a few paces. "You know, Madison was right about you. You're a nosy pain the ass."

"Mad did not say that about me."

He laughed, not an alluring sound. "He sure as hell did."

"Oh, yeah? When?"

"That day he got canned. Right in Bill's office."

I exhaled, normal breathing abilities returning in a rush. "Come on, that doesn't count. He was drunk out of his mind. It doesn't count."

"Whatever." He started walking again.

"Jesus, what did I do to piss you off so much?"

"Nothing. You didn't do anything. Now just leave me alone, all right? Just let me do my job and you do yours and we'll get along fine."

"This is psychotic." He ignored me, and very effectively

too. "You don't just go sloughing off your friends like this. It's not normal human behavior."

"We aren't friends."

"Of course we are. What the hell are you talking about?"

No response. Fortunately or unfortunately, at this point we were at the front door of the so-called Criminal Justice Building, so the meaningful talk was at an end. We went inside and walked into your garden-variety media frenzy.

I should've been tipped off by all the TV trucks outside, but I'd been so intent on cracking the Ochoa nut I'd barely even noticed. But there were at least a dozen cameras there, with call letters from stations all over upstate New York, network affiliates and everything. The NPR reporter was present and accounted for, as were a bunch of local radio guys, somebody from the A.P., and a certain, very contented fellow named Gordon Band.

I ditched Ochoa and went to stand next to him, all the chairs having been cleared out to make room for a veritable ton of TV equipment. "So when you gotta file?" I asked. He just smirked at me. "Come on, Gordon, what's the big deal? I was just wondering, that's all."

More smirking. "Try four hours ago."

"Excuse me?"

"You asked me when I was gonna file. And the answer is, four hours ago."

"What?"

"Most of it, anyway. Gotta leave room for whatever crap they shovel out here, right?"

"Somebody tipped you off." Not a question.

"It's called having sources."

"Hey, I've got some of my own, you know."

"No offense, sweetheart, but being in the pocket of the local cops doesn't quite compare to having an in with the F.B.I."

He dragged out the acronym—*eff-bee-aye*—just to make me squirm.

"Well, bully for you. It's a miracle you even bothered to show up to the press conference."

"Gotta dot your i's and cross your t's, right?"

"Right. So what'd this guy tell you?"

He whistled a little tune, looking so self-satisfied as to invite a good pillow smothering.

"Come on," I said, "give me a break. We're all gonna hear it in about five minutes."

"Read all about it in tomorrow's *Times*."

"He give you a bunch of stuff off the record?"

"Wouldn't you like to know," he said, and smirked some more.

The conference lasted less than half an hour. It was presided over by someone named Special Agent Douglas Broderick, a clean-cut chap who looked like he never enjoyed anything, ever. His hair was cropped marine-style, his jaw was so square it resembled something off the comics page, and his entire demeanor said he held the media in slightly lower esteem than the Branch Davidians.

Still, he was a font of information, delivered in a staccato style that let you know you were getting what he wanted to give you and not a syllable more. He stood at the front of the room, wearing a blue F.B.I. windbreaker (as though the sprinkler system threatened to drench him any second) and flanked by a cadre of white guys. I counted nine, but the only ones I recognized were Cody and the chief. I heard later the negotiations about how many men each agency could send—not to mention where they'd stand in relation to Broderick—took two whole hours. Behold my tax dollars at work.

"Thank you for coming," he said. "I'm going to read a statement, then take questions. Remember this is an ongoing investigation. Some subjects should and will be off-limits. Understand?"

There was generalized nodding, and Broderick turned his attention to the TV cameras.

"At six A.M., as a result of a joint investigation by the Federal Bureau of Investigation, the Gabriel Police Department, the New York State Police, the Walden County Sheriff's Department, Benson University security, and the Bureau of Alcohol, Tobacco, and Firearms"—I could swear he grimaced a little over that last bit—"an arrest was made in the June twenty-first bombing of the Benson University plant-science building. Four individuals were apprehended at their homes this morning, three here in Gabriel, New York, and one in Rutland, Vermont. Those individuals are Richard Daniel Krikstein, Elaine Dillon Gilbert, and Harlin Mott, no middle name, in Gabriel. In Vermont, the brother of Harlin Mott, Ethan Mott, also no middle name, was apprehended. All four are believed to be members of a group called the Organic Activist Tribe. At this time, they're being charged with . . ."

He rattled off a laundry list of misbehavior, starting off with one count of homicide in the death of Philip Herzog, and including seven more (albeit attempted) for the people with the most serious injuries. Throw in the blowing-up of the building itself, the transportation of bomb-making materials across state lines, and conspiracy to do all of the above—and, well, the four suspects were clearly in a heap of trouble.

I wrote down all the info, and when I got to Elaine Gilbert's name, it stopped me cold. I got the feeling I'd heard it before . . . but where? I flipped through the previous pages in my notebook, but I couldn't find it. Had it been in the one I dropped in the scuffle with Kahan? I sure as hell hoped not. But since I've never been good about labeling them, I'd have to go back through all the others on my desk (and in my backpack and at my house) to be sure.

When it came time for Q & A, though, it occurred to me that there was a shortcut to the Gilbert question. To wit: acting like a goddamn reporter.

Unfortunately, Special Agent Tank McNamara didn't seem inclined to call on the waggling hand of anybody without a klieg light. He passed me over ten times before I finally got my chance. No offense to my colleagues in the coiffure-and-lip-gloss set, but I couldn't believe none of them thought to ask the question themselves.

"I was wondering," I said, "if you could tell us something about who these four people are."

I promptly got glared at by a girl in a dark green suit whose hair was a shade of red not found in nature. But Broderick didn't miss a beat, just pulled a sheet of paper from the middle of the pile in front of him with the fluidity of a magician in mid-card-trick.

"Richard Krikstein," he said, "is a member of the Ecstatic Eggplant Vegetarian Restaurant Collective and a journalist for the *Gabriel Monitor*." *Thanks a lot, buddy.* "Harlin Mott is unemployed. Ethan Mott operates an apple orchard in Rutland, Vermont. And Elaine Gilbert . . ."

He spoke slowly, and I realized my snap judgment about Broderick's capacity for joy had been somewhat mistaken. He might not have fun on general principle, but he was sure as hell enjoying this.

"Elaine Gilbert," he said, "is a graduate student in plant science at Benson University."

❧❧❧

The gasp that spread through the crowd was satisfying to everybody in the know, except one. There went Gordon's big scoop—though why he thought the rest of us were too dumb to put two and two together in time for deadline was beyond me.

Anyway, my little question catapulted the room into a frenzy of raised hands and poking microphones, at which point the powers that be ended the press conference toot-sweet. Cody barely had a chance to shoot me a covert salute before he was hustled out with the rest of the law-enforcement types, and Ochoa promptly hightailed it back to the paper. That left me to put in some valuable gloating time with Gordon, who appeared mad enough to spit.

"Son of a bitch told me they weren't releasing the names today," he said, rubbing at his eyes under his glasses. "They goddamn well weren't supposed to release the goddamn names. They were supposed to announce the arrest today and release the actual names tomorrow."

"Why would they do that?"

"I don't know. That's just what I heard they were gonna do. Man, this *sucks*."

"Poor baby."

"Like you care. Aren't you supposed to be back in the newsroom writing right about now?"

"It's Ochoa's story. I was just along for the ride. Bill sent me."

"What for?"

I shrugged. "Either to teach Ochoa some humility, or to make the *Monitor* look like Johnny-on-the-spot. Most likely, both."

He took off his glasses and wiped the finger smudges with his shirttail. "Wanna go grab some coffee?"

"Don't you have to go file something?"

"Yeah, but right now I wanna go jump in one of those gorges of yours," he said as we walked out of the building toward the Green. "Jesus, I am *never* gonna get off this stupid beat. 'Upstate correspondent,' my ass. . . ."

"You were counting on the Ellie Gilbert thing to do you some good, huh?"

He nodded, looking increasingly miserable. "Her name's Elaine."

"Her friends call her Ellie."

Gordon stopped in his tracks. "How the hell would you know?"

"Met her already. Just in passing, though."

"Son of a . . ." He shook his head. "I never even heard of her until my source called me this morning."

"So whatcha got in your piece on her, anyway?"

"Like I'm gonna tell you."

"What's the problem?"

"Problem is you've got plenty of time till deadline to screw me over. *That's* what's the problem."

"Thanks for the vote of confidence. For that, you're buying the coffee."

"No, I'm not."

"Chivalry is truly dead."

"Screw chivalry. You're buying *me* coffee because I'm about to tell *you* something interesting."

I stopped and cocked an eyebrow at him. "About what?"

"About Lane Freeman."

"But . . . I thought you weren't even working on that. I mean, I haven't even come up with anything for you to—"

He offered a derisive snort. "Like I'm gonna sit around and wait for you to hand me an assignment. Who do you think you are, my fucking editor? God, I *hate* my fucking editor. . . ."

"So you've remarked. Now what gives?"

"Am I getting a coffee out of it or aren't I?"

"Oh, hell. Yes, you're getting a coffee out of it. Don't you do anything just to be nice?"

"No."

"Color me surprised."

We went to Café Whatever, where I blew major bucks on a double mocha with a shot of amaretto syrup for the gentleman and all of a dollar on a small java for myself. He made noises about wanting a biscotti in the bargain, but I told him to go to hell.

"So spill," I said once we'd sat down at one of the tables, whose glass tops covered a collection of artsy cut-paper question marks. "What's so hot it earns you a four-dollar drink?"

"Lane Freeman," he said, "was a very naughty boy."

"What do you mean? Naughty how?"

"I'm not entirely sure. But let's just say if he'd lived, he might be the one on his way to the big house right about now."

"Huh?"

"Okay," he said, wiping residual foam off his upper lip, "I've got this source at the I.R.S. Now, he won't go telling me anything about anybody's personal finances, not as such, but he'll tip me off if somebody's in the shit."

"And Freeman was."

"You got it. The man was on a one-way trip to audit city." He paused so I could appreciate the cleverness of the phrase. "Next stop, Club Fed minimum-security prison."

"You're kidding. What did he do?"

"It's more like what he didn't do, which is pay his taxes in a thorough and timely fashion."

"He was a tax cheat?" He nodded. "Man, I hate tax cheats. . . ."

"Then you wouldn't have cared for Mr. Freeman. Apparently, he reported about a third of his income."

"How'd he get caught?"

"Random audit," he said. "Sucks, huh? But from what this guy told me, Freeman was living way beyond his means—big house in Benson Heights, Catholic school for all the kids, two new cars, swimming pool. . . ."

"Doesn't exactly sound like Hugh Hefner to me."

"Yeah, but remember, Benson doesn't pay the really big bucks unless you're a tip-top administrator. No way they could afford that lifestyle on their paychecks, and zip in the way of family money. Plus, he tried to deduct a bunch of stupid stuff, which sent up a red flag. The I.R.S. may be a kinder, gentler outfit nowadays, but this guy had 'bust me' written in big letters on his 1040."

"Wild. So where was all the rest of the money coming from?"

"Good question. I have no idea."

"How do we find out?"

"You know what bank he used? Know anybody there who might give us a little peek at his—"

"No and no."

"Well," he said with a longing look at the biscotti jar, "I'm open to ideas."

"That makes two of us."

He scratched at his scalp for a while. I whirled the metal spoon around my cup (disposable stirrers being distinctly unkosher in these parts) and tried to come up with something brilliant.

"There's a guy he worked with up at the news service, the one who told me Freeman was in cahoots with Kahan. He worked over at the next desk. He might know something."

"Worth a try."

"It'll require the showing of some cleavage."

"I'm sure you'll persevere. What else?"

"We could ask around where he bought all his fancy toys, find out if he paid cash or what."

"What good would that do?"

"I don't know. I'm desperate."

"And I'm gonna be covering greater Rochester for the rest of my natural life."

I played with my spoon some more. "Hold on a second," I said. "I'm a moron. I'm totally ignoring the obvious."

"Meaning?"

"Meaning who the hell knows everything there is to know about a man's finances?"

"His accountant?"

"The right answer," I said, "is the lady who spends the cash."

CHAPTER
27

The stomachache started around three A.M.

At first, I wasn't especially worried—yeah, it was bad enough to wake me up, but I chalked it up to my closing of the Citizen at one-thirty after ingesting two gin and tonics and half a margarita. Then there was the fact that dinner had consisted of some leftover Szechuan tofu that was probably past its prime, and which I had chased with some equally iffy Velveeta Shells & Cheese right out of the Tupperware.

Around three-thirty, I felt like I was going to throw up, and couldn't.

By four, I was doubled over on the bathroom floor, wondering whether I was going to die right then and there.

I hollered for Melissa, but she didn't answer; she was off at Drew's as usual. Still, for some idiotic reason I was inspired to crawl to her room on my hands and knees, in the hope that maybe she just hadn't heard me. Her room looked like it hadn't been occupied in weeks, which it hadn't.

I was starting to lose my higher brain power. No, scratch that; it was already mostly gone.

It dawned on me that I needed help—real, actual, professional, medical help—but curled up there, moaning on the hall floor, I couldn't for the life of me figure out how to get it.

I had a dim thought that finding a phone would be a good idea, but I couldn't remember where the cordless was. I could picture the desktop phone perched on a table in the living room, and that maybe if I made it there and pushed some buttons somebody might come and save me, but the concept of making it down the stairs was downright ridiculous.

It was about then that I realized I was also having trouble breathing, and that my arms and legs were a lot heavier and more prickly than usual. I felt like I was swimming through extremely thick Jell-O, though why this analogy presented itself I couldn't tell you.

You're in trouble, I thought. *You're in very, very big trouble.*

It occurred to me that maybe I was having a stroke, which is one of the myriad horrors you find in the fine print on a package of birth-control pills. *I can't have a stroke,* I thought. *I'm only twenty-seven.* Not the most medically sound concept, I know—and how I was rationalizing the gut-wrenching stomachache into the bargain I have no clue.

I lay there on the hall floor, moaning and whimpering like a damn wounded puppy, and tried like hell to remember where the phone was. But like I said, my brain no longer felt like my own; to say I wasn't thinking clearly implies I was thinking at all.

I'm not sure how I made it back to my room, but the next thing I remember is lying on the ground staring up at my bed, which looked to be about ten feet off the floor. I reached up and felt around for the phone, but it wasn't in the square foot of bed I appeared to be able to reach. My

hand must've moved over to the nightstand, because the
next thing I remember is my alarm clock hitting me on
the head just as a glass of cranberry juice came crashing to
the floor. But there was the phone—cold and sticky and
beautiful—and I managed to press what I hoped was the
right button.

*Hello and thank you for calling Gabriel Cinema Ten,
where you're the star! The following movies and show-
times are good for Friday—*

I'd hit redial. I tried to focus on the keypad, but it was
all blurry. I brought it closer to my face and looked for the
little blue-cross symbol that meant an ambulance—Cody
having supervised the phone programming when we
moved in—but for the life of me, I couldn't find it.

Nine-one-one, I thought. *Dial 911. Come on, you can do
it. You better do it, or you're gonna die.*

I pushed what felt like random buttons, but it rang. I
don't remember who answered, but I do recall that when it
came time for me to ask for help I couldn't talk. I opened
my mouth, at least I thought I did, but no words came out.

Which is probably no surprise, considering the fact that
I was no longer able to feel my tongue.

✎✎✎

The next thing I remember is waking up. Where I was
seemed comparatively unimportant; the very fact that I
woke up at all was a pleasant surprise, and my ability to
use my arms and legs was an unexpected bonus.

For the record, I was in the hospital. I was, in actual
truth, in intensive care—a first even for me. Sitting in a
nearby chair was Detective Brian Cody, whose presence at
my bedside was a depressingly regular occurrence. When I
woke up, I found him slumped down in one of those now-

familiar plastic chairs, apparently asleep. But he opened his eyes almost immediately, blinked, and then just stared at me.

"Hey," I said.

"You're awake."

"I don't feel so good." My voice was raspy and weird, a lot like Mad's when he'd first returned from la-la land. "How . . . How long have I been here?"

"Less than a day."

"What happened to me?"

"Don't worry about that right now."

"Cody . . ."

"How are you feeling?"

"Like I got run over by a truck. What's going on?"

"It was, um . . . food poisoning."

"Jesus, I *knew* that leftover Chinese tasted funny."

"That was it."

"How do you know?"

"We had it tested."

"Already? That's incredibly . . ." Something in his voice pulled me up short. "Wait a minute. What are you not telling me?"

"Sweetheart, just lie back and relax. We can talk about all this later."

"Tell me the truth."

"Honey—"

"Tell me the goddamn truth."

"There's plenty of time to—"

"Tell me."

He stared at his feet for a while. "It wasn't food poisoning," he said. "It was poisoned food."

"Son of a *bitch*."

"Alex, please, try not to get yourself all upset. The doctor said you need to—"

"Upset? Somebody tried to *kill* me. Of course I'm upset. . . ."

"Shh . . ." He came over to sit next to me on the bed, which if you ask me he should've done a hell of a lot earlier. And since we've been together for a while, why he hadn't was pretty damn obvious: It's easier to lie from six feet away. "Honey, listen," he said. "You're going to be fine."

"Then why am I in the I.C.U.?"

"They're just about to move you. You don't need to be here anymore, honest."

"Please, Cody, you gotta tell me what happened. The last thing I remember is . . . I was in all this pain and I was looking for the phone. . . ."

"You got the nine-one-one operator, but all she could hear were these . . . sounds. They sent an ambulance and the cops over, and when nobody answered the door, they broke in."

"They busted the door down? Landlord's gonna love that. . . ."

"It was unlocked."

"I guess . . . I forgot to lock it. I'm such a—"

"Shh . . . Don't worry about it. Don't worry about anything."

"Except that somebody tried to poison me."

"I'll get them, honey. I promise."

Usually, that sort of manly Cody-talk makes me feel better. This time, for whatever reason, it didn't. "Are you really telling me it was in the leftover Chinese?"

"Yeah."

"How do you know already?"

"When they brought you into the E.R., it was obvious to the docs on duty that you'd taken something, and—"

"I did *not*—"

He waved me off. "I know. Of course you didn't. What I should've said was that it was obvious you had something in your system. By the time they had you stabilized and upstairs, one of the uniforms had tracked me down, so I got over here as fast as I could. And once I heard what was wrong with you, and after what you told me about Madison . . ."

"You put two and two together."

He nodded. "You were out cold, so there was nothing I could do here, and I thought if we moved fast we might be able to figure out how it got into you. First thing I could think of was to clean out your refrigerator to see if there was anything in there, and we got lucky."

"Speak for yourself."

"Honey, according to the tox guys, you got damn lucky. Considering what you had in you, well . . . things might not have come out so well."

"Since when does the lab turn around stuff this fast?"

"They can work really fast if they've got a crazy man screaming at them."

"I see."

"We're talking way too much. I should get out of here and let you sleep."

"My head hurts."

"Want me to get a nurse to give you something?"

"Stay here."

He brushed my hair back from my forehead. "All right."

"My God . . . Somebody broke into my house and put—what was it, anyway?" He grimaced, looked back down at his shoes. "Tell me."

"Toxicology isn't final—"

"Cody . . ."

He took in a long breath and let it out in a sigh. "It was

abrin," he said. "The same thing that killed Lane Freeman."

✦✦✦

I got out of the hospital the next day, the *Monitor*'s health
plan having moved me from I.C.U. to the sidewalk in less
than twenty-four hours. It was fine with me, though; if I
was going to feel weak and miserable, I'd just as soon do
it on my couch watching *The Twilight Zone*. Plus, I was
sick to death of people telling me how lucky I was—how
if I hadn't gotten help, I could've wound up dead or shopping for a new set of internal organs.

The fact that I've become something of a household
name in this wee burgh made my near miss a hospital
cause célèbre, so there were nurses and med students and
perky little candy stripers popping in and out of my room
ad nauseam. Being home, with Shakespeare on my lap and
a load of tapioca in the fridge (my guts still being mighty
tender), seemed like a little slice of heaven. Then there
were the doctor's orders to force down as many carbs as
possible—somehow this was supposed to protect me
against postpoisoning liver damage—meaning that I got
to eat glazed doughnuts for the sake of my health.

You might be getting the impression that I shook off my
near-death experience like a case of strep. You'd be wrong.

As a matter of fact, the whole thing shook me up but
good. To be specific, it made me (a) furious and (b) determined to find out who put the poison in my goddamn spicy
tofu so I could (c) kill him. And though sitting on my
couch with my dog is indeed my idea of a good time, I
would prefer to do it without a panic button around my
neck, a humiliating device Cody had insisted upon in lieu
of a twenty-four-hour guard of volunteer G.P.D. officers.

(Which, come to think of it, wouldn't have been a first, either.)

But it wasn't just a thirst for revenge that was coursing through my recently rescued brain. The whole experience had kind of crystallized things for me vis-à-vis the stories I'd been covering — or, more to the point, pussyfooted around covering — for the past month. My thinking, muddled though it may be, went something like this:

I was not dead.

Somebody, however, wanted me dead.

Whoever that somebody was had a reason.

This reason probably didn't involve either my movie reviews or my charming personality.

Therefore, it had to be related to something I was covering.

Something nasty.

Which meant it had to involve Lane Freeman, Kate Barnett, or the plant-science explosions.

Probably also the near death of one Jake Madison.

Or all of the above.

In other words, that somebody did not want me to find out the truth.

Which meant that I was damn well going to do just that.

In other words, nearly dying put a fire under my backside — a zeal to get it all over with and out in the open.

This, by the way, was probably not what the poisoners had intended.

Speaking of which . . . Finding the bastards who'd done it seemed like a damn fine starting point. So as I sat there surrounded by pudding and fried dough, I tried to picture just who the hell wanted me out of the way. Unfortunately, a fringe benefit of thinking about the who and why was that I started contemplating the *how*. It may sound idiotic, but for the first time it really hit me that somebody had broken into my house and tampered with the food in my goddamn refrigerator.

Now, Melissa's and my place isn't what you'd call a high-security building. It's your average little run-down professorial bungalow, pretty much indistinguishable from two hundred others sprinkled about greater Gabriel. One of the upstairs windows doesn't close all the way (the landlord is supposed to fix this before winter), and since until the deadly tofu incident no one had threatened to kill me in at least two months, I hadn't been particularly security conscious. Don't tell my mom, but half the time I don't even remember to lock the front door.

In short, if somebody wanted to practice the art of breaking and entering . . . Well, it would mostly involve entering.

I tried to picture that somebody slipping into my house in the middle of the day, dumping what was (as I'd learned from the Freeman trial) one of the most toxic substances on the planet into my leftover Chinese, and sneaking out again. It was hard not to imagine that whoever this person was, it was the same somebody who'd pulled a similar stunt with a stealth hike up Mad's dingy staircase. As far as I was concerned, the two crimes (three, counting Lane) were way too alike for it to be a coincidence.

But at least Mad lived alone. Whoever poisoned the leftovers either didn't know Melissa might eat them, or didn't care.

That made me ponder the nature of poison itself—a coward's weapon if there ever was one. No blood, no violence, no looking your victim in the eye. You don't even have to be there for the big event. Just pull out your little bottle with the skull and crossbones on it and do the deed without even getting your hands dirty. This lovely train of thought reminded me of a movie I'd once reviewed, a

British art film about a teenager who gets off on concocting various witch's brews and then watching people die slowly. He kills his mom, nearly blinds his sister, then starts picking off his coworkers by dosing their afternoon tea.

It's based on a true story.

But back to my own personal melodrama, made somewhat more palatable by the consumption of a chocolate-glazed doughnut, softened by dunking in Lady Grey tea. I chewed, wondered how much dietary leeway you get from having your guts cleaned out by the herbal equivalent of Drāno, and tried to figure out who wanted to kill me.

My first choice, of course, was Tobias Kahan; no further explanation needed. But as much as I wanted to pin all manner of misbehavior on him, I had to admit that I couldn't picture him adopting the no-muss-no-fuss method of assassination; he seemed far more likely to strangle me with his big hairy hands and laugh while he was doing it. So who else?

Well, there was whoever had really killed Lane—and presumably wouldn't appreciate having to swap places with Shelley. (Speaking of which: Getting good and poisoned had, at least, obviated the need to hit up Cody about her probable innocence; although he hadn't said much, and I'd felt too lousy to push it, the fact that I'd been dosed with the same stuff clearly had him doing mental gymnastics about the entire investigation.) And on top of Lane, there was the guilty party behind the Barnett murder, whoever the hell that was. But had I really done enough snooping on either point to get myself, as they say, terminated with extreme prejudice?

And what about Mad? The attempt on his life predated Barnett's death, so that couldn't have been it. No, he was working on the whole G.M.O. thing, the protests, and all the Frankenfood stuff going on in her lab. And then there was Lane, who died from the same poison that had so recently wreaked havoc on my innards. Gordon and I had discussed the possibility that Lane was offed because he'd stumbled onto something ugly at the ag school — and sure enough, the plant-science bombing turned out to be an inside job. Could Ellie Gilbert, recently apprehended conspirator in the explosion that killed one and wounded many, have poisoned Lane and framed Shelley for it?

I picked up the paper from a couple of days ago, the one with Ochoa's story about the bombing arrests. There was a long mainbar, naturally, and a decent-size sidebar devoted to each of the suspects. Ellie's life story was right there on the page, or at least as much of it as he'd been able to dig up in an afternoon with a little help (unsought and unappreciated) from yours truly.

Ellie had grown up in some West Texas town called New Braunfels, graduated first in her high-school class, and gotten a full scholarship to A & M, where she'd been even more of an overachiever: She'd double-majored in organic chemistry and plant science, with a minor in biology. As pedigrees for the plant-based poisoner go, it was hard to beat.

Why she'd decided to come to Benson to get her Ph.D. only to wind up destroying the building that housed her department was very much an open question. And it didn't look to be answered soon: Having acquired a long-haired legal team at the expense of Don't Break the Food Chain, none of the four was talking to the cops.

It didn't take Perry Mason to figure out what the Feds were going to try next. They'd work on getting one of them to flip on the others, with the aim of cracking the whole Organic Activist Tribe wide open.

So should I call Cody and spout my theories about the

connection between the bombings and Lane's death? I still hadn't even had the guts to talk to him about Shelley's potential innocence; our recent encounters had been so charged (what with me either threatening to weep like a woman or just plain die), I hadn't found the right moment to suggest that he might have bungled the Freeman case in a big way.

I glanced at the phone, thought about it a minute longer, and picked up another doughnut instead.

CHAPTER
28

The next morning, I felt a whole lot better. So much better, in fact, that I decided it was time to go to the fertility doctor.

Note to Mom: Don't get excited. My visit to Oren Kravitz was indeed professional — but it was my profession, not his.

With my newfound determination percolating in my belly (far more pleasantly, might I add, than the abrin), I decided to take Lillian's advice and give Barnett's ex-husband the old frontal assault. The nice thing about doctors is that you can call them up for an appointment, and they don't think it's weird. The truth is, though, my meeting with Dr. Kravitz turned weird within five minutes.

I suppose the ability to create life in a petri dish is bound to turn a person into a megalomaniac of one sort or another. As I found out later, Kravitz's particular quirk is an ability to size up his patients inside of thirty seconds. Like a hyper-educated version of the lady who guesses your weight at the county fair, Kravitz likes to assess how many children his patients aspire to produce, not to mention the kids' respective genders, and, occasionally, the root cause of the couple's infertility.

The man, in other words, is both brilliant and something

of a wack-job. And if his New York clinic didn't have one of the highest success rates in the world, people might mind.

His prescience, however, is not infallible. Case in point: When I walked in there, twenty-seven years old and wearing no wedding ring, he took one look at me and decided I was a lesbian seeking a withdrawal from Benson's famed genius sperm-bank.

And no, he doesn't generally share these prognostications with his patients; he told me later, after he'd spent half an hour talking about his ex-wife.

How did I get an appointment with him so fast? That was plain old luck; he'd canceled a conference trip and suddenly had the day open. Why I got in to see the doctor himself, without a phalanx of nurses getting in the way, was yet another aspect of his quirky character; Kravitz likes to size up his prospective patients fresh, before they start to get stressed out by the medical machine—a fact I'd learned from the package Mad had done on him and the clinic five or so years ago.

The question of why he decided to spill his guts is considerably more complicated. It definitely wasn't sour grapes; sitting there in his yarmulke in front of an entire wall's worth of baby pictures, eating jelly beans by the fistful, he really didn't strike me as that kind of guy. No, my guess is that, kind of like the coach over at Griffin Academy, Kravitz had an urge to unburden himself on a topic that meant a lot to him, and that nobody had ever asked him about.

It didn't hurt that I made it clear the conversation was entirely off the record and on the Q.T. Oh, and one other thing: I'm fairly sure the man was still rather madly in love with his dead ex-wife.

The scene went something like this:

I go up to the Benson med school—which, due to the generosity of one very rich animal freak, appears a rather shabby cousin to the vet school. But never mind the crumbling fifties-era building; the school is consistently rated in the top twenty, and some of its affiliated programs (the infertility clinic being one of them) are in the top five.

So . . . I walk into the reception room, and barely manage to remember not to say I'm from the *Monitor*. I sit there for a while, flipping through a well-thumbed copy of *A Lovers' Guide to Baby-Making* before I notice Kravitz wrote it. Then the man himself comes out, offers a firm handshake, and I note that he has a sweet but goofy-looking face atop a reedy runner's body. He invites me into his comfy office with a partial view of the football crescent, whereupon he stares at me for thirty seconds and, apparently, concludes that I am both gay and desirous to breed.

"So you want to have a baby," he says.

"Actually, no," I say.

At this point, he stares at me like I've just grown a second head.

"You don't?"

"Not at the moment, no."

"Then, uh, might I ask what you're doing here?"

"I want to talk to you about Kate Barnett."

Another dumbfounded stare, as though the aforementioned second head has just opened its mouth and started singing *"Hava Nagila."*

"Really?"

"Yeah."

"Whatever for?"

"I want to understand her."

"You want to . . . Ah, I thought your name was familiar. You're Alex Bernier from the *Gabriel Monitor*."

"That's right."

"And you really came up here on the pretext of being treated as one of my—"

"I didn't lie or anything. I just called for an appointment, and I got one."

"So you did." He laughed all of a sudden, shook his head, and went for the candy jar. "My colleagues tell me it's an unfortunate idiosyncrasy of mine, not wanting to know any preliminary information before I meet a patient. But I like to start with a clean slate. It's simply my way."

"Well, from what I've heard, it seems to work."

"So it does. Jelly bean?"

"Thanks." I dug in, trying to avoid the yucky black ones.

He leaned back in his big leather chair. "*Kate*. You want to know about Kate. *Unbelievable*."

"Why's that?"

"Because . . . Oh, hell, I don't know. It just is. Kate is from another lifetime. Another lifetime entirely."

"You didn't keep in touch?"

"Hardly."

"How come?"

"I see the interview has begun, eh?"

"Do you mind talking about it? I promise, this is completely off the record."

"Do I mind talking about Kate? Hmm . . . That's a good question. And I suppose the answer is . . . not really. Not terribly much, anyway. Though I doubt my wife would approve." His eyes darted to a photo of himself, a pleasant outdoorsy-looking lady, and a gaggle of kids standing in front of a sailboat. "It's called the *Blessed Event*."

"Huh?"

"The boat. It's called the *Blessed Event*. My wife named it after what pays for it. Get it?"

"Oh, yeah."

"What were you asking me before?"

"Whether or not you were in touch with Professor Barnett. You said you weren't."

He laughed, though he didn't sound happy. "Anyone familiar with the situation would know that's a fundamentally ridiculous question."

"Why is that?"

"Think about what Kate did with her life. Now think about what I do with mine. Kate didn't exactly approve."

"She was worried about overpopulation, and you—"

"And I was helping rich white people spend tens of thousands of dollars to bring more rich white kids into the world."

"Is that really the way you look at it?"

"No. That's the way she did."

"But why . . . Look, I know this is probably way too personal, but if she didn't approve of what you do, why would she—"

"Why would she marry me?" I nodded. "When we met, I was in med school—we were both spending our winter break doing volunteer work down South, rural Alabama. I was working in a free clinic, and Kate was on an agriculture project—it was all under the same program. Anyway, they held a party for everybody on Christmas Eve, and that's how we met." He laughed, and this time it sounded more genuine. "My mother wasn't amused."

"Why not?"

"How do you think a woman named Edna Kravitz would feel about her son meeting his future wife at a Christmas party?"

"Ah."

"Ah is right." He started for the candy jar, then seemed to change his mind. "So that's how we met. She finished her Ph.D., I graduated from med school, and we got married."

He was silent for a while, and I had a bad feeling the interview was over. I figured I had nothing to lose, so I prodded him a little. "But it didn't work out?"

"No."

"How come?"

"Because . . . Oh, because we wanted different things."

He gazed out at the football field, looking like a poster child for the word *wistful*. I sat there and watched him, afraid to nudge him any more than I already had. Finally, he turned back to look at me.

"You see . . . Kate had certain ideas about how our life was supposed to be, about the kind of man she thought I was—she thought I ought to be, at any rate. When we met, it was in this dismal little town in Alabama, tar-paper shotgun shacks, the worst poverty you can imagine. That *I* could imagine, anyway . . . And Kate, she assumed that was the way I wanted to live—practicing medicine in places like that all over the world. She thought I'd be this crusading doctor, and she'd be this crusading researcher. . . . I suppose she really liked that picture in her mind. But it wasn't the real world—it wasn't *me*. She held on to the image, but I just wasn't that guy. I mean, I grew up in *Scarsdale,* for Pete's sake. . . ." He rubbed at the back of his neck. "This probably sounds awful, I know."

"You can't change a person," I said. "Going from refugee camp to refugee camp is a noble thing, but it isn't for everybody."

"*Yes,*" he said, and slapped his hand on the desk so hard I nearly jumped out of my chair. "That's what I told her. That's what I always told her, but she'd never really listen. And she'd say . . . She'd always say this thing that drove me out of my mind. She'd say, 'I love you, and I believe in you, and I know you'll do what's right.' Do you have any idea how . . . how . . ."

"How manipulative that is?"

"*Yes.*" Another desk smack. "How did you know?"

"Just how it strikes me, that's all."

"It was as though I was constantly letting her down. But I

didn't want to live that way. I wanted to have a family and a nice house and maybe a little boat. . . ." He gazed back at the *Blessed Event* and sighed, though not as deeply as you might think. "I should've known Kate would never fit into something that . . . I suppose she would have called it bourgeois. Come to think of it, she *did* call it that."

"But you still came here together to work at—"

He snorted. "Not remotely. Kate and I were divorced long before either one of us came to Benson."

"I don't understand."

"I came here first, to teach at the med school. I always wanted to do both academic medicine and work with patients, which was another thing Kate never understood. . . ."

"So the fact that you're both here, that was just a coincidence?"

"You could say she came *despite* the fact that I was here. When Benson was wooing her to be their star rice-breeder, one of the major strikes against the job was that she'd be in the same city as me. You're probably wondering why I know that. The answer is that when she was deciding which offer to take, she called me up. It was the first time she'd contacted me since the divorce—and it was also the last, by the way. At first, I thought . . . I hoped she wanted to be friends, but what she really wanted was to find out if I might be leaving anytime soon. I told her I wasn't. Then she asked me if I was out of town a lot, and I told her I was. That seemed to mollify her enough to take the job. But she made it very clear that if she moved here she wanted nothing to do with me."

"Just because of the line of work you're in?"

"That, and all the other water under the bridge."

"Let me ask you this: Do you think she was the kind of person who would've stolen somebody else's research and tried to pass it off as her own?"

"Are you serious?"

"An accusation's been made, but so far it's an anonymous one and I'm not saying it deserves a whole lot of weight. I was just wondering if you thought it was possible."

"Absolutely not. Kate was nothing if not morally upright—some might even say morally superior. It was . . . Well, for her, I suppose I'd say it was air and water. She couldn't live without it."

"How come you didn't go to the memorial service? I mean, obviously you still think pretty highly of her. . . ."

He laughed. "And, obviously, you're not married."

"Not even close."

"Well, first off, my wife wouldn't have appreciated it. She would never have said anything; in fact, she probably would have told me it was a *mitzvah* to go, but it wouldn't have made her happy. But the main reason is, I didn't go out of respect for Kate. She didn't want me in her life, so I doubt she would've wanted me at her funeral."

"I see."

He came forward in his chair and leaned his elbows on the wide maple desk. "You asked me if it was all about my job, but the truth is, it wasn't. As I've already implied, Kate didn't approve of my lifestyle. The house in Benson Heights, the sailboat, the job at the big university hospital . . ."

"And the three kids." Don't ask me why I said it; I just opened my mouth and it popped out.

"What?"

"I said . . . Look, I'm sorry, I know it was rude. All I meant was, considering Professor Barnett's choices, she probably wouldn't approve of having a big family."

"What choices are you referring to?"

"You know, adopting those two kids from the refugee camp . . . plus what she did when she was in her twenties . . ." He looked genuinely confused. "I don't mean to get too personal, but it's been in some of the stories about her—"

"I've never read any of the stories about her. It wouldn't make me happy, so I don't."

"Oh. Well, what I meant was, how she made such a political statement out of not having her own biological children—how she had her, um, had herself sterilized when she was young so she wouldn't contribute to the overpop—"

"Are you serious?"

"I'm definitely not making it up."

"Look, Ms. Bernier . . . You agreed this is all off the record, correct?" I nodded. "Then . . . I have to tell you, I've heard a lot of sad stories in my line of work, but that's got to be the saddest of them all."

"How do you mean?"

He shook his head, jaw clenched tight. "You know, it's damn ironic. Kate never really understood how she helped shape what it is I do. Or at least if she did, she never told me."

"I still don't understand."

"Kate did not have herself sterilized," he said. "She was unable to have children—it was medically impossible, at least it was back when we were married. In fact, if I'm going to be honest with myself, it was the other major reason the marriage failed. I very much wanted to be a father."

"But I thought . . . I mean, she made such a point about—"

"And the very idea that she took that—this horrendously painful situation that I see couples grappling with every day—and twisted it into some sociopolitical badge of courage . . . Honestly, I never would have believed it of her. But maybe . . . Well, maybe it was the only way she could cope. I suppose, knowing Kate, I can see that—the idea that she'd try to turn it into something voluntary rather than a tragedy that happened to her and she couldn't do anything about it."

"You mean she really wanted kids as much as you did?"

"Maybe her feelings changed as she got older, as her work began to dominate her life even more than it had before," he said. "But I know one thing for sure. The Kate Barnett I married didn't just want kids. She wanted them more than anything in the world."

CHAPTER
29

Apparently, after you get poisoned with something that could potentially do quite the hatchet job on your liver, you're not supposed to drink for a while. At least, that's what the doctor told me—to, quote, "avoid alcoholic beverages for the next several weeks." It'd barely registered among the various discharge orders I got on my way out the door, but now it was foremost in my brain.

Because, you see, I wanted a drink very badly.

Kate Barnett did not have herself fixed. Kate Barnett, in actual fact, had been sterile. Which meant that, at least on this one point, Kate Barnett was a big fat liar.

Did that make it any more likely that she'd been guilty of what the anonymous grad student had accused her of? Oren Kravitz didn't think so, and he'd probably known Kate better than anyone. But had she changed so much in the intervening years that his instinct was just plain wrong? Or, as he implied, had her work become so important to her that she would never, ever compromise her professional ethics? And did any of it have anything to do with her death?

Good questions all. Too bad no answers manifested themselves on the drive down the hill.

In no mood to wrestle this particular alligator all by myself, I went over to Mad's place.

"Jesus, Bernier," he said as he opened the door, "where in the hell have you been?"

"Up on campus," I said, more than a little bit wary. "What's going on?"

"I was looking for you."

"Oh. Well, you found me." I took a good look at him; he was plenty agitated, pacing and hopping like a kid with thirty-six hours to go until Christmas. "What's up with you, anyway?"

"I got news."

"Yeah? So spill it."

"I got *good* news."

"You got your job back."

"Aw, damn, Bernier. You killed the surprise. How the hell did you guess?"

"I dunno." I flopped down onto the couch with a shrug. "What else could it be?"

"I am once again gainfully employed. *Very* gainfully."

"Man, don't tell me she went and gave you a raise."

"Well, no, but . . . I got my old job back."

"Good. I mean, that's fabulous. Congratulations."

"Let's go celebrate. Citizen's on me."

"Hey, I'd love to. But no drinkie-drinkie for me for a while, remember? Christ, at this point I'm ready to take up smoking crack. . . ."

"Huh? What's eating you?"

"I just had the weirdest conversation with Kate Barnett's ex-husband. He told me—"

"Kravitz talked to you? No way. How'd you pull that off?"

"I just went up to his office and asked him about her."

"Really? You chicks are *diabolical.* So what did he tell you?"

I gave him the sixty-second version which—predictably enough, knowing me—wound up taking fifteen minutes. When I was done, he stretched his legs across the hideous coffee table and gave a long whistle.

"So Barnett's story wasn't all it was cracked up to be, eh? Interesting. Very damn interesting . . ."

"That make you think our mystery grad student has something on the ball?"

"Who can say? Public and private don't necessarily mix, you know? Man can be a fine upstanding citizen in the boardroom and still be diddling his secretary behind the credenza." He waggled his eyebrows at me. "If you get my drift."

"Yeah, I get it. But what do you think it means?"

"Hey, don't ask me. I slept through most of this, remember?"

"This crap is all connected, Mad. I just know it is."

"You mean Barnett and Freeman?"

"I mean Barnett and Freeman and you and me and goddamn Phil Herzog. . . . It's all tied up together somehow. Don't you think?"

"Yeah, I do. But don't go asking me how. And definitely don't go asking me how to figure it out."

"Okay, riddle me this. You feel like you're in danger?"

"Huh?"

"You heard me. Somebody poisoned you, for chrissake. Do you—"

"They poisoned you too, you know."

"No shit. I asked you a question."

He gave me a dirty look. Or maybe it was directed at the TV stand. "Look," he said finally, "I've been thinking about it a little bit—okay, a *lot*. And I've been figuring that, you know, maybe I kind of asked for it."

"Excuse me?"

"Come on, Bernier, I was a fucking mess. I totally had my guard down, you know? If I'd been at the top of my game, I never would've—"

"Never would've what? Swallowed some shit you didn't even know was there? What are you, Clark Kent all of a sudden?"

"Don't be a bitch. I mean, whoever did it obviously knew what was up with me, right? Not that I made much of a secret of it . . . I just think I gave them an opening, that's all."

"And if you hadn't, they would've hit you with something else. Look what happened to me."

"Yeah, but you're . . ."

"If you say 'a girl,' I'm gonna kick your ass."

"Nah, not that exactly. You're just . . . Hell, I dunno. Not me."

"And you're supposed to be invincible? News flash, Mad. You're human like everybody else."

I thought he was going to take it badly, but he just laughed. "After all those goddamn hours in the gym? No way."

"Hate to break it to you, but yeah."

"You know, that's pretty much what your boyo said."

"You didn't tell me you talked to him."

"I don't tell you everything, okay?"

"You gonna tell me what he said?"

"Just that, you know, I shouldn't feel like a pussy because—"

"He did not use the word *pussy.*"

"Nah, he didn't. He just said I shouldn't feel like, you know, a wimp because of what happened. But he said the cops were looking into it and I should watch my back for the time being."

"And you weren't going to tell me this?" He shrugged. "I know one thing for sure. From now on, we gotta all be working together instead of against each other."

"Meaning us and the cops? You gotta be kid—"

"Hell no," I said, "not us and the cops. Meaning we've gotta bring in Gordon. Not just on the Shelley thing, but all the way. Besides, I really think once you pull one string on this the whole thing's gonna come unraveled."

"Ain't you the poet. . . ."

"And we need Ochoa too. Enough of this lone gunman bullshit."

"What do we need him for?"

"As far as I can tell, he's spent the past month digging into the activist groups. Of course he won't tell me jack, but that's what I think. So we need him."

"Fine. But how do we get him? And how do we get him and Gordon to work together when they're two of the most competitive bastards we know? Not to mention, how the hell do we have time to do this when you and I are both back to work tomorrow and Gordon's off covering how Rochester's building the world's biggest water slide?"

"If that's what he's covering, he's gonna be begging to join up. Trust me."

"And what about Ochoa? How do you propose we draft him if he wants to go solo?"

"You could threaten him. Physically, I mean."

"Next idea."

"Oh, hell, I don't know."

"Hmm . . . Well, I guess we could try blackmail."

"With what?"

"I know something you don't know."

"Which is?"

"I know why Ochoa's been such a son of a bitch to be around lately. Also why he's been such a freak about taking the Barnett thing all on himself."

"No way. What? Come on, you're killing me here. What is it?"

"His girlfriend dumped him on his ass."

"You're kidding. How did you know?"

"Let's just say it takes one to know one."

"Details."

"I ran into him a couple of days ago. Poor bastard was putting up flyers looking for a roommate. I said, you know, 'Isn't the old ball and chain moving out here soon?' and I could tell what was whatting. He did the hem-and-haw. 'Hey, man, she got delayed a semester,' but I could tell. She dumped his ass, and the man is not happy."

"I guess that explains a few things."

"Yeah," he said, "and get this. When I called him on it, he copped to what went down."

"Which was?"

"You."

"Excuse me?"

"Apparently, his ex was the jealous type, *really* the jealous type, and when Ochoa dropped your name one time too many, she decided there was something going on. When he refused to admit it, she called him a goddamn liar and that was the end of that."

"You're joking."

"Nope."

"Jesus Christ. So how's that possibly gonna help us get him in our foxhole?"

"Ochoa's a prideful guy. I assume he doesn't want his bad fortune spread around the newsroom."

"Mad, you *wouldn't*. That is lower than low. Besides,

doesn't that violate some sacred male creed or something? I
mean, you *couldn't.*"

"No, I couldn't," he said. "But you could."

The four of us got together the very next night. It was, if anybody asked, a little celebration in honor of Mad's return to
the world of work. In actual fact, it felt more like some cockeyed version of a Brothers Grimm story; call it "Alex and the
Three Boy Reporters." At certain moments, I'd swear I was
in danger of getting eaten by the Big Bad Wolf.

Speaking of whom . . . If Ochoa didn't truly despise me
before, he sure did now. The only mitigating factor was my
pesto sauce, my culinary ace in the hole. This, however, was
the first time I'd ever employed it to seduce men I didn't actually want to sleep with.

"Okay," I said once I had them somewhat sedated with fat
and carbs, "let's lay it all out on the table. We work together,
write some kick-ass stories, and nail ourselves some bad
guys. *Capice?*"

Ochoa made a face and reached for his Dos Equis. "Who
the hell are we supposed to be, the motherfucking Scooby
gang?"

"You promised you'd play nice."

"I don't even know what you think I can tell you," he said.
"All I've been doing is working my contacts in the D.B.F.C.
and the OATs, and most of them just went to jail."

"You mean you knew about Ellie Gilbert? That she was in
on it?"

"Not her. Krikstein and Harlin Mott."

"How did you get in with them, anyway? I mean, obviously Krikstein knew you were a reporter. . . ."

"I kept at it. Started with him, convinced him I was sympathetic to the cause and I needed to talk to some true believers. Mott called me out of the blue, so there was never any direct contact through Krikstein—that's the way they work. One night, my phone just rang and it was Mott, talking about how there was going to be this special camp for anti-G.M.O. protesters outside Gabriel this summer where they'd teach you how to climb buildings and chain yourself to something with a bike lock around your neck. He wanted me to go through it and write about it for the paper, first-person thing. I told him I would."

"Not a bad story," Gordon said.

"Bunch of freaks," Mad said.

I passed Ochoa the pasta bowl, my version of the olive branch. "So that's what first got them to open up to you?"

"Yeah. But mainly I hung out with the Chain people. The OATs are a squirrelly bunch, *tu sabes?*"

"So I've heard."

"The Chain's just the opposite—they want to get their names in the papers and their faces on TV. Totally live for it. You remember a guy name of Tobias Kahan?"

"Unfortunately, yes."

Ochoa offered his fellow menfolk a nasty smile. "He's not gonna be president of the Alex Bernier Fan Club, trust me."

"Was that before or after I had him picked up for assault?"

"He says you symbolize everything that's wrong with modern journalism."

"And what the hell does that mean?"

"I don't know," he said, "but I sure like the sound of it."

"Great. Anything else you'd like to share with the group?"

"He got ahold of one of your notebooks, was crowing about it to anybody who'd listen—which is basically everybody, since he's the top hombre. Said he was going to expose the inner workings of a corrupt media."

"Shit."

"Yeah, well, I hate to say it, but it didn't do him a whole lot of good. Couldn't barely read a damn word."

"Excellent. What else?"

"Hell, woman, I don't know. You dragged me into this, remember?"

"And during all the time you spent with these people, you never had any idea about Ellie Gilbert?"

"No, I mean . . . They definitely referred to somebody they had on the inside, somebody who could help them, quote, 'conduct appropriate actions.' But I never heard anybody cop to the bombings or mention her by name. Remember, I was mostly hanging with The Chain. The OATs people were just about impossible to pin down. I was working on getting to a cell meeting—I told Krikstein they could blindfold me or whatever they wanted—but then the cops busted them for the bombing and that was that."

"Okay, anybody hear anything about the investigation?"

Ochoa favored me with a sneer. "Like you need to ask *us*."

"What's that supposed to mean?"

"You're in bed with the cops. Literally."

"We try to keep things sep—"

"*Right.*"

"Look, I really don't know how the case is shaping up. Cody wouldn't tell me and I wouldn't ask him."

"You are such a hyp—"

"Somebody's copping to it," Gordon said, prompting us to stop bickering and stare at him. "Source of mine says somebody's flipping. He wouldn't say who, but I think it's one of the Mott brothers."

I drank some water, gazing longingly at the two wineglasses. "What makes you think that?"

"Just the way he talked about it. My bet's that one

brother's flipping to get the other one off. But that's not the really interesting part."

"Come on, Band," Mad said. "Don't be a prick, just spit it out for chrissake."

"The really interesting part, to me at least, is that this person's only copping to one of the bombings."

"Well, that makes sense," I said. "The first one didn't actually kill anybody, so the charges would be a lot less—"

Gordon interrupted with a game-show buzz. "Incorrect. Source tells me they're copping to the other bombing. The big one."

"The one that killed Herzog?"

"The very one."

"Are you being serious? Come on, Gordon, you must've gotten it wrong. Why the hell would they cop to the really heinous one and deny the other?"

"Only one reason I can think of," he said. "And that's because they didn't do it."

Mad, Ochoa, and I made simultaneous noises that translated into *no way*.

"Come on, Band," Mad said. "That's ridiculous. Don't tell me two separate parties just happen to blow up the same building on the same night. What are the odds?"

"Hey," Gordon said with a shrug, "I never said it was a coincidence. I'm just saying maybe that's the way it played out."

Ochoa drained his beer. "I'm still not following."

"Me neither," Gordon said. "I'm not the answer man here. I'm just telling you my impressions based on what the source told me. I mean, think about the differences between the two bombs—"

"But there wasn't any difference," Mad said. "They were made of the same shit."

"I mean the different objectives," Gordon shot back. "Think about it."

"Wait a second," I said. "I think I get it. The first bomb was . . . how to put it . . . *targeted*. It blew up the lab where Kate Barnett was supposed to be. Everybody figured it was supposed to kill her, and since she eventually got killed, that probably wasn't such a stupid thing to think. But everybody also assumed the first bomb was also intended to bring more people to the scene to get blown to smithereens by the second bomb. And maybe *that* wasn't right after all. Is that what you're getting at?"

"Give the girl a Kewpie doll," Gordon said.

"Shh . . . You're gonna kill my train of thought. Now, one of the things nobody could believe about the second bombing, the big one, was that these granola-crunching morons were so vicious they'd want to blow up a whole bunch of innocent people. But what if they weren't? What if it was just a really horrible . . . not coincidence exactly, but . . . What if they never intended it that way? What if they just planned to blow the building up in the middle of the night when nobody'd be there? And then . . . Oh, hell, I don't know. Come on, Mad, help me out here."

"Well," he said, "if it's not a coincidence, which we all agree is a dumb idea . . . and Gordon's source is right, *and* whoever's flipping is telling the truth . . . Where does that leave us?"

I scratched my head, and realized I was using my pesto fork to do it. Oops. "Okay, let me think. I guess that means that one bombing prompted the other. Either the OATs people heard about the plan to kill Barnett, or the other way around. Right?"

"If you ask me," said Ochoa, "it's the second version. I've spent a fair amount of time with these people, and most of them just don't strike me as killers. Yeah, they talk a big game about 'by any means necessary,' but I can't believe a majority of them would plan to murder her or anybody else."

"Hold up," Mad said. "I'm not sure I follow."

"The question is, did the idea of killing Barnett inspire the idea to blow up the building, or was it the opposite? And I'm saying, I think it's a hell of a lot more likely that a bunch of people got together and decided to eighty-six the building, and then somebody else took it upon themselves to make sure Barnett went with it. The other version—planning the big explosion when you knew the first bomb would bring a bunch of people to the scene—it's just too evil. It doesn't fit with what I've been seeing."

Gordon reached for the serving spoon and plopped more pesto into his bowl. "And what have you been seeing?"

"Bunch of true believers, kids mostly, a lot of them not quite sure what they believe in the first place."

"Meaning?"

"Look, I'm not gonna say none of them know what they're talking about. But all these issues are tangled up together—Frankenfoods and the W.T.O. and the I.M.F. just for starters. Hard to get your message straight with so many bad guys."

"Okay," I said. "Let's concentrate on something else. Which is, how do we think this all ties up? I mean, on top of Barnett and the bombings, we've got three—count 'em, three—poisonings, two of which involved the same stuff. First there's Lane, who we know was not only working with Kahan but also getting a ton of money on the side *and* cheating on his taxes over it. And by the way, I talked to his wife. She was pretty furious—said she had no idea about the money or where it came from. Apparently, he'd been making up stories about his family paying for the kids' tuition and a bunch of other stuff, and now on top of being in the clink she finds out she's in deep with the I.R.S. I also talked to this guy at the news service who worshiped Lane like he was Jesus-meets-Superman, the same one who told me about Lane and Kahan in the first place. He didn't know a thing about cash changing hands. Said he was, get this, 'offended at the inference.' "

"Flacks can't write for shit," Mad offered. The other two nodded as though he'd read a line from the Taoist handbook.

"So," I went on, "what'd Lane do to get that money? And was it the same thing that got him killed? What'd he know exactly? Was it that Gilbert was dipping her toe in both ponds? Maybe he found out about the plans for the bombing or for killing Barnett. But he must've known something he wasn't supposed to, right?" Nods all around. "Then there's Mad here, who starts digging into plant science, and the next thing he knows he wakes up in the hospital. And, finally, yours truly. I was, well . . . I was kind of sticking my nose into all of it, and somebody slips me the same shit that killed Lane. So what's question number one?"

"That," said Mad, "would be whether the same individual perpetrated all the aforementioned bad acts." Gordon raised an eyebrow at him. "Hey, I banged a law student once, okay?"

"So fine," I said. "Let's ponder the concept that the same person—or more likely people—is behind all of it. The next question is why?"

"Maybe," Ochoa said in a deeply patronizing tone, "they didn't feel like going to prison."

"Yeah, but we gotta look at it logically. By the time somebody got to me, they'd already made arrests in the plant-science bombing. And as for Barnett and Freeman . . . Hell, I don't even know anything useful."

"Or maybe," said Ochoa, "they just wanted to get you out of the way as a service to mankind."

I stuck my tongue out at him, but with great dignity. Mad laughed. That left it to Gordon to defend my honor.

"First off," he said, "whoever's behind this probably has no idea how much we know or don't know. And practically speaking . . . How long could the poison have been in your refrigerator?"

"Um . . . well, you know me. I'm the leftover queen. Maybe a week."

"That's what I figured. Could be it predated the plant-science arrests, right?"

"I guess. But you know what kills me? Wait, scratch that. Totally bad pun. What I was going to say is, it makes me furious to think that whoever did that had no idea if I'd eat it or if Melissa would, you know? That's pretty cold-blooded."

Mad took a sip of his wine. Amazingly, he was only on his second glass. "Truth is, though, she's been hanging with that Drew guy a lot, right?"

"I don't think she's spent a night in the house since we moved in. Her cat's in need of some serious therapy."

"Then maybe whoever did it didn't know you even had a roommate. Maybe they watched the house and only ever saw you coming and going."

"So they only staked out my house and put poison in my food," I said. "Thanks, Mad. That makes me feel a whole lot better."

CHAPTER
30

Two days later, and courtesy of a dirt-cheap fare procured over the Internet, I was on a plane to Los Angeles. So was Mad.

Our mission, should we choose to accept it, was to track down and interview one Ann Tucker. To this end, we were also prepared to sleep on the floor of one of my myriad ex-boyfriends and, if possible, take the studio tour at Universal.

Mad had tracked down two of the three possible mystery grad students, one to Monsanto (or, as the OATs call it, *Mon-Satan*), the other to a Baltimore suburb where she'd detoured onto the mommy track. That left Ann Tucker as the only likely candidate—and sure enough, he learned via the wonders of the Web that a woman of that name was teaching high-school biology in Santa Monica. And lest you think we were on a six-thousand mile (round-trip) goose chase, her personal home page revealed she had a master's in plant science from Benson University.

The *Monitor,* like the Mounties, always gets their man.

Or woman. You get the idea.

So there we were, renting a car at the L.A. airport, which Mad had every intention of making me drive, our visions of a cherry-red convertible marred by financial reality. We wound up with an aqua-blue GEO Metro, and managed to get lost approximately twenty-five times on the way to Devon's place, including a scenic tour of lovely downtown Encino.

"This better not get all weird," Mad said. "You guys aren't going to hook up again or anything, right? I mean, Cody's a buddy of mine now and—"

"Not bloody likely."

"Good. Cause I wouldn't wanna be—"

"He's gay."

"Huh?"

"He plays shortstop for the other team. You know, he—"

"Christ, I know what gay means. I thought you said he was your ex."

"I went to Vassar, remember? Everybody's freshman boyfriend came out sophomore year. It was kind of a rite of passage."

"*Man.*"

"But he is gonna *love* you. . . ."

"You mighta mentioned this before I agreed to flop on the guy's . . . Oh, hell. I really don't wanna finish that sentence."

"Hey, I told you he lived in West Hollywood."

"So?"

"So that's like the West Coast version of Chelsea."

"How the hell am I supposed to know that?"

"Look, don't worry about it. You're not his type anyway."

"Honestly?"

"No, I'm lying. You're actually his dream guy and he'd jump your bones soon as look at you. I was just trying to make you feel more comfortable."

"Yeah, well, how about keeping your eyes on the road?"

We eventually found Devon's apartment, and once my ex had enough of ogling Mad, the three of us went out to Jamba for frozen juice drinks, which as far as I can tell is the main reason for allowing California to remain in the Union. I got a yummy watermelon thing with orange sherbet and something called spirulina; I'm not sure what that is, but a strapping young man in shiny disco-era short-shorts and a fanny pack ordered it in line before me, so I figured it must be good for you.

"You look hot, sweetie," Devon said to me—at least, I *think* it was to me.

"Thanks. So do you."

"Do I rethink the sideburns?" He turned his head left and right. "Are they working for me?"

"Jesus, this place is turning you into one of the tragically hip."

He kissed the air in our general direction. "Behold the male animal in his native habitat."

"Auditions going okay?" I turned to Mad. "Devon's an actor. Didn't I mention that?"

"You did not."

Devon shot a glance at Mad and winked at me. "You know," he told him, "you could be in the business yourself. You've got great bone structure." He reached over and squeezed a bicep. "And do you work out?"

Mad turned a lovely shade of red and sucked on his banana-yogurt shake.

"Come on, Devon," I said. "Stop torturing him with the horny-queen act." I turned to Mad. "He's not really like this. He's just doing it to get a rise out of you."

"In a manner of speaking," said Devon. "Okay, I'll be good. Now tell me, what brings you two here to grace my doorstep?"

"Like I said on the phone, there's this lady in Santa Monica we want to interview."

"And you couldn't just call?"

"It's a delicate matter. Besides, the tickets only cost ninety-nine bucks."

"And," said Devon, "I'm extraordinarily charming."

"That goes without saying."

"So what time's your appointment?"

"Um, we don't actually have one."

"You flew three thousand miles so you could drop in on the off chance she's home?"

"If we said we were coming, we figured she'd tell us to get lost."

"You, my darling, have *such* an exciting job."

"Not as glamorous as being a movie star."

"Oh, hardly. Though there was that little thing I did with Sean . . ."

I twisted my neck to look at Mad. "He means Connery."

"No *way.*" Devon gave a little nod. I thought Mad's tongue was actually going to hit the somewhat-sticky table. "He's my *hero.* What's he like? I mean, what's he *really* like? I gotta know. . . ."

"Well," said Devon, leaning in and speaking sotto voce, "he is absolutely *manly.*"

"I *knew* it," Mad said. "I knew Connery was no pussy."

Devon looked around the store, saw nobody he knew within earshot, and relaxed a little. "Not a word you want to say real loud around here, *o-kay?* "

"It was Mad who found this girl," I said. "First he figured out her name was Ann Tucker; then he searched a ton of schools and colleges in the L.A. area until he tracked her down. And then he figured out where she lived, 'cause at first we were gonna go to the school, but we had to come on the weekend to get the fare, so he found her home address."

Devon leaned back in his chair and sucked on the bright orange straw. "And how, pray tell, did he do that?"

"Tell him, Mad."

"Well," he said, "we found a ton of Ann Tuckers and A. Tuckers in the L.A. area, so we had to narrow them down, right? Now, we knew the one we wanted had a master's from Benson. So I had this idea to call them up and say I was from the Benson alumni association and did they want to make a donation. Most of them said, 'You made a mistake, I didn't go there,' right? But finally, bingo, I got to one who said, 'I didn't like Benson that much, so please take me off your mailing list.'"

I patted Devon on the cheek. "Pretty much what I say when old V.C. comes calling."

"Listen to this girl. She had no school spirit then and she still doesn't. College was the best years of my life."

"If I thought that," I said, "I would've jumped in the gorge long ago."

⁂

Ann Tucker lived in a building a block off Santa Monica Boulevard that smelled of curry and cardamom. Like just about every middle-class dwelling in L.A., it had a gated parking garage opened via remote control. The front door, which seemed like an afterthought since nobody ever came on foot anyway, looked like the entrance to a doctor's office. I didn't think buzzing was the best idea, so we waited until somebody came out. It was a long wait. Finally, an Indian lady in a sari walked out with a white toy poodle on a leash, and we were in.

Tucker's apartment was on the first floor, maybe twelve steps from where we'd been standing. We knocked, held our breath to see if we'd flown across an entire continent for nothing, and heard a voice ask *who is it*. I nudged Mad, who gave the answer we'd rehearsed in the car on the way over.

"Ms. Tucker? It's Jake Madison. You sent me a letter." No response. I nudged him again. "I'm a reporter at the *Gabriel Monitor*. You sent me a letter about Professor Kate Barnett." Still no response. "I'm here with another reporter from the paper, Alex Bernier. We were really hoping we could come in and talk with you for a few minutes. It won't take long,

and it'll all be off the record. Your name never has to go in
the newspaper if you don't want. Just a few minutes, and
we'll be out of your hair, okay?"

I was standing there wondering whether we were going to
find ourselves evicted by the L.A.P.D. when the door opened.
Not a few inches on a chain, but all the way.

The woman standing there was about my age, but maybe
six inches taller. She had curly brown hair held back in an un-
ruly ponytail, no makeup, wearing a T-shirt and sweat-
pants—perfectly normal for nine-thirty on Sunday morning.
She was barefoot, no toenail polish, and her fingernails
looked like she bit them a lot.

"How did you find me?" was the first thing she said. "The
letter I sent you was anonymous."

"It had some clues," Mad said. "We kind of thought
maybe you wanted to be found."

Actually, the two of us had discussed no such thing—and
the fact that Mad came out with something that touchy-feely
nearly knocked me flat. However, it must've been damn in-
sightful, because her eyes got big and wide.

"Maybe I did," she said. "But how did you find me? Really, I have to know." Mad told her. She seemed impressed.
"And you came out all this way just to talk to me?"

"That's right," Mad said.

"Then I guess I better ask you to sit down. You want some
orange juice? Oh, and I've got some blueberry muffins. . . ."

Now, this was what I call promising. Sources who plan to
clam up on you don't offer you breakfast first.

So we sat out on the tiny slab of cement that passed as Ann
Tucker's back deck, overflowing with flowerpots and smelling
slightly of the curry from down the hall. She and I were on a
pair of rickety lawn chairs, while Mad (still complaining about
the crick in his back from the coach-class seats) opted to lean
against the eight-foot wooden privacy fence.

"I still can't believe you found me," she said. "That's really amazing."

"It wasn't that hard," Mad said. "Would've been a lot easier if the plant-science people hadn't stonewalled us."

Her juice stopped in midsip. "They didn't want you to find me?"

"Well, it didn't come down to you in particular," he said. "After all that's happened up there, nobody was feeling especially friendly, you know?"

"All that's happened?"

We both stared at her. "The building getting blown up," I said, "and Professor Barnett getting killed. Didn't you hear about—"

"Oh, yeah, sure. Of course I did. I was just wondering if that's what you were talking about."

"Um . . . yeah. That's what we're talking about."

"Okay. I just wanted to make sure there wasn't anything else."

"No," I said. "That's pretty much it."

"Seems like enough to me." She pulled the wrapping off a homemade muffin bit by bit so it stayed in one piece. She turned it upside down on the little plate on her lap and spread it out so the folds went flat. "So what do you want from me?"

"We want to talk to you about your letter."

"But . . . What's the right term? 'Off the record,' right?"

"Right. Nothing gets published if that's what you want."

"I wouldn't want my name in the paper."

"No problem. This is just between us."

"But . . . Alex, is it?" I nodded. "I don't understand. Why would you come all this way just to talk to me?"

"Because we had a feeling you knew a lot about what was going on in the department, stuff that might shed some light on why what happened, happened."

"But I don't. Like I told the F.B.I.—"

Mad snapped to attention. "The Feds were here?"

"They said they were talking to everybody who'd been in the department over the past five years, kind of a security check to see if anybody might have been involved in the bombing. They asked me if I'd ever been part of a terrorist group. Can you believe that? And anyway, if I had been, did they really think I'd tell *them?*"

"Did they ask you about the letter?"

"No, not specifically. They just asked if I knew anybody who had a grudge against Kate. Then they asked me if *I* had a grudge against Kate, so I sort of wondered if they knew about the letter somehow. But then I thought since it was anonymous there was no way anyway. But now you're here, so obviously it's possible. . . . Would you like some marijuana?"

I really, really thought I'd heard her wrong. "Excuse me?"

"Some marijuana. Some pot. I don't really like to call it that, though. *Marijuana* is such a pretty word, don't you think? So would you like some? I grow it myself." She indicated a spiky-leafed plant in the corner.

"Um, no thanks," I said. "It's a little early in the day."

She looked to Mad, who shook his head. "I prefer my drugs in glass bottles."

"Do you mind?"

We said we didn't. She went inside for a second and came out with a small red lacquer box, from which she pulled a neatly rolled doobie. She lit it up, and as the smoke wafted toward us, I wondered if we were in danger of a contact high. Doubtful; I hadn't smoked dope since shortly after Adam died, Cody being far too upright to indulge in such things. Ann Tucker must smoke a lot of it, though, because she didn't even get silly—just calmer, like me after two Marlboro Lights.

"I think it should be legalized," she said. "Don't you?"

"Yeah," I said.

"Definitely," said Mad. "I think everything should be legalized."

"So where were we?" she asked, exhaling after holding the smoke in longer than I would have thought humanly possible. "Oh, the letter. You were wondering why I wrote it, right?"

I tried to wave the smoke back at her without being rude. "That sounds like a good place to start."

"I wrote it," she said, "because I believed in Kate and she let me down. She *really* let me down."

"How come?"

"You know, I didn't even know who Kate was when I applied to grad school. I didn't go to Benson hoping to work with this world-famous rice-breeder or anything. I just wanted to do some solid research and get my Ph.D. so I could teach college. Not even a fancy college—it didn't have to be Ivy League or anything, just maybe a state school. Don't get me wrong, though. I kind of like teaching high school. The kids like me and all, so I guess it's fulfilling in its own way, you know?"

"You didn't think about transferring to another grad program?"

"That's not as easy as it sounds. You'd basically have to start from scratch. Kate said she'd give me any kind of recommendation I wanted, but I just didn't feel like—"

Now it was my turn to snap to attention. "She did? But I thought she . . . I mean, from your letter, it sounded like she—"

"Ran me out of town on a rail? I guess she sort of did. But maybe a better description would be the golden parachute. Kate didn't necessarily want to ruin me or anything," she said, puffing on the joint and the memory. "She just wanted me gone."

CHAPTER
31

And like my friend the physics teacher might say," Ann Tucker continued, "she wanted me gone at the speed of light."

"Why?" I said. "What was the big rush?"

"Honestly, I don't even know. I thought at first it was because she just didn't like me personally, which really hurt my feelings. I really looked up to Kate. There still aren't too many role models for women in the sciences, and she was mine. I remember when she asked me to work with her and said she'd be on my committee, I was just so honored, you know? And when she told me I had to leave, I was just *crushed.*

"And I started to wonder why, whether I'd done or said anything or just hadn't worked hard enough. But I couldn't see how that could be true, because I'd always tried to be really pleasant and I worked almost every weekend. And then this boy I was dating said . . . He said maybe she wanted to, you know, steal my research. I kind of . . . made noises about that to some friends in the department, and that's what I've been telling myself ever since it happened, maybe to stroke my ego." She waved the joint toward Mad. "Then when I saw that article you wrote on her, and it made her look like such a paragon, I just couldn't take it—I wrote that letter so at least somebody would know that she wasn't all sugar and spice. But since she died, I've thought about it some more and done a little reading, and she never published on any work of mine or anything like that, so that couldn't have been it."

She gazed out over the fence for a while. Finally, I got sick of waiting. "You mean she just asked you to leave and that was it?"

"One day, just out of the blue, she called me into her office and said my work wasn't up to her standards and I should do a terminal master's. She said she was trying to spare me the pain of working on a dissertation she didn't think I could ever finish, or getting shot down during my orals. She made it sound like she was doing me a favor, actually. But when I said I wouldn't go, that I wanted to stay and try harder and maybe take a little longer to get my degree, she got kind of mad—I think she wasn't used to having her academic decisions questioned by anyone, certainly not by a grad student. Anyhow, she told me she'd help me get into another program on the West Coast. . . ."

"Why the West Coast?"

"I guess because she knew I had family here."

"And not because it was really far away from Benson?"

"I don't know. I never thought about it like that."

"So what happened next?"

"She told me I was being really stubborn and stupid, and that if I left, then I might have a chance of salvaging my career. But if I stayed at Benson and failed, it'd be too late. I asked if the other people on the faculty agreed with her and she said that didn't matter—nobody would ever go against her decision about who to keep and who to get rid of. I was pretty upset, crying and all, and I know she felt sorry for me because that's when she offered to help me out."

"Help you out?"

She nodded, the tiny stub of the joint clasped expertly between thumb and forefinger. "She said she felt guilty for voting to admit me in the first place. She said it'd been a mistake and it wasn't fair to raise my hopes like that, so she felt responsible for it, especially since my parents were dead and I didn't have anybody to help me out. That was why she gave me ten thousand dollars to help me get back on my feet and get settled someplace."

"She gave you ten grand to get out of town?" Mad asked.

"Yeah, I guess. . . . I just had to sign a paper promising never to sue her or the university, and that I'd never talk to anybody about why I had to leave or any of the research I'd done. Since I'd been funded, all my work was their property; Kate told me it was fairly standard."

"So why are you talking to us now?" I asked.

She shrugged. "Well . . . I mean, Kate's dead now, and you promised none of this was going in the paper. And I suppose . . . Well, I have to admit it feels good to finally tell my side of the story. I've kept it bottled up a long time, and I don't think that's too good for a person. You want some more O.J.?"

She jumped up with far more agility than I would have after an equal amount of THC and returned with the carton.

"Listen," I said when she'd refilled my glass, "let me ask you about something else. Did you know a girl named Elaine Gilbert?"

"Ellie? Sure. She's the one who sent me the article about Kate."

"What did you think of her?"

"I don't know. We started about the same time, but we weren't that close. I was pretty surprised when she sent me the story, 'cause we'd totally lost touch. She was serious, I remember. Didn't socialize a lot. I was surprised when I heard she got engaged, 'cause she didn't seem like the dating kind. How come you're asking about her?"

"I guess you haven't heard. She was one of the people arrested for blowing up the building. Apparently, she was a member of the Organic Activist Tribe. You've heard of them?"

She nodded, then shook her head, so it sort of came out on a diagonal. "Yeah, but . . . I can't believe Ellie would do something like that, or anybody else in the department, either. I mean, the OATs are basically against everything we do, aren't they?"

"Pretty much. Was there anybody else in the department you'd consider more likely to go that route?"

"Oh, my God, no."

"Ever heard of a man named Lane Freeman? He was a writer for the university news service." She shook her head. "Okay . . . tough question. Can you think of anyone who'd want to kill Professor Barnett?"

"You mean, did she have enemies?"

"Those," offered Mad, "are generally the sort of people who want to kill you."

"Oh. Right. Um . . . no. She was definitely abrasive sometimes, but I can't think of anybody who'd want to kill her. Except . . ."

I leaned in closer. "Except who?"

"Well, she had this son, who was kind of a handful. People talked about . . . Well, it's not very nice to say, but they'd talk about how they couldn't believe somebody as smart as Kate had made such a stupid decision and got saddled with this really difficult kid."

"Difficult how?"

"I think he was just really mad at her all the time. Sometimes if you were waiting for an appointment outside her office, you could hear them arguing. Other students, they'd talk about it and kind of, you know, compare notes. I remember this one time he said something really terrible, like 'You're so selfish; everything you do is so selfish. You were selfish to bring us here.' And then he said something even worse. He said, 'You should've left us to die in Africa. We would've been happier that way.' I couldn't even believe what I was hearing; it was so awful."

"Did he threaten her?"

"Kind of. He said something about how he was going to make her sorry for what she'd done to his sister."

"But his sister died in a car accident."

"I know, but he said . . . Look, I don't even feel right about repeating this. It's just too awful."

"I know, but Kate's dead. This can't hurt her anymore, okay?"

She chewed on that for a while. "Well," she said finally, "he basically said that the sister hadn't been in an accident, that she'd killed herself. The two of them, the brother and the sister, they'd made, you know . . . a suicide pact. But it didn't go like it was supposed to, and only one of them died."

"Jesus."

"I felt like a creep just sitting there listening to all that, but I didn't know what to do. I sure never told anyone else about it. And you know . . . I felt really sorry for him, and for Kate too. She worked so hard, and then to have this person you'd tried to help hate you so much . . . It just seemed unfair."

"Is there anything else you can think of that might help us out? Anything about Kate or anyone else in the department?"

She shook her head, then just sat there, this time staring at a night-blooming jasmine in a square ceramic pot.

"Well, if you can't think of anything else," Mad started, "I

guess we'll be going. There's a tour of Universal Studios I—
I mean *Alex* wants to take. . . ."

No response. Either the jasmine bush was truly fascinat-
ing or Ann Tucker was suddenly very, very stoned.

Mad looked at me. I looked at Mad. Neither one of us
knew quite what to say. Finally, just when I was trying to
remember if there really was such a thing as a marijuana
overdose, she spoke up.

"Don't go," she said. "There's something else."

Mad, who apparently had had enough of leaning against
the wall, dropped down and sat cross-legged on the concrete.
"Shoot," he said. "We're listening."

"There could be another reason Kate made me go. It
wasn't something I really wanted to think about, so I didn't.
But now that we're talking about it . . . Well, I think it would
be best for me to just come clean."

"We're listening," Mad said again.

"One time, a week or so before Kate told me to leave, she
and I were having this long conversation in the lab late one
night. I'd just come in to pick up some things, but she was
there working, and I sat down to talk to her. I'd had a little
bit to smoke, so I probably said more than I would have otherwise. But we got to talking about the overpopulation problem and people's misconceptions about it and everything.
Like, there are still plenty of people who'll tell you 'Don't
feed starving people, because they'll just have more babies
and then there'll be even more starving people than before.'
But that's totally wrongheaded. History has always shown
that once people aren't starving anymore, once their lives
have meaning and they can count on most of their children
living to adulthood, birthrates go way down. Women start to
see they can do more with their lives, and they practice con-
traception.

"So that's the sort of thing we were talking about, and

that's when I said . . . I told Kate about this idea I'd been having for my dissertation. And I'm kind of afraid that's why she kicked me out."

Another long pause, another nudge from me. "What makes you think that?"

"Well . . . When she told me to leave, I tried to ask her about it, say I was sorry, but she wouldn't even listen. She just said she never wanted to hear a word about it ever again."

"About what?"

She drew in a long breath. It made her cough. "It . . . You have to understand. The whole genetic-engineering thing was just beginning to explode back then, and people were throwing around all these crazy ideas—you know, crossing an apple with a pork chop and cloning your dead grandmother. And we were doing all this amazing stuff with rice, or just starting to, and I thought . . . Well, what if you could feed people and deal with the birthrate at the same time?

"So I suggested to Kate, did she think we could . . . Couldn't we genetically engineer a kind of rice that made people sterile—at least temporarily? I mean, I know it sounds like science fiction, but even Kate agreed it was theoretically possible. You maybe could do it with hormones, sort of like dropping birth-control bait to reduce deer populations—the trick would be finding something that didn't have bad side effects. And if you were targeting it to work on the women, which you probably would because of all the research that's already been done on the pill, you'd have to make sure that somehow men and kids could metabolize it without having it harm them.

"So I told Kate this, and I guess I expected her to laugh at me. Or else I expected her to scream at me and tell me it was the most disgusting idea she'd ever heard—that it was like eugenics or Nazi Germany. But she didn't, and I remember I was really grateful. She was just kind of thoughtful about the whole thing, talking to me about the pros and cons—not only medically but politically too. How would the international scientific community react? How would donor agencies feel about it? Would it be considered yet another attempt by Western white people to wipe blacks off the planet? That sort of thing . . .

"And I also remember . . . Her main reaction was sort of wistful—that there was this terrible famine on the horizon, and something like what we were talking about might be able to relieve a lot of suffering. But it would never be permitted because of what she called 'wrongheaded liberalism.'

"Anyway, I never got the chance to talk about it again, because the next week she asked me to leave. And at first I thought she was just completely disgusted with me, even though she hadn't acted that way—I thought on reflection she was horrified by what I'd suggested. I sure never told anyone else about it, because I didn't want them to think badly of me too. But I did mention to that boy I was dating that she'd told me to leave right after I told her a concept for a research project, and that's when he got me started on the idea that she wanted to take it for herself."

She'd addressed the entire soliloquy to the jasmine bush. Finally, she looked back at us. "I haven't talked about this to anybody ever, not since I told Kate. Do you think I'm a terrible person?"

"Look," I said, "I'm not gonna lie to you. What you suggested sounds pretty creepy to me."

"But it was just an idea," she said. "All right, yes, I wondered if it could work on a practical level. But mostly it was just a theoretical argument. Could it be done? And if it could, would anybody ever allow it?"

"They never would," said Mad, "and they never should, either."

"But people were starving," she said. "People *are* starving, right now, today. I know what I talked about sounds extreme, but what's going on is a really extreme situation. You know the expression. Desperate times call for desperate measures."

"Jesus," Mad said. "You sound just like Kate Barnett."

Then Ann Tucker opened her mouth and said something I totally didn't expect.

"Wow," she said. "Thanks."

CHAPTER 32

After that conversation, I was greatly in need of an animatronic shark.

Luckily, one was readily available over at Universal, where we did the touristy thing for the rest of the day. Mad, who was very happy to soak up the fun while blaming our presence there entirely on me—he'd done the same thing on the Maid of the Mist ride at Niagara Falls—took it upon himself to point out that real sharks, with whom he'd scuba dived, were actually much more frightening. I didn't argue, particularly since my mouth was full of a chocolate-covered banana on a stick.

It wasn't my first time at Universal. I'd gone there once before, when I was seven and my mom had a legal conference out in L.A. and I got to tag along. I distinctly recall that it rained like a son of a bitch, and my fashionable white polyester bell-bottoms got all water stained. I also remember practically leaping out of the tram with glee at the sight of the eighteen-wheeler from *B.J. and the Bear,* and my mom being so mortified, she practically threw herself under the tires.

This time, I was far less exuberant. In fact, despite the frozen banana, I was kind of depressed.

"What the hell," I asked Mad as we made our way back to the airport to catch the red-eye home, "do you think Kate Barnett was up to?"

"I don't know."

"Then do me a favor and hazard a guess."

He sighed, either at the question or the scenic bumper-to-bumper traffic. "Okay . . . First off, I think your instincts have been right all along. I think understanding Barnett is essential to cracking this, and I think understanding what really went down between her and Tucker is, well . . ."

"The soft, creamy center of it all?"

"What do you think are the odds I was about to use those particular words?"

"Pretty long."

"Yeah," he said. "But you got the gist of it."

"Damn, but it'd be nice to talk to somebody who actually knew the woman. You ever track down that engineering prof you talked about? The one from the ladies who lunch?"

"Mehta? Yeah, I talked to her. Didn't do me much good."

"What'd she say?"

"She said Kate Barnett was a very special person."

"No *way*. What the hell is up with that?"

"I asked her that too, since it didn't sound like her style, and she told me U-relations has been spreading around talking points about Barnett. Not the news service, U-relations—we're talking the double-speak big guns here."

"And they said everybody should just say Kate was special? What kind of crap is that?"

"Your garden-variety P.R. crap, I guess."

"She really gave you nothing useful?"

"Bunch of junk about how she was a role model for babes in the sciences, yadda-yadda."

"Wait a minute. . . . Before, you said what *really* went

down between Tucker and Barnett. You think Tucker's holding out on us?"

"Nah. You?" I shook my head. "Honestly, Bernier, I don't
think *she* knows what really went down."

"Then let's think about it logically. Tucker gets into the
Benson grad program. Came from U.C. Davis, where she
had a pretty good average. Probably, she's no slouch."

"Which doesn't necessarily mean she was qualified to
work under Barnett."

"True," I said. "Maybe she did get canned for academic
reasons. But then there's Tucker's two instincts. First she
thinks Kate was horrified by what she suggested—but let's
face it. If you're gonna be horrified, you usually just go 'Eek'
right away, right? You probably don't chew on it and then get
horrified later. But Tucker also thought maybe Barnett
wanted to steal her work, only she scraps that idea because
what's the point in stealing if you're not gonna take the
credit? In this publish-or-perish world of ours, Barnett never
published."

"Because she was horrified."

"Or because she wasn't."

"Huh?"

"Come on, Mad, don't be so dense. You heard Tucker
back there rhapsodizing about curing the ills of the Third
World. You said yourself she sounded just like Barnett."

"So?"

"So what if she didn't get rid of her because she hated the
idea? What if she got rid of her because she *loved* it? Like, so
much she maybe wanted to give it a try?"

"That's ludicrous."

"I've heard crazier and so have you."

"Crazier than feeding people rice that makes them sterile?"

"Okay, I admit, it's right up there."

A two-seater cherry-red convertible—the very car we were supposed to be driving—crawled past us on the left. Inside were two disturbingly gorgeous blond girls, each chattering madly on her own cell phone.

"And why would she get rid of Tucker, anyway?" Mad was saying. "Wouldn't she, you know, just recruit her? It was her idea, after all."

"Good question. Maybe, I don't know . . . Maybe Tucker wasn't all that academically sound, and Barnett really thought she couldn't pull her weight. But more likely . . . What if she didn't want her in on the plan, maybe because she just didn't think she could trust a second-year grad student? And if she didn't want her in on it, she sure as hell wouldn't want her *around* it, right? If she was in the department, she'd be bound to figure it out eventually. And something like that . . . Christ, you'd want as few people in on it as possible, don't you think?"

"Definitely," he said. "But come on . . . Would she?"

"How the hell do I know? But you gotta admit, as much as I admired the woman, she was a total zealot. She would've done anything and everything to feed the hungry. The desire to do it . . . I'm tempted to say it sucked all the air out of a room, but it was just the opposite. Her dedication kind of lit everything up. But . . . God, it's so complicated. She adopts these kids as a quote-unquote 'political act,' then doesn't even give them the time of day. She finds out she can't have kids of her own, then turns it into some radical choice she supposedly made.

"And trust me, Mad, I may not be brimming with the maternal instinct, but finding out you can't have kids can definitely catalyze a woman one way or the other. I did a story on a support group in town one time, and I can still remember how intense these people were about it. Some of them spent all their money trying like hell to have them biologically, other ones adopted and got real activist about it, so they looked at in vitro people like a bunch of selfish jerks. Then there were the women who totally threw themselves into their careers as if they wanted it that way in the first place."

"And you're implying Barnett was the latter?"

"I don't know. All I'm saying is the woman was a true believer."

"You really think she might've signed on for what Tucker was suggesting?"

"Again, I don't know. But she said something to me once, about how once you see suffering like that, it changes you. So I guess it's within the realm of possibility that she might have done just about anything to stop it."

"Shit, Bernier, it just seems so, I don't know . . . condescending somehow. Dictating people's lives like that."

"Yeah," I said, "and the Chain folks are ready to stage a riot over making a better broccoli. Imagine how nuts they'd go about something like this. 'Brave new world' is right. They'd stop her at all costs."

Mad stared at me, and I stared back at him. This was not a wise thing to do on the L.A. freeway.

"Bernier," he said, "are you thinking what I'm thinking?"

"Obviously."

"Everybody's been wondering how these 'Kumbaya' creeps could go from sit-ins to bombings to cold-blooded murder. What Tucker said is one hell of a motive, don't you think?"

"But where does Lane come into all of it?"

"Hey, it kind of all shakes out. We wondered what he could've found out about. This sure fits the bill."

"And the money?"

"Maybe the OATs were paying him off to tell them what he knew."

"Or maybe somebody else was paying him off not to."

"Huh?"

"Look," I said, "maybe I'm reaching here. But what if he wasn't getting paid for giving the protesters the inside scoop? What if he somehow stumbled onto something—either the bombing plans or this nutsy rice idea—and somebody was paying him to keep his mouth *shut?* Or hell, who knows? Maybe he was double dipping, playing both sides of the fence."

"So why would somebody kill him?"

"Could be he got greedy. Or maybe he *was* playing both sides against the middle, and he got found out."

"But you're forgetting something, Bernier. There already was someone playing both sides, remember? Unless the Feds are full of it, Ellie Gilbert was a grad student in plant science *and* a member of the OATs."

"You saying you think Lane figured that out and she offed him?" He nodded. "You know, that crossed my mind a while ago. Also crossed my mind that maybe she tried to do the both of us in, to boot. We were both digging around the department, which could definitely have made her nervous. And like Ochoa was saying the other day, the timing vis-à-vis the arrests works out."

We pulled up alongside the red convertible again. This time, both the passenger and the driver were putting on lipstick, making kissy faces into their compacts. The car, by the way, was still moving.

"Speaking of Ochoa," Mad said, "are we gonna let him and Gordon in on what we found out?"

"Of course. We have to. I mean, we said we were gonna work as a team."

Mad eyed the traffic, which had recently upgraded from molasses to ketchup. "Are we gonna miss our flight?"

"I damn well hope not."

He finally noticed the two mobile supermodels. "Might not be such a bad thing. . . ."

"Hey," I said, "what about what Tucker told us about Kenny?"

"Who?"

"Barnett's son. Tucker said she heard him say the accident his sister died in was no accident."

"What happened again?"

"Car did a header into a tree; sister was driving, younger brother was a passenger."

"And according to Tucker, the kid said they were trying to do themselves in."

"Right."

"What's your point?"

"Well . . . just that here's damn good reason for Kenny to hate his mother. First he blames her for bringing them over here, and apparently the two of them are so miserable they want to die; then even that gets screwed up—he survives and gets left all alone. He probably blames his mother for all of it, the sister's death and everything."

"You saying you think he killed her after all?"

"Oh, man, I don't know. It sure leaves out a lot of other stuff, doesn't it?"

"It surely do."

"Then let's just forget him for the moment and go over the rest of it from the start, okay?"

Another visit from the red convertible. This time, the two girls were necking. Mad shook his head and sighed.

"Whatever you want," he said. "Just get us out of this town."

"Okay, let's begin with Ann Tucker. She gets to grad school, and one night she tells Barnett about this wild idea she had. Barnett doesn't freak out or tell her it's impossible, but a week later, she gets rid of her—sends her three thousand miles away with a promise to keep her mouth shut. Meanwhile, at some point, Ellie Gilbert . . . Jesus Christ."

"What?"

"Maybe that's it. Maybe that's why Gilbert goes over to the other side. Maybe somehow she got wind of the idea and she was so totally appalled she joined the OATs."

"And she tells them all about it and they decide Barnett has to go. But where does the order of the two bombings come in? And that whole thing about whoever the cops flipped only copping to one of them?"

"I got no idea," I said. "Let's just keep going. So Gilbert becomes the OATs' little undercover angel. She keeps them up on what's going on in the department. Maybe . . . You know, I keep hearing about the OATs as this pretty fragmented network. Maybe the right hand didn't know what the left hand was doing."

"Which," he said, "brings us right back to the idiotic idea about two coincidental bombs."

"Could be it kind of went like Gordon said. One faction decides to blow up the building and screw up the research— either this creepy stuff Tucker talked about or just the Frankenfoods thing in general—and some other faction finds out about it and decides it's the perfect opportunity to get rid of Barnett. If Gilbert were in on it, she was in an ideal position to say where and when Barnett was gonna be, right?"

"And then when it didn't go off the way they planned, they bashed her head in?"

"Hey, like the man said, 'by any means necessary.' But you know what's bugging me? Gilbert was engaged to somebody from the department, Ron What's-his-name."

"So?"

"So the guy wasn't arrested too. And I'm sure the Feds would've rounded up as many suspects as they could."

"Meaning she was in on it and he wasn't. Why's that bother you so much?"

"Don't you think it's a little weird that they're engaged to be married, and they're both in the same department, and by the way she's trying to blow up the building and maybe kill their most famous prof and he doesn't know anything about it?"

"No," he said. "But then again, nobody ever called me a romantic."

We got back to Gabriel after an overnight flight (which we made by mere seconds) and a three-hour drive from the Buffalo airport. I can never sleep on planes, but Mad rested comfortably in the arms of Morpheus—and he still didn't offer to split the driving.

I got home exhausted and cranky, took a shower, called Cody to tell him I was back, and found he couldn't sneak away from the Feds to have dinner with me. Then I went to work.

Among the messages on my newly acquired *Monitor* voice mail was one from Coach Laughton. I was so tired it took me a minute to remember who he was.

I played phone tag with him for the better part of the day while, with very few neurons firing, I tried to write a story on neighborhood traffic barriers. I finally got him around three, just as he was going off to lacrosse practice.

"I've been thinking a lot about Kenny Barnett since we spoke," he said. "So much so that I decided to try to track him down. I know someone in the Department of Corrections—we were in the service together—so I asked if he could tell me what became of Kenny after Spofford. It was pretty much what I was afraid of. He got picked up again over in Cortland, three months after he got out. It wasn't anything violent this time, just drug possession, and not enough to kick in the Rockefeller Drug Laws, thank God. He got sentenced to a year and a day and he served eight months minimum security, then got sent to a halfway house downtown."

"Downtown where?"

"Gabriel."

"Isn't that kind of a weird coincidence?"

"I suspect it was his mother's influence again."

"When did all this happen?"

"He got out of jail about four months ago. After you and I talked, I went down to the group home to see him, but he was gone."

"Do they know where he went?"

"The residents are encouraged to leave a forwarding address, but they aren't required to."

"Well, thanks for trying."

"No offense, Ms. Bernier, but I didn't do it on your behalf or even mine," he said. "I did it for Kenny."

After we hung up, I sat there trying to get excited about the traffic story and failing miserably. All I could think about was Kenny Barnett—no, not just him, his sister and his adoptive mother too. If what Tucker said were true, the two of them had been desperately unhappy. And Barnett, brilliant scientist though she was, had been either unwilling or unable to help them. The end result was that the girl was dead and the boy was a walking disaster.

Yet again, Barnett's words flashed across my brain—about how witnessing extreme human suffering changes a person. That was undoubtedly true. But what more would it do when you see the effects of that suffering under your own roof? Would it be enough to make you do something—there was that word again—something *desperate?*

CHAPTER
33

I was putting the finishing touches on what proved to be a deeply mediocre story about traffic barriers when a blond-haired, clean-cut young guy came up the newsroom stairs. Now, at a lot of papers you have to go through at least nominal security to get to where the action is, but Marilyn feels strongly about the editorial benefits of an open-door policy. So when this vaguely familiar-looking, bunny-cute fellow arrived, I wasn't sure who he was.

He asked for Ochoa. The newsroom secretary was already gone, Ochoa was out on a story, and I was closest to the staircase. That's how he landed in my clutches — and how my byline wound up on a certain story on page one of the next day's paper. Headline: FIANCÉ DEFENDS ACCUSED BOMBER.

Yes, it was Ron Bozier. He'd come down the hill all by his lonesome, determined to talk to the cop reporter. When he got me instead, he seemed relieved.

"I've heard . . . People have told me this Cal Ochoa is kind of a scary guy."

"Oh, yeah?" I had to suppress a snicker. "Scary how?"

"I guess . . . tenacious. Tenacious and scary."

"Sounds like the right person."

"Listen, do we have to talk here?"

"Would you rather go somewhere else?" He nodded. "How about if I buy you some coffee?"

I took the guy to Café Whatever, where, despite the July heat, he opted for a hot chocolate. I got a frozen coffee slushie thing with cinnamon in it. I asked him if he wanted to sit outside, but he said he burned really easily and didn't have any sunblock with him. That meant we had the place to ourselves, most Gabrielites being unwilling to miss a molecule of all-too-rare sunshine.

"Thanks for talking to me," he said.

"It's kind of my job. So what do you want to talk about?"

"I wanted to . . . I feel like I need to tell people about Ellie. About what she's really like."

I pulled out my notebook. "All right."

"You see, she's not this . . . this radical crazy person like the police are making her out to be. She's a really nice girl. She's a good girl. Honest, she is."

He turned a pair of earnest, pale blue eyes on me, and I wondered if he was about to tell me Ellie was not only nice and good but also really, really swell.

"So tell me about her."

"Ellie grew up in Texas, and she worked really hard and she was really smart. She got a full scholarship to college, and then she got into grad school and Benson, which isn't easy. I mean . . . I don't mean to sound like I'm bragging or anything. I wouldn't do that. I don't mean to say I'm so—"

"It's okay. I get your drift."

"Oh. Like I said, Ellie worked really hard all her life, and she worked really hard at Benson too. We both started our Ph.D.'s the same year, and we kind of hung out. . . ." He was actually blushing, as though he'd just told me the two of them had had carnal congress in the hydroponic greenhouse. "So we, you know, we dated, and after a few years, I asked her to marry me and she said she would. But we're having a long engagement because—"

"Um, Ron . . . Are you telling me you didn't know Ellie was involved in the OATs?"

"No, of course not. I mean, I don't believe she really was. I think this whole thing has been a terrible mistake."

"Is that what Ellie told you?"

He stared down at the whipped cream dissolving on top of his drink. "No. Since she got arrested, she won't even talk to me. Except . . . except to . . ." He reached into his shirt pocket and pulled out the ring I'd seen on Ellie's finger, the gem so small it was barely a chip, and laid it in the center of the table. "Except to give this back."

"She broke off the engagement?"

He nodded, then gave me a panicked look. "Please don't print that. I'm hoping she'll change her mind, so I don't want anybody to know she . . . You won't print that, will you? Please?"

"We can consider it off the record. Look, Ron, I want to ask you a tough question, okay? Let's just say for the sake of argument that Ellie did participate in the bombing. . . ."

"But she—"

"I said just for the sake of argument, okay? If she did, do you have any idea why?"

He ran a hand along the tabletop toward the ring, but stopped short of touching it. "For a while, the whole past year almost, she's been kind of . . . different."

"Different how?"

"Distant. Quiet a lot. I kept asking what was wrong, but she always said it was nothing."

"And now you wonder if maybe it was that she was involved in something she knew you wouldn't approve of?"

"No . . . I don't know."

"And if she were, can you think of why she might've done it?"

"She said . . . one time she . . . You have to understand. Ellie isn't the kind of person ever to say anything bad about anybody. But one time, I was invited to this picnic when the governor of Iowa was here giving a speech. The university invited all the students from Iowa to meet him, and that's where I'm from, so I asked Ellie to go with me and she said she wouldn't. And when I asked her why, she said it was because Professor Barnett was his official host and she was sick of hearing how great she was. I told her she shouldn't say something like that about somebody who does so much good for the world, and Ellie just got really quiet. She never said anything else bad about Professor Barnett, though, so I guess it was nothing."

"And what did you think of Professor Barnett?"

"Me? I thought she was an amazing lady—I mean, an amazing *scientist*." He cringed, like he was afraid the P.C. police were about to slap the cuffs on him. "Everybody respected her a whole lot, you know? Especially her students. So much that they even . . ." He cut himself off and turned his attention back to his hot cocoa.

"They even what?"

"Um . . . I'm probably not supposed to say."

"Come on, Ron. It's okay. You can tell me."

"It's . . . Well, it's just that her students all thought really highly of her. They believed in what she was trying to do, trying to feed hungry people, so much that they . . . Hey, you won't put this in the paper, will you?"

No, but I may kill you.

"It's completely off the record."

"Okay . . . Well, what I was going to say is, they admired her so much they started the Secret Garden."

"You mean, that anti-G.M.O. group, the Secret Garden-ers—"

"Oh, *gosh* no. It's nothing to do with them. It's just named after that kid's book, you know, the one about the little girl who—"

"So what's the Secret Garden exactly?"

"See . . . Professor Barnett was always warning us about how the anti-G.M.O. people were out to sabotage our work. And after those explosions, everybody knew it was true. So a couple of grad students went to her and said they wanted to help, and Professor Barnett gave them some samples of her experimental plants. She said to put them in different spots, places even she didn't know about—that way if anything ever happened to her, everything she'd worked for wouldn't be lost, right?"

"Did Ellie know about this?"

"I don't think so. I mean, we never talked about it. And like I said, she seemed like she was angry at Professor Barnett for some reason, so I didn't think she'd like it, and I didn't want her to be mad at me. . . ."

"So where are they?"

He didn't answer. I was trying very hard not to grab him by the collar of his polyester polo shirt and shake it out of him.

"Look, Ron," I said, opting to turn on the charm instead. "It sounds like what you guys did is really admirable. What's the harm in telling me about it? I promise, none of it's going into the paper."

"You promise?"

"Cross my heart."

"Well . . . I only know about one. Professor Barnett wanted it that way, so no one person knew where they all were, see?"

"And the one you know about would be . . . ?"

"Um, you know that big old grad student greenhouse? The kind of crummy one you can see from biotech? Everybody figures it's gonna get torn down one of these days to make room for—"

"The greenhouse right next to biotech? Isn't that kind of too close for comfort?"

He shrugged. "Hardly anybody ever goes in there. I mean, professors never do. Like I said, it's kind of crummy. Besides, it's not *right* next to biotech, you can just sort of see it from there. Anyway, the rice is all down at one end, and they hid Professor Barnett's stuff right in the center of it. You couldn't even see it if you didn't know it was there."

"But wouldn't it, I don't know . . . crossbreed with the other kinds?"

"Professor Barnett's modified strains don't work that way. It's one of the safeguards she—"

I stood up. "Thanks, Ron, this has been really helpful."

"But what about Ellie?" Blank look from me, soulful look from him. "You said you'd write a story about how she isn't—"

"You've already given me plenty of stuff to work with."

He favored me with the watery blue eyes again. *"Please?"*

I sat back down and proceeded to spend the next hour hearing about Ellie's myriad virtues—from regular attendance at the Lutheran church to taking her cat to visit nursing-home patients. As soon as he showed the first sign of running out of steam, I made good my escape and headed across the Green to the Citizen Kane in search of Mad. He wasn't there, but I found him at home, where he answered the door in a pair of tropical-print boxers.

"Go put some clothes on."

"What for?" He waved his wine-filled salsa jar at the

couch, covered in newspapers fluttering in the breeze of the window fan. "I'm lounging."

"Great. Get dressed."

"Bernier—"

"Remember on the plane when you said how cool it would be if we could get a sample of Barnett's wacked-out rice, so we'd actually have some proof of what she'd been up to?"

"Yeah."

"Remember how I said no way the people who killed her would leave any of that shit lying around?"

"Yeah."

"Well, I'm a moron. Get dressed."

"What gives?"

I told him. He still didn't move. "Come on, Mad. What's your problem?"

"It's eight o'clock."

"So what? It's past your bedtime?"

"So," he said, "maybe it'd be better to wait until there's nobody around to catch us."

⁊⳿⳿⳿⳿⳿⳿ᘓ

We got to the greenhouse around two A.M., toting a pair of flashlights and a plastic wastebasket. The place was indeed crummy; the white paint was flaking off the wooden frame and the foundation was crumbling.

"Hey, Mad," I whispered, "why's it so dark in there?"

"I told you, some of these places are on timers to simulate night and day. Why do you think we brought the flashlights?"

"Oh."

We'd been prepared to force our way in, but considering the greenhouse's state of dilapidation, it didn't take much. The door was locked, but all Mad had to do was jerk the handle upward; it shifted feebly on its hinges and we were inside.

The place was hot as hell, the air so humid it felt like you could ladle it with a soup spoon. I started sweating the second I walked in the door.

"What the hell are we doing in here again?" I asked, swiping at my forehead with the neck of my T-shirt.

"Gathering evidence."

"Wonderful. Let's get it over with."

"Just watch out for the snakes."

"The *what?*"

"I'm joking, Bernier. Jesus, lighten up."

We ventured farther into the greenhouse, inching down one of the two dirty concrete paths that ran the length of the thing. From the inside, it seemed enormous—gigantic and dark and icky and wet. I must've been dragging my feet, because Mad grabbed my wrist and drew me along behind him. "Where did that kid say Barnett's plants were?"

"The rice is at the far end. Her stuff is supposed to be hidden smack in the middle of it."

We kept going down the narrow aisle, our flashlights casting weird shadows off leaves and stalks and branches. The windows themselves were opaque—why, I couldn't tell you—and the reflections of our flashlights made the mood even creepier. Eventually, we got to what looked like a big, boxy wading pool maybe two feet deep, filled with spindly green plants.

I poked Mad with the butt of my flashlight. "Is this what rice looks like?"

"I guess. Go get it."

"Me?"

"You want me to ruin my loafers?"

"So take them off."

"And go in barefoot? No *way.*"

"But—"

"You've got those waterproof sandals on. So go."

I growled at him; his response was to shove the waste-basket at me and give me an encouraging pat on the butt. I reached in and felt the water, which was lukewarm and distressingly slimy. He patted me on the butt again; I elbowed him in the ribs and stepped into the water. It felt heavy and alive with tendrils of God-knows-what, and I recalled Mad's reference to snakes. Thanks a *lot*.

"Hey, watch it," he said. "You're stepping on stuff."

"I'm in a goddamn rice paddy, Mad. How the hell am I supposed to avoid it?"

"Just be careful."

"Whatever." I made my way toward the interior, which was just about the last place I wanted to go. "How am I supposed to tell what's Barnett's stuff and what's normal rice?"

"Maybe you'll know it when you see it."

"Terrific . . . Oh, *shit*."

"What?"

"Hey, Mad . . . Was that flashlight waterproof?"

"Don't tell me you dropped it."

"Er . . ."

"Then pick it up."

"I can't find it. The light went out."

"Then I guess it wasn't waterproof, was it?"

"Come on, give me a—"

"*Shhh.*"

"Look, I didn't mean to—"

"*Shhh.*"

"What?"

"Be quiet," he shot back in a whisper. "Did you hear that?"

"Hear what?"

He shushed me again and clicked off his flashlight. I stood

there frozen in the middle of the icky wading pool, trying to ignore whatever was tickling my ankles.

"Don't move," he said, so low I could barely make it out. "I think somebody's in here."

He crouched down next to the hard plastic rim and motioned for me to do the same. I shook my head at him in what little illumination was coming from outside, and he jerked his index finger toward the ground. I did as he said, and the slimy water promptly soaked me to the waist.

"Don't move," he mouthed at me again, and a few seconds later, I caught what he'd been hearing: the sound of someone rummaging around near the entrance.

Then the lights went on.

CHAPTER
34

I blinked in the sudden brightness, now not only wet and miserable but partially blind as well. I wanted to jump out of the pool, since there was no way I could explain what I was doing in a bunch of experimental rice. But I couldn't really see, and there were slimy green things between my toes, and the best I could do was just shove the wastebasket underwater and stay put.

I heard footsteps coming down the aisle toward us — actually, coming down *both* aisles. Whoever it was, there was more than one of them. I saw the rustle of leafy greenness, and the next thing I knew, we were face to face with Lindsay McDaniel.

I expected her to ask us what we were doing there. She didn't. She just shook her head — looking, if possible, even more miserable than I was. Then another bunch of greenery started to wiggle, and out popped Shep Robinson.

"Er . . . hello," Mad said. "You're probably wondering what we're doing here. . . ."

"That's a damn good question," Robinson said.

"Um, you see —" I started.

"What the hell are you doing in there?" said Robinson,

who clearly hadn't even noticed I was there until I opened my big mouth.

I stood up and waded my way out.

"We're really sorry," I said. "We're . . . You see, we're doing this story on grad students who . . . who . . ." My severe lack of science caught up with me. I gave Mad a pleading look.

"Who . . . ," he started, then stumbled. "Who work in the greenhouses at night, and . . ."

Robinson's Abercrombie & Fitch T-shirt fit tightly across his pecs, and the crevices were already sweaty. "Then where are they?"

I looked at Mad. Mad looked at me. It didn't do either of us any good.

"Where are who?" I said.

Robinson's jaw clenched, marring an otherwise-hunky face. "Where are the students?"

"Oh, um . . . They're not here yet."

"Look," Mad said, "I know we shouldn't have been in here without somebody to show us around. . . ."

I glanced at McDaniel, who seemed . . . nervous.

"But the door was open," Mad went on, "so we figured we'd just come on in and wait for . . ."

He kept babbling, but I could tell something wasn't kosher—something beyond us getting caught red-handed. I mean, Robinson was saying all the right things, but McDaniel wasn't even listening. She just seemed agitated, like she was . . . Well, like she was waiting for something really *bad* to happen.

"This is private property," Robinson was saying. "And I happen to know that the door is always locked."

"You're right," Mad said, "we should probably just go. We can do the interview some other time."

He took a step, but Robinson blocked his way. "Whom were you going to speak to?"

That's when I noticed that something in his voice wasn't quite right. He was asking a lot of questions, but something told me he didn't really give a damn about the answers.

He's stalling for time, I thought. Mad must've figured out the same thing, because when we exchanged glances again, he jerked his chin toward the door in a way that clearly said *Let's get out of here.*

"How, um . . . ," I mumbled at Robinson. "How did you know we were in here, anyway?"

"Lindsay saw your flashlights from her office window."

I was inching away from the edge of the pool when all of a sudden Mad made a run for it. He threw himself at Robinson while I scrambled past them and headed toward McDaniel at a moist jog. I shoved her out of the way and into a row of plants—she was slight and I caught her off guard, so it wasn't that tough. Mad decked Robinson with one punch, and the two of us went careening toward the door.

Mad beat me there, and when I heard the door open, I assumed he was on his way out.

No such luck.

I got there just in time to see him struggling with a big bear of a guy who turned out to be Jack Cerretani. Based on Mad's performance with Robinson, I expected him to knock the guy flat, but he didn't. He still wasn't at the top of his game, and after he got in a couple of swings, Cerretani shoved him hard and knocked him off balance. Mad got up but was barely on his feet before Cerretani nailed him right across the jaw, and he went down again. Then Robinson came down the aisle at a run, and he was clearly pissed off; he didn't even wait for Mad to stand back up before he decked him.

Mad hit the ground, and he stayed there. This time, he took a whole row of tomato plants down with him.

Robinson and Cerretani looked us over, the expressions on their faces in no way positive. Robinson appeared to want to give the unconscious Mad a swift kick in the ribs, while his colleague eyed me like a germ in a petri dish. Finally, Cerretani rubbed his raw knuckle and sighed.

"Miss Bernier," he said, "you truly are an unbelievable pain in the ass."

"Um . . . What's this about?"

"I'm sure that you know exactly what this is about. You've been running around campus thinking your little head off for weeks, so do us a favor and don't waste our time by acting stupid." He shook his head, like I gave him a migraine. "If we'd wanted to kill you before this, we could've done it, you know. How much abrin we gave you was completely up to us. But Lindsay said no, just scare her off and she'll give up. It's not as though you know anything about science. But you do know how to be nosy, I'll give you that."

I tried to think of something useful to say, and came up short.

"Listen to me, Alex," he said. "We don't want to be here any more than you do. You don't know what it's like, the burden of science at its highest level. People want answers, and it's up to us to come up with them—and do it before the grant money runs out. Do you have any idea how much guilt we feel when we can't deliver?"

"Um . . . A lot?"

"Can you believe that there are as many people starving *now* as there were before the Green Revolution? How can the world live with that?"

He'd dropped the "Miss Bernier" bit. He'd also gone from creepy villain to bleeding-heart zealot in under sixty seconds, and I had no idea what to make of it. I did, however, wonder if there was any chance of me running through his legs and out the door before he could catch me. Highly unlikely.

"So you see," Cerretani was saying, "when someone presents you with an idea that could alleviate that suffering, no matter how outrageous, you have to give it due consideration. Don't you agree?"

"Come on, Jack," Robinson said, putting a hand on Cerretani's shoulder. "Let's just get this over with."

Cerretani shook him off. "We will," he said. "But Alex isn't stupid. Neither is Madison." He glanced at the heap of useless muscle on the floor. "I want them to understand they aren't the only victims here. They have to see that we're waging a war, and wars have collateral damage. We were willing to put ourselves on the line to help people. Every one of us risked our careers to do it. But it's over, and we just wanted to let it rest. But you had to keep digging."

Mad was starting to stir then. Cerretani gave Robinson some sort of signal, and he pulled some rope out of his pocket and tied Mad's hands behind his back. Mad put up some resistance, but not much. I tried to look him in the eye, tried to see how bad he was hurt, but he didn't seem to be able to focus on anything.

Then Robinson tied me up too. I tried a trick Cody had shown me—you flex your wrists so there'll be some slack afterward—but it didn't do much good. I glanced at McDaniel, who'd finally emerged from the row of plants, but she just looked away.

Then they marched us back down the aisle to the rice paddy—Mad, they half dragged—and had us sit on the ground with our backs against the big plastic pool.

"All right," Cerretani said. "Now we need you to tell us what you know."

I glared back at him. Mad's head drooped against his chest.

"Don't be difficult," Cerretani said. "Just tell us what you know and this will go a whole lot easier."

"Go to hell," I said.

It was obviously a bad thing to say, because Cerretani strode over and lifted me up by the shoulders so I was perched on the edge of the pool. Then he pushed me back-ward until my head was underwater in a tangle of plants. I tried to hold my breath, but somehow I panicked and swallowed what felt like a gallon of slimy water. I thrashed around, hands tied behind my back and the horrible feeling I was about to die screaming in my brain. Just when I was sure I was done for, he pulled me up again and I sat on the edge, coughing and sputtering and blinking.

"All right," he said. "Let me put the question to you again."

Now, maybe a braver person would have told him to *really* go to hell. I, however, didn't need to be drowned like a rat twice in one night to get his point.

"Honestly," I said once I got my breath back, "we don't know much. All we know is, Professor Barnett got this idea to engineer rice to make people sterile, to try to lower the birthrate so people wouldn't starve. Somebody found out about it and they probably killed her to stop it."

"And what do you know about Lane Freeman?" I breathed in hard, and went into another coughing fit. "Don't look so surprised," he said. "It's a small campus. We know you've been asking around."

"He . . . I don't know. We thought maybe he found out about it and . . . was silenced." The thought of it pissed me off enough to say something stupid. "I'm sure," I said, "that you three know a lot more about it than I do."

"Is that what you think?" Robinson said. "You think *we* killed him?"

His tone was, of all things, offended.

"Are you saying you didn't?"

"As far as the state of New York is concerned, the Lane Freeman case is closed," Cerretani said. "According to a jury of her peers, his wife did it. It's not our fault that—"

"Stop it," McDaniel said, and turned to me. "You've got it all wrong. We didn't kill Lane Freeman. Kate did."

CHAPTER
35

We didn't kill Lane Freeman. Kate did.

I heard the words, but they were so absurd I practically laughed out loud. Then I got well and truly pissed; the only thing that stopped me from telling them all to kiss my ass was the threat of another dunking.

But, I mean, who the hell did they think they were? It wasn't enough that the evil creeps had taken out Lane—they were going to go blaming it on a woman who'd had her goddamn brains bashed in?

I looked from McDaniel to Cerretani and back again. "I don't believe you."

"If that's the case," he said, "then you obviously don't know much after all." He turned to Robinson. "Go get the materials we discussed. Do you remember everything we—"

"I have a goddamn Ph.D.," Robinson said in a tone that sounded more whiny than self-righteous. "I think I can put together a simple bomb."

"A *what?*" This from me. I was summarily ignored.

"But come on," Robinson went on, "do we really have to be so *theatrical?*" He pulled his sticky shirt away from his chest and checked his watch. "Why can't we, you know . . ."

He eyed the rice pool and my dripping wet hair, and I had a bad feeling I knew what he had in mind.

Cerretani shook his head, like he was coping with a tiresome child. "We agreed we'd blame it on the OATs, and that's what we're going to do," he said. "It's a perfectly plausible story: The two of them were nosing around the greenhouse when the bomb went off. . . ."

Son of a bitch, I thought. *Some of the greatest scientific minds in the world put their heads together and what do they come up with? Blowing me and Mad to smithereens. Wonderful.*

"I know," Robinson was saying. "But why do we have to keep them around until we—"

"Because there's such a thing as forensic science. You don't want the coroner to decide that a couple of bombing victims died by drowning, do you?"

Robinson shrugged and took off, and Cerretani sent McDaniel to lock the door behind him. After she got back, the two of them put their heads together and had some sort of earnest confab.

"Mad," I whispered, "are you okay?" He groaned something that sounded like *yeah.* "Listen, I . . . I'm really sorry."

"What?"

"I'm sorry I dragged you into this. I mean, you just got out of the . . . And now we're gonna get . . ."

"We goddamn well are *not.*"

"I'm just sorry I—"

"We are *not* gonna get killed by these fucking *eggheads.*"

"You're my best friend, you know."

"For chrissake," he whispered, "will you *please* shut up?"

Our captors finished talking and just stood there staring at us, McDaniel looking despondent and Cerretani sporting some expression I preferred not to contemplate.

"You really . . . ," McDaniel began.

Cerretani shook his head at her, like nothing she said could possibly make any difference. She was quiet for a minute, but then she opened her mouth again.

"You really need to understand what happened," she said. "Kate . . . didn't mean to do it. I mean, she did, but she never wanted it to turn out that way. She just saw so much suffering, and it got to her—it *really* got to her, until she was desperate for a solution. You have to remember what she'd been through, adopting those children and one of them dying and the other having so many problems. And being unable to have kids of her own, and blaming herself for it . . ."

"What are you talking about?" I said. "Why would she blame herself?"

"Because of the abortion."

"The *what?*"

"Back when she was in high school. It was against the law, but she knew she'd lose her scholarship if she had a baby. And there were complications . . ."

"Are you telling me not being able to have kids of her own justified—"

"I was horrified too at first, but later I came around. And so did the others, here and in France and in the Philippines. . . ."

She took in a deep breath, exhaled. Cerretani looked vaguely bored.

"But it wasn't easy," she went on. "Scientifically, it was a really tough problem—how do you do it without side effects? How do you make it undetectable? And I don't know the answers, because even though we worked for almost three years, we got only so far and no further.

"Then somehow, about two years ago, Lane Freeman found out about it. He was covering the ag school for the news service, and he was hanging around the department a lot. The rest of us were really worried, but Kate said not to panic. She gave him fifty thousand dollars to keep quiet, but then he came back for more, and then more again."

"And then," Cerretani said, "she decided to get rid of him."

"Why didn't you say anything?" I said. "After his wife went to jail for it, how could you just keep your mouths shut?" Neither one of them answered. "And what about Mad? Somebody poisoned him too, and he —"

"And I nearly fucking died," Mad chimed in, sounding hale and hearty all of a sudden. "Are you saying that was also Barnett?"

"It was your own damn fault," Cerretani said.

"Oh, yeah?" Mad growled. "How do you figure that?"

"You came marauding into the department, on fire to write the definitive story about her lab. It set off all kinds of alarm bells for her. She thought you were going to be Freeman all over again. She just couldn't risk it, particularly at that time. Everyone knows how much you drink, so she thought an overdose would seem —"

"You miserable bastards," Mad said, wrists twitching against the rope. "I swear, I'm gonna —"

"You're gonna what?" Cerretani towered over him, the vein in his temple beating a tango. I decided distracting him was a good idea.

"You said she couldn't have Mad sniffing around 'particularly at that time,'" I said. "What did you mean?"

He gave me a look that said I wasn't worth the oxygen. McDaniel answered. "At that time," she said, "she was about to release the rice."

"But . . . I thought you said it didn't work."

"It didn't work the way it was supposed to," she said. "It didn't work without side effects. But it worked—at least the animal testing was promising. But there were problems. We saw an increase in uterine and mammary tumors, but

Kate . . . She wanted to go ahead. She said the situation was too pressing to wait for the internal peer review we'd planned on. She basically said . . . that the ends justified the means."

"Kate knew that the work she was doing could benefit millions, and that the greatest enemy was time," Cerretani said, sounding surprisingly calm all of a sudden. "Every day, more children were being born only to die of starvation. She was working herself to death trying to feed them, to raise them up so their standard of living would cause the birthrate to drop naturally. But things were so bad, she felt she had to jump-start the process."

"Tell me something else," I said. "Why the hell did you use abrin on me, of all goddamn things? Weren't you afraid it'd get linked right to Lane Freeman?"

"That was my idea," McDaniel told her fingernails. "I thought it might help his wife. I thought if the same poison was used on someone else, with her in jail, maybe it would make the police take another look at her case. . . ."

Cerretani's head swung around. "You said it was because you knew the dosage. You said you could get it just right if—"

"I know what I said."

There was a long silence—which, unfortunately, Mad decided to fill.

"You know what I think?" he said. "I think you people are pathetic. Here you are playing God, justifying yourselves with all sorts of high-minded bullshit, when all you really care about is saving your own ass."

Cerretani grimaced down at him. "You don't know what the hell you're talking about."

"Come on," Mad said, "you already said your precious experiment is over. The only reason to get rid of us is to get yourself off the hook, you pathetic son of a bitch."

I sat there gaping at him, not quite sure what to do. I

mean, it was nice to see Mad in fighting form—but not with both hands tied behind his back.

"Come on, Mad," I said. "Don't even bother. It's not worth the—"

"Fuck him," Mad said. One look in his eyes told me he was beyond reason. "Come to think of it, fuck the *both* of them. Fuck all *three* of them. What are you gonna do, blow us up and walk away and wash your hands of it? If you want to kill me, why don't you do it like a man, you cowardly fuck? Why don't you do it to my *face?*"

"Don't tempt me."

Cerretani's face was reddening rapidly, his hands clenching into fists at his sides. I hoped Mad would shut up soon.

"You wouldn't have the *balls,*" Mad spat back at him. "All you can manage is to poison people and rough up a woman half your size, you goddamn *pussy.*"

That did it. Cerretani hit him, *hard,* and when Mad threatened to fall over backward into the water, he grabbed him by his shirtfront. They stayed like that for a while, Cerretani holding on to Mad's shirt with his left hand and pummeling him with his right. Blood came streaming out of the corner of Mad's mouth and from a cut near his left eye. Cerretani apparently didn't like the sight of it, because he pushed him back into the water and held his thrashing torso down for a while, then pulled him back up and hit him some more.

I'm not sure how long this went on, but it was way longer than I would have thought possible.

He's going to kill him, I thought. *He's really going to kill him right in front of me, and there's not a damn thing I can do about it.*

I stood up and tried to throw my body between the two of them, but Cerretani just knocked me out of the way and the next thing I knew I was back in the goddamn pool. I landed facedown and tried to turn myself over, but I got caught in the plants and for a panicked minute I thought I was done for too. But I managed to flip myself over and sit up, hands still shackled tight behind my back.

I sputtered and coughed and blinked the water out of my eyes all over again, and the next thing I saw was McDaniel whacking Cerretani over the head with a shovel.

I'm not kidding. It was a beautiful sight.

She hit him once, twice, and he turned to her with a confused look on his face before he crumpled to the ground. She gaped at him bug-eyed, as though she couldn't quite believe what she'd just done. Come to think of it, neither could I.

I stood up and waded over to Mad, who was lying faceup among the battered plants. He was half zonked, but breathing.

"Thanks," I said to her, but she didn't answer—just pulled a knife out of her pocket and cut my hands free. "Thanks," I said again. She didn't even nod, just leaned over and did the same for Mad. Then she sat on her haunches and stared at the two of us, the shock on her face not even starting to fade.

"Um . . . Lindsay," I said. "What are you planning on doing right now?"

"I . . . I suppose I'm going to let you walk out of here. Then I'm going to call my fiancé and we're going to move to a country where there's no extradition."

"Are you serious?"

"He knew it might come to this. We're not like Ellie and Ron." She shook her head, like there was a bad memory knocking around in there. "We have some friends who can help us. All I'm asking is, don't call the police for a couple of hours. Just give me time to get away."

"Listen, Lindsay . . . I'm incredibly grateful. You just saved our lives."

"Yes."

"I've gotta ask. . . . Why?"

She shrugged and commenced chewing on her lower lip. "When I signed on for Kate's plan, it was partly because she made it sound like a really brave, altruistic thing to do. But I also have to admit . . . that wasn't the main reason. I mostly did it because it was so . . . It was such a hard scientific problem, I wanted to be the one who solved it."

"And you saved us because you felt guilty?"

"Partially, yes. But it was also because . . . Watching Jack beating him like that . . . was just so *brutal*. And I just couldn't be a part of it anymore. I just couldn't do it. I couldn't let them kill you," she said. "I just couldn't stand by and let them kill you like we killed Kate."

CHAPTER
36

We did as she asked. First, however, we got the hell out of there.

Doctor's orders be damned, we went down the hill and made a beeline for Mad's apartment, with a strategic stop at the all-night liquor store. He sat on the couch downing a Junipero and tonic while I cleaned up his face, ascertained that he (probably) hadn't broken any facial bones, and swilled a very large drink of my own.

By mutual agreement, we barely talked at all. God only knows what Mad had on his mind, but as for me . . . I sat there tippling away, trying not to think about the theoretical condition of my liver and doing a damn good job of it too. I was also trying not to think about the conversation we'd just had with Lindsay McDaniel. At this, though, I was failing miserably.

It'd gone something like this:

Her: "I just couldn't stand by and let them kill you like we killed Kate."

Me: *"What?"*

At that point, she'd glanced toward the door like she was poised to flee, then didn't. In fact, she'd leaned down and used the remains of the rope to lash Professor Jack Cerretani like a prize hog. Then she just knelt there, shaking her head and staring at the pool of smashed-up rice plants.

Mad seemed to be doing okay, if a bit groggy, but Cerretani's head wound was another question. I thought maybe I should point out that if we didn't get him to a hospital, he might die. Then I decided I didn't give a damn.

After wasting a few more of her precious getaway minutes, McDaniel looked up at us and said, "You heard me."

"Who do you mean 'we'?"

"Jack and Shep. And Arnie Kim. And me."

"Arnie Kim?" The name sounded vaguely familiar. "He's another professor in the department?"

She nodded. "He used to work at the Rice Institute in the Philippines. Kate needed him too." She glanced over at Cerretani, out cold on the ground. "I don't know why I'm still here. I don't have much time. But I need to explain this to you, to somebody, at least the short version. What you do with it is up to you." She checked her watch. "Ten minutes. That's all. Shep'll be back in another half hour anyway."

She drew in a deep breath, exhaled.

"You already know what Kate was up to. She called it Project Eve, if you can believe it—some romantic notion about Africa being the cradle of life. At the time that she . . . When Madison got sick, she was getting ready to release the rice—not for testing, not a small control group, just to release it on the public. She knew the animal tests hadn't been great. Yes, the fertility rates went way down, but the side effects . . . They might have been considerable.

"But Kate said these people couldn't afford to wait. She said she was sure her science was sound and the animal protocols were flawed. She even started eating the rice herself, two cups every day, just to prove it was all right, but we thought it needed more time in the lab. I mean, science isn't supposed to work that way. There's methodology to be followed, and she swore we'd follow it when we all signed on. But almost up until the end, we didn't even know how bad things really were."

"What do you mean?"

"I told you the rice hadn't gone into human trials. It turned out that wasn't quite true. You see . . . Kate was on the board of a battered women's shelter in Gabriel. She gave them some of the rice, and then she monitored the health of the women who ate it."

"Are you telling me she used them as human guinea pigs?"

McDaniel gave a reluctant nod. "She . . . only told us about it to justify releasing the rice, since none of the women had gotten sick. But she knew it was too soon to tell—the secondary effects might not come for years. I told her that, and . . . She didn't even seem that concerned. She said that these women had been born with chances poor African women never had, and they still made stupid choices that ruined their lives—they'd just keep going back to the same abusive man. . . ."

Son of a bitch, I thought. *Kate Barnett was not a nice person.*

It may seem like the silliest of sentences, but that's what slid across my mind as I sat there on the floor of the greenhouse, still soaking wet, Mad's head on my lap.

Kate Barnett was not one of the good guys, I thought. *She may have had her reasons for what she did, but so do the people who blow up buses in Tel Aviv.*

How could she do it? How the hell could she?

"And you know the strange thing?"

It took me a minute to realize McDaniel was expecting an answer.

"Uh . . . no. What?"

"Vavilov's seed bank."

"What about it?"

"Kate always talked about the value of sacrifice, the *beauty* of it, how those scientists had given their lives to protect the seeds, how the women in the shelter might be making a sacrifice for the greater good. And after the plant-science explosions, she gave that ridiculous speech practically daring whoever did it to come and get her. But you know what? I don't believe for one minute that she actually thought she was in any danger. Her lab got blown up, for God's sake, and she still thought she was untouchable. Even at the end, even when we . . ."

Her voice trailed off. For a second, I thought she was actually going to cry, but she just shook her head and looked me right in the eye.

"Jack came to me," she said. "He told me he'd thought about it and she had to be stopped." Her voice was clipped, precise, totally dispassionate all of a sudden. "Shep agreed. So did Arnie. We were the only project members in the country. It was up to us. That was the agreement—we'd do it together or we wouldn't do it at all. I couldn't. . . . I said I couldn't be a part of it, not physically. But we agreed I'd be there, so I'd be just as guilty as they were.

"We went into her lab at around two in the morning. It took less than five minutes. We were all wearing lab coats and we burned them in the incinerator. That's all."

She stood up. "Wait a minute," I said. "I've still got a ton of questions. Like, what about the bombings? Was that you or the OATs or what?"

She looked at her watch again, and that's when it struck me: Through the whole conversation, Lindsay's demeanor had hardly changed at all. There she was, braining one of her coconspirators and describing their little murder plot—all the while still slouching and fidgeting with her gum ball of an engagement ring.

Looks sure as hell can be deceiving.

"Tell Ellie," she said, "that I told her to take the deal."

"What?"

"Once this all comes out, Kate and the whole department are going to look a lot less sympathetic. I'm not saying anyone is going to consider the bombings justified, but at least it's a mitigating factor. Ellie also knows some things about what Kate was up to that might do her some good. So if they offer her a deal, whatever it is, tell her to take it."

"She'd never believe me."

For the first time that night, she smiled. "You're probably right," she said. "But you can prove it to her. Just tell her that I also told you . . . Tell her it's not the number of karats, it's the quality of the stone. She'll know what it means."

Then she left. The next time I saw her, it was on a flyer at the post office.

That's what was running through my unwilling brain as I sat on Mad's couch, trying to have the self-control to stay much more sober than I wished to be. Once the promised minutes had elapsed, I left Mad with a frozen steak on his face and walked to the police station, where I asked for a certain detective.

"Cody," I said once I'd dragged him out of earshot of the rest of the constabulary, "do you love me?"

"You gotta ask?"

"No, but . . . I just want you to keep that in mind."

I told all, and his usually pale skin turned a rather disturbing shade of crimson.

"If I weren't so goddamn glad you're not dead," he said, "I'd slap the goddamn cuffs on you."

"On what charge?"

"I'd think of something."

"Oh."

"I can't believe you really let that woman go. And Madison—"

"Mad said fuck her. But I said, you know . . . we gave her our word."

"That's ridiculous."

"I'd think a military guy like you would get the honor thing."

"Just because she did the right thing where you're concerned doesn't mean she gets off the hook for murder."

"I know, but . . . Oh, hell, I don't know."

"Really," he said, "why'd you do it?"

"It's pretty simple," I said. "I gave her two hours. She gave me my life. Seemed like a pretty fair trade."

Then, of course, all hell broke loose. A swarm of cops from a glorious tapestry of jurisdictions descended upon the greenhouse, where Cerretani was still trussed up. They found Robinson in his bedroom, packing his Brooks Brothers shirts in anticipation of a getaway. They also went to Arnie Kim's house, but he was gone, presumably tipped off by McDaniel—though his underground railroad was clearly less efficient, because he got snagged at the Canadian border.

I discharged the rest of my debt via Ron Bozier, since there was zero chance the Feds were going to let a reporter anywhere near Ellie. It took four tries before she finally agreed to see him, but when she did, the message must've had the desired effect. The rumored deal with one of the Mott brothers dematerialized and, since Ellie was a hell of a lot smarter and less of a tongue-lolling nincompoop than her coconspirators, she got a deal of her own: In exchange for taking full responsibility for the smaller explosion, she got off the hook for the big one. This may sound like a sweet arrangement, but she still wound up with a whole slew of charges, topped off by attempted murder.

I wish I could say I got the chance to interview her, but I sure as hell didn't. I only know what everybody else knows from goddamn *60 Minutes*—how she spent so much time hanging around Barnett's lab she put two and two together about Project Eve, and got so wildly disillusioned she went off and joined the OATs but never quite trusted them enough to tell all. And how when she learned about the plan to blow up the building, she took it as a sign she had to screw up her courage and deal with Barnett herself. Unfortunately for Phil Herzog and the others, she was a bush-league terrorist; it never even crossed her mind that the first bomb would attract victims for the second.

And for you incurable romantics out there: Last thing I heard, Ron Bozier was sticking by her. He even held her hand on *60 Minutes*.

My story on the internecine intrigues of the Benson plant-science department ran two days after our *menage à cinque* with Cerretani et al. It could've run the next day, but it didn't for two reasons: One, I was so exhausted I could barely see straight, and two, I had to give Gordon and his *Times* editors a heads-up. A deal, after all, is a deal.

"You know," the newshound in question was saying to me in the Citizen the day the story broke, "you go to some ridiculous lengths sometimes."

"How do you mean?"

"Practically getting drowned and blown up and all."

"It's not like I did it on purpose."

"Tell me," he said, "was it worth it?"

"Worth what?"

He drank his Corona and grinned. "Scooping me."

※

There was one interview I *did* get on exclusive. No—make that two. The first was with an extremely grateful Shelley Freeman, freshly liberated from the hoosegow. They say the wheels of justice turn slowly, but in Shelley's case the jailhouse door just about sprung open. It didn't hurt that the cops found traces of abrin in Kate's house, which had been sealed up pending a sale to benefit various charities. It also didn't hurt that the original investigating officer on the case ran around like a maniac demanding Shelley be released; Cody is nothing if not morally upright.

So Shelley came back to Gabriel, retrieved her (extremely traumatized) kids from the various relatives to whom they'd been shunted, and moved them all right back into the family home. Benson even offered her her old job back and, amazingly enough, she took it.

The interview I did with her took place out on her back deck as the kids splashed around the pool and Shelley grilled a pile of hot dogs (veggie for me) on Lane's beloved barbecue. If you're expecting she said a lot of mushy stuff about forgiving and forgetting, think again. She basically said that everybody who thought she was guilty were a bunch of dickless, witless, nasty-minded morons and she hoped they all got theirs someday.

She said these things, by the way, on the record.

And my other exclusive interview? That one was conducted where I'd originally met Shelley: behind bars. The subject? A very, very unhappy young man named Kenny Barnett.

Tracking him down was, if I may say so myself, no easy

trick. And frankly, the story wasn't particularly vital, journalistically speaking; by the time I got to him, the Kate Barnett exposé had been on the front page for what felt like weeks.

So why did I do it? I'm not quite sure, except as some last-ditch attempt to understand what made the woman tick. I'd heard from her ex-husband, her ex-students, her ex-colleagues; I'd even met her myself. But it still didn't add up. How could somebody who obviously cared so much about alleviating human suffering risk people's lives like that? How could she actually commit murder? How could the Kate who lit up the lecture hall with her good intentions really think the ends justified the means?

Unsurprisingly, I couldn't answer those questions. And I'll be straight with you: I still can't. Kate Barnett may have seen the world in black and white, but the mess she left behind was more complicated. And although the Sunday-morning chat shows have given her story plenty of airtime, there was only one person I could think of who might fill in the shades of gray.

I looked for him everyplace I could think of, from Red Cross shelters to county jails. I asked Coach Laughton to call in another favor from his buddy in the D.O.C., but as far as he could tell, Kenny wasn't in the state system. I thought about what I'd heard about him, tried to figure out where he might land, and the only common denominator I could come up with was *trouble*.

This prompted me to keep up a daily vigil in the Benson library. Every night after work, I'd go up there and glance through the police blotters of every decent-size paper in New York State and look for his name. One day toward the end of July I got lucky: Kenny had been arrested for robbing parking meters in Oneonta. The paper said he was being held on a hundred-fifty dollars bail, so the next morning I got up early, drove the two hours, and got to the police station just as it was opening. When I said I was there to bail out Kenny Barnett, a middle-aged cop with a gut worthy of triplets looked me up and down and muttered something about "jungle fever."

Ten minutes later, he came back with my money, and without Kenny.

"Boy says he doesn't know you."

"Tell him I'm a friend of his mother's."

"Tell him yourself."

We went down a long hallway to the back of the building and down a staircase, then through another hall. He unlocked a door to reveal a row of cells with little mesh-covered windows up high; the whole scene was such a jailhouse stereotype I expected to hear some guy playing the harmonica and yelling for a lawyer. After we walked past two cells whose occupants smelled violently of stale beer, my guide stopped so suddenly I almost banged into his gun belt.

"Barnett, front and center," he barked, though I have no idea why; Kenny was already standing at the bars, gripping one in each hand and leaning his head into the space between. "You got ten minutes. Bail him out or don't, doesn't matter to me."

The cop took off and I was left there against the cinderblock wall, Kenny Barnett staring at me through the bars and across the four feet of space. I took a long look at him, this troubled young guy I'd been searching for for weeks, and the first thing I thought was *He's so small*. The second thing was *He's so black*.

Now, I don't mean anything racially offensive by this. But I grew up in a white-bread world, and though I have some African-American friends, they're all comparatively light skinned. But Kenny Barnett's skin was this beautiful, intense, bitter-chocolate color—so dark it made the whites of his eyes seem to glow out of his head. Okay, maybe this is terribly un-P.C.; I'm just telling you what I saw.

I also saw that although he had to be nineteen by now he honest to God could've passed for twelve. He was wearing a pair of raggedy denim cutoffs and a faded Chicago Bulls tank top, the kind that hangs way under your armpit and looks awful on everybody but Michael Jordan. His fingernails were filthy even by my standards, and his left knee was raw and scabby—a mixture of old and new wounds that made me think he couldn't stop picking at it.

He looked at me for a long time, like he couldn't imagine what I was doing there. Finally, he just asked, "Who are you?"

"My name is Alex Bernier. I'm a reporter for the *Gabriel Monitor*."

"A reporter's here to bail me out?" He had a slight accent, sort of a pretty, lilting tone that would've been easy to miss. But there was also a slowness to his speech, like he had to concentrate hard on stringing the words together in the right order. "How come?"

"I want to talk to you."

"Talk?"

"About your mother."

I watched his jaw clench. "My mothers are dead," he said. "Both of them."

"I mean Professor Barnett."

He eyed me like I was the one in the cage. "Is that why you came here to get me out of jail? To talk about her?"

"Yeah."

"Maybe I don't want you to get me out."

"Why not?"

"Maybe this is where I belong."

"What makes you say that?"

He shrugged and leaned back from the bars until his arms

stretched out, then pulled himself back up. "Makes sense," he said.

It was a psychological hornet's nest, and I decided not to stick my foot in it. "So how about it?" I said. "You talk to me, and I'll bail you out of here."

"Talk to you for the newspaper? To run in the newspaper?"

"If that's okay with you."

Honestly, it never occurred to me that he'd go along with it. But since I was mostly here for my own curiosity, I figured I could always do it off the record if I had to.

"Okay," he said. "I'll talk to you for the paper, but that's all."

"Huh?"

"I'll talk to you, but no bail. I want to stay here."

"What? Why?"

"Because I don't have anyplace else to go."

I tried to think of something inspirational, and came up short. "Coach Laughton might help you," I said. "From Griffin Academy."

Kenny smiled, just a little, and I caught a glimpse of teeth so white they didn't look real. Considering what I'd heard about the aftereffects of childhood starvation, maybe they weren't.

"Nice guy," he said. "He was . . . He was the only one who ever . . ." He bit his lower lip, hard. "Why do you want to talk to me?"

"I've been hearing about you a long time. I wanted to get to know you in person."

"To talk about Kate."

"To talk about her, yeah."

"Why do you want to know about her? She's dead and gone."

I tried to think of how to put it. "I knew her a little when she was alive," I said, "and now that she's dead . . . I guess she seems like a mystery."

"Yeah."

"You heard about what happened to her?"

"The cops said."

"The cops?"

"They talked to me . . . after. Wanted to know where I was. Thought maybe I did it."

"And you heard . . . what she did? What she was trying to do?" He gave me a blank look. "Her experiments with the rice?"

He nodded. "She wanted to feed people. She didn't want them to go hungry."

He hasn't heard about it, I thought. Well, I wasn't going to be the one to tell him.

"Listen, Kenny, I have to ask you. . . . If you don't want to get out of this place, how come you're even talking to me?"

Another shrug, followed by a look around his cell. "It's boring in here."

"And that's why?"

"There's nobody else to talk to."

"All right. I guess we have to talk fast, because that cop said I only had ten minutes, and I have a lot of—"

"He'll forget," he said with a head shake. "They forget everything. Like, I never even got my bologna sandwiches last night. In jail, they're supposed to bring you bologna sandwiches. It's the law. Somebody told me that."

"So," I said, "will you tell me about her?"

He dropped down to the floor in one swift motion and wound up sitting cross-legged. I did the same, but with less grace. The floor was cold, hard, and dirty.

"What do you want to know?" he asked.

"What was she like?"

Yet another shrug. "She was Kate."

"You didn't call her 'Mom'?"

"She didn't want us to."

That kind of threw me for a loop. "And, um, how old were you when she adopted you?"

"I don't know for sure. They decided I was eleven."

"And what was—"

"I remember . . . At the camp, they never asked us if we wanted to go. One of the nuns said there was this wonderful white lady who wanted to take a boy and a girl back home with her, and how we were so lucky because they'd chosen us and we were going to this wonderful place where there'd always be enough food to eat."

"Was she nice to you? Kate, I mean?"

"We always had enough food to eat," he said, as though it were the definitive answer.

"Yeah, but, you know, did she treat you kindly? Did she make you feel welcome?"

"We had . . . We had big rooms to sleep in, one for each one of us. I couldn't believe it, that there was a room just for me." He fiddled with the bars in front of him. "I don't want to talk about this anymore."

So much for the impromptu therapy session. I was scrambling to regroup when he started speaking again.

"I don't want to talk about me," he said. "You didn't say I had to. You just said you wanted to know about Kate."

"That's fine."

He just sat there for a while, running his hand up and down the bars. When he started talking again, he didn't look me in the eye.

"I think . . . I think we made her mad."

"How come?"

"I think we disappointed her. She got up so early every morning, five o'clock, and we . . . especially at the beginning, we just wanted to sleep all day, just to eat and to sleep.

But she wanted us to do lots of things, go to places and meet people, but we weren't any good.

"And I think we made her sad too, because some nights, most nights, she'd be in her room and we'd hear her crying for a long time, crying real loud. When I asked her about it once, she said she'd seen so many bad things in her life, that when she tried to go to bed she'd see them behind her eyes so she couldn't sleep. Sometimes she'd stay awake and work all night or use her exercise machine for hours and hours. . . ." He shook his head, the way people do when they think they're about to cry and really want to avoid it. "But that probably isn't what you wanted to know."

"Actually, it's . . . Go on."

"You want?" I nodded. "I . . . I asked her once why she didn't have a man, a husband, and she said she was like the nuns back at the camp. She said they gave up that part of their life so they could concentrate on God and doing good things, and she said she didn't believe in any God that would let people suffer like she'd seen them suffer, but she was kind of like them because she gave up that part of her life so she could concentrate on her science and make the world better for people like us."

Yikes. "You said you thought you made her mad. Did she ever make you mad too?"

He looked down at the soles of his feet, and for the first time, I noticed he was barefoot. "I get mad sometimes."

"Everybody gets mad sometimes."

He shook his head again, hard. "Not like me."

"Why did she make you mad?"

"I dunno."

"Don't you think she treated you well?"

"We had plenty of food to eat," he said again.

I decided not to push the issue, mostly because I wasn't sure how.

"Okay, let me ask you something else. Do you think she was ever happy?" He seemed to think about it for a long time, then just shook his head. "Didn't her science make her happy? Her research?"

"It just . . . It made her upset."

"How do you mean?"

"I dunno," he said. "Maybe she was afraid she wouldn't do it right."

"You mean because the stakes were so high?"

"I guess. Whatever you say."

His eyes darted around the cell, and I got the distinct feeling I was about to lose his attention. "Listen, Kenny . . . What are you going to do now? After you get out?"

He shrugged again. "I dunno. Go someplace."

"Don't you have any plans, stuff you'd like to do for the future?"

He recommenced chewing his lip, then cracked a smile. "Later on," he said, "they're supposed to bring me another bologna sandwich."

EPILOGUE

As far as I can calculate, there was only one advantage to the whole plant-science mess: After our story about the collusion between Lane Freeman and the protesters came out, Don't Break the Food Chain packed up and headed west.

This, merciful heavens, meant the exodus of Tobias Kahan. I never did get my notebook back, though — Kahan having reportedly burned it in some farcical shamanistic ceremony in front of the entire D.B.F.C. crowd. And by the way: From what I hear, he's sticking to his story about how I subjected him to unwanted touching behind the Ecstatic Eggplant. Oh, hell.

What ultimately became of the Project Eve rice, I couldn't really say. The university swore up and down that it seized and destroyed every last sprig of the stuff, but I have my doubts. A lot of brainpower was expended on it, and a fair amount blood as well; I can't believe they'd just toss it in the incinerator. Besides, Lindsay had said people were working on it all over the world, so somebody somewhere must have their own samples. I'm willing to bet we haven't seen the last of it, God help us.

On the positive side, Ochoa and I appear to have made our

peace. At least, he's willing to imbibe alcohol in my presence again, which passes for friendship in my world. His girlfriend never did show her face, though, so maybe at this point the poor guy's lonely enough to drink with just about anybody.

I wish I could report that Mad's near-death experience inspired him to make positive, fundamental life-changes. That, however, would be a whole lot of hooey. Mad is Mad, and I suspect 'twill be ever thus. For a while there, I thought he might at least pick up the phone and call Emma, but as far as I know, he never has. He did, however, max out his credit card to go scuba diving off the Florida Keys.

I also wish I could report that Detective Brian Cody is in fine fettle, but he's not; truth be told, the guy is as depressed as I've ever seen him. First he put the wrong person in jail for the Lane Freeman murder; then the Feds shunted him to the sidelines for the rest of the action. It may be enough to make a man want to pull up stakes and move to Boston, which is something I dearly want to avoid thinking about.

One rather torpid night when we were sitting on a bench by the lake, I tried to convince him that having the guts to face the music on the Shelley thing was damn impressive, that he should be proud of himself for that much at least. He wasn't buying it, though; in fact, he told me that pretty much the only bright spot in his summer so far was that his girlfriend didn't actually die on the three occasions (bombing plus poisoning plus drowning) when it seemed most likely.

"You know," I said, "that sounds pretty positive to me."

"That's true."

"My summer would've been a lot worse if I'd croaked."

"Mine too."

I couldn't think of anything remotely conciliatory. So I grabbed his chin, turned his head around to face me instead of the water, and kissed him for a while.

"What can I do to cheer you up?" I said when it was obvious the smooching was getting me nowhere. "Come on, you name it. We gotta celebrate my imminent nondemise."

"This is pretty good right here."

"Yeah?"

"Yeah, it's nice. What else you got in mind?"

"I could take you out to dinner."

"Or," he said, "we could just eat in."

"There's the spirit. What do you feel like?"

"Pizza?"

"Nah. Kinda heavy for blazing heat."

"Good point. How about Chinese?"

"Works for me. Nicely symbolic, actually."

"Huh?"

"Haven't touched the stuff since somebody tried to kill me with it."

"I'm sorry, baby. I didn't think—"

"It's okay. Come on, don't look at me like that, I mean it. I kinda like the idea, actually."

"You're ridiculous."

"Which is why you love me."

"The girl speaks the truth." He pulled his cell phone out of his jacket. "What do you feel like? That tofu thing you always get?"

"Yeah, that sounds . . . Nah, wait a minute. Get me veggie lo mein instead."

"You sure?"

"Yeah," I said. "I really, really don't feel like anything that comes with rice."

ABOUT THE AUTHOR

BETH SAULNIER is an editor at *Cornell Alumni Magazine* and a film critic for *The Ithaca Journal*. A graduate of Vassar College, she lives in Ithaca, New York.

More
Beth Saulnier!

Please turn this page
for a
bonus excerpt
from

ECSTASY

available
wherever books are sold.

PROLOGUE

I still wonder what it was like for him in those last minutes — lying there alone, the nylon walls close against him in the dark, the only light coming from the kaleidoscope in his own head. I wonder if he was scared; did he know what was happening to him was the *end,* or was he just too out of it to realize? And if he did know, did he kick himself for it?

His death, after all, can in great measure be chalked up to his own stupidity. You can argue all you want about the fundamental nature of justice, you can point out that the punishment didn't really fit the crime, but the bottom line is that although other people were obviously responsible for his death, he damn well helped; somehow, this clueless seventeen-year-old boy managed to be both victim and accomplice.

I barely knew him, so it's probably nuts even to speculate, but at the moment I can't seem to stop. Maybe that's because lately I've come across so many kids just like him, or because I've spent so many hours trying to walk in his patched-up Birkenstocks. Either way, right now his last hour or so on earth is incredibly vivid in my imagination. And I'll tell you the truth: I really, really wish it weren't.

But it is. And I picture it like this:

He crawls into the tent, strips down the childish white underpants they'll find him in. He's full, probably uncomfortably so; the coroner will find a gigantic amount of food in his stomach—falafel and veggie chili and peanut butter cups he put away a couple of hours before, probably in an attack of the munchies from all the grass he smoked that afternoon.

A different sort of guy might want company, but later his friends will say that wasn't his style. He likes to be by himself, savor the moment—open his mind to new realities, I suppose he'd say. He prefers to lie by himself in the dark and wait for the universe to open up and swallow him, to take him on some dopey journey of the imagination; the next morning (or more likely afternoon) he'll tell his friends all about it over a whole wheat bagel with extra honey.

So he pins a sign to the tent that says—no kidding—TRIPPING, DO NOT DISTURB. He zips up the flap and lies on top of his sleeping bag mostly naked, since the late-August heat is all but unbearable, even if you're in your right mind. He pulls his long corkscrew curls out of their usual ponytail and wraps the elastic around his flashlight. He lights the candle on the milk crate beside him, but only long enough to let the scent of sage waft over to him. He blows it out after a minute or so, not only because he craves the dark but because he knows you're never supposed to have an open flame inside a tent; later, when his friends are called upon to eulogize, they'll say he was a kick-ass camper.

He's happy, at least that's the way I imagine it. He's utterly in his element, a skinny little fish gliding in his favorite pond. Within a few hundred yards are most of the people on the planet who really matter to him—guys he's been skateboarding with since he was ten, girls he's danced with and gotten high with and screwed, and no hard feelings afterward.

The night feels alive around him; it's loud with laughter and bits of conversations, all of them important—some pondering the next band on the playlist, others the fundamental meaning of the universe. There's music everywhere, coming from so many sources and directions it's impossible to separate them, innumerable voices and bass lines and drum beats going *thump-thump-thump* inside his chest.

He closes his eyes, because even before the candle goes out there's no need for vision. His other senses are on overload, and he likes it. If he's feeling this much even before the drug really kicks in, he knows he's in for one hell of a ride.

This is the moment he likes best, when it's just starting and he's not quite sure which world he's in. At first, the sensations are slow, sneaky, subtle—fictions masquerading as fact. The beginning of a trip is like crossing a river, he's always said; you can try to stay on the rocks of reality, but the closer you get to the other side, the wetter you're going to get.

I have no idea how long he balances in the netherworld between here and elsewhere; for his sake, I hope it's a while. But eventually, he segues into something infinitely wilder—and since my personal experience with mind-expanding drugs is essentially nil (my head being kooky enough without the addition of psychotropics), I have a hard time imagining it. When I ponder the usual stereotypes—shooting stars and melting walls and talking rhinos and such—it just seems pathetic, and I know he didn't see it that way. To him it was something profound, something worth stretching yourself, maybe even scaring yourself, just for the sake of the experience.

But was it something worth dying for? That much I seriously doubt. But there's no arguing with the fact that that's precisely what happened.

At some point, quite when I don't know, things start to go

wrong. His mouth goes dry. He gets a raging headache. Maybe his stomach starts to hurt; then it starts to hurt *bad*. He can barely breathe. Eventually, he can't breathe at all.

I wonder if he thinks it's all just part of the experience—that he's taking some dark spirit journey to the edge of his own demise. (And, okay, I know that sounds like your typical druggie-hippie crap; it just goes to show you how much time I've been spending with these people.) How nasty a surprise must it have been to realize that it wasn't a fantasy version of death, but the real thing?

But there's another possibility—one that's even more unpleasant, if such a thing is possible. From what I've been told, physical well-being is essential to the enjoyment of your average acid trip. The symptoms he must have experienced, then, could very well have sent him spiraling into the same mental purgatory that keeps cowards like me limited to gin, Marlboro Lights, and the (very) occasional joint.

This seventeen-year-old boy, in other words, may not have died in just physical agony; he may well have died in mental agony as well. *Serious* mental agony. Through the magic of chemistry, his was an anguish not necessarily bounded by the normal limits of the human mind. It's a horrible thing to contemplate, to tell you the truth. There's plenty of pain in the conscious world, after all; how much must there be when the pit is well and truly bottomless?

When they finally found him, he was in the fetal position—curled up tight, knees against his chest, stringy arms wrapped around each other. The doctors say this doesn't necessarily mean anything about his last moments, but frankly, I don't buy it. As far as I'm concerned, it means he didn't go peacefully.

Because, after all, neither did any of the others.

CHAPTER
1

August in a college town is its own special brand of torture. The living is easy, the weather is still gorgeous, and the students have been gone so long you have a hard time remembering what the place is really like nine months out of the year. You have these vaguely distasteful images of crowded restaurants and SUV-driving frat boys and gaggles of tummy-shirted coeds, but none of it seems real. You soak up the delicious moments—when you get a parking place right smack in front of the multiplex, say, or you go out for a drink without having some postadolescent moron comment on your cleavage—and you fantasize that maybe, just maybe, they're never coming back. Maybe the leaves will stay on the trees forever, and the streets will always be open and empty, and the new semester will never come.

But deep down, you know it will. Damn it all, it will—and it always does.

It used to be that October made me feel wistful, what with impending winter and the smell of decay in the air and the knowledge that you weren't going to get to wear shorts again for a very long time. But since I moved to Gabriel five or so years ago, my wistfulness threshold has been pushed back a good two months. Maybe it's just because people around here are too smart to ever really be happy, but we townies tend to start feeling blue three weeks before Labor Day, and we don't really shake it until graduation.

I mention al this by way of explaining that although late summer early fall in this ZIP code can be a tough pill to swallow, by all that's holy, last August should've been comparatively jolly. I was, after all, celebrating the fact that I had recently avoided being killed on three separate occasions within a matter of weeks — rather a nifty accomplishment, if you ask me. The newspaper where I work was, for the first time in recent memory, fully staffed. And — here's the cherry on the sundae — my boyfriend, who I'd been fearing was about to move away and break my little heart, showed every sign of staying put. Even the imminent return of fifteen thousand undergraduates couldn't put the kibosh on my good mood.

If I tried to put my finger on when everything went to hell, well . . . it wouldn't be too hard. That would be when I walked into the newsroom around eleven on a Wednesday morning in mid-August. I'd walked out of there precisely ten hours earlier, after covering a particularly pissy county board meeting that went until nearly midnight, then scrambling to slap together three (mercifully short) stories by my one A.M. deadline. Then I'd gone home to hold the crying towel for my roommate, Melissa, whose boyfriend had recently — you guessed it — moved away and broken her little heart.

So it was without a whole lot of sleep that I went back to work, toting a bagel with diet olive cream cheese and blissfully unaware of how much my life was about to suck. I poured some coffee into my big Gabriel Police Department mug, one of several recent gifts my aforementioned boyfriend had proffered to celebrate the fact of me not being dead. Then I sat down at my desk and tried to figure out which of the county board stories was going to need a follow-up for the next day's paper.

I'm not sure how long it took me to figure out something weird was up. I do recall that my first clue was that I was the only reporter on the cityside desk; come to think of it, I was the only reporter in the entire newsroom. It was way too early for the sports guys, but there should've at least been someone else around *somewhere;* as it was, though, the owner of every single *Gabriel Monitor* byline was nowhere to be found.

To round them up: There's Jake Madison (aka "Mad"), the science writer and my best buddy; Cal Ochoa, the cops reporter and one moody hombre; Lillian, the elderly-but-steely schools reporter; Marshall, the Dixie-born business writer; and—both last and least—Brad, an ambitious, scandal-mongering young fellow who's on the towns beat, and whom I avoid whenever possible.

Where was everybody? In a word: Hiding. And if I'd known better, I damn well would've been hiding too.

But there I was, sitting at my desk with the kind of clueless-but-doomed expression you see on a cow peeking out of the airholes in a livestock truck. At some point, my catlike instincts must've registered the fact that someone was breathing down my neck; when I looked up, there were three of them.

Three *editors.* As any reporter can tell you, there was no way this was going to end well.

"Alex," one of them said, and way too brightly. "You're here."

This from the shorter and rounder of the two women. Her name is Sondra, and she's the editor of (among other things) *Pastimes,* the paper's deeply mediocre arts-and-leisure magazine. Except for the weekly processing of my movie review column, I don't have a lot to do with her; she mostly lives in her own little universe, eternally beset by underpaid free-lancers.

She was already making me nervous.

Standing next to her were both of my bosses — Bill, the city editor, and his own overlord, the managing editor. Marilyn is not short, and she's in no way round; in fact, she has a black belt in tae kwon do.

"Um . . . ," I said, "Where is everybody?"

"My office," she said.

"They're all in your—"

"Come *into* my office," she said, and turned her well-exercised tail on me.

I followed, with Bill and Sondra bringing up the rear. In retrospect, they were probably trying to make sure I didn't make a run for it.

"Um . . . ," I said when we'd sat down, "So where is everybody?"

"Alex," Sondra said, sounding even more scary-friendly than before, "what are you doing for the next few days?"

"Huh?" I looked to Bill, who was taking a passionate interest in the pointy end of his necktie. "You mean, what am I covering?" Sondra nodded and leaned in closer, so I had a clear view right down her blouse to her tattletale-gray mini-mizer bra. "Today? Maybe a couple follows from last night's board meeting. Tomorrow . . . I think another stupid Deep Lake Cooling thing. Why?"

"And do you have any plans for this weekend?"

Uh-oh. Say something clever. Say . . . you have to donate a kidney to homeless mental patients.

That's what one side of my brain told the other. Bit I wasn't quick enough on the uptake, so all I said was, "Um . . . no."

Sondra squeezed my upper arm, harder than I would've thought she could. "That's *great*."

"Huh?"

"*Alex,*" she positively cooed at me, "I was hoping you could do me this teeny-tiny favor. . . ."

Now, at this point my hackles well and truly hit the ceiling. Because when an editor asks you for a *teeny-tiny favor,* it generally means you've about to get screwed without so much as a box of chocolates.

"Listen," I said, "I'm actually pretty busy at the moment, so—"

"You're covering Melting Rock," Marilyn said, sounding nowhere near as nice as Sondra, but considerably more genuine. "Starts today. So—"

"*What?*"

"Haven't you heard of it?" Sondra chirped at me. "You know, the official name is the Melting Rock Music Festival, but lots of people just call it—"

"Hell yes, I've heard of it. But what do you mean I'm—"

"Freelancer flaked out," Marilyn said into her mug of terrifyingly black coffee. "Chester says we gotta deliver the goods. So go."

Chester is our publisher—and there are guys in the pressroom with better news judgment. Things were not looking up.

"Go where? You mean go *now?* And where *is* everybody, anyway?"

I must've sounded either very desperate or very pathetic, because Bill finally took pity on me. "Here's the deal," he said. "You know Sim Marchesi?"

"Er . . . I dunno."

"He covers pop music for me," Sondra offered. "I mean he *covered* it. Right now I wouldn't hire that miserable—"

"Listen," Bill said, "Marchesi pitched us this story, and

when Chester got wind of the thing, he ate it up—promoted it up the wazoo. Then Marchesi bailed."

"Bailed how?"

"He was gonna cover the days and nights of Melting Rock, camp out there with the rest of the freaks and send us dispatches from the front. It was on the budget at the cityside meeting yesterday. Remember?"

"Vaguely."

"So the thing starts today. He was supposed to get there last night to cover the setup—was gonna file right before deadline for today's paper."

"And he blew it off?"

"Blew it off?" Marilyn growled with a whack of her mug onto the desktop. "Little prick flew the coop."

"You mean he hasn't filed yet? But maybe he just—"

Sondra waved me off. "He never even came by to pick up the laptop or the cell phone we were lending him. I tried his apartment and the number's disconnected. Then I tracked down the fellow in charge of the Melting Rock campground and . . . it looks like he never showed up yesterday."

"So spike the story," I said. It turned out to be a poor choice of words.

"What are you, deaf?" Marilyn said, segueing to something resembling a snarl. "We *can't* spike it. Don't you think I wish we could spike it? Chester's really got his undershorts in a twist. He thinks it's gonna be the goddamn miracle cure for our circulation with the under-thirty crowd. He's been flogging this thing all over cable commercials and house ads and mother-humping rack cards. . . . Don't you even read the paper?"

"Er . . . Yeah, sure I do. I guess I've been kind of busy."

"Okay, here's how it is," she said. "Chester's been promoting this package like it's the Second Coming, you got it?

Marchesi's AWOL, so somebody else's gotta cover it. And that somebody would be you."

"Why me?"

Another arm squeeze from Sondra. "Because," she said, "you're a really good feature writer. I mean, I know you mostly cover news, but you always have lot of great color in your—"

"Give me a break." I glanced out the window, which is not the kind you can open. Leaping to my death did not appear to be an option. "Listen, like I said, I gotta do some follows on board stuff, so—"

Marilyn didn't even blink. "Give it to Brad."

"*Brad?* You gotta be—"

"Anything else?"

"Um . . . yeah. There's gonna be another town meeting for Deep Lake Cooling on Friday night, so I really have to—"

She turned to Bill. "Who's weekend reporter?"

"Madison."

"Perfect. He's been covering the science end anyway. Hand it off to him." She turned back to me. "That all?"

"Er . . ." I racked my noggin for something good enough to spring me, and came up short. "I guess not."

"Super. So be a good girl and go put on your love beads and get the hell out there."

"But why can't we just—"

"Stop whining and hop to it," she said.

I'm not kidding. That's actually what she said. I decided to get the hell out of there before she told me to shake my tail feather, or worse.

Bill, being no fool, beat a hasty retreat to his office. I followed Sondra back to the arts-and-leisure desk, which is at the opposite end of the newsroom from Marilyn's domain. The commute took ten seconds, during which Sondra said,

"This is going to be just great!" more times than I cared to count.

Sometimes I think that journalists, like double agents, should be issued a suicide pill.

You may be wondering just why I was being such a baby about this. To put it succinctly: The Melting Pot Music Festival is my idea of hell. Until I was conscripted by the *Gabriel Monitor*'s editorial staff, I'd been there exactly once, and for a grand total of four hours.

It was the summer I'd moved to Gabriel five years ago, back when I didn't know any better. Melting Rock sounded kind of charming, and . . . well . . . this cute Canadian grad student in materials science asked me to go with him. So I put on a flowy skirt and a tank top to get into the spirit of the thing, and proceeded to experience what was, at least at that time, just about the worst day of my life.

First off, the guy's primary purpose for attending the festival proved not so much to be rocking to the groovy beat but hunting down his ex-girlfriend, whom he'd met there the year before. He didn't actually inform me of this at the time, though I had a sneaking suspicion something was up since I spent most of the afternoon looking at his back as he dragged me from stage to stage.

You might think, therefore, that my negative feelings toward Melting Rock amount to sour grapes. But the fact remains that the whole event gave me both a stomachache *and* a migraine. I'm not quite sure what my personal "scene" is, but I can tell you this much: Whatever it is, Melting Rock is the opposite.

So what's it like? To start with, it's hot as Satan's rec room, and sanitary facilities consist of overtaxed Porta-Johns and rusty taps sticking out the side of a barn. Consequently, the whole place stinks—not only of urine and sweat but also frying foodstuffs, incense, stale beer, and veritable gallons of patchouli. It's also one of the most crowded events I've ever had the misfortune to attend, so there's no escaping the aforementioned aromas. You're constantly elbow-to-elbow with young ladies who've never heard the words *brassiere* or *disposable razor* and gentlemen who equate their shoulder tattoos with the goddamn Sistine Chapel.

The music is okay, I guess, though I can't say I paid much attention to it. It all kind of blended in together to make this incredibly tedious, drum-heavy soundtrack that was impossible to escape; within an hour I felt like the guy from "The Tell-Tale Heart" who goes stark raving nuts because he can't get the beat out of his head.

After about four hours of this, I decided I'd had enough. I told my quote-unquote date that I needed to go home, whereupon he said that was fine with him and went back to searching for his erstwhile ladyfriend. Which might not have been so bad—if Melting Rock weren't held in a little village ten miles outside Gabriel.

I walked home. Honest to God. It was either that or hitch-hike, which is something my mother would not approve of. I got back to my apartment after midnight and got into the shower with my stinky clothes on.

These memories were, shall we say, plenty vivid as I sat at the leisure desk listening to Sondra prattle on about what a humdinger of an assignment I'd just been shafted with. To summarize the various points of my misery:

- I was not only going to the goddamn Melting Rock Music Festival, I was going there for the next *five days.*
- I was actually going to have to talk to people who frequent such events. Then I was going to have to write down what they said and churn out stories that presumably made it look like I gave a damn.

- I was going to have to eat a lot of greasy carnival food. (Okay, maybe this part wasn't so bad.)
- Any plans to spend the weekend in the boudoir of a very attractive policeman named Brian Cody were out the window.

And, worst of all.
- I was going to spend the next four nights in a tent. *Four.* In a *tent.*

I was pondering this litany of misfortune when my newsroom compadres finally started filing in. I was on the point of unloading on one Jake Madison when I realized that—big surprise—he was already very much in the know.

"So you guys knew she was gonna sandbag me and you didn't even give me a heads-up? Thanks a lot."

"Hey, every man for himself."

"Lovely."

Mad took a seat on the edge of my desk and unwrapped his tuna sandwich. "Human nature."

"Yeah, maybe *yours.*"

"Come on, you know," he said, "it's like that story about the two guys and the bear."

"What the hell are you talking about?"

"Two guys are walking in the woods and they see this bear, right? So one of them pulls his sneakers out of his backpack and puts them on. And the other guy says to him, 'What are you doing? You know you can't outrun a bear.'"

"And?"

"And the first guy goes, 'Hey, man, I don't have to outrun the bear.'" He smiled his wolfish Mad smile and poised to take a bite. "'I just have to outrun you.'"

VISIT US ONLINE @
WWW.TWBOOKMARK.COM

AT THE TIME WARNER BOOKMARK
WEB SITE YOU'LL FIND:

- CHAPTER EXCERPTS FROM SELECTED NEW RELEASES

- ORIGINAL AUTHOR AND EDITOR ARTICLES

- AUDIO EXCERPTS

- BESTSELLER NEWS

- ELECTRONIC NEWSLETTERS

- AUTHOR TOUR INFORMATION

- CONTESTS, QUIZZES, AND POLLS

- FUN, QUIRKY RECOMMENDATION CENTER

- PLUS MUCH MORE!

Bookmark AOL Time Warner Book Group @ www.twbookmark.com